DYING INSIDE

DAMIEN BOYD

Text copyright © 2021 by Damien Boyd
All rights reserved.

Published by Thomas & Mercer, Seattle

www.apub.com

Amazon, the Amazon logo, and Thomas & Mercer are trademarks of Amazon.com, Inc., or its affiliates.

ISBN-13: 9781542023597
ISBN-10: 1542023599

Cover design by Ghost Design

Printed in the United States of America

For Jeanie

Prologue

It was a simple enough question, surely?

Can you kill someone with an eighty-pound draw weight pistol crossbow?

Hours he'd spent, trawling the internet looking for the answer. In the end, he had posted on an American preppers forum and waited, refreshing the page every couple of minutes, even though they'd still be asleep over there. Crossbows seemed to be the weapon of choice for those prepping for the end of the world.

The first response came from a sarcastic git hiding behind the username WildBill: 'You could always beat him to death with it!' followed by a smiley face.

You should've stayed in bed, mate.

Next came Trashcan, who had clearly been watching too much of The Walking Dead: *'If it's a zombie that's been dead for a while the skull will have gone soft so you should be alright.'*

Some people . . .

Another tried a more scientific approach. 'Force equals mass times acceleration,' whatever the hell that was supposed to mean. Maybe he should have paid more attention in physics class; although going to school in the first place might have been a good start. 'It's all about the weight of the bolt and the speed it's traveling. Don't be confused by the draw weight, that's just the effort needed to cock it. What's the fps?'

Fps turned out to be feet per second – the speed the bolt leaves the bow – so it was back to the specification on the online archery shop listing: Scorpion 80lb draw weight pistol crossbow – he scrolled down – 145 fps.

'That won't be enough,' came the reply. 'A 6.5 inch bolt is light as a feather and traveling at that speed it certainly won't penetrate bone. A Coke can maybe, but not a skull. You might get lucky and hit soft tissue, so the eye socket is your best bet. If you aim for the heart and hit a rib, you're in deep trouble. What's the range? It'd need to be pretty much point blank, in which case you might just as well stab him and be done with it.'

It was a pleasant surprise how helpful some people could be – sort of restored his faith in human nature – but stabbing was out of the question; far too up close and personal.

'At the very least make sure you get the aluminum bolts with the steel tips. The plastic ones they come with are useless. And don't forget to sharpen them,' offered another user calling himself Urthe14me. 'Really it'd be best to get a more powerful bow to be on the safe side. What's your budget?'

That was a good question. What was his budget?

A Scorpion pistol crossbow was only £15.99, but what good was that if it didn't do the job?

'You can get an Anglo Arms Jaguar for 154 bucks. That should be enough. It comes with a red dot sight that's not too bad – good battery life and the red dot is easy to acquire. Go for a carbon fiber bolt (less wobble in the flight); minimum 20 inches with a broadhead on it, nice and sharp. That'll leave a decent drip trail to follow if your quarry gets away. And remember a heavier bolt will hit harder even if it's traveling

2

at a slightly slower speed. That's what you're looking for in a kill shot. A Desert Hawk is a bit more expensive but will do the job at 30 yards.'

Thirty yards? He'd won his wife a small teddy bear at the fairground once, but that had only been about five yards and she'd had to snatch the gun, hitting most of the ducks herself.

Unclesam76 had been very helpful all the same, although he clearly hadn't read the original post properly.

'What are you hunting by the way, bud? Deer?'

Chapter One

'Highbridge Neighbourhood Watch Liaison Committee.' Detective Chief Inspector Nick Dixon slammed his papers down on a vacant desk in the Safeguarding Unit, on the second floor of the police centre at Express Park, Bridgwater. 'Two bloody hours,' he said, slumping down on to the chair opposite Detective Sergeant Jane Winter.

'How was the meeting with Building Maintenance?' she asked, without looking away from her computer.

'Forty minutes on the state of the changing rooms. As if I give a flying—'

'Charlesworth's got you by the short and curlies now your promotion's been confirmed.' Jane almost stifled her chuckle.

'The crafty sod.'

'How d'you think he got to assistant chief constable?'

Dixon began tearing a piece of paper into strips, folding each strip neatly before dropping it in the bin with a flourish. He was watching Jane out of the corner of his eye, her frown growing ever deeper.

Curiosity finally got the better of her. 'What's that?'

'The meeting agenda. Antisocial behaviour at Highbridge Railway Station; boy racers in the car park; graffiti; any other business; date of next meeting. Two bloody hours.'

'You know what you've got to do.'

'I am not going to work at Portishead.'

'What's so wrong with HQ? And I rather like the idea of being engaged to a detective superintendent. Think of the salary. It's either that or you're stuck here as the office manager.' She shrugged, trying to soften the blow. Or rub it in, perhaps. Dixon couldn't tell.

'I'd rather go back to being a DI.'

'What've you got on this afternoon?'

'Performance reviews, then a webinar on building better teams.'

The Safeguarding Unit may have been soundproofed, but the walls were glass and the sight of Police Constable Nigel Cole shifting from one foot to the other on the landing outside did little to improve Dixon's mood.

'Sorry, Sir.' Cole had finally summoned up the courage and was pushing open the door inch by inch.

'What is it?'

'Dead sheep.'

Dixon ignored Jane's laughter, instead preferring to enjoy the choking on her coffee that followed.

'Is she all right?' asked Cole.

'Pat her on the back.'

'I'm fine,' spluttered Jane, wiping away the tears streaming down her cheeks with the palms of her hands.

Dixon turned back to Cole, determined to take him seriously, and not just because it was only nine months or so ago that Cole had saved his life, jumping into an icy drain out on the Somerset Levels and pulling him to safety. The truth was that dead mutton was far more interesting than building better teams. 'What's with the sheep then?'

'There's a farmer outside with six of them on the back of his tractor. He says he either gets to see someone senior or he's going to dump them on the steps. They don't half stink, and you're the most senior officer in the building. I thought about nicking him but then we've still got the problem of the sheep.'

They left Jane dabbing the coffee off her keyboard with a tissue and walked along the landing, Dixon stopping in the floor to ceiling windows at the front of the building while Cole summoned the lift. He looked down at six rotting sheep carcasses stretched out on a flatbed trailer hitched to a huge green tractor parked across the entrance. A small crowd had gathered on the far side of the visitors' car park to enjoy the spectacle, some holding iPhones aloft.

'His name's Gordon Bragg, Sir,' said Cole when they stepped out of the lift on the ground floor. 'He's locked himself in his cab.'

The receptionist was unlocking the front doors to let them out. 'He's not bringing those bloody sheep in here.'

'Quite,' replied Dixon.

An elderly lady waiting upwind of the trailer rushed forward, hoping to get in. 'I've got to report a missing dog,' she said.

Dixon stepped back to let her in, then followed Cole down the steps, listening to the jangle of keys in the lock behind him. He headed for the trailer while Cole banged on the door of the tractor.

Not that he needed to; the old farmer had been watching their every move. 'I seen you on the telly.' He was climbing out of the cab on the opposite side to Cole. 'What rank are you?'

'Detective chief inspector,' replied Dixon, staring at a neat hole in the forehead of the sheep at the back of the trailer. 'Nick Dixon.'

'You'll do.' The old farmer had come dressed for battle: clean shirt, tweed jacket and tie, grubby corduroys, baler twine belt and wellington boots. 'Now, what the bloody hell's going on with my sheep? This is the third lot.'

'Gordon Bragg, isn't it, Sir?' interrupted Dixon, taking the opportunity to put his opponent on the back foot.

'Er, yes, sorry.' The weather-beaten face made it impossible to tell if the old man was blushing.

'What breed are they?' Not that Dixon knew many, apart from the Herdwick, perhaps, a familiar sight on the fells of the Lake District.

'Dorset Downs.' Bragg was following Dixon around the back of the trailer. 'The rams are worth five hundred quid each and I've lost four. The ewes two-fifty.' He pulled a torn envelope from his jacket pocket and looked at the back. 'So, that's five thousand five hundred pound I've lost all told.'

The fleeces were matted with blood, maggots visible in gaping wounds on their flanks.

'Are you insured, Sir?' Cole was standing on the bottom step, upwind and keeping a safe distance.

'Yes, but that's not the point, is it. Dorset Downs are a rare breed.'

'Where d'you keep them?' asked Dixon, changing the subject with a sideways glance at Cole.

'I lives over at Mark, but I've got ten acres just east of Blackford and the flock's over there. I does a bit of contracting too.'

'And it's happened three times?'

'It's all on your records. I reported it each time and was told it'd be referred to the Rural Crimes Unit.'

'He's retired, Sir,' mumbled Cole. 'And Mr Bateman hasn't replaced him yet.'

'Oh, that's bloody marvellous.' Bragg folded his arms and leaned back against his trailer, apparently oblivious to the smell of rotting sheep. 'Well, I said it before and I'll say it again, I ain't shifting this lot 'til something's done.'

'Has a vet looked at them?'

'I had to have a post mortem done for the insurance. You've had the reports from the first two.'

'Not this time?' asked Cole.

Dixon winced. He knew the answer to that question before Cole asked it and braced himself for the sarcastic jibe.

'I was waiting for you useless buggers to come and 'ave a look before I got the vet out.'

'And who is your vet?' Dixon asked, changing the subject again.

'Clive Docherty over at Beaumont Agricultural. They're on the industrial estate at Cheddar. He said they were killed with a cross-bow, before you ask.'

'I thought you were going to say it was a dog attack,' said Cole. 'The injuries . . .'

'He's using bolts with broadheads on 'em and cuts 'em out when he's finished.'

'When did this happen?' asked Dixon.

'The first lot was a couple of months ago, then maybe a month or so ago – you've got the dates – and this lot was last Thursday.'

'Six days ago,' said Cole.

'I'm staying over there in my caravan now, to keep an eye on 'em.'

Dixon spun round at the sound of tapping on the window behind him to find Jane pointing towards the visitors' car park, where Charlesworth was parking his car. 'All right, I've heard enough. The assistant chief constable's here. Get this lot shifted and I'll look into it. You have my word.'

Bragg hesitated.

'The new Rural Crimes Unit here will help me,' continued Dixon, pointing to Cole.

'I have your word on it?'

'You do.' Dixon slid his phone out of his pocket and walked along the trailer taking several photographs of the sheep carcasses.

It was enough for Bragg, who climbed into the cab of his tractor.

'I'll need to speak to your vet, if you could let him know,' said Dixon, reaching up and holding the door open when the old man tried to close it.

'I will, thank you.' Bragg tore the used envelope in half and passed one piece down to him. 'These are the crime numbers they gave me.'

Dixon slammed the door just as Charlesworth appeared at his elbow, the sight of the assistant chief constable in uniform striding towards him prompting Bragg to start his engine and accelerate away, the trailer bouncing over the pavement as he turned for the exit.

'Everything under control, Nick?' Charlesworth suddenly noticed the receptionist unlocking the doors of the police centre and the smell lingering in the air. Not even the diesel fumes had been enough to mask it.

'Yes, Sir.'

'Jolly good. I gather you're joining us for the webinar later?'

'I am, Sir.'

'Building better teams; it should be very exciting.'

Stinging nettles up to his armpits and a short-sleeved shirt.

Sod it.

He should have known better and would have to come back later with the strimmer.

Shafts of light flooded through the lush green canopy, the familiar screech of a buzzard wheeling overhead cutting through the chatter of blackbirds as he weaved his way along the path, the chainsaw held above his head to keep his arms clear of the nettles.

The path took him further into the wood, not a breath of wind to rustle the trees; the air colder, the birdsong louder, the puddles deeper, brambles to contend with now too. He stopped to take off his sunglasses, hooking them over the collar of his shirt.

A short detour along a deer run below the path to check on the badger sett; several large tunnels dug deep into the hillside beneath the stumps of trees long since cut down. Something had been digging at the top entrance, scattering the carpet of ivy, leaves and twigs.

Bloody dogs.

Branches above his head sprang back under the weight of squirrels leaping to safety when he jerked back the cord and the chainsaw spluttered into life. He cut through the trunks of a large ivy strangling a big oak, careful not to damage the bark of the old tree, and switched off the motor just in time to hear something crashing through the undergrowth below him. He peered through the trees, catching sight of a small herd of deer bounding off across the field at the bottom of the wood.

Eight; one more than the last time he'd seen them, in the spring.

He was back on the path when his phone rang in the pocket of his jeans.

'Where the hell are you?' barked Mike, before he'd even put the phone to his ear.

'Harptree Combe,' he replied, flicking a dog turd into the bushes with the toe of his boot. 'We had that call about a tree down across the bottom path.'

'Have you finished clearing up at Priddy?'

'Yes.'

'Then you're supposed to be helping me over at Cheddar. We don't get effing well paid to ponce about in that wood.'

'You said we get five hundred quid a year to keep the paths clear. A container, or something.'

'*Retainer*, and we get that anyway, that's the whole point. Now get over to Cheddar. You'll have to meet me there; I'll text you the address.'

Mike rang off, leaving him searching for the woodpecker some-where above him, the telltale knocking echoing in the trees. He spun around, his phone still clamped to his ear in his right hand, the chainsaw in his left.

'The traffic was shite.' He looked at his watch as he contin-ued along the path, the bottom track now visible as the vegetation thinned out. 'Roadworks.' Rehearsing his excuses.

Not much of a tree, as it turned out; long dead, the ivy had been holding it up, most likely, until that storm blew in. Hugo, or whatever it had been called.

The chainsaw made short work of the rotten wood; a cut just above the path, another below and the trunk dropped to the ground. Then he rolled it clear with his foot, watching it tumble down into the bushes, coming to rest on the edge of the stream at the bottom of the combe. Well off the beaten track.

Job done.

Take the shortcut back to the car park and he'd be on his way to Cheddar in twenty minutes or so. Mike would just have to lump it.

He followed a deer run, weaving his way up the hillside and through the undergrowth, arms above his head again to keep his elbows clear of the brambles and stinging nettles. Twigs and ivy crunched under his feet as he picked his way carefully up the slope, always at risk of sliding back down.

The barking started before he emerged from the bushes on to the top path.

'What the—?' An elderly lady looked startled by the sight of the chainsaw held aloft, but his Mendip Tree Services T-shirt seemed to calm her nerves.

'Shortcut,' he said, smiling, although he wasn't sure she heard it over the yapping of her terrier. And he certainly didn't hear any reply.

Then he was off, scrambling up the steep slope, his boots slid-ing on the dry earth; the dog still barking, but far below him now and out of sight as he headed for a gap in the hedge at the top of the wood. The chainsaw would soon clear a path through the nettles and his van was on the other side of the field. He checked his watch again: Cheddar by eleven-thirty; plenty of time.

He glanced along a deer run that followed the brow of the hill off to his right, a flash of fluorescent orange at the base of a tree stopping him in his tracks.

Orange?

He left the chainsaw on a tree stump and picked his way along the narrow track, stepping over roots and ducking under holly branches. Footprints in the mud were out of place too.

Nobody comes up here, surely?

At last able to stand up straight, he sighed at the unmistakeable outline of fletching, the arrow shaft black.

Bow hunting. Here?

Bastards.

He ducked under the last of the holly branches and looked down at the base of the tree.

'Too short to be arrows,' he whispered, oddly matter of fact. 'Must be crossbow bolts.' There were four, three in the man's chest and one sticking out of his eye socket – that was the orange one; the others were fluorescent green.

A trickle of blood from the corner of the eye had congealed in the man's beard, the mouth and eyes wide open; taken by surprise, killed mid-sentence maybe. He leaned over and examined the exit wound; the bolt was buried in the eye almost up to the fletching and had gone clean through, pinning the man's skull to the tree.

He took out his phone and dialled 999, then thought better of it. A quick check all around, then he squatted down next to the body and grinned at the camera in his outstretched hand, careful to angle it just right for a couple of selfies.

The lads on WhatsApp will love this.

Chapter Two

'Lamb hotpot?'

'You've got coffee all down your front,' said Dixon, smirking.

'Go and grab that table over there. I'll get you a bacon roll.'

'And a KitKat, please.'

'Oh, that's great news.' Jane pecked him on the cheek, her delight loaded with sarcasm. 'When were you going to tell me?'

'Tell you what?'

'That your diabetes had gone.'

Dixon knew resistance was futile, so he left her queuing and sat down at a vacant table in the corner of the canteen. There was a distinct smell of ripe mutton, but lamb hotpot wasn't on the specials board. He sniffed the sleeve of his jacket; the stench of death always lingers.

Jane placed a can of Diet Coke on the table in front of him and sat down. 'What's the story with the sheep then?'

'Someone's been killing them with a crossbow. Eighteen of them over the last couple of months.' Dixon was turning the Coke can, wiping away the condensation with the tips of his fingers. 'Poor bug—' The rest of his expletive was lost in the snap of the ring pull.

'There's not a lot you can do about it. The Rural Crimes team'll be looking into it, surely?'

'He's retired and Bateman's not got around to replacing him yet.'

'Please tell me you didn't say *you'd* look into it.'

'I had to tell the old boy something to get rid of him. Cole's getting me copies of everything, just to have a look at, you know; and he's checking for anything else involving a crossbow in the last three months.' He hesitated. 'And besides, there's something bugging me about it.'

'Charlesworth'll do his bloody nut. A DCI investigating a few dead sheep?' Jane sighed. 'Is there no one you can give it to? You can delegate now, you know.'

'All four teams are flat out as it is. And you said so yourself, it's just a few dead sheep.'

'So, what's bugging you?'

'Bacon roll?'

Jane spun round in her seat and raised her hand. 'Over here.'

'Any sauce?' asked the kitchen assistant, placing the plate on the table.

Jane's 'no, thank you' beat Dixon's 'yes, please' by a split second. 'Ketchup is rammed full of sugar,' she said, frowning at him.

'No, thank you,' he mumbled, ignoring her sheep reference; he wasn't sure the pun was deliberate anyway.

'So, are you really going to look into it?' asked Jane, when the coast was clear. 'Or did you just say that?'

'I gave him my word.' Dixon bit into the roll. 'And I'll tell you what's bugging me: ask yourself why someone would be killing sheep with a crossbow,' he said, spraying crumbs across the table.

'Well, they're obviously a sick f—'

'Either that or they're rehearsing for something.' Dixon spotted Cole hovering in the doorway and gestured to a vacant chair at the table. 'And it's not going to be the Christmas panto.' He took another mouthful of bacon roll.

Cole looked at his watch. 'I'm going off duty in a minute, Sir, thank you.'

'Have you got the files?'

'I was in the middle of printing them off when I saw the log pop up on the system; I thought you'd like to know straight away.'

Dixon raised his eyebrows.

'Harptree Combe, Sir; it's on the far side of the Mendips, East Harptree way. Adult male, mid-fifties; no ident so far; pinned to a tree with four crossbow bolts in him.'

Three emails sent cancelling the performance reviews, another to the training officer apologising profusely for missing the webinar, and Dixon was speeding north on the M5, wondering whether his sheep killer's rehearsals were over or whether organised crime might really be involved.

That had come as an unpleasant surprise. Cole had handed him the files on the sheep killings just as he was leaving Express Park, at the same time breaking the news that Zephyr had taken over the murder investigation. Dixon had crossed paths with the organised crime squad twice before; the first time Detective Chief Superintendent Collyer had offered him a job, the second he had threatened to nick him for obstruction.

Happy days.

He would have driven straight past it were it not for the patrol car parked across the entrance to the lane.

'I'm under orders not to let anyone up there, Sir,' the uniformed officer said, almost apologetically. It was worth a try, perhaps, but in the end, he had to agree it was unlikely that instruction extended to a detective chief inspector. That said, Dixon felt sure there would be a welcoming committee waiting for him in the car park.

He parked next to the Mendip Tree Services van and watched in his rear view mirror as the suit leaning up against a BMW stubbed out his cigarette on a fence post and walked towards him, dialling a number on his mobile phone. The dark sunglasses and red braces were the giveaway: Zephyr.

Dixon wound down the window and held out his warrant card.

'He's here, guv,' said the suit into his phone, leaning over and peering at the card. 'It's a DCI from Bridgwater.' Straightening up. 'Dixon, yes.'

Dixon waited, listening to the voice on the other end of the line, not that he could make out what was being said.

The suit took a step back. 'Yeah, it's a Land Rover Defender. Sort of vomit green, with a white bonnet.'

Jane had called it mushy pea green, but 'vomit green'? Cheeky sod.

Then the suit looked in the back window. 'A Staffie, guv, a big white one curled up in a dog bed.' The tap on the window had been a mistake, the suit stepping back sharply when Monty jumped up on the bench seat and started barking at him.

Dixon had been passing his cottage and it had only taken a minute to swing by and pick up his dog. There might even be time for a walk in the woods on the way home.

The suit rang off and dropped his phone back into his jacket pocket. 'DCS Collyer says that you can go down. Follow that path.' He pointed to a gap in the post and rail fence. 'Cross the field and there's a gap in the hedge. They're just inside there. If you stay on the path it's miles round.'

'Keep an eye on my dog, will you?' asked Dixon, as he set off across the car park.

The stubble crunched under his feet as he weaved his way between the large round bales of hay in the field. He was heading towards the trees at the top of the wood, the gap in the hedge on the far side obvious only because of the Scientific Services team in hazmat suits milling about. He recognised Donald Watson, the senior scenes of crime officer, and Leo Petersen, the Bristol pathologist.

'Shouldn't you be sitting behind a comfy desk somewhere, shuffling paper clips?' Watson pulled his face mask down below his chin, revealing a goatee beard; that was new, but then Dixon hadn't seen him since the funeral.

'I was sorry to hear about Peter Lewis.' Petersen forced a smile. 'Big shoes to fill.'

'That they are.' Dixon had met Petersen once before, but couldn't have picked him out of an ID parade. Still, they'd been bobbing about on Chew Valley Reservoir in a small boat at the time, which might explain it.

'Does Collyer know you're here?' asked Watson. 'He doesn't usually like people sticking their noses in.'

'He'll get used to it.'

Petersen handed a set of overalls to Dixon in a sealed plastic bag. 'Bung these on and I'll show you what we've got.'

'Not so fast.' Collyer emerged from the undergrowth, brambles clawing at the sleeves of his overalls. 'I need to know what you're doing here first.' He hadn't changed a bit: short dark hair, sharp moustache and horn-rimmed glasses. Dixon thought he could make out a pair of red braces under his translucent hazmat suit too.

'I'm just interested in the crossbow,' replied Dixon. 'We've got someone killing sheep wi—'

'Look, I appreciate you're bored. I get that. But this is a gangland execution, a professional hit, not some kid out hunting Shaun the Sheep.'

Dixon decided to rise above it. 'Who is he?'

'The victim is Godfrey Collins. He's an accountant – *was* an accountant – from Congresbury.'

'And what's his connection to organised crime?'

Collyer sighed. Loudly. 'He was in it up to his neck. He owned a yacht that was being used in a drug run. It capsized mid-Atlantic; the keel fell off and our intel says two hundred and sixty kilos of cocaine went to the bottom, so that's a street value of twenty million, give or take.'

'The name of the yacht?'

'What the f—?' Collyer turned away, remembering just in time that was no way to speak to a DCI in public, perhaps. Dixon had been about to remind him and was relieved to have been saved the trouble.

'*Sunset Boulevard II*,' continued Collyer. 'Google it; it was all over the bloody news. Still is, now the memorial services are coming round. We've managed to keep the drugs out of it, so far anyway, but this'll probably put paid to that.'

'May I?' Dixon gestured to the gap in the hedge with the overalls in his hand.

Collyer leaned back against a bale of hay and folded his arms. 'Go ahead.'

'We haven't moved him yet,' said Petersen, watching Dixon wriggle into the hazmat suit. 'We're going to bring the tree down so we can cut out the section behind his head. The bolt's deep into the wood and the tree might well come down anyway if we try to cut it out.'

'Make sure you stick to the stepping plates,' said Watson. 'We've got two sets of shoe prints, although one belongs to the lad who found him.'

'Where is he?'

'Gone with one of my lot to trace his route into the wood,' replied Collyer. 'He'd been in to clear a fallen tree off the bottom path and was taking a shortcut back to his van.'

'When his boss gets here they're going to take the tree down for us,' said Watson.

Dixon nodded, then turned and followed Petersen into the trees, the stepping plates adjacent to a line of yellow flags on the narrow track leading out into the field. The conversation behind him just carried over the wind and the birdsong.

'He's wasting his bloody time,' Collyer grumbled.

'He's the best we've got,' replied Watson. 'And if he thinks there's something—'

'Bollocks.'

Petersen was standing over the body. 'Looks like he was in the middle of saying something. I'd love to know what.'

'*Please don't shoot,*' muttered Dixon, teetering on the edge of the stepping plate nearest to the body. 'Have you got a time of death?'

'Last night between eight and midnight. Sunset was quarter to eight and it was light until about twenty past. There's very little blood from the chest wounds so it looks like the shot to the head came first; that would have killed him instantly, although I won't know for sure until I open him up, of course. The shot to the eye is just an ordinary bolt, but the others have got broadheads on them. You can see the patterns on the entry wounds: a double, a treble and one with three curved blades. Never seen one of those before – seriously nasty stuff.'

'What about the bow?' Dixon squatted down and looked at the exit wound at the back of the skull. 'Will we be able to tell anything about that?'

'Not really. There's no ballistics, no gunshot residue, and without knowing how far away the shooter was we'll be hard pressed to get any idea of the power, if that's what you're asking.'

'We might get something from the bolts, though,' said Watson, appearing along the line of stepping plates. 'When we get them out, that is.'

Dixon stared into the trees beyond the body.

'No footprints over there either,' continued Watson. 'Just ivy and dead leaves. He picked his spot carefully; we've been over it with a fine-toothed comb and there's nothing. The only prints we've got are next to the body there' – gesturing to small red flags at the base of the tree – 'and over there. The red ones are the lad who found him; we haven't been able to identify the yellow ones.' A line of red flags followed a narrow track along the top of the wood, inside the hedge line. 'The lad said he came along the deer run, heading for the gap in the hedge, and saw the orange fletch on the bolt.'

'Looks like he squatted down here.' Dixon turned back to the body and pointed into the trees. 'Facing that way.'

'That was when he dialled 999,' said Petersen.

'Of course it was.'

'Seen enough?' shouted Collyer from the other side of the hedge.

'I'd better not outstay my welcome.' Dixon straightened up. 'Thank you, Doctor.'

'Leo, please.'

'Satisfied?' snapped Collyer, when Dixon emerged from the trees.

'I'm satisfied he was killed with a crossbow.'

'Good, now piss off back to Bridgwater and keep your nose out of it.'

Dixon rolled up his hazmat suit and dropped it into a plastic crate. 'The lad who found the body.'

'What about him?'

'I'd check his phone if I were you,' he replied, with a wave of his hand as he set off back to his car. 'I'm guessing you'll find a couple of selfies with your victim in the background; it'll be a trifle embarrassing for you when they go viral.'

'The little scrote—'

Chapter Three

Charlesworth's on the prowl wondering where you are. He asked me if you understood the importance of management training. I said you did! Jx

Jane's text arrived when Dixon was sitting in the car park outside Beaumont Agricultural, flicking through the post mortem reports on the sheep. He could have done without the photographs, and wasn't entirely sure the insurance company would have needed them either. The cause of death in each case had been a foregone conclusion too, the injuries inflicted by crossbow bolts.

He was about to reply to Jane's text when the door at the side of the unit opened and an elderly man in a waxed jacket shuffled towards a mud spattered car. Well into his eighties would have been a reasonable guess; far too old to be sticking his hand up a cow's backside for a living. Still, if he ever retired, the shock'd probably kill him.

'Mr Docherty?' Dixon was striding across the car park with his warrant card at the ready.

'Yes.'

'Mr Bragg was going to ring you and give you his permission to speak to me.'

'You'll be the police then?'

'Yes, Sir.'

Docherty dumped his bag on the bonnet of his car and began adjusting his hearing aid. 'How can I help you?'

'The first incident a couple of months ago, the injuries were far less severe, and I'm wondering how you arrived at the conclusion it was a crossbow?'

'It was a penetrating injury, so I suppose it could have been a metal rod or a screwdriver or something similar, but there were marks either side of the entry wound – you can just see them in the photographs – caused by the flights.'

'The fletchings, you mean?'

'Flights, fletchings, it's all the same.' Docherty pointedly failed to hide his impatience. 'I've seen it before, a few years ago; it was cats that time and your lot arrested some local yob for it. Got community service or something useless like that. I tell you I'd have wrung his bloody—'

'When exactly was that?' asked Dixon. 'Can you remember?'

'Five years ago, maybe. The cats came in to our small animal clinic in the town, but they were already dead. One had been left by the side of the road to make it look like it'd been hit by a car.'

'And the injuries were the same?'

'The lout had been using a pistol crossbow with six and a half inch plastic bolts. A bow and four bolts for under a tenner it was back then; no age checks, nothing. You can still get them on the internet for under twenty quid, would you believe it? I wrote to our MP about it, but a fat lot of good that did.' Docherty took out his keys and unlocked his car. 'The injuries on the first lot of sheep were four inches deep, so that's about right, isn't it, if the bolt went in up to the fletchings?'

23

'I suppose it is,' agreed Dixon.

'There wasn't a lot of power behind it either. There were wounds on the forehead where the bolts had failed to penetrate the skull. So, my best guess is he was using a pistol crossbow.'

'But you can't tell how far away he fired from, surely?'

'The sheep were in a pen, so pretty much point blank range would have been easy. You could say he had a captive audience.'

'And the second time?'

'Something much more powerful. The bolts penetrated the skull easily and to quite a depth. They were longer too; a couple went clean through – those that didn't hit bone. He'd fitted broadheads on some of them as well.' Docherty opened the back door of his car and threw his bag on to the seat. 'Have you seen them?'

'I can imagine.' Dixon blinked away the image of a body pinned to a tree.

'No, you can't. Take it from me; the damage they do internally.' Docherty breathed in sharply through gritted teeth. 'Vile bloody things. Hunting with a bow is illegal in this country so can you please tell me how on earth it's legal to own them, let alone sell them? They're not used for target shooting so what the hell are they used for?'

'Were you able to tell what sort of broadheads he was using?'

'Two and three blade; the ones that had gone clean through left the incisions from the blades. With the rest, the flesh was lacerated almost beyond recognition by the time he'd cut the bolts out, so I really couldn't say what they were, I'm afraid.'

'Do you recall seeing any curved incisions?'

'No, sorry.' Docherty shook his head. 'What's your interest in it?' he asked. 'A detective chief inspector, no less.'

'These things have the potential to escalate.'

'Ah, the old psychopath.' Docherty dropped into the driver's seat of his car. 'He starts out pulling the wings off daddy long legs as a child and before you know it he's a serial killer.'

'Something like that, Sir. It wouldn't be the first time.'

And it's far more interesting than building better teams.

'Gordon told me there's been a third lot.' Docherty slammed his car door and wound down the window. 'I'm over there in the morning to have a look and do another report for his insurers.'

Dixon handed him his business card. 'Will you let me know if you see any sign of a curve in the broadhead? Three curved blades, so the entry wound looks a bit like a clover leaf.'

Docherty looked at him quizzically as he started his engine. 'There's something you're not telling me, isn't there?'

'Yes, Sir.'

Half an hour on the beach with Monty had been perfect, getting him back to Express Park while the webinar was still going on. In and out in two minutes flat, provided Jane was ready to go; an encounter with Charlesworth was to be avoided at all costs.

Dixon parked across the entrance, leaving the engine running, and sent her a text – *outside take back stairs Nx* – keeping a careful watch on the front doors as he did so. Charlesworth's car was still in the visitors' car park, but that was where it should be if he was in the training session. It made Dixon nervous all the same, his eyes darting from wing mirror to front doors to rear view mirror and back round again.

As it turned out, Jane was late and Charlesworth was early, the tap on the driver's window catching him unawares as he watched her emerging from the side entrance in his rear view mirror. Still, there was an argument for getting it over with before Collyer could complain about his appearance at Harptree Combe.

He undid his seatbelt and opened the door.

'I had a call from DCS Collyer this afternoon,' said Charlesworth, before Dixon's feet had touched the ground.

Oh, shit.

'Yes, Sir.'

'Let me run through it for you one more time, Nick.' Charlesworth put down his briefcase, took off his hat and tucked it under his arm. 'You're the detective chief inspector in charge of the Bridgwater Criminal Investigation Department. That is a managerial role. There are four teams of eighteen detectives, which means you're responsible for the wellbeing of seventy-two officers, and then there are the fifty-six civilian staff as well. It is an onerous task.'

Dixon was watching Jane sneaking across the car park, until she disappeared silently behind the Land Rover.

'Is. That. Clear?' continued Charlesworth. It didn't help that he was standing on the bottom step, towering over Dixon.

'What happened to the webinar?' he asked.

'There was only me in the end so we've put it back to Friday afternoon. I hardly need tell you I expect you to attend.'

'No, Sir.'

Charlesworth took a deep breath. 'Look, we know the gangs are using crossbows; they're cheap as chips, readily available, easy to use and silent. We also know that kids sometimes play with them.'

'Play?' Dixon knew a conciliatory tone was called for, but try as he might . . . 'Eighteen sheep isn't *playing.*'

'Of course it isn't,' said Charlesworth, menacingly. 'I've spoken to Chief Inspector Bateman and he's going to make sure that the Rural Crimes team looks into it as a priority. You did well defusing that situation this afternoon; dead sheep on the front steps would have been a PR disaster, but it is not your job to go gallivanting off investigating the matter. If it warrants CID involvement – which it does not – you delegate it to one of your teams.'

'There's a clear escalation in the power of the crossbow and the destructiveness of the bolts. It's always been leading up to something, Sir, and now we've got a dead accountant on our hands.'

'*Zephyr* have got a dead accountant on *their* hands.'

'And who's to say this isn't just the start?'

Charlesworth stepped down on to the pavement and made eye contact with Dixon. 'I'm not an idiot, Nick. I've been a police officer for twenty-seven years and I know the way these things work; and yes, sometimes there is an escalation.' He sighed. 'There is a way out of this and you know very well what it is.'

'Portishead.'

'Peter Lewis's death leaves a vacancy for a detective superintendent and you are the outstanding candidate for the job, head and shoulders above the rest, only you're not a candidate for the job because you haven't applied for it.'

'No, Sir.'

'Apply for it and you'll get it.' Charlesworth picked up his briefcase in his free hand. 'Then you'll have all the resources of your own major investigation team behind you. Applications close on the twenty-seventh, so you've got two weeks. In the meantime, you've got some performance reviews to catch up on, haven't you?'

Dixon grimaced.

'You didn't even tell your assistant where you'd gone today. He tried ringing you three times while I was there.'

'It was one of the first things I learnt in the legal profession, Sir.' Dixon tried a wry smile. 'The fact that someone is ringing to speak to you doesn't necessarily mean you want to speak to them.'

'That explains why solicitors never return telephone calls.' Charlesworth smiled back. 'And don't think I don't know what happens now,' he said, as he turned for his car.

'What's that, Sir?'

'You look into it anyway and hope I don't notice.'

Chapter Four

The final credits were rolling on *A Matter of Life and Death* when Dixon finally looked up from his phone.

Jane was lining up the gizmo on the arm of the sofa, nudging it until it was exactly parallel to the pattern on the fabric. 'I had a visit from Charlesworth today. He wanted me to get you to apply for the superintendent's position at Portishead.'

'What did you tell him?'

'That it was your decision.'

'What did he offer you?'

'A return to CID. Once you were out of the way, there'd be no conflict of interest, he said, and I could transfer.'

'You don't like safeguarding then?'

'It's hardly real police work, is it? Monitoring people. I'm just a filing clerk for reports that come in from Social Services. Would you like it?'

'I'd rather shove wasps up my—'

'It can be arranged.' Jane smiled. 'Anyway, it's up to you. I told Charlesworth I wouldn't try to persuade you one way or the other.'

Dixon pushed Monty off the sofa and stood up. 'He doesn't need you to and I shouldn't think for a minute he expected you to, either.'

'What was it all about then?'

'He wanted to let me know it was your route out of safeguarding; the crafty sod knew you'd tell me.'

'Oh.'

'Fancy a turn round the field at the back?' Dixon picked up Monty's lead.

The dog was easy to follow even before their eyes had adjusted to the darkness, his white coat reflecting the moonlight and almost glowing. Dixon lifted him over the fence behind the shed in the corner of the yard behind his cottage and then climbed over, turning to hold the single strand of barbed wire clear of Jane's trousers as she followed.

The strand of barbed wire on the top of the fence had appeared at some point over the summer, so maybe the farmer had been trying to tell him something, particularly given that the field had never had livestock in it.

'Are you going to tell me what's so fascinating on your phone?' said Jane, weaving between the thistles along the edge of the field. 'You've hardly said a word all evening.'

'I was researching that accountant. He's found pinned to a tree with a crossbow bolt through his skull, three more buried in his chest, and before I get a look in, Zephyr steam in and take over the investigation.'

'Collyer?'

'I shall have to get myself a pair of red braces if I go to Portishead.'

'Your birthday's coming up.'

'Don't you dare.' Dixon gave Monty a shove with his foot when the dog stopped in the middle of the path, sniffing something in the undergrowth at the base of the hedge. 'The victim's yacht sank mid-Atlantic. There's lots of stuff about it online, but no mention of the twenty million quid's worth of cocaine that went to the bottom, according to Collyer. He seems to think it's got something to do with that.'

'A reasonable enough assumption, I'd have thought.'

'Possibly.'

'Maybe he knows something you don't?'

'There's somebody on our patch killing sheep with a crossbow and I don't believe in coincidence.' He flicked on the light on his phone and leaned over to see what was distracting Monty. 'Leave that,' he snapped. Then he turned, shining the torch in Jane's face. 'There's a dead rat there.'

'It could be the Albanians are back,' said Jane, blinking furiously.

'Collyer wouldn't say. And I can't look at the file or he'll see I've logged in to the system and grass me up to Charlesworth again.'

'Collyer was behind that?'

'Yeah, 'fraid so. Charlesworth told me to keep my nose out of it and gave me a lecture about the importance of management; how many people I'm responsible for, etcetera, etcetera. Then he reminded me applications for the super's job close in two weeks.' Dixon turned, careful not to shine the light in Jane's eyes again. 'Told me he'd be watching me, he did.'

'So what're you going to do?'

'Be careful. I'll need to monitor the sheep thing to see whether it warrants CID involvement and the rest I'll have to do on Google. Which reminds me, you went to Weston College, didn't you?'

'Yes, why?'

'We're going to a memorial service tomorrow afternoon.'

There weren't many places in the area that Dixon hadn't visited at some point, but West Stoughton was one of them. A tiny village tucked away off the beaten track, it would be about a forty minute commute to Weston-super-Mare. An early bird who liked to avoid the morning rush hour and arrive in the office bright and early, coffee in hand, might leave home at seven-thirty. It had made for an early start, Dixon parking across the drive just before twenty past seven.

Myrtle House was on the edge of the village, standing in its own grounds, a thin barbed wire fence separating it from the fields behind. Dixon couldn't tell if it was old or a new build made to look old, not that it mattered. The owner had certainly made an effort with old stone toadstools in the garden and a wisteria just getting going up the front porch. Worth a bob or too as well.

The electric gates started to open just after 7.30 a.m. – inwards, mercifully, otherwise they'd have clattered into the side of Dixon's Land Rover – revealing a car on the gravel drive, engine running. Dixon ignored the blast of the horn, instead waiting for the driver to approach and tap on his passenger window.

'Would you mind moving? You're blocking my drive and I've got to get to work.'

A light blue shirt, open at the neck; fifty or so, balding with wire-rimmed glasses. Polite too.

The electric windows on his new Land Rover were a bonus, thought Dixon, holding his warrant card out in his left hand as he opened the passenger window with his right. 'Mr Staveley?'

'Yes.'

'I wonder whether I might have a word with you about your business partner, Godfrey Collins.'

Staveley sniffed. 'I've got some of your lot coming to see me at ten.'

'Different lot, I'm afraid, Sir. It won't take long.'

Dixon's disarming smile seemed to work. Staveley looked at his watch, then sighed. 'D'you want to come in?'

'No, that's fine, Sir, thank you. It won't take long, if you'd like to hop in.'

'Let me just switch mine off.' Staveley walked back to his new Audi estate. Gunmetal grey with alloy wheels and low profile tyres – lot of money in accountancy, even in a small firm above a charity shop in the arse end of Weston; Dixon had checked Google Street View.

'If you've got someone coming to see you at ten, I'm guessing you know what's happened to Mr Collins?' he said, watching Staveley slide into the passenger seat of his Land Rover.

'Yes, and I can't say I'm surprised.' Dixon opened his mouth to speak but Staveley beat him to it. 'This is where you ask me who might have wanted to kill him and it'd probably be easier if I told you who *didn't*.'

'Like that, is it, Sir?'

'Yes, it bloody well is. He's lucky I didn't do it.' Staveley frowned at Dixon. 'And I didn't, before you start.'

Dixon turned in his seat to face Staveley. 'How did you come to be in partnership with him?'

'We were both sole practitioners and we met at Wedmore Golf Club. That was about fifteen years ago. We were originally just sharing office space, pooling resources, but then we went into partnership proper in 2010. It seemed like a good idea at the time. We kept our practices separate, so I never really knew what he was up to.'

'And what was he up to?'

Staveley puffed out his cheeks. 'He was running tax avoidance schemes, or perhaps I should say he was running schemes that were borderline at the time but have since been clamped down on by HM Revenue and Customs. The end result is I've had the Investigations Unit crawling in and out of every orifice pretty much ever since.'

'What did these tax avoidance schemes involve? Keeping it simple for a humble police officer.'

'It's what they call the "loan scheme". It's fairly simple, really. Basically, the employer doesn't pay their staff, they give them loans instead. Loans aren't subject to income tax and national insurance so there's nothing for either the employer or the employee to pay to HMRC.'

'But surely they have to pay the loans back?'

'No, they don't, that's the whole point. Everybody's happy, except the taxman.' Staveley was watching a neighbour turning out of a driveway further along the lane. 'It's a little bit more complicated than that in the precise mechanism, but that's the gist of it. Anyway, as you can imagine, the taxman wasn't having any of it and has since gone after everyone paid under these schemes for the back tax. All outstanding loans are now treated as income and taxed accordingly – they call that the "loan charge". They went after the advisers too. An adviser is liable if he is the "enabler" of tax avoidance, and the fine is up to one hundred per cent of the tax avoided.'

'How much was Mr Collins fined?' asked Dixon.

'One point four million.'

'A lot of money. Did he have it?'

'No, but he managed to pay just enough of it to keep himself out of prison.'

'How many employees were there?'

'They're the ones I feel sorry for. It's not just footballers and celebrities using these schemes to duck millions, y'know. There was even a care agency, ordinary people earning ten pounds an hour doing agency work suddenly finding themselves with a four or five grand bill for back tax. And it's not as if they were given any choice. "That's the way the agency pays its staff and if you don't like it you can go elsewhere." What were they supposed to do?'

'How many were there?'

'A couple of hundred. The taxman's being reasonable with some of them, giving them time to pay, but some of them just can't. The government were supposed to be looking into it; there was a review to see whether it was reasonable to claw back this money, but that just decided they couldn't go back further than 2010, which is still leaving some people with whopping great bills.'

'And you were never involved in any of these schemes?'

'Certainly not! The Institute took a bit of convincing, mind you. They hauled us both up before a disciplinary panel. Godfrey was struck off for the tax avoidance and misappropriating clients' funds, but I was cleared of any dishonesty.'

'But that still leaves hundreds of people with a motive to kill him?'

'I suppose it does. But, having said that, I'd be surprised if many of them knew who he was. He was just the accountant who administered the scheme. If they were going to blame anyone it would have been their employer, I'd have thought.'

'Collins is struck off,' said Dixon, nodding. 'Fined one point four million pounds. Was he bankrupt?'

'Not yet. It was in the pipeline though. He'd made some payments towards it using clients' funds, it turned out. He used to do a bit of probate work, administering estates, and stole some of the money. I got a bit of stick for that; the tribunal said I should have kept a closer eye on the books. Sort of ironic, for an accountant, don't you think?'

'The beneficiaries who lost out would've been covered by your professional indemnity insurance, so there's hardly a motive there.'

'The bloody premium shot up.'

'So, that's when he starts letting someone use his yacht for drug runs?'

'So I gather, but that's all news to me.' Staveley checked his watch. 'It was an old heap; he kept it at Burnham Yacht Club and

34

the thing used to spend most of its life out of the water anyway. It was a good size, thirty-something feet or so. I went on it once, when we first met.'

'Did he ever mention to you who he was dealing with?'

'Lord, no. The last time I saw him was at the Chartered Institute's disciplinary panel eighteen months ago and we certainly didn't discuss his drug running, or anything else for that matter.' Staveley checked his watch again. 'Look, I really need to be . . .'

'One last thing, Sir. When you meet my colleagues at ten, if you could see your way clear not to mention this meeting I'd be most grateful.'

'Why?'

'Just a bit of internal police politics, you know how it is.'

Chapter Five

A couple of performance reviews before lunch and Dixon was sitting in the corner of the canteen when Jane caught up with him.

'Where's this memorial service then?' She placed a bowl of soup on the table and sat down next to him.

'St Andrew's in Burnham. It's one of the crew on the yacht that sank. Laura Dicken – she was a couple of years younger than you; pregnant too.'

'Oh God. Do we know what happened?'

'The keel fell off and the boat capsized in a storm. The crew would've had no warning and it happened in the middle of the night, so some of them might even have been asleep.'

'Doesn't bear thinking about.' Jane shuddered. 'How many were there?'

'Four.'

'But it was a drug run?'

'According to Zephyr's intelligence, yes, but there's no evidence and nothing was found to suggest there were any drugs on board.'

'I thought you said the boat sank?'

'A container ship stumbled on it three hundred and fifty miles north-east of the Azores. They got a rope on it, but it sank when they tried to tow it. There are some photos of the bottom and the keel's gone; just some holes where the bolts would've been.' Dixon pushed his empty plate into the middle of the table and picked up his can of Diet Coke. 'It's hardly rocket science to work out what Zephyr are thinking: the keel's taken off somewhere in the Caribbean, packed with the drugs and then not put back on properly.'

'Either that or they were coopering,' said Jane, between slurps of soup.

'And what's that when it's at home?'

'It's where a local yacht goes out, collects the drugs from the ocean-going vessel and then slips back into a small place like Burnham.'

'With next to no chance of a customs check.'

'Leaving the larger yacht to breeze into Southampton or some-where, clean as a whistle.'

'Yes, but they couldn't pack the keel with drugs at sea, could they?'

'Maybe they didn't.'

Dixon breathed out slowly through his nose. 'We need to have a word with somebody at the Marine Accident Investigation Branch.'

'We?' Jane turned to Dixon, soup dripping off the end of her spoon on to the table. 'With Charlesworth on your tail?'

'Since when did you care about that?' he replied, standing up. 'You know as well as I do this accountant is just the start.'

'Back stairs or out through the front?' asked Jane, as they walked along the landing.

Dixon paused in the large windows at the front of the building and looked down. He had used the visitors' car park again, which, on reflection, had not been a good idea. Charlesworth never used the staff car park either, and there he was, sitting in his car next to Dixon's Land Rover. 'He's like a trapdoor spider,' he whispered.

'We're going to a memorial service,' said Jane, her finger on the button summoning the lift. 'He can't very well grumble about that.'

'He's not to know we won't know anybody there.'

'Not even the deceased.'

Charlesworth's car door opened right on cue, just as they were walking across the car park. 'Where are you off to?' he demanded.

'A memorial service, Sir,' replied Dixon.

'Laura and I were both at Weston College, Sir,' offered Jane. 'It's very sad; someone so young.'

'Oh, I see.' Charlesworth blushed. 'I'm very sorry to hear that. Please accept my condolences.'

'Thank you, Sir.'

'That makes you a co-conspirator,' Dixon said, when they were both sitting in his Land Rover.

'I didn't lie.' Jane was putting on her seatbelt. 'We were both at Weston College. I never said we were there at the same time, did I?'

'I'm sure Professional Standards will take that into account at your gross misconduct hearing.'

Dixon hadn't expected television cameras; local ones only, mercifully, but it was still an unpleasant surprise.

'Keep an eye out for Collyer,' he said, as they walked along the narrow path around the back of St Andrew's Church, the tower leaning over them, the result of building on sand dunes. Most of the gravestones were at odd angles too.

A large group was filing in from the road, shuffling along the wide path towards the main entrance, their faces turned away from the TV cameras on the pavement outside. Dixon and Jane would need to do the same, if only because the side door of the church had been locked, much to his irritation.

Two men were standing unusually close together out in the road – waiting for something, that much was obvious; presumably for the crowd to disperse before they followed them into the church. Both wore black ties under dark suits, the older man looking bored and disinterested, the younger embarrassed. Dixon watched an elderly woman walk over and put her arms around the young man, beaming through her tears. He simply blushed, forced a smile and put one arm around her.

'Looks like a prison escort to me.' Dixon nudged Jane with his elbow and pointed in their direction.

'Who is he?'

'We'll soon find out.'

They slotted into a gap in the line of mourners on the main path and filed into the church, heading straight for a pew at the back.

Jane picked up a hymn book and turned to number 325, the first on the order of service. 'Eternal Father, Strong to Save,' she read aloud. '*Oh, hear us when we cry to Thee, for those in peril on the sea.*'

'Had to be, didn't it.'

The church was full, although the pews along the north wall had been ripped out since the last time Dixon had been in St Andrew's. Stacks of plastic chairs and boxes of toys now replaced what had once been ornate carved oak pews, a pile of soft rubber mats placed against the wall where he had sat on that last occasion: midnight one Christmas Eve, slightly the worse for wear.

No one from Zephyr had seen fit to come, although Dixon might not have recognised them if they had taken off their red braces. He wondered whether they wore black braces to funerals as he looked around the congregation. Collyer certainly wasn't there, nor was the twat from the car park.

Family to the front was the usual order of things; an older couple who had been holding hands on the way in and a young boy and girl were sitting on the front pew. Mother and father of the deceased with her brother and sister, possibly. Grandparents, aunts, uncles and cousins in the rows behind.

The older couple in the front row on the other side of the aisle were in-laws, perhaps; not that Laura was married. Parents of her boyfriend, then; the father of her unborn child, possibly the lad waiting outside with his prison escort?

All were staring at a large photograph of Laura on a stand at the top of the steps at the front of the church.

Dixon had seen the same picture on the internet – of Laura wearing a lifejacket and smiling at the camera, at sea somewhere in Bridgwater Bay, the unmistakeable outline of Steep Holm just visible in the background and the water that familiar murky grey colour.

He recognised a couple from the yacht club he had spoken to on a previous investigation nine months ago, so the chances of them recognising him were small. The yacht club seemed to have turned out in force too, most of them having made a deliberate effort not to wear black.

Then came the pair in dark suits, walking slowly down the aisle, this time the older man looking embarrassed as the congregation turned to glare at him. Who'd be a prison officer, thought Dixon, as he watched the scene unfold, each row turning at the sound of footsteps behind them until finally the pair sat down on the front pew.

The deceased's mother sitting on the other side of the aisle reached out and took the younger man's hand; a nice touch. Must be category D, otherwise he'd be handcuffed.

'No hard feelings, obviously,' whispered Jane.

A few prayers, then the yacht club really put their backs into 'Eternal Father, Strong to Save'. After that came the eulogy, from which Dixon learned a lot. Laura's mother was sitting at the front with her second husband, making him Laura's stepfather; the young boy and girl, her half-brother and half-sister. Wearing the dark suit was Laura's fiancé, Craig, who currently had the misfortune to be detained at Her Majesty's pleasure and hadn't even had the chance to say goodbye to her.

Twenty-nine years of age, Laura had been four months pregnant when she had set sail in late March, her last communication with anyone an email sent by satellite phone to her mother as the yacht rounded Land's End a week before it lost contact.

The eulogy was given by her uncle, who only just managed to keep his composure; the sound of sobbing providing the backdrop to his tribute.

'I've always hated the sea.' Dixon was watching the uncle squat down in front of Laura's mother on his way back to his seat.

Another hymn, a collection for the local RNLI, a few more prayers and then a rousing blast of 'All Things Bright and Beautiful' – Laura's favourite, apparently – and they were filing out of the church in silence, Laura's mother thanking each of the mourners in turn on their way out.

'Thank you for coming.' Her eyes were filled with tears when Jane reached her. 'How did you know Laura?'

'Weston College.'

'Oh, yes, I remember.' Already looking along the line to see how many more were behind Jane. 'You're welcome to join us at the yacht club for a drink.'

'I'm afraid I've got to get back to work.'

The woman released Jane's hand and shook Dixon's. 'Thank you for coming.'

He smiled and kept moving.

◆ ◆ ◆

'I feel awful.' Jane shifted uneasily in the passenger seat of Dixon's Land Rover as he turned into Express Park twenty minutes later, the journey from Burnham having passed in silence. 'Misleading the mother like that.'

'Not my finest hour, but we didn't have a lot of choice.'

'And what about Laura? Four months pregnant when she set sail on a transatlantic crossing. I'm not sure I'd do that.'

'Someone climbed the north face of the Eiger six months pregnant.'

'I'm not doing that either.'

'Charlesworth's still here, so we'd better use the staff car park.' Dixon slid his phone out of his jacket pocket while he waited on the ramp for the electric gates to open, the diesel engine straining as he held the Land Rover on the clutch. 'Three missed calls from a Bristol number; don't recognise it,' he said, dropping it back into his pocket. 'I think I'll leave it on silent though.'

'Mine's ringing now.' Jane put her phone to her ear. 'Jane Winter.' She turned to Dixon and raised her eyebrows. 'Who's calling?' she asked, mouthing 'It's Collyer' before continuing, 'He's driving, I'm afraid, Sir.' She flinched, then passed her phone to Dixon. 'He says he doesn't give a fuck.'

Dixon pulled on the handbrake. 'Yes, Sir.'

'What the bloody hell are you playing at?'

'Not sure I follow you.'

'We were watching the funeral.'

'Which one, Sir?' He glanced in his rear view mirror as another car appeared behind them on the ramp.

'It's only Dave and Mark,' whispered Jane, looking over her shoulder.

'You know very well which one, you were bloody well there.' Collyer's voice was gathering momentum and increasing in volume at the same time; a dangerous combination.

'You mean the memorial service?'

'Is there a difference?'

'There needs to be a body for a funeral, otherwise it's a memorial serv—'

'Are you trying to wind me up?'

'No, Sir. And we were there in a personal capacity.'

'Don't give me that Weston College crap. Laura Dicken was twenty-nine and Sergeant Winter is thirty-two so they weren't even there at the same time.'

Dixon could hear fingers clicking in the background.

'Just keep your nose out of it, all right? This is your last bloody warning. Is that clear?'

'Yes, Sir.'

'I'd be making this a formal disciplinary matter if you hadn't tipped me off about that little scrotum and his selfies with my victim. I owe you one for that. Then there's the fact Charlesworth seems to think the sun shines out of your arse.'

Collyer rang off.

'Better back off, then.' Jane dropped her phone into her handbag.

'Just block his number,' replied Dixon, accelerating up the ramp. 'And ask yourself this: if Zephyr are so convinced the accountant's murder was a gangland execution, why are they watching the memorial service of one of the crew from his yacht?'

Chapter Six

Dixon stood in the floor to ceiling windows on the far side of the Safeguarding Unit, watching Charlesworth walking across the visitors' car park below. Briefcase in the boot, jacket on a hanger in the rear passenger compartment, then he climbed into the driver's seat and reversed out of his parking space.

'Has he gone?' Jane was peering over the top of her computer screen.

Dixon hesitated, watching Charlesworth turn out of the car park and into the petrol station on the corner of the entrance road. 'Not quite.'

'So, what happens now?'

'We investigate what we can.'

'You keep saying *we*!'

'The victim was an accountant running tax avoidance schemes that landed several hundred people with large tax bills, but we've hardly got the manpower to start going through them one by one. And we need to keep out of Zephyr's way, so looking into the Bristol drug gangs is a non-starter as well.'

'What does that leave?'

'Bugger all, really,' he replied. 'Except the yacht, the fiancé in prison and the crossbow bolts.'

'And you're sure there's someone out there armed with a crossbow who's going to kill again?' Jane leaned back in her swivel chair. 'Because otherwise you'll be making a nuisance of yourself and pissing everybody off for no real reason.'

'I've got another performance review in ten minutes.'

'Just be careful,' said Jane, raising her voice as the door slammed behind Dixon.

Two performance reviews, followed by a meeting of the clerical officer team leaders, the main items on the agenda being the coffee machine and quality of the paper on offer in the ladies' loos. Some bright spark had asked whether the toilets ought to be gender neutral, but the discussion was quickly shut down by Chief Inspector Bateman, who had the misfortune to be chairing the meeting. Dixon's eyes had glazed over long before then anyway.

He sent a text message to pathologist Dr Roger Poland during 'Any other business': *Where are you in about half an hour?*

Roger's reply arrived during the argument over 'Date of next meeting', which seemed to be the longest item on the agenda: *At the lab all evening doing a PM.*

There was a hint of sarcasm in Bateman's 'thank you for your contribution' as Dixon was leaving; he couldn't recall having said anything at all, except perhaps 'sorry I'm late'.

The pathology lab at Musgrove Park Hospital was locked when Dixon and Jane arrived half an hour later. She rang the bell and then leaned back against the door. 'He's not going to thank you, dragging him out of a post mortem to look at pictures of dead sheep.'

'He owes me one.'

'He does, but you can't keep calling in the same favour over and over again. And besides, he sorted you out the night of the fire.'

'Roger won't mind.'

'Won't mind what?' Poland was standing behind the glass door listening to their conversation, his translucent green apron smeared with blood. At least he'd taken his latex gloves off.

'Can you see a PM report from Bristol on your system?' asked Dixon.

Poland pulled his face mask down below his chin. 'When from?'

'Today, or maybe late yesterday.'

'If it's been typed up, then yes.'

'What about the photos?'

'If they've been uploaded.' Hands on hips now. 'What's this all about? I thought you were supposed to be putting your feet up?'

'Tell me about it,' said Jane, tipping her head.

'Can we come in?'

'Course you can.' Poland unlocked the door. 'I'm in the middle of a bit of a nasty one, I'm afraid. The bloody Ilminster bypass again; that's three this year. This one had a blood alcohol level off the charts, mind you.'

They followed him along the corridor to an open plan office area with four vacant desks. Poland leaned over and flicked on a computer. 'Name?'

'Godfrey Collins,' replied Dixon. 'He was found yesterday in woods on the north side of the Mendips; Leo Petersen was there when I got there. D'you know him?'

'I do. And what is it that's got your feathers all ruffled?'

'Collins was killed with a crossbow and one of the bolts had an unusual broadhead on it, one that Petersen said he'd never seen before. It's got three curved blades, so the entry wound looks like a clover leaf or three of the Olympic rings.' Dixon was drawing the pattern in the air with his index finger, watching Poland scroll through a series of photographs on the computer screen.

'Like this.' Poland gestured to the screen and an image of a man's bare chest, the flesh greying. 'These are just the usual type, that one's got two blades and that's a three-blader.' He jabbed his finger at the screen. 'There's your circular pattern; designed to bring down a deer I should imagine, although hunting with a bow is illegal in this country.'

'Forty pence each online.' Dixon shook his head. 'And it was used to bring down an accountant.'

'Well, I've never seen a broadhead like that before either.' Poland was sucking his teeth. 'You need to get whoever's using it off the bloody streets sooner rather than later.'

'Zephyr have taken over on the assumption it's gang related. Collins was up to his neck in drug running and his yacht sank with a consignment of cocaine on board apparently, so—'

Poland frowned. 'What's the problem then?'

'We've got someone on our patch killing sheep with a crossbow.'

'Sheep?'

'It's not as daft as it sounds, Roger,' said Jane, diving in.

'All right, all right.' Poland raised his hands in mock surrender, revealing blood on the sleeves of his blue smock. 'Let's hear it.'

'Three lots of six each time, over a period of a couple of months.' Dixon sat down on the edge of Poland's workstation. 'The power of the bow increasing and then broadheads start to make an appearance.'

'With curved blades?'

'That's your department, as you like to say to me often enough.'

Poland didn't take the bait. 'You've got photos of the sheep?'

Dixon slid across an envelope from under his arm. 'These are the vet's reports from the first two lots and then I've got some photos on my phone of the most recent, a week ago they were now.'

Poland flicked straight to the photos at the back of the first report.

'The vet reckoned those were inflicted by a pistol crossbow with six and a half inch bolts. Not very powerful either, as the bolts bounced off the skull.'

Poland pointed to a scuff mark on the forehead of one of the sheep. 'You can see that there.'

'The next lot have got deeper injuries from longer bolts and a more powerful bow. There are simple two-bladed broadheads, but they're not easy to see because they've been cut out.'

'You can see a fine incision there,' said Poland, 'where the vet has clipped away the fleece.'

'The last lot are on my phone.'

'Email them to me and we can look at them on the bigger screen.' Poland stood up and opened the door. 'I'd better go and let them know in the lab what's going on.'

'We'll be ten minutes, Roger, that's all.'

Poland reappeared in the doorway a few seconds later. 'That's fine, they're going to have a cup of tea,' he said.

Dixon clicked 'send' on the email, then opened a web browser. 'A crossbow is a common enough weapon, but these broadheads are a different kettle of fish. I looked up the listing online. Listen to this,' he said, holding up his phone. *'Curved blades for a larger cutting surface; massive wound channel for highly visible blood trail; bone crushing chisel tip for increased penetration.'*

'Forty pence each?' Poland sneered. 'Have you sent the email?'

'Yes.'

A couple of clicks and Poland was scrolling through Dixon's photographs of the rotting sheep. 'It's a bit difficult because the fleeces are matted with blood and you can't really see . . . there.' He stood up, sending his chair sliding into the desk behind him. 'There are your Olympic rings. Plain as day. One's been cut away but the others are still there if you look at that flap of skin and marry it up with that bit. Where are the sheep now?'

'The farmer's got them,' replied Dixon. 'And the vet was going over there last night.'

'It should be in his post mortem report then, and hopefully he'll have cut away the fleece for the photos.'

'Nice work if you can get it,' mumbled Jane.

'It doesn't really prove anything though, does it?' asked Poland. 'I mean, if Zephyr are right, the executioner could just have been practising on the sheep, surely?'

'The broadhead's a signature, Roger,' replied Dixon, sliding the reports back into the envelope. 'And professionals don't leave signatures.'

'Fancy a walk with Monty and a bag of fish and chips?' Dixon had said when they got back to their cottage in Brent Knoll.

'Lovely,' Jane had replied. 'Where d'you fancy going?'

'How about down by the sailing club for a change?'

Now they had finished their food and were watching the yachts gradually being lifted off the mud by the incoming tide, the pontoons lying flat on the sloping sludge; the occasional gust of wind rattling the rigging. A couple of people were moving about near the waterline, weaving in and out of piles of seaweed, picking up litter and placing it in large sacks.

The sailing club was open, the double doors hooked back to the walls on either side, a few people visible propping up the bar. The gates to the yard were open too, although it seemed empty compared to the last time Dixon had seen it, but then that had been January when most of the yachts were out of the water for the winter. He recognised two Cornish pilot gigs on the far side of the yard sitting on their trailers, rowers taking the covers off ready for launch when the tide was far enough in.

By now he had edged several paces into the yard, hoping to be challenged by the woman he had seen watching him from the window.

'They might get an hour's rowing in before it gets too dark,' she said, coming down the steps. 'Can I help you?'

'It's Mrs Sumner, isn't it?' asked Dixon.

'Do I know you?' she asked, with the same frown, short dark hair and orange Musto jacket Dixon had seen last winter.

'We met during the by-election in January. Mr Perry's wife was murdered.'

'Of course, the police.'

Time for the warrant card. 'Off duty at the moment, I'm pleased to say.'

Mrs Sumner looked at Jane, who was waiting at the gate with Monty. 'Didn't I see you at Laura's memorial service this afternoon?'

'Jane was at Weston College too.' Dixon got the white lie in before Jane had to. 'I was interested in the yacht Laura was on.'

'The bloody thing should never have been at sea and certainly not for an ocean passage. If Godfrey hadn't been killed I'm sure he'd have been prosecuted; manslaughter by gross negligence, they said.'

'They?'

'The Marine Accident Investigation Branch. *Sunset Boulevard* was a wreck when he bought it. He had it in the water a couple of years, then after that it was craned out and never went back in, it just sat over there,' she said, gesturing to the far corner of the yard. 'Rotting away.'

'Did you know Mr Collins well?'

'Not really. He paid his subs, crane fees and rented the yard space, but that was about it. He wasn't what you'd call a social member, at least not for the last ten years. God knows how much money he wasted on the damned thing.'

'When did he put it back in the water?'

'Last season, I think. And he left it on a mooring for the winter. He actually started living on it for a time, but then we had to ask him to stop and he moved out. No idea where to, I'm afraid.'

Dixon stepped back to allow four rowers to pull one of the gigs past on its trailer. 'What's the thinking on the cause of the accident; why the keel fell off?'

'You'd better have a word with my husband,' replied Mrs Sumner, turning and waving to the man sitting in the window above.

His and hers Musto jackets. Nice.

'Bob, this is the police and he wants to know about the accident – you know, *Sunset Boulevard*.'

'Design flaw.' Sumner was sucking on a pipe, tamping the tobacco down with the tip of his thumb. 'Big yacht, big keel, ten bolts. It was asking for trouble. Not the first time it's happened either.'

'Really?'

'It was a Geronde Six, at least twenty years old. The keel fell off another after it had grounded. Mercifully that was at a regatta and everyone on board was picked up. Imagine the stresses on those bolts grounding a yacht of that size, and he left *Sunset Boulevard* in the water on a pontoon where it effectively grounded twice a day on the tide.'

'Did you tell all this to the Marine Accident Investigation Branch?'

'We had a couple of people here for a couple of days – May time, maybe. They spoke to several of us and took copies of the relevant documents: craning records, yard rentals, that sort of thing.'

'Did you ever see any maintenance work being done on the boat?' asked Dixon.

Sumner winced. 'Yacht. *Sunset Boulevard* was *not* a boat.'

'Sorry.'

'Maintenance, no. Never.'

'Taking the keel off, perhaps?'

'You'd have to have drilled the bolts out, I expect; rusted to buggery they must have been. It's no wonder they sheared off in a heavy swell.' Sumner shook his head. 'They wouldn't have stood a chance. The French coastguard got a diver on board apparently, the day before it sank, and they said the life raft was still stowed away aft.'

'How often did Mr Collins go out in it after he'd put it back in the water?'

'A couple of times, maybe. He had a captain who took it out a few times as well, but they were never out for very long – a few days, maybe a week, at most.'

'Who is this captain?'

'Richard Page. He'd take a couple of youngsters from the club with him as crew.'

'Laura was one of them.' Mrs Sumner was zipping up her coat. 'We tried to warn them about the condition of the boat.'

Dixon watched Sumner scowling at his wife – calling a yacht a boat was clearly a cardinal sin. 'And where can I find him?'

'You can't. He went down with the rest of them,' replied Sumner.

'So, there's no one left who went out with him.'

Sumner shook his head solemnly. 'All dead.'

'One last thing. Mrs Sumner, you said that Mr Collins would have been prosecuted if he hadn't been killed and I was wondering how you knew he was dead?'

'It was on the local evening news.'

◆ ◆ ◆

'You were doing so well until that last question.' Jane laughed to herself as they walked across the road to the Land Rover.

'I wonder if Zephyr have spoken to the Marine Accident Investigation Branch.'

'Does it matter?'

'Probably not.' Dixon was rummaging in his pockets for his car keys. 'Collyer wouldn't give a toss why the boat sank, just that it did, with somebody else's cocaine on board.'

'So, what's this all about then?' Jane was frowning at Dixon through the passenger window when she opened the door.

'I keep thinking about the sheep.' He shrugged. 'And that crossbow bolt.'

'Thank you for putting that image back in my head.'

'My pleasure.' Dixon smiled. 'Fancy a beer?'

Chapter Seven

It had been a simple enough plan. A two hour meeting with the Citizens in Policing scheme volunteer coordinators starting at 9 a.m. was bad enough, but it left no time to ring the Marine Accident Investigation Branch before his second meeting at 11 a.m. with the Forensics Liaison team. And after lunch it was straight into a Family Liaison meeting.

'Ring me on my mobile at ten and make out there's been some emergency, will you?' Dixon had asked, as he and Jane left the canteen just before nine after a breakfast of bacon rolls and coffee.

He checked his phone at ten, five past and then ten past, trying not to make it look too obvious to the other attendees, his phone finally buzzing on the table at quarter past the hour.

'Sorry,' he mumbled, turning away with his phone to his ear.

'How's the meeting?' Jane chuckled.

'Oh no, really?' An exaggerated sigh. 'Is he still there?'

'Who?'

'Yes, yes, all right, I'm on my way. Just keep him there.' Dixon rang off. 'I really have to go, I'm afraid.' He stood up, offering an apologetic smile to the other attendees now glaring at him. 'I'll try to get back as quickly as I can.'

He was already dialling the number when the door of meeting room 2 closed behind him.

'Marine Accident Investigation Branch, can I help you?'

Dixon would have preferred to visit, but Southampton and back would take all day; a phone call would have to do, for the time being. 'I'd like to speak to whoever's in charge of the *Sunset Boulevard* investigation, please.'

Name and rank convinced the receptionist to take his call seriously. 'Please hold.'

He was beginning to wonder whether he'd been cut off when the line finally crackled. 'John Taylor. *Sunset Boulevard* is my investigation. How can I help?'

'It's been suggested the yacht was carrying drugs when it sank?' asked Dixon, cutting to the chase.

'News to me.'

'About two hundred and sixty kilos of cocaine; twenty million quid's worth.'

'Where was it supposed to be taking this cocaine?' asked Taylor, the legs of a chair being scraped along a hard floor in the background.

'Here.'

'Couldn't have been. *Sunset Boulevard* was heading away from the UK when it capsized.'

'Away?' Dixon perched on the table in the meeting room, watching Charlesworth watching him from the landing on the other side of the atrium.

'Yes, the crew was exchanging emails with Collins via a satellite phone – we've got his laptop – and they were clearly moving southwest towards the Azores. They were a little further east than they might have been initially, perhaps, if they'd been taking a direct route. I've got a map with their positions marked on it, if that would help?'

'It certainly would.' Charlesworth was still watching him while he recited his email address.

'There are some internal photographs too; I'll ping them over as well, although they're strictly confidential. The French coast-guard found the upturned hull and got a diver on board the day before the container ship tried to take it under tow. There's not much to see, though. No bags of cocaine floating about.' Taylor's attempt to stifle a chuckle failed dismally.

Dixon cleared his throat. 'What about in the keel?'

'Well, we'll never know now, will we?' replied Taylor. 'Although it's highly unlikely, for a whole host of reasons. We spent two days at Burnham Sailing Club, took statements from twelve club members and they all said they never saw any maintenance work being done on the yacht, let alone the keel coming off. And it had been in the water for at least a year anyway. It would've had to have come out for that.'

It sounded a daft question, but Dixon thought it worth the risk. 'There's no way you can do it with the yacht in the water?'

'God, no.' Another chuckle. 'Look, it set sail from Burnham on the evening of the twelfth of March and capsized on the nineteenth, north-east of the Azores; it would have to have been under sail the whole time to have got to that position, so there'd have been no time to do it, even if it was possible, which it isn't.'

'What else?'

'It was a Geronde Six, the 1998 model.' It sounded as though Taylor was tapping his desk with a pen. 'And the keel isn't hollow, so that's the end of that theory, isn't it?'

'Could it have rendezvoused with another yacht, perhaps, or even something bigger, that had brought the drugs across the Atlantic?'

'There was nothing else in the area, nothing that was reporting its position via GPS anyway, and I say again, *Sunset Boulevard* was still heading away from home when the accident happened. If she'd been carrying drugs destined for the UK, I imagine she would have been heading towards the UK, don't you think?'

Dixon hoped it was a rhetorical question.

'I'll send you the emails so you can see for yourself,' continued Taylor.

'Thank you.'

'I tell you what is a bit odd, although it's probably nothing.' Taylor hesitated. 'There are no hard and fast rules, but an east to west Atlantic crossing is usually made starting November time. You head south to the Canaries, getting across the Bay of Biscay before winter sets in, and then have a nice jolly across to the Caribbean on the trade winds. You come *back* via the Azores, so what they were doing out there in March is anyone's guess.'

'So it could have been drugs?'

'I still don't see how. The captain gave a position via email on the evening of the eighteenth and three PLBs activated further to the south-west, which means they were sailing away from the UK the whole time. Even a couple of hours transferring drugs to the *Sunset Boulevard* and they couldn't have got to that position.'

'What's a PLB?'

'Personal locator beacon; it's an emergency radio beacon. It emits a GPS signal too. You attach it to your life jacket and activate it if you go into the water; nice and easy, pull up the aerial, remove a tamper seal and press "on". They all had the RescueMe PLB1 with a seven year battery life on it.'

'Have you concluded your investigation?'

'Pretty much,' replied Taylor. 'We're just looking at a man-slaughter prosecution at the moment; waiting to hear from the Crown Prosecution Service.'

'And the cause of the accident?'

'Gross negligence; failure to maintain; unsafe operation. The bolts failed – no doubt stressed by age and multiple groundings – and the keel detached, resulting in a sudden capsize and the loss of four crew.'

'No trace of them was ever found?' asked Dixon.

'They didn't even have a chance to get the life raft out.' Taylor sighed down the phone line. 'The search was called off after three days; they'd have survived eight hours max in that water temperature.'

'Just one last question.' Dixon was watching Charlesworth walking along the landing. He'd lose sight of him beyond the canteen; discomforting to say the least. 'Has anyone from our organised crime unit been in touch with you about the suggestion that drugs were on board *Sunset Boulevard*?'

'No.' He could almost hear Taylor's frown. 'What's your interest in it then, if not the drugs?'

'I'm making preliminary enquiries into the murder of Godfrey Collins.'

'Collins is dead? When did this happen?'

'Three days ago.'

'Three days? When the bloody hell was someone going to tell us?'

Light the blue touch paper; stand well back.

The knock on the door was pure politeness; Charlesworth could see him sitting at his desk through the glass partition. In fact it was more of a goldfish bowl than an office, and Dixon still regarded it as Peter Lewis's anyway. 'Dead man's shoes' was a punch in the stomach when the deceased had been more of a friend than a colleague.

'Settling in?'

'No.' Suitably blunt.

'You can take down his pictures, surely, Nick?' Charlesworth was looking at the photographs on the wall to either side of the only window: Greek island holiday snaps. 'Doesn't his wife want them back?'

'I offered, but she said she couldn't face it yet.'

The view out of the window wasn't much to write home about either – of the large caged enclosure at the back of the custody suite, the familiar sound of the rear doors of a prison van parked inside the cage slamming shut.

'More happy customers.' Charlesworth had his back to Dixon as he watched the scene unfold below. 'I'm assuming that was the Marine Accident Investigation Branch you were on the phone to earlier?'

'Yes, Sir.' Dixon had learned early on that it was best to come clean straight away when it was obvious the interrogator knew the answer to the question anyway. It had been his first term at school when his housemaster had seen him in town after lights out, and he remembered the conversation well: 'I reckon you were in the White Hart, the Rising Sun or the Forrester's Arms, now how am I doing?' Dixon had opted for the honest answer: 'All three, Sir,' and had got off lightly, spending a day of his half term holiday painting the corridor.

'Oh, I see.' It clearly took the wind out of Charlesworth's sails too. 'Well, at least you didn't try to deny it.'

'There were no drugs on *Sunset Boulevard*.' Dixon turned his computer to face Charlesworth and pointed to the screen. 'These are photos of the inside taken by the French Coastguard the day before it sank, and everything's stowed away where it should be. You tell me, where the hell are you going to hide two hundred and sixty kilos of cocaine in there?'

Charlesworth peered at Dixon over his reading glasses before turning to the screen. 'Not according to DCS Collyer's informant.'

'Some crackhead feeding him false information, probably to put him off the scent of something bigger.'

'What about the keel then?'

Dixon could sense a seed of doubt creeping in. Time to go in for the kill. 'It's not even hollow on this model of yacht. And it was sailing away from the UK when it capsized. I accept entirely that Collins has connections, is a "known associate" or whatever phrase you care to use, but it does not automatically follow that his murder was a gangland execution. Zephyr have gone steaming in with their blinkers on, ignoring every other possibility. He was an accountant running tax avoidance schemes, for a start. Then there are the families of the crew lost at sea.'

Charlesworth was still facing the computer screen, although Dixon could see he was no longer focused on the photographs. *When you've got someone on the ropes, keep hitting them*: it was good advice, but some boxers were better at it than others.

'And then there's the crossbow broadhead with the circular pattern,' continued Dixon. 'It's on the last lot of sheep, according to Roger Poland.'

'You've been to see Dr Poland?'

'It's on Godfrey Collins too, you can see it plain as day on the post mortem photographs. Roger's never seen a broadhead like it, and neither has Leo Petersen.'

Charlesworth folded up his glasses and slid them into his top pocket. 'So, you're saying there's some maniac out there with a crossbow and he's going to kill again?'

'He's killed once, that's all I can say with any degree of certainty, but my gut feeling is this is just the start.'

'You've never been wrong before.' Charlesworth let out a long sigh. 'What do we do?'

The question was probably rhetorical, given that he was staring out of the window, but what the hell? 'Take the case off Zephyr,' said Dixon, 'and put a major investigation team in place.'

'We can't possibly do that.'

'Then you'll just have to hope he doesn't kill again before you *can* do that.'

He let that one hang in the air, watching Charlesworth mull it over.

'What's your next move?'

'I'm going to see Craig Pengelly at Leyhill open prison tomorrow,' replied Dixon.

'And who's he?'

'The fiancé of one of the crew lost on *Sunset Boulevard*. He's doing eighteen months for fraud; he was at the memorial service with a prison escort.'

'I thought you'd be out somewhere with your dog; it is a Saturday.'

'Time is of the essence, Sir. If I'm right.'

'Well,' Charlesworth said, turning on his heels, 'Peter Lewis watched your back often enough and now it's my turn.'

'Thank you, Sir.'

'Just keep out of DCS Collyer's way. You leave him to me.' Charlesworth stopped in the open doorway, his eyes narrowing. 'There is a price, Nick.'

'Portishead?'

'Applications close in twelve days.'

Chapter Eight

Dixon turned in to the visitors' car park at HM Prison Leyhill just before nine the following morning. Monty had snored through most of the hour-long journey and Jane had been engrossed in her phone, which gave him plenty of time to think.

Crucial time had been lost by Zephyr wading in with their size tens. A major investigation team was the proper response to a murder, unless and until a connection with organised crime was proven, not the other way around; but at least Charlesworth was beginning to see sense.

Monty woke up when Dixon turned off the engine, the patter of rain on the roof the only sound once the diesel engine had stopped rattling.

Jane glanced up at the windscreen, raindrops running down the glass. 'Bloody typical, isn't it. Lovely all week then it pisses down at the weekend.'

'It'll have stopped by the time I've finished here.'

'D'you want me to come in with you?'

'No point in us both losing our jobs.'

'I thought Charlesworth was on side now?'

'He's no Peter Lewis.' Dixon dropped the car keys into Jane's lap with a sigh as he opened the driver's door. 'I can't make up my mind if he's watching my back, or deciding where to stick the knife.'

He left his insulin pen and phone with Jane, dropping just door keys and coins in the tray when he went through the security scanner, much to the prison officer's surprise.

'No phone?'

'I left it in the car.'

Then he was shown in to an interview room – a table, two chairs, and a camera mounted on the wall just under the ceiling. There was a tape machine too, but he wouldn't need that.

It was true what they said, thought Dixon: time passed slowly in prison. He'd checked his watch five or six times before the door finally opened and Craig Pengelly shuffled in and sat down opposite him. The prison officer escorting him gestured to the wall beside the door. 'D'you want me to . . .'

'Outside's fine.' Dixon was watching Craig. 'Thanks.'

Craig had looked him up and down when he'd first walked in, and he was now sitting with his arms folded and his eyes fixed on the table in front of him.

Dixon waited.

'Do I need a solicitor for this?' Craig spoke without looking up.

'You can have one if you want one,' Dixon replied. 'I just wanted to talk to you about Laura, really. I saw you at her memorial service on Thursday.'

'What about her?'

'How's it been?' He slid a packet of cigarettes across the table; the obligatory sweetener, useful currency even if Craig didn't smoke. 'Your time.'

'Shite.' Craig looked up, his bloodshot eyes darting around the room, the pupils dilated; hair cropped with clippers; standard issue light blue top and jogging bottoms. Someone had given him a thick lip too. 'Five months at Bristol, then here surrounded by nonces. I'm not sure which is worse.'

'How long have you got left?'

'Days, not that it matters. I've got nothing left to come out to now.'

'Didn't I see you sitting with your parents at the church?'

'They'll not have me back. Not now.'

'Spice?' Dixon knew the signs only too well; few drugs were more addictive than synthetic cannabis.

'Gets you through the day.'

'What will you do?'

'I've got a friend in Bristol, so I'll go there, see what happens.'

'Tell me about the fraud.' Another packet of cigarettes slid across the table.

'Don't you know?'

'I'd rather hear it from you.'

'I was a trainee financial adviser.' Craig started picking at the skin at the base of his thumbnail. 'How was I to know the whole thing was a scam, for fuck's sake? Fucking pensions.' He blinked, tears appearing in the corners of his eyes. 'Then they all bugger off and I'm left to carry the can. Eighteen bloody months and the judge knew I wasn't the brains behind it.'

'You serve nine of that, and it's nearly up, isn't it?'

'Four of them in here surrounded by perverts.'

'When did you last see Laura?'

'It was before I came here. I'd not long been in Bristol, a couple of months maybe, and she came to see me; told me she'd been offered ten grand to crew a boat down to the Caribbean and back. She said the money would pay off all our debts and we'd be able to start again when I got out.' Craig was kicking the table leg.

'Nothing I said made a difference. She was adamant she was going and that was that.'

'What debts?'

'She'd gone to her parents, but we still owed rent on the flat, credit cards, the usual shit. And then there was the spice. It all has to be paid for one way or the other. Cash or credit, and you really don't want to owe these people anything; they *own* you when you get out.'

'These people?'

Craig frowned. 'You're not seriously asking me to—?'

'Sorry.' Dixon waved away the question with the back of his hand. 'Was Laura a member of the sailing club?'

'Had been since she was a kid. She was good at it too; used to race lasers, they're the small dinghies. She'd been on bigger boats as well, crossed the Atlantic before so she wasn't worried.'

'And you?'

'Not my thing, but I joined to keep her happy, ended up doing a bit of gig rowing.'

'What did she say about the yacht?'

'Not a lot, just that it was plenty big enough for an Atlantic crossing. I begged her not to go.' His jaw clenched. 'She never said it was that wreck *Sunset Boulevard*.'

'She knew the condition of the boat?'

'Everybody did.' He blinked, releasing the tears from the corners of his eyes. 'It's all my fault.' Flowing freely now. 'She said we needed the money, otherwise we'd never be free of them. "Here, mate, have some of this," they said. "It'll help pass the time", and before you know it . . .'

'*Don't worry, you can pay us later,*' said Dixon.

'They'll be waiting for me when I get out.'

'Who gave you the thick lip?' Dixon asked, changing the subject.

'Just some nonce in the shower. He slipped on a bar of soap and hit his head on the sink; in hospital now, he is, if you catch my drift.' Craig ran his tongue along his lower lip. 'It'll be two or three of them next time and I won't be so lucky. Unless I get out of here first.'

'When did you hear from Laura last?'

'She emailed her parents and they printed it off and sent it to me,' Craig replied, sliding a tightly folded piece of paper out of his back pocket. 'Here it is.'

Dixon watched him smooth the piece of paper over his thigh and slide it across the table.

'They were just going round Land's End,' continued Craig. 'She says she can see it in the distance.'

It was short, to the point and read more like a postcard: *Weather lovely, favourable winds, can see Land's End, tell Craig I love him and to look after himself.*

Dixon handed back the email. 'When did you find out she was pregnant?'

'We knew before Christmas. I was sent down in January so it was a couple of weeks before that, I suppose. We never told anyone else.'

'And you were pleased?'

'She said it gave me something to live for, and it did. She was going to try and hang on so I'd be out for the birth, only it didn't work out like that, did it?'

'Does the name Godfrey Collins mean anything to you?'

'He's the bloke who owned the boat.' Craig folded his arms again. 'They're supposed to be investigating him for manslaughter.'

'Would it surprise you to learn that's he's dead?'

'Surprise, no; disappoint, yes.' Craig managed a smile, although it was loaded with contradiction; the eyes gave him away. 'I had thought it might be fun to catch up with him when I got out.'

◆ ◆ ◆

'How was he?' asked Jane, when Dixon opened the driver's door.

'Off his box on spice and in debt to drug dealers up to his armpits. It's why Laura was crewing the yacht – for the money.'

'How much was she being paid?'

'Ten grand.' He reached into the back as he climbed in, rubbing Monty behind the ears.

'When's he due out?'

'The next few days, he hasn't got a date yet. Until then he's in there, convicted of a fraud he says he knew nothing about and surrounded by sex offenders.'

'Ninety per cent according to the last prison census. I googled it.'

Dixon sighed. 'All he's got to hold on to is an email she sent as they passed Land's End.'

'And drug dealers waiting for him when he gets out.' Jane was putting on her seatbelt. 'Life really stinks sometimes.'

'How about a walk somewhere in the Cotswolds now we're up here, and lunch in a pub?' Dixon turned the key and the diesel engine rumbled into life.

'You have forgotten, haven't you?' Jane frowned. 'I knew you would.'

'What?'

'We're supposed to be picking Lucy up at Temple Meads on the way back. Her train gets in at eleven.'

Dixon felt his face tighten. It had been a long hot summer and Jane had spent most of it trying to keep tabs on Lucy's comings and goings, acting more like her mother than her half-sister. That said, neither of them knew who their real father was, so they were full sisters in every way that mattered, or so Lucy insisted, usually when she was trying to borrow money.

The end of her exams in July had coincided with the confirmation of Dixon's promotion and he had got home from his first day of management bollocks to find Lucy had moved into the cottage for the summer, bringing her *Walking Dead* box set with her. She had, at least, enrolled in college to sit her A levels, so there had been that light at the end of the tunnel, and the peace and quiet this week had been blissful. Now it was weekends only, her foster parents dropping her at Manchester Piccadilly for the train *home* – that was a change that had crept in over the summer too: 'home during the week and Somerset at weekends' had morphed into 'Manchester during the week and home at weekends'.

Jane was happy, all the same, although Dixon felt sure Lucy was really coming down to see her boyfriend, Billy; there are some things best kept to yourself.

'Where to?' he asked, when he turned off the M5 at Burnham.

Lucy was sitting in the back of the Land Rover, her arm around Monty who looked none too chuffed in his seatbelt harness. That was the deal: no seatbelt, no sitting on the seat. 'I said I'd meet Billy at the Pavilion.' She looked at her phone. 'Ten minutes ago.'

'Have you got any money?'

'No.'

'Your sister will give you some.'

'Oh, thanks,' muttered Jane, picking up her handbag.

Dixon parked on the seafront.

'Make sure you're home by ten!' shouted Jane, although Lucy was already out of earshot. She sighed. 'It's like a scene from one of your old films,' she said, peering over her shoulder at Lucy and Billy running into each other's arms.

'There was a time when we did that.' Dixon was watching the same scene unfold in his wing mirror. 'The night of the fire; it was just down there.' He pointed over the sea wall. 'You ran the full length of the beach.'

'I did, didn't I.' Jane blushed. 'I thought you were dead. And you were running too, remember?'

'Then there was the time—'

'Don't start.'

He grinned. 'We're like an old married couple.'

'And we're not even married yet.'

'We should set a date.' Dixon started the engine and continued along the seafront towards the sailing club.

'When?'

'It's September now, so that depends on whether you want winter, spring or summer. And you must walk down an aisle; Rod would never forgive us if he didn't get to walk you down the aisle.'

Jane's parents, Rod and Sue, had adopted her as a baby, a decision taken out of love, not forced on them by circumstance. Jane knew she was adopted. What she didn't know was that her parents could have had a child of their own, but instead chose to adopt her. One day they would tell her; on her wedding day maybe? That would make for quite a speech from the father of the bride.

'Let's get this crossbow business sorted first. Besides, if you lose your job you might not be worth marrying.' She sighed when it dawned on her they weren't heading home. 'Where are we going now?'

'Express Park,' replied Dixon. 'Louise is in this afternoon.'

'You're not going to rope her into this as well?'

Chapter Nine

'Three missed calls from a Bristol number,' said Dixon, holding out his phone in front of Jane as she swiped her pass to open the staff entrance. 'No messages though.'

'Nothing on mine,' she replied, heading for the back stairs, only stopping when she noticed Detective Constable Louise Willmott on her way up.

'I saw you drive in,' said Louise. 'I've had the ACC on the phone wondering if you were in. I think he was hoping to catch you on your way home from Leyhill.'

It sounded like an ambush and, whatever it was, it could wait. 'What time does your shift finish?' asked Dixon.

'Four.' Louise's short dark hair was tied back in an elastic band, a pen tucked behind her left ear. She was young and keen, transferring from uniform to CID when Jane had been shunted off to Safeguarding. It had been dressed up as the only vacancy for a newly promoted detective sergeant, but Dixon knew Jane's move had been forced on her by their relationship.

Charlesworth had once described Louise as 'Dixon's protégé', which was absurd, although he was happy to take the credit. 'What's Janice got you doing?'

'Watching CCTV.' Louise shrugged. 'The only good thing is there's no overtime, so I'm seeing lots of Katie at the moment. She's three next week, would you believe it?'

'Can you spare me an hour or two?'

'Er, yes,' she replied, nervously.

Dixon handed her a scrap of paper with the names of the four crew from the *Sunset Boulevard* scribbled on it. 'This is the crew from that yacht that sank a few months back. The owner is dead.'

'The crossbow?' Louise was following them along the landing. 'Dave and Mark said you were up to something.'

'The families have got serious motive, so I'd like you to—'

'Find out everything I can about them?'

'Thanks.'

'What about the victims of the tax avoidance scheme?' asked Jane.

'There are hundreds of them, so we'll have to start with the families and see where we go from there.' Dixon flicked on the kettle in the CID Area. 'After all, we're not exactly awash with resources, are we?'

'I'd better get that,' mumbled Louise, gesturing to the landline ringing on her desk. 'Yes, Sir.' The phone pressed to her ear. 'I don't know, Sir, let me have a look.' She put her hand over the mouthpiece and stared at Dixon, her eyes wide.

'You can't ask her to lie to the assistant chief constable,' whispered Jane.

'I wasn't going to,' he said, stepping forward, his hand outstretched.

'Yes, he's here, Sir, over by the kettle. Hang on.'

Dixon took the phone from Louise. 'Yes, Sir,' he said with a wince.

'You weren't answering your mobile, Nick.'

'I was driving, Sir, sorry.'

'Oh, well, I need you here as quick as you can. Whatever it is you're doing, drop it and leave now. We're in conference room five in Ops.'

'We?' Dixon couldn't help himself.

Charlesworth cleared his throat. 'I'm here with Deborah Potter and Dick Collyer. Vicky Thomas is here too, and there's someone on the way from Operational HR for two o'clock.'

'I'm leaving now, Sir.' Dixon looked at Jane and drew his index finger across his throat as he handed the phone back to Louise. Detective Chief Superintendent Potter was his boss, or 'line manager' according to the manual; and what was the press officer there for? That left someone from HR and Collyer. At least there was no one from Professional Standards.

Yet.

Dixon dropped Jane and Monty at the beach on the way to Portishead, her parting shot still ringing in his ears. 'You'll be checking parking meters in Martinique by this time tomorrow.'

She'd obviously been watching his old *Pink Panther* films again.

What was even more disturbing was that he was waved through the main gate before he'd even had a chance to get his warrant card out, the officer on duty raising the barrier and letting him straight through. Perhaps he'd been told to look out for a 'vomit green' Land Rover?

It was just before two when Dixon finally looked through the small window in the conference room door; stern faces all around the table, the remains of a sandwich lunch in the middle of the table. Vicky Thomas was sitting with her back to him, but the press officer was no doubt enjoying his misfortune. Collyer didn't look like he was enjoying himself much though, turning the coffee cup on its saucer and clearly not listening to the discussion taking place between Deborah Potter and Charlesworth. Notes were being taken by the person from HR, either that or Charlesworth was having minutes taken by Professional Standards; they do that at disciplinary meetings.

Sod it.

He could always get a job on the door of some supermarket somewhere; or even go back to the legal profession if push came to shove and there really wasn't anything else going. Someone would give him a job as a criminal defence solicitor somewhere and it wouldn't take a jiffy to get police station accredited. Now, that really would piss Charlesworth off.

He knocked on the door and opened it.

'Come in, Nick.' Charlesworth gestured to the vacant chair opposite Deborah Potter, the grey streaks in her hair still matching the pinstripe of her suit.

He sat down, trying to look relaxed, but the beads of sweat on his forehead probably gave him away. Potter smiled at him from behind the reading glasses perched on the end of her nose – a feeble attempt to put him at his ease – then slid her phone across the table.

Dixon picked it up and stared at the photograph on the screen: a middle aged man, a tree and two crossbow bolts, one through the cheek and the other the eye socket; mouth open, a drip of blood congealed on the end of his chin like an icicle.

Charlesworth was introducing Dixon to whoever it was from HR, but he wasn't listening – instead reeling from yet another blow to the pit of his stomach, his relief that he had been right after all quickly turning to guilt that a man had died to prove it.

'Yes, there's been another one.' Charlesworth sighed. 'It seems you were right.'

'And I was wrong.' Collyer was still staring into the empty coffee cup on the table in front of him.

'There's no blame here, Dick,' said Charlesworth. 'We all did what we thought was right at the time and it was perfectly reasonable to proceed on the assumption that it was gang related.'

'Doesn't look good, though, does it.' Vicky Thomas's face flushed, her eyes darting from Charlesworth to Collyer and back again, clearly embarrassed she had said that out loud.

'When was this?' asked Dixon, using his fingers to zoom in on the back of the victim's head, both bolts clean through and buried deep in the tree.

'He was found at ten this morning by his wife,' replied Potter. 'He was supposed to be doing a bit of deadheading, and when he didn't come in for his coffee, she went to look for him. The call came in from a neighbour at ten-twelve. She heard screaming and went to investigate, as any good neighbour would. His wife was still screaming when uniform got there eight minutes later.'

Dixon zoomed back out, a conservatory now visible in the background, a tray of coffee sitting on the table beyond the open doors. 'Who was he?'

'Keith Finch.' Potter again. 'An enforcement officer at HM Revenue and Customs in Cardiff.'

'You know what this means, Nick?' asked Charlesworth.

The bloody boat's got nothing to do with it.

'I do, Sir.' Dixon was already halfway through tapping out a text message to Louise: *Stop what you're doing ta*

'Collins was up to his neck in a failed tax avoidance scheme that landed hundreds of people with large tax bills,' continued Charlesworth. 'And now the officer pursuing the payment of those bills has been killed.'

'Perhaps I could clarify, Sir.' Potter leaned forward. 'It's not been established exactly what work Mr Finch was doing at the tax office, but it is the same office that's handling recovery of the loan charge scheme debts. I think that's all we can say at this stage.'

'That's enough, isn't it?' Collyer took a sip from his empty coffee cup, more for something to do with his hands than anything else, probably.

'Where is he?' Dixon slid Potter's phone back across the table.

'In his back garden,' she replied. 'It's a bungalow on the edge of Bradley Stoke so it's in our patch. I suppose he commuted over the Severn Crossing every day. Nice and convenient, especially now there's no toll.'

Dixon turned to Charlesworth and fixed him with a steely glare. Mercifully he got the message before Dixon had to ask, an abrupt 'Well?' proving unnecessary.

'We're going to make Janice Courtenay up to acting DCI and move her across to the managerial role at Express Park. I think she's probably more suited to that anyway and it leaves you free to head up the major investigation team we're putting in place. All right?'

'Yes, Sir.'

'You're more suited to the senior investigating officer role, so everyone's happy.' Now it was Charlesworth's turn to glare at Dixon. 'And you haven't forgotten our little understanding?'

'No, Sir.'

'Eleven days.'

'Yes, Sir.'

'Staffing's going to be difficult, that's why Jesminder's here from HR,' said Potter.

'Call me Jez,' she said, her long dark hair tied back in a ponytail. 'We can spare you eight from Portishead and a few more from Bristol, but it's going to be really tight for an investigation of this size. I gather the victims of Godfrey Collins's tax avoidance schemes run into the hundreds, so we'll need to take some people from Bridgwater too. Is there anyone specific you'd want on the team?'

'Louise Willmott, Dave Harding and Mark Pearce.' Dixon noticed Potter smiling. He must be getting predictable.

'Got them,' said Jez, still hovering her pen over her notebook. 'Anyone else?'

'It might be useful if the Bridgwater Rural Crimes team was seconded to the MIT as well. That's Nigel Cole. He's been looking into the sheep killings.'

'A representative from Zephyr for liaison purposes would be sensible as well,' said Charlesworth. 'At least to begin with.'

Dixon stifled a sigh. *Not the twat from the car park, please.*

'I've asked DS Turner to drop the files down to you,' said Collyer. 'You met him in the car park at Harptree Combe.'

'Of course I did, Sir. But I'm not sure we'll need to liaise with Zephyr.'

'Don't push your luck,' snapped Charlesworth, his face quickly softening into a smile. 'The last question then is where we put the incident room, here or Express Park?'

'There's space upstairs,' offered Jez. 'And I'm sure we could find room in the accommodation block for anyone from Bridgwater who didn't want the daily commute.'

'I think I'd rather Express Park, Sir,' said Dixon. 'The top floor's vacant at the moment.'

'Jolly good, that's settled then.' Charlesworth rubbed his hands together. 'Portishead it is; second floor, ops building.'

'Area J,' said Jez.

'Reporting to Deborah as usual,' continued Charlesworth. 'Now, you'd better get up to Bradley Stoke.'

'Scientific Services will be there for a while and Leo Petersen's on scene,' said Potter. 'The wife's gone to the neighbour's; family liaison are with her and the daughter's on her way down from Birmingham.'

Chapter Ten

'It's a cedar of Lebanon.'

Dixon recognised Leo Petersen's voice, and the rustle of overalls behind him. 'It's not coming down, is it?' He was craning his neck to see the upper branches towering over the rear of the red brick bungalow.

'Can't,' replied Petersen. 'There's a tree preservation order on it. It may look nice from a distance, but I wouldn't want it in my garden, the bloody thing drops needles and crap everywhere.'

The front door of the bungalow was standing open.

'No, you don't.' Petersen stopped him in his tracks. 'Follow the path round the side. And you'll need these.'

Dixon turned to find a sealed packet of overalls flying towards him like a frisbee.

'I'll see you round the back when you've put those on.' Petersen opened the wrought iron gate between the corner of the bungalow and the double garage and disappeared from view.

'DCI Dixon?'

He was wriggling into the overalls when he heard footsteps on the gravel behind him. 'Yes.'

'DS Bennett, Sir; Patchway Police Centre. The wife's next door and would like a word when you've got a minute. And I've sent two lads over to his place of work. We've got hold of one of the senior tax inspectors who's going to open up for us.'

'Have you seen him?'

'No, Sir. We just sealed it off and were waiting for you. Scientific are in there though.'

Dixon pulled the elasticated hood over his head and followed the path alongside the bungalow, stopping to peer in the side window of the garage: a BMW and a British racing green Mini with Union Jack wing mirrors; standard his and hers.

He ducked under the washing line, admiring the roses along the hedge to his left as he set off across the perfectly manicured lawn until the grass thinned out under the cedar, the ground covered in needles.

'See what I mean?' Petersen was standing on the edge of a stepping plate. 'It's taking the sun off the conservatory too.'

'Well, Mr Finch doesn't have to worry about that now,' said Dixon, following the line of plates.

'Mrs does though.' Petersen spoke without looking away from the entry wound in the eye, examining it at disturbingly close quarters with an ophthalmoscope, his index finger rotating the dial to change the focus as he moved still closer.

'Eye, eye.'

Dixon spun round to find DS Bennett laughing at his own joke on the stepping plate behind him, wearing a set of hastily put on overalls; the sleeves were rucked up showing the cuffs of his shirt and the zip had only been done up as far as his neck, which Dixon could cheerfully have wrung. 'Show some respect, Sergeant.'

'Sorry, Sir, it's just that we don't usually get too many murders round these parts; it makes a change from shoplifting at Cribbs Causeway.'

'And do your suit up properly,' snapped Petersen.

Bennett backed away, wrestling with the cuffs on his overalls.

It was no more than three paces from the flower bed at the bottom of the garden to the base of the tree, a pair of secateurs lying on the bare earth in amongst the roses, two Scientific Services officers crawling on their hands and knees in the long grass of the field beyond. A patrol car blocking a tarmac lane was visible through a five bar gate in the far hedge line.

Dixon turned to Bennett, who was still fidgeting with his hazmat suit. 'Let's get a team out for a full fingertip search of the field, and I want that lane checked for tyre tracks; the nearest traffic cameras in both directions too.'

'Now, Sir?'

He resisted the temptation. 'Yes, please.'

Finch himself was upright, although his legs had buckled under him, his full weight now being taken by the crossbow bolts.

Petersen stepped back. 'He was killed by the second bolt through the eye; the first one pinned him to the tree, but he was probably alive at that point. Just.'

'The second bolt's a lot further in,' noted Dixon.

'Eight point two centimetres,' replied Petersen.

'Three and a bit inches then.'

'The entry wounds tell you a lot.' Petersen pointed to the lower bolt. 'It's a clean hole so an ordinary steel head, I suspect. Certainly not a broadhead of any shape or description, which explains why it's gone clean through the cheekbone and the back of the skull. It was probably shot from a greater range too. Then the killer moved in for the second. Closer range and the eye is soft, of course, which explains the penetration.'

'Is the second one a broadhead?'

'See for yourself.' Petersen was holding the ophthalmoscope in his outstretched hand.

Dixon would have told Roger Poland to get knotted if he'd suggested it, but wasn't entirely convinced Petersen would take kindly to that. And he needed to be sure it was the same pattern. He took a deep breath and flicked on the light, moving in close to the base of the bolt buried in Finch's eyeball. He was usually on the other end of this sort of examination at the diabetic centre, and the urge to blink was almost irresistible.

Petersen was standing on the plate directly behind him, peering over his shoulder. 'Can you see the incisions on the eyeball?'

'Yes.' The circles around the bolt where the broadhead had gone in. No blood, just clean cuts.

'You can see the same pattern on the exit wound, although it's obscured by hair and congealed blood. I'll get a better look when I've shaved his head.'

Dixon had skipped lunch, instead keeping his blood sugar levels from dropping with the occasional fruit pastille; far from ideal when it came to diabetes control, but a bloody good thing, as it turned out.

Petersen snatched the ophthalmoscope from Dixon's hand. 'You look as if you're about to throw up.'

'I'll be fine, thank you.'

'What are you thinking then?'

'He's deadheading the roses, looks up and sees someone in the field pointing a crossbow at him. He drops the secateurs and starts stumbling back, maybe intending to hide behind the tree, we'll never know, then the first shot's fired, hitting him in the cheek and pinning him to the tree.' Dixon sighed. 'He's still alive at this point, so he gets to watch his killer advance and reload.'

'We should get an idea of the range.' Petersen gestured to a series of flags in the field. 'Scientific have identified footprints in the grass by the looks of things.' A cluster of red flags maybe thirty yards away, then a line forwards to another cluster nearer the hedge, at most twenty yards away. 'That's pretty much point blank for some of the more powerful bows; you can get some that'll put a bolt clean through you at two hundred yards, let alone twenty.'

'With the extra weight of the broadhead?'

'Maybe not, which might explain why he fired the ordinary bolt first from further away, before moving in to fire the broadhead.' Petersen frowned. 'Actually, I think it's "shot" rather than "fired", to be technically correct.'

Donald Watson, the senior Scientific Services officer, stood up twenty yards away in the field, camera in hand. 'He reloaded here,' he shouted, pointing at the ground. 'You can see the imprint of the metal bar. No boot prints, I'm afraid.'

'The more powerful bows have a stirrup on the front,' said Petersen. 'You put your foot in it and then pull the string with cocking ropes to give you greater leverage. Anything with a draw weight of over a hundred and seventy-five pounds requires a good deal of strength to cock; I did a bit of research after the last one and there are plenty of videos on YouTube.'

'I'd better go and see his widow.' Dixon turned away. 'When's the PM?'

'Tomorrow morning now,' replied Petersen, turning the sleeve of his overalls back to see his watch. 'It's going to be another couple of hours before we get him out of here, at least.'

Next door was pretty much a carbon copy of the Finch's bungalow, but without the conservatory or the cedar of Lebanon. The neighbour meant well too and, more often than not, it was intended as a compliment, but it wasn't the first time someone had pointed out that Dixon was very young for a chief inspector; the youngest in the history of Avon and Somerset Police, by a few weeks, although he didn't feel the need to mention it and just smiled.

'She's through in the back bedroom, having a lie down,' the neighbour said, closing the door behind Dixon.

'Does Mrs Finch need a doctor?' He was following her along the corridor.

'She's had one of my Valium and her daughter will be here in half an hour or so anyway.'

Mrs Finch was in the bed fully clothed when the neighbour pushed open the door.

'This is Chief Inspector Dixon, Mary.'

Mary Finch's eyes were glazed over, either by the tears, the Valium, or a combination of the two. 'He said there'd been somebody watching the house.' She was trying to sit up, the neighbour lurching forward to prop up the pillows. 'The last couple of days – a red car in the lane at the back and then someone standing in the middle of the field.'

'Did he call the police?'

'I said to, but he wouldn't.'

'Had he seen this person before?'

'He didn't say so. The field was going to be sold a couple of years back, for development, and there were people in it all the time back then. He was worried because he thought it might have gone back on the market.'

'Did he mention a make or model of car?'

'Just that it was red.'

Dixon sat down on the arm of a chair next to the bed. 'What about at work?'

'He was the head of enforcement, so there was always bad feeling coming from somewhere, but he'd stopped case work long ago. He was winding down to retirement; only had a couple of months to go.'

'Did he ever mention the loan charge?'

She nodded her head on the pillow.

'What about the name Godfrey Collins?'

'No.'

The neighbour pointed to the door and Dixon took the hint. 'Mary's struggling to keep her eyes open.' She closed the door softly behind them. 'Can you do this another time?'

'Yes, of course. There was supposed to be a family liaison officer here?'

'She left when Mary took the Valium; said she'd be back later.'

Cardiff city centre was reasonably quiet for late on a Saturday afternoon, although the autumn rugby internationals didn't start for another couple of weeks, so that was to be expected, perhaps. And why couldn't architects build out of anything except glass these days, Dixon had thought, standing on the pavement looking up at the new HM Revenue and Customs building.

DS Bennett had telephoned his colleagues to let them know the SIO was on the way, and one had been waiting outside.

'Detective Constable Walker, Sir,' she had said, presumably recognising Dixon's Land Rover. 'DC Shannon is upstairs with one of the tax inspectors, a Mr Fox; he's a key holder and emergency contact.'

A glass lift up to the fifth floor and two people sitting at the far end of a long conference table were visible through the glass partition. 'There they are, Sir.'

David Fox looked like a tax inspector, even in jeans and a polo shirt. 'I'm hoping I might get some sense out of you.' He stood up and offered Dixon his hand. 'These two won't tell me anything.'

'I'm afraid Mr Finch is dead, Sir,' replied Dixon.

'How?'

'He was murdered in his back garden at Bradley Stoke. Just before ten this morning.'

'Oh, God, no.' A sharp intake of breath. 'The poor sod.'

'Does the name Godfrey Collins mean anything to you?'

'No. I should clarify I'm not on the enforcement team though.'

'He was an accountant who'd been running loan charge schemes with several hundred people now facing large tax bills as a result. He was found dead three days ago, also murdered, and we believe the killings are connected.'

'You need to speak to someone in the loan charge team. I'll see if I've got a number.' Fox was scrolling through the list of contacts on his phone. 'There are several sub-teams in enforcement, and loan charge is one of the biggest.'

Dixon glanced out of the window at his Land Rover parked in the loading bay below, a traffic warden circling it with intent.

'We need a complete list of all the taxpayers owing money to HMRC as a result of schemes run by Godfrey Collins,' he said to Walker as he stood up, Fox on the telephone in the background. 'I'd better get back to Portishead.'

Chapter Eleven

Area J turned out to be little more than the far end of an open plan office on the second floor of the operations building. Someone had taken the trouble to put in place some partitioning, a laminated 'J' pinned to it, but that was about it.

'There's no coffee machine,' grumbled Louise, her back to Dixon as he weaved his way through the vacant workstations. She was standing by an empty desk, an overnight bag on the chair.

Turner – the twat from the car park – was there, leaning back in a chair, his hands behind his head and his feet resting on a box on the floor. Without the sharp suit and red braces this time; perhaps Dixon would reserve judgement until Monday morning to see whether they reappeared.

'The canteen's closed, but I found this lying around.' Mark Pearce was holding a kettle in his outstretched hand. 'It said "Transport Services" on the door, so we've got until Monday to put it back.'

'Where's Dave?' asked Dixon.

'He was stopping to get some beer; something about there not being a bloody pub for miles around.'

Dave Harding and Mark Pearce had been on his team since his first outing with Avon and Somerset Police nearly a year ago. Dave Harding in his crumpled grey suit and brown suede shoes, closing in on his thirty years' time served, all of them as a detective constable; happy with his lot. Mark Pearce was younger – thirty perhaps – but seemed content with his lot too; enjoyed his beer a bit too much, turning up unshaven and with a hangover more times than Dixon cared to remember, his blond hair unkempt more often than not – he wouldn't have looked out of place on a surfboard or on Bondi Beach maybe. Still, both could be relied on to do their jobs, and that was all that mattered.

Had Nigel Cole been in uniform, Dixon would have recognised him straight away, but the jeans and open necked shirt threw him fleetingly; not that Cole noticed, mercifully. 'Ah, the Rural Crimes Unit is here.'

'I suppose I've got you to thank for that, Sir?' Cole was sitting on the windowsill, his back to the grandstand view of the sports hall.

'I may have suggested your name to Inspector Bateman. Why, don't you want it?'

'No, I do,' replied Cole. 'Thank you. And my wife's chuffed to bits. No more Saturday nights and missing teeth. I had to have a bloody implant for this one.' He pointed to his front tooth. 'Hurt like hell.'

Jez appeared behind him, Louise alerting Dixon to her presence with a nod.

'I've got you twelve more for Monday, and there may be four more by the middle of the week; there's something big wrapping up tomorrow so that should free them up.'

'Is that it?'

'For the time being.' Jez was hiding behind her clipboard. 'But I'll see what I can do.'

'Thank you.' Dixon didn't bother to hide the tinge of resignation in his voice. 'Looks like it's just us, until Monday anyway.'

'Let's get this party started,' said Pearce, gleefully rubbing his hands together.

'Shut up, Mark.'

'Yes, Sir.'

The rattle of beer cans announced Dave Harding's arrival, a carrier bag dumped on the floor next to his overnight bag. 'There's an off licence in that petrol station back towards Clevedon,' he said, smiling. 'All you can get in the restaurant here is those poxy little bottles of wine and ginger beer; indigestion in a bottle.' He curled his lip. 'I've fallen for that one before.'

Jez was still loitering. 'Not on duty, I hope.'

'He never does,' replied Dixon, without looking over his shoulder.

'I'll email you your room numbers in the accommodation block.' Jez was backing away. 'Will you be staying over, Chief Inspector?'

'I'm just a couple of junctions down the M5 so probably not, thank you.'

'Me neither,' said Turner. 'I'm only just up the road.'

'Four then. Give me half an hour.' Jez's voice increased in volume as she backed further away.

'Right then.' Dixon waited while they all sat down. 'Let's start at the beginning.'

'Godfrey Collins?' asked Turner, sitting up.

'Sheep. Over to you, Nigel.'

'Me?' Cole looked nervous. 'The statements and post mortem reports from the vet are all on the system.' He was fumbling with his notebook. 'The first lot were killed on the eighteenth of July.

They were fine when Mr Bragg left them on the evening of the seventeenth and he found them dead the following morning, so the early hours is most likely. It wasn't a powerful bow, possibly a pistol crossbow, and the wounds were four inches deep, so six point five inch bolts, allowing for them stopping at the fletch. No broadheads. Then we've got another six a month later on seventeenth August, again overnight; the bow more powerful this time and it's the first use of broadheads, two and three-bladed in the classic arrowhead pattern. The last lot was nine days ago now, and that's when we first get the curved blade pattern you see on Godfrey Collins.'

'And on Keith Finch.' Dixon looked at Turner. 'How far did Zephyr get with Collins?'

'House to house in the vicinity of the woods and his bed-sit; plenty of statements on the file but nothing of much use. We looked at hours of CCTV too, but we would've been focusing on certain vehicles, don't forget; known associates and gang members. Scientific Services have finished and their reports are due by Monday. The post mortem's done too, of course.'

'What about his phone?'

'Never found one.'

'And a computer?'

'Never found one of those either.'

Dixon turned to Louise. 'His laptop's at the Marine Accident Investigation Branch in Southampton. Get it, will you?'

'Yes, Sir.'

'And I'm guessing his office computers are at HM Revenue and Customs. I want the lot with High Tech by the end of tomorrow.'

'So, that's what this is about,' said Mark. 'Tax?'

'Zephyr seems to think Collins's yacht had been used for drug runs,' replied Dixon, 'and there was a suspicion it was carrying cocaine when it sank, which explains their interest in his murder, but that's got nothing to do with it. Before the drugs he was an accountant running several loan charge schemes. Basically people were paid with loans, which are tax free, instead of the salary you and I receive which is not tax free. We're taxed on Pay As You Earn, aren't we? Then, having been given the loans, they were told that they didn't have to pay them back, so everybody's happy except the taxman.'

'And who gives a toss about him?' Mark ducked down behind a computer. 'I'll shut up, Sir.'

'The problem is that these schemes have since been clamped down on and HMRC is pursuing the back tax, treating the loans as income and landing, in Collins's case, a couple of hundred people with large bills for tax going back to 2010. Finch was the enforcement officer at the tax office responsible for recovering the back tax.'

'A couple of hundred people?'

'Yes, Dave.'

'And one of them's got the hump about it.' Mark again.

'Where do we start?' asked Louise.

'There are a couple of officers from Patchway over at the tax office in Cardiff now, so can you get over there and stay there until you get a complete list of all of the debtors owing tax from one of Collins's schemes? You can try to track down his old office computers while you're there too.'

'Yes, Sir.'

Turner was sitting up now.

'I can't keep calling you DS Turner' – *or the twat from the car park* – 'so what's your name?'

'Kevin, Sir.'

'Dave's our car and CCTV bod, so can you team up with him, Kevin, and go back through the footage looking for a red car? We also need to trace Collins's movements the night before he was killed.'

'We never got very far with that, Sir.' Kevin shrugged. 'You'll see why when you see where he lived. And there'll be hundreds of red cars.'

'In Congresbury?'

'That was repossessed.'

'Mark, get over to Finch's bungalow and see what you can find there. Scientific will have finished at the scene, but they should still be in the house. You know what to look for, and see if you can get anything more out of his widow about the person in the field the husband said he saw; and the red car. Get his phone too – if Scientific haven't already – he may have taken a picture of it. Landline phone records too, while I think of it.'

'Yes, Sir.'

'Make sure the local lot have got the house to house going, and see if anyone else saw anything at the back of the bungalows.'

'What about me, Sir?' asked Cole.

'Focus on the broadheads, Nigel. Archery shops, bricks and mortar and online. Find out who they've been selling the bloody things to.'

'Since when?'

'Eighteenth of July,' replied Dixon. 'We know he didn't have them when he killed the first lot of sheep so he must have bought them after that. And the more powerful bow. Find out how many have been sold and who to.'

'Which type?'

'All of them. Start with buyers in Avon and Somerset. Archery clubs too; get membership lists.'

'Where will you be, Sir?' asked Louise.

'I'm going to see where Mr Collins used to live.'

'Good luck with that,' muttered Kevin.

'An accountant from Congresbury,' Collyer had said when Dixon popped up at Harptree Combe. Maybe once upon a time, but Collins had fallen far, judging by the bedsit Dixon found in St Paul's.

The landlord was standing in the doorway, his eyes following Dixon around the room. 'Shall I leave you to it?'

'Yes, that's fine.'

'Just pull the door to on your way out.'

'These are all his belongings?'

'The council came for the mattress, but I haven't got round to clearing the rest yet. There's someone coming on Monday. The pictures on the walls are mine.'

Dixon waited for the door to close and then looked around the room. A dark oak double bed frame, the mattress gone, revealing springs underneath; an antique, almost. A few clothes were hanging in the wardrobe, the pockets all turned inside out, either by Zephyr or the landlord perhaps. Fingerprints on the white painted mantelpiece over the electric fire stood out in the grey powder left by Scientific Services. The sink in the corner doubled as a urinal, judging by the yellow stains on the porcelain. And the smell.

A few letters and other post lay on a table in the bay window, all of it rifled through and none of it remotely interesting. Two empty window envelopes of the type that usually contain bank or credit card statements reminded Dixon to get Collins's bank records, unless Zephyr already had, not that they would be terribly enlightening.

The drawers of the bedside cabinets were open, revealing nothing inside except a box of paracetamol one side and an empty glasses case the other.

Dixon stood in the bay window, watching the world go by. It was easy to see why Zephyr hadn't got very far with Collins's movements the night he died. It was the sort of place where the neighbours heard nothing and saw nothing, even before they'd been asked the question. And the nearest CCTV cameras were out on Lower Ashley Road.

He glanced around the walls: a tarnished mirror in a chipped frame above the mantelpiece, a faded watercolour either side; above the bed was a pair of etchings of Bristol scenes covered in damp spots. He recognised the suspension bridge and Bristol Cathedral.

A postcard had been stuck to the window frame with a blob of Blu Tack; a beach scene somewhere, Scotland perhaps. Many weeks in the sunlight had warped the card, curling it over so Dixon could see it was blank; no stamp in the top corner or any writing. He pulled it off the frame and turned it over.

Maybe his visit hadn't been a complete waste of time after all, he thought, smiling at the sight of the Blu Tack flattened against the back of the card, a micro SIM card embedded in it.

Chapter Twelve

'Where are you?' Dixon was sitting in his Land Rover on a garage forecourt on the A369; mercifully he'd had a pound coin for the toll on the Clifton Suspension Bridge, although the crossing had brought back memories he'd rather have left forgotten – of standing on the rail looking down over the suicide fence at two coastguard officers recovering a body from the mud below.

'Portishead,' replied Louise. 'The tax office will let us have the list by the end of tomorrow, they said. Collins's computers are in store and we can't get our hands on those until Monday.'

'What about the Marine Accident Investigation Branch?'

'I got them on the emergency contact number. They're sending over his laptop by courier first thing on Monday. How did you get on?'

'Good.' The micro SIM card was burning a hole in Dixon's jacket pocket.

'Nige says there's an archery shop at Puxton, in an old barn. It's got a range behind it and there's a club that meets there on a Sunday; opens at ten.'

'Tell him to meet me there in the morning.'

'Will do.'

'Is your computer on?'

'Yes, Sir.'

'About five years ago there was a young twerp shooting cats with a pistol crossbow in Cheddar. I'd like to pay him a visit.'

'At this time of night?'

Forty minutes later Dixon parked on the pavement outside a small terraced cottage in the middle of Cheddar, oddly enough opposite the vet's surgery.

'Who is it?' came the shout when Dixon banged on the door.

'Police. I need to speak to Luke.'

'Can't you bloody people leave him alone?' The door was snatched open from the inside, the woman's anger soon dissipating when she saw the smile on Dixon's face. 'What is it?' She was peering at his warrant card.

'I'm just here to rule him out of some sheep killings, Mrs Bales.'

'Sheep?'

'And two people.' Cool and calm.

'A crossbow, I suppose?' She stepped back into the hall, opening the door wider. 'He's in the back. There's a copper here to see you, Luke.' Shouted over her shoulder.

Smart trousers, snappy shirt open at the neck; Saturday night uniform. 'I was just going out.' Luke was brushing his short dark hair in the mirror over the fireplace.

'Where were you on the night of seventeenth July?' asked Dixon.

'What day of the week was it?'

'Monday, between say ten on the Monday through to six the following morning, Tuesday.'

'That's easy, I was at work. I do nights at Morrisons – eight till six. It's on the Express Park industrial estate, not far from the pig farm.' Luke was watching Dixon in the mirror.

'Do you still own a crossbow?'

'No. Look, when are you people going to let me forget that? I was fifteen, for fuck's sake!'

'These cats are his.' Mrs Bales gestured to a tortoiseshell and a tabby, their faces buried in a feeding bowl, their tails gently swishing in the air.

'I rescued them as kittens. To make up for . . .' Luke's voice tailed off.

'What about last Thursday night?'

'If it's a weekday night I'll be at work; check with Morrisons if you don't believe me.'

'I believe you, Luke, but I'll have to check anyway.'

'Fine, now can I go? I'll miss the bus into Weston.'

'You've forgotten, haven't you?'

Louise had entered the micro SIM, the Blu Tack and the postcard into the evidence log and then headed for the accommodation block for a FaceTime session with Katie, late for the child's bedtime, leaving Dixon sifting through the box of papers that had come over from Zephyr. Dave and Kevin were still watching the CCTV and Mark was on his way back from Bradley Stoke, bringing pizza.

Dixon dropped a file back into the box. 'Forgotten what?'

'We're sitting in the Zalshah,' Jane huffed down the phone. 'Your best man's birthday. Where are you?'

'Portishead.'

'Give me the phone.' Roger Poland's voice in the background. 'I quite understand, Nick. Don't worry about it.'

'I'm sorry, Roger,' replied Dixon. 'I'm on my way.'

I need a word with you anyway.

He parked on the forecourt of the bookmaker's opposite the restaurant forty minutes later and ran across the road.

'Kingfisher?' asked Ravi, when he burst in.

'Yes, please.'

'They're in the far corner.'

'We've eaten, but I've ordered for you.' Jane scowled at Dixon as he sat down next to Poland.

'Thanks.'

'You two'll be going on *Mr and Mrs* before you know it.' Poland was holding aloft the dregs of a pint of lager. 'I had David Charlesworth on the phone earlier; wanted to know what I thought about the crossbow business.'

'What did you tell him?'

'Same as I told you.' Poland drained his glass. 'The same pattern of broadhead was used on the sheep and on Godfrey Collins.'

'And on a taxman from Bradley Stoke,' said Dixon, looking in the direction of the bar. 'I still can't get my head around the fact you can buy the bloody things at all.'

'I had a look online,' said Jane. 'It seems most of them are coming into the UK direct from sellers in China. I only found one archery shop selling them. Leicester somewhere.'

'Well, they'll be getting a visit.' Dixon smiled at the waiter placing a pint of lager in front of him. 'Cole's putting together a list.'

'Cole?' Jane frowned. 'He's on your major investigation team?'

'Bridgwater's new Rural Crimes team. He's been working on the sheep killings.'

'He'll be insufferable.'

'Jane said you were talking about setting a date.'

'We are,' said Dixon, allowing Poland to change the subject, for the time being at least. 'It'll be next year now, I expect.'

'What about Christmas Eve, or Valentine's Day?' Poland flashed a mischievous grin at Jane, a conspiratorial glint in his eye. 'And the honeymoon somewhere exotic, I think.'

'The Lakes, or Scotland possibly.'

'Scotland?'

'He won't leave Monty,' mumbled Jane. 'And neither will I, for that matter.'

'Quite right too.' Poland raised his empty glass. 'Here's to Monty.'

Dixon's food had come and gone before he brought the conversation around to where he wanted it. 'Did you get a chance to have a look at my email?'

'The vet had been very thorough,' replied Poland. 'And the broadheads are clearly visible in the photographs, where he'd cut away the fleece. It's interesting that they don't penetrate the bone at the front of the skull.' He was pointing at the middle of his forehead with his index finger. 'An ordinary bolt clearly does, but not the curved broadhead, which may explain why your killer is hitting his victims in the eye.'

'But, why use them at all?' asked Jane. 'And why when the victim is already dead?'

'Collins certainly was,' said Dixon. 'And the taxman, Finch, possibly, according to Petersen; let's hope so anyway.'

'Then your killer is sending a message, isn't he?' Poland was staring at the dessert menu.

'Who's he sending this message to?' Jane took the menu from Poland before he could pass it to Dixon.

'I gave myself a couple of extra units,' Dixon grumbled, snatching it from Jane's hand.

'To you lot, I suppose,' said Poland.

'Or his next victims.'

◆ ◆ ◆

'Last one for a while, old son,' Dixon said when he dropped Monty at home after an early Sunday morning walk along the beach to

Brean Down. It was never time wasted – he did all his best thinking when following his dog along the beach; not that there had been that much to think about this morning. It all seemed straightforward – too straightforward, almost: two murders, the motive obvious and the killer almost certainly coming from a pool of two hundred or so taxpayers who had been landed with hefty bills. It still left an uneasy feeling in his gut, but he couldn't work out whether that was down to him missing something or because he knew there were surely more killings to come; and two hours on the beach hadn't been able to answer that question.

He turned into the large gravel car park of Bowman Archery at Puxton to find Cole waiting for him, leaning against a patrol car and watching a small group putting up archery targets on trestles on the far side of the field adjacent to the converted barn. Beyond the targets a long low haystack waited for those who missed.

Cole clearly hadn't been able to resist the burger van.

'Bacon butty, Sir?' He was holding up a half-eaten roll in a paper serviette. 'Damned good. He comes on a Sunday morning for the club meets.'

The blob of ketchup running down Cole's chin turned Dixon's stomach. 'No, thanks.' He blinked away the vision of Finch and the blood congealed on his chin.

The front doors of the barn were standing open, a few people milling about inside.

'Did you tell him we were coming?'

'No, Sir,' replied Cole, spraying crumbs over the bonnet of the patrol car. 'I know what you're thinking, but he's used to seeing a marked car on a Sunday morning. This place was on my patch when I was over at Cheddar and I'd always stop for a bacon roll if I had the chance.'

'And what's his name?'

'Aaron Bowman.'

'Bowman?'

'Yeah, I know. I asked him once and he said he'd changed it by deed poll. You can't miss him, he's the one with the tattoos.'

'I'm going in to have a wander round. You'd better wait out here.'

Dixon made a beeline for the crossbows, the irony of arrows on the floor directing him up a flight of steel steps to a mezzanine floor not lost on him. A bewildering array of bows of all shapes and sizes were locked in glass cabinets on the far side, some with telescopic sights, some with red dot sights. He decided that price must be a good measure of the power of the bow, quickly navigating along the display to the compound bows at the far end; a complex system of pulleys offering the archer even more power, at a price.

The bolts were arranged in wooden trays under the counter; aluminium, carbon fibre and wood of varying lengths, some smaller ones – the pistol crossbow bolts – hanging in packets on hooks mounted on the back wall. Packets of broadheads too; two and three-bladed, some with prongs, but none curved.

'Would you like to try one?'

Dixon spun round, his eyes immediately drawn to the tattoos: Bard the Bowman slaying Smaug the Dragon on the right arm; Cupid on the left, with a woman's name that looked like it had been changed more than once. The Bowman Archery T-shirt confirmed it.

'Mr Bowman?'

'Yes.'

Time for the warrant card.

'The offer still stands.' Bowman looked unimpressed. 'I've got a range out the back.'

'Maybe later, Sir,' replied Dixon. 'D'you have a minute?'

'Yeah, sure.' Bowman nodded, obligingly. 'The archery club lot are all recurve bow people anyway and Ryan's downstairs.'

'Recurve?'

'The tips of the bow curve away from the archer, for more power. Some of the crossbows have got it too.'

'Do you sell many of these?' Dixon gestured to the compound crossbows.

'We sell a few online; rarely in store, to be honest. Actually, most of our sales are on the internet. And I always get ID to prove they're over eighteen. We're a reputable business.'

'Of course you are, Sir. And which of these bows would be powerful enough to kill?'

'I assume you're talking about deer,' replied Bowman, frowning, 'which is illegal in this country anyway.'

Dixon stared at him, letting the question hang.

'Oh, shit . . .' Bowman took a deep breath. 'Well, pretty much any of them to be honest. Even the pistol crossbows at close range would do it.'

'Am I right in assuming the more expensive bows are the more powerful?'

'Basically, although there are several ways of measuring the power of a crossbow.' Bowman unlocked a cabinet and took out a bow. 'Put your toe in that stirrup and try to cock it.'

Dixon put his left foot in the stirrup and pulled on the string with both hands, managing to get it halfway up at most.

'Sorry, I should have said.' Bowman leaned over and took the bow from an out of breath Dixon. 'This is the Excalibur Micro Axe. It's got a draw weight of two hundred and seventy pounds; you'll never cock it without a rope. Some of the medieval ones used to have a pulley system called a windlass to cock 'em, they were that powerful, but then they were trying to kill through a suit of armour.'

'So, it's about the draw weight?'

'It's about the kinetic energy, really. Force equals mass times acceleration and all that. People look at the draw weight and the FPS, but they're misleading.'

'FPS?'

'Feet per second, the speed of the bolt when it leaves the bow. People think the faster the better, but that's not necessarily true. A heavier bolt will fly slower but hits harder; more force behind it.' Bowman slammed his right fist into the palm of his left hand. 'That's much better for hunting. It's about finding the right balance for your quarry, whether it's a deer or a rabbit.'

'Or a human being.'

'Please tell me someone's not been using one of my bows to kill—'

'We don't know whose bow it is, Sir,' said Dixon. 'Yet. That's why I'm here.'

Bowman replaced the crossbow in the cabinet and locked it with the key dangling from his belt. 'You're going to want a list of everyone I've sold a crossbow to, aren't you?'

'Three months, please.' Dixon opted for the friendly smile.

'And it's a murder investigation?'

'*Double* murder investigation.' Dixon walked behind the counter and took a packet of broadheads off the rack. 'What d'you sell these for?'

'The price?'

'Use.'

'Field archery. There's a place on the other side of the Mendips; you're shooting at targets in the trees, varying distances, on the move, that sort of thing. This lot outside know the target's exactly fifty yards away, but in field archery you're constantly moving.'

'Why the broadheads though?'

'It's simulated hunting, really, and that's what you'd use if you were out for real.'

Dixon slid a piece of paper out of his pocket and unfolded it, laying it flat on the countertop. 'Have you ever sold any of these?'

'Shit, is that what the killer's using?' Bowman bared his teeth at the photograph of a red painted broadhead with three curved blades. 'No, I wouldn't give them house room. I've seen them before; bought some online once to see what they were like, y'know, but I'd never stock them myself. Never have, never will. You don't need those things for field archery.'

'Have you still got them?'

'Yes, I think so.' Bowman opened a cabinet behind the counter and started rummaging about inside. 'They're in here somewhere, I'm sure they are. I got 'em on an auction site, the seller in China. How we're supposed to compete with that I don't know, but then that's not your problem, is it?'

'No, Sir.'

'Here they are.' Bowman handed Dixon a small padded envelope slit open at one end. 'It's come in from China. Look, under "detailed description of contents" it says "metal plugs".'

'Six.'

'They're all there. They're on the heavy side, which reduces the effective range, even with a more powerful bow.'

Dixon slid a small plastic bag out of the envelope and counted them. 'May I?' he asked.

'Go ahead,' replied Bowman, watching Dixon drop the broadheads into his jacket pocket. 'You still haven't said how you know it's a crossbow.'

'We're going by the length of the bolt,' he replied. 'He started with sheep, using a pistol crossbow and some of these, I suppose.' Dixon was pointing at a packet of twenty bolts, each six and a half inches long, with a gold painted shaft, steel tip and black plastic fletch. 'Then he moved up to a more powerful bow and broadheads. These' – gesturing to the two and three-bladed tips – 'and some of these.' Tapping his pocket. 'He's also moved on from sheep to people.'

'You can fire a short arrow from a longbow using a Turkish siper; it's like a glove with a grooved piece of wood on the back of the thumb for the arrow.' Bowman extended his left arm, miming the holding of a longbow. 'It's so you can overdraw the short arrow, but it's unlikely, to be honest. You're not going to want to lug all that around when a crossbow is small and compact.'

'It makes the perfect murder weapon,' said Dixon, airily. 'You could add that to your marketing material.'

'Now, hang on a minute.'

'Which of these bows would you choose, Sir? If you wanted to kill someone?'

'At what range?'

Cole appeared at the top of the stairs.

'Thirty yards,' replied Dixon.

'You'd want something that's easy to cock, so nothing overly powerful.' Bowman was looking along the cabinets. 'There'd be no need for a compound bow, so probably the Anglo Arms Jaguar. One hundred and seventy-five pound draw weight, so quick and most people could manage it. Light too. And accurate up to thirty-five yards with a four-twenty grain bolt with one of those broadheads on it. Or maybe something with a bit more poke, say a Desert Hawk – that's a two-twenty-five draw.'

'Powerful enough?'

'Plenty.'

'How much is it?' asked Cole.

'A hundred and ten quid for the Jaguar,' replied Bowman. 'A hundred and twenty-seven with the red dot sight. The Desert Hawk is three hundred and thirty.'

'The Jaguar's not too expensive if you had to leave it behind,' said Dixon. 'Can we try it?'

'Yeah, sure. I've got one set up down on the range.'

It looked more like a skittle alley, except that it was lined with chipboard and a large carpet was hanging at the far end in front of yet more hay bales.

'I'll set up a target,' said Bowman, handing the bow to Cole. 'What d'you fancy? I've got a cardboard police officer.'

'Just the usual, thank you.' Dixon would allow him that one, after his jibe about the perfect murder weapon.

Cole went first, managing to cock the bow with comparative ease.

'Twenty yards from that line.' Bowman gestured to a line on the floor. 'Squeeze, don't snatch.'

Cole put two in the inner gold and one in the outer. 'Must be something wrong with these sights,' he said indignantly. 'I'm firearms trained.'

'What about you, Inspector? D'you fancy a go?'

'I've seen enough, thank you, Sir. You were going to let me have a list of buyers of crossbows for the last three months.'

'Yes, give me a minute.'

'Do you run the archery club as well?'

'You want a list of the members, I suppose.'

'Thank you.'

Dixon waited until Bowman had left the range and then turned back to Cole, who was still checking the sights on the crossbow. 'Do me a favour, will you, Nigel. Fire it and then reload as fast as you can; hold the spare bolt between your teeth.' He looked at his watch. 'Go!'

Another bolt in the inner gold, then Cole started to reload. 'Shit,' he hissed, fumbling with the second bolt.

'Six seconds,' said Dixon, when it thwacked into the target. 'A fraction less if you hadn't fluffed it.'

'It's pretty fiddly.'

'Let's say five seconds with practice. We may need to know one day.'

Chapter Thirteen

Dixon decided to risk the loading bay outside the tax office in Cardiff city centre. After all, it was a Sunday, and he'd been able to talk his way out of trouble the day before. Just.

Cole had gone back to Portishead armed with the lists of customers and members at Bowman Archery, leaving Dixon to head over to Cardiff, where Louise was due back at the tax office, this time for a meeting with the senior manager at 2 p.m.

Fox was there again, still wearing the same jeans and polo shirt, but the manager had taken the trouble to put on a suit and tie, even on a Sunday. He certainly looked the part.

'This is Owen Jones, Sir.' Louise had met Dixon on the landing when he stepped out of the lift, and was making the introductions. 'He's the general manager.'

'Senior officer.' Jones looked down his nose at Louise, although that may have been the bifocals. 'The equivalent of a superintendent in the police.'

They were sitting around one end of the conference table, Dixon standing in the window admiring the view of the Millennium Stadium. 'How many staff do you have here?'

'Three thousand two hundred,' replied Jones. 'And we're recruiting at the moment. We're one of thirteen regional tax centres.'

'And Keith Finch was in charge of enforcement?'

'He was.' Jones slid his fingers under his glasses and rubbed the bridge of his nose. 'We have lots of teams in the building; self assessment, trusts and estates, VAT, corporate, tax avoidance, stamp duty land tax, environmental and enforcement. We've even got a regional prosecutions office. Each one is looked after by a manager.' Jones let out an impatient sigh, as if he had far more important things he could and should be doing. Golf, probably, thought Dixon. 'Then you've got the sub-teams, so in enforcement you've got loan charge – disguised remuneration, to give it its proper name – pension transfer, VAT, offshore, as well as the general avoidance and evasion.'

'And the film scheme,' offered Fox.

'And the film scheme,' repeated Jones. 'But don't ask me to explain that, for God's sake.'

Dixon sat down next to Louise. 'I assume you mean the use of investments in the film industry to generate artificial losses and claim the tax relief on them.'

'Er, yes.' Jones sat up.

'I qualified as a solicitor before I joined the police, Mr Jones.'

'Oh, I see, sorry.'

'We're interested in the loan charge or disguised remuneration.'

'That's a comparatively small team,' replied Jones. 'Eighty-seven at the last count, some of them part-time, and we also offer job share.'

'How many taxpayers were affected by it?'

'About fifty thousand; we've been recovering back tax and national insurance from both the employer and the employee.

106

Employers were dodging their national insurance contributions as well, of course.'

'And the attitude taken?'

'Firm but fair, as you would expect.' Jones folded his arms. 'If the taxpayer engages with us and we're able to arrive at a settlement agreement with them then they can pay by instalments over five or seven years, depending on their current salary. We've agreed longer settlement periods with some too. You have to remember it's not all management consultants and locum doctors, there are construction workers and agency staff too.'

'A bill for back tax of five grand is a lot of money to someone earning twenty pounds an hour,' said Fox. 'Some were even on the minimum wage. So, we try to be reasonable.'

'Keith was always very clear about that with his team.'

'How many taxpayers have taken their own lives?' asked Dixon.

'Seven, sadly,' said Jones, a hint of regret in his voice. 'We referred each to the police conduct office. They investigate us, as well as you.'

'And how many taxpayers have been made bankrupt?'

'None. Some have declared themselves bankrupt, but we haven't bankrupted anyone.' Jones puffed out his chest. 'Are these questions really necessary?'

'I'm trying to gauge whether it would be a sufficient motive for murder,' replied Dixon. 'And it seems to be.'

'Then they should go after George Osborne. He was the Chancellor who brought in the charge in 2016, and made it retrospective.' Jones closed his eyes. 'For God's sake don't quote me on that.'

'I won't, Sir.'

'Keith was just doing his job.'

'What about Godfrey Collins?'

Jones gave a dismissive wave of his hand. 'David's got the list.'

'He ran the schemes using offshore trusts in the Cayman Islands,' said Fox. 'He had three main clients, all of them employment agencies – two in Bristol and one in Weston-super-Mare. All told, there were two hundred and sixty-seven staff affected.'

Jones began shifting in his seat, unable to contain himself any longer. 'Are they seriously expecting us to believe that it never occurred to them there was anything wrong with receiving loans they didn't have to pay back from an offshore trust?'

'Some didn't have any choice,' replied Louise. 'And others were told it was perfectly legal by their accountants.'

'Which it was at the time the schemes started,' said Fox. 'Technically. It was only in 2016 when the law was tightened up and backdated.'

Dixon decided to move the conversation along. 'How many of the Collins taxpayers have cooperated with you?'

'We've got settlement agreements in place with two-thirds of them,' replied Fox. 'I've marked them on the list.'

'What about the agencies?'

'Them too. Their details are there as well.'

'And Collins himself?'

'We threw the book at him,' replied Jones. 'Keith referred him to the prosecutions office and they went for the maximum fine; made an example of him.'

'Most of the debts are in the under ten thousand bracket.' Fox slid the bundle of documents across the table. 'But there are some bigger ones where we've been unable to get any response from the taxpayer. I've marked them too. One of the agencies in Bristol recruited sales and IT staff and their bills tend to be bigger.'

'And which of them was Keith Finch pursuing?' asked Dixon, flicking through the list.

'None of them,' replied Jones, frowning. 'He was just the enforcement team line manager. He didn't do any of the casework himself. He was probably targeted for no other reason than all of the correspondence went out with his electronic signature on it.'

'So, whoever killed him thought he was the caseworker when in fact he wasn't.' Louise sighed. 'That makes it almost mistaken identity.'

'Just to clarify, then.' Dixon was trying to hide his pained expression. 'Mr Finch's signature would've been on all the correspondence from the whole enforcement team: loan charge, pensions, VAT, even the film scheme?'

'That's right,' said Jones, an apologetic smile the best he had to offer.

◆ ◆ ◆

'Start by cross referencing the loan charge list with the archery stuff Cole's got. Then tomorrow we should have the boots on the ground to start knocking on doors.'

That had been Dixon's parting shot when he left Louise outside the tax office.

'You'll be in trouble if they issue tickets by CCTV,' she had said, gesturing to the loading bay opposite before heading for the multistorey car park.

Now Dixon was on his way to see Keith Finch's widow in Bradley Stoke. Her daughter was with her and she felt up to it, apparently.

It was a sobering thought that Finch could very well have been killed by any of the thousands of taxpayers being pursued by the enforcement team for anything from the loan charge to VAT fraud. His only crime had been to have his signature printed on every letter that went out. Granted, it gave the individual caseworker some degree of anonymity, but at what cost? That said, he had been killed with the same type of crossbow broadhead used on Collins, and the loan charge was the obvious connection between the two of them.

The last of the Scientific Services vans had gone by the time he arrived at Bradley Stoke, the cedar of Lebanon in the back garden still towering over the bungalow. The sleek Mercedes was new and probably belonged to the daughter; it was a younger woman who answered the door, tall and with short blonde hair.

'God, you are young, aren't you? I thought Gaynor next door was joking.' She gave a nervous laugh. 'Sorry, it's one of those things you say, isn't it?'

'Is it, really.'

'Have you caught him yet?'

'We're working on it, Mrs . . . ?'

'Jessop.' She was shutting the front door behind Dixon. 'My mother's in bed.'

'Is there a family liaison officer here?'

'There was, but we sent her home. I've got her mobile number and she'll be back in the morning,' she said.

'Are you staying long?' Dixon was following her along the passageway.

'I'll be here as long as she needs me, although I did suggest she come home with me. She can't face sitting in the living room or the conservatory . . .' Her voice softened to a whisper. 'You can see the tree from there.'

Dixon nodded his understanding.

'Mum, the chief inspector's here,' she said, pushing open the door.

Propped up in bed, fully clothed, the duvet covering only her feet; a kitchen roll was on the sheet beside her, the television on the chest of drawers against the wall opposite on, but with the sound turned down.

Mary Finch looked up at him, her eyes bloodshot and dry. 'I still can't believe it's . . .'

Mrs Jessop went to stand by the bed on the far side, gently rubbing the back of her mother's hand. 'Take your time, Mum.'

'I gave your colleague Keith's phone. I remembered him saying he'd taken a photo of the red car, so you've got that to go on.'

'What have you been told?' asked Dixon.

'Nothing,' replied Mrs Jessop. 'Karen, the liaison officer, is great. She said she'd tell us everything she can, but she doesn't know anything either at the moment.'

'May I?' Dixon gestured to the chair by the bed, waited a moment for Mrs Finch to turn her head, then sat down. 'When I saw you yesterday you'd taken one of your neighbour's Valium.'

'I don't really remember, I'm afraid. It's all a bit of a blur; someone asked me about the car.'

'I also asked you about someone called Godfrey Collins. Does that name mean anything to you?'

'No, sorry.'

'Me neither,' said Mrs Jessop.

'He was an accountant formerly from Congresbury.'

Mrs Finch shook her head on the pillow. 'What's his connection to Keith?'

'Mr Collins was murdered with a crossbow five days ago. The pattern of what they call the "broadhead" on the bolt was identical, so we're working on the basis that his murder and your husband's are connected.'

'I've never heard of him.'

'This is highly sensitive information, so if you do talk to the press I'd be very grateful if you kept this to yourself.'

'Mum won't be talking to them. One of the sods came knocking earlier and I sent him packing; from the local rag.'

'Godfrey Collins ran what is known as loan charge schemes,' continued Dixon. 'And they landed a couple of hundred people with large tax bills that your husband's enforcement team at Cardiff were pursuing.'

'He'd huff and puff whenever the loan charge came on the news, wouldn't he, Mum?'

'That and the film thing were his pet hates.' Mrs Finch was staring at a photograph of her husband on the bedside table. 'He had more sympathy for those caught up in the pension transfer scam.'

'You also mentioned that your husband saw someone standing in the field. Did he tell you what this man looked like?'

'He was too far away. I seem to recall him saying he was tall with dark hair, but that's about it.'

'Did any of the neighbours see him?' asked Mrs Jessop.

'House to house hasn't come up with anything yet,' replied Dixon. 'Did he ever mention any trouble at work, any particular incidents or individuals threatening him, or anyone else for that matter?'

'No.' Mrs Finch forced a faint smile. 'He always used to say that most people were sensible enough to know the taxman was just doing his job.'

Chapter Fourteen

'Look everywhere, you never know where you'll find it.'

It was good advice, although he'd been looking for the last piece of a jigsaw puzzle at the time. That said, it applied to police work too, although it did make for the odd late night. He'd finished the box of papers from Zephyr at gone midnight and the house to house statements by 2 a.m. – another sighting of the mysterious red car, but that was about it – his evening punctuated by a microwaved sausage roll from the garage. Mercifully, he'd remembered to bring his night insulin with him.

Four hours' sleep on the sofa in the Transport Services staff room would have to do, Mark waking him up when he burst in to return the kettle. Dixon cupped his hands together and exhaled sharply, sniffing the air and wincing; a toothbrush and toothpaste might have been a good idea too.

'Transport start at seven, so I thought I'd better get it back.' Mark was plugging in the kettle. 'The restaurant's open for breakfast and they sell toothpaste. Cheap razors too.'

'That bad is it.'

A fry-up for breakfast and clean teeth; he felt almost human again, although he skipped the shave. The last time he'd tried one of those cheap plastic razors he'd looked like he'd been dragged through brambles face first.

There was a buzz to Area J when he arrived back on the second floor of the operations building, the murmur gradually decreasing as he made his way to the front, taking up position by the white-board. He counted twelve new faces, which was a start.

'You're all up to speed with where we've got to?' he asked, looking at the jacket and tie sitting nearest to him.

'Yes, Sir.'

'We've got two hundred and sixty-seven people owing money to the taxman; these are the people caught up in Collins's schemes who were being pursued by Finch, or at least might have thought they were. One hundred and seventy-one of them have entered into settlement agreements with HMRC, so we start with the other ninety-six. Find them, interview them, alibi them; DNA swabs too, if they consent.'

'And if they don't?' asked the jacket and tie.

'We put a giant asterisk by their name.' Dixon turned to Cole. 'How have you got on with the archery retailers?'

'I've emailed the sellers of the broadheads, but they're all in China, so I'm not holding my breath. Only one UK retailer has them listed on his site, but they're out of stock.'

Dixon slid the padded envelope he'd picked up at Bowman Archery the day before out of his jacket pocket, took out one of the broadheads and passed it to the jacket and tie. 'Just so you all know, this is what we're talking about.'

'Fucking hell.'

'Pass it round,' said Dixon. 'One of these went straight through Keith Finch's eyeball. The tip is sharp and those are curved blades on the side, so be careful.' He waited while the broadhead made its way around Area J, watching the reactions as it passed from hand to hand; if he hadn't had everyone's attention before, he certainly did now. 'Nigel, what about crossbows?'

'I've come up with seven so far, sold to people living in Avon and Somerset in the last three months; all of them online. Bowman sold two, again both online but to people out of the area.'

'I don't suppose any of them are on the loan charge list?'

'No, Sir.'

'That would've been too good to be true. What about the red car, Dave?'

'We've checked all the CCTV and number plate recognition cameras nearest to the bungalow in Bradley Stoke and come up with one hundred and seventeen red cars in the two hours either side of Finch's murder. That's CCTV on Winterbourne Academy and ANPR cameras on the intersection of Beacon Lane and the Old Gloucester Road; there's one on the Bristol Road too.'

'If he ducked out into the country we're buggered, though,' said Kevin, sitting next to Dave.

'Could he?'

Dave nodded. 'If he knew his way around; residential streets will take you out the back and into the country lanes.'

'We have to assume he did know his way around. Finch spotted him scoping the place days earlier. Check them anyway. I don't suppose anyone on the crossbow list owns a red car?'

'I'm afraid not, Sir.' Dave slumped back in his chair. 'We've already cross-checked the lists.'

'Computers, Lou?'

'All with High Tech, Sir.' She glanced across at Kevin. 'And the micro SIM that Zephyr missed.'

'Right, let's get on with it. We all know what we've got to do.'

The twelve new faces dispersed to vacant workstations in Area J, leaving Louise and Mark staring at Dixon. 'We don't, Sir,' said Louise, frowning.

'I've got an accountant telling me the agency workers wouldn't have known who Collins was and I've got the senior officer at HMRC Cardiff telling me Finch wasn't a caseworker, his name was just printed on the letters, so I'm not entirely convinced by the loan charge. It's all we've got at the moment, and we'll go with it, but I want you two to find another connection between Finch and Collins.'

'And what if there isn't one?' asked Mark.

'Then we're stuck with the loan charge, aren't we?'

'What about me?'

'You're with me, Nige.'

'Really?'

'We're going to visit the agencies and then start working through your crossbow buyers.' Dixon was holding the broadhead between his thumb and index finger, turning it by the thread, the blades glinting in the morning sunlight streaming in through the windows. 'We'll need some discreet body armour too; a stab vest isn't going to stop one of these.'

'They're always above a shop, aren't they.' Cole looked up. 'With one of these on the pavement.' He kicked the A-board, the poster of job listings spattered with what Dixon hoped was coffee, or Coke perhaps.

He glanced down at the vacancies: C++ developer; digital officer, facilities management; database manager (Oracle/Postgres); cyber security engineer. None of them less than fifty pounds an hour. 'I'm in the wrong business.'

'Do they know we're coming?'

'You can't wrong-foot someone if they know you're coming, Nige.'

The door between the bookshop and the coffee bar in Small Street was standing open, a flight of stairs leading up to a glazed door etched with *Bristol Recruitment Solutions* and their logo, a sort of speech bubble that left Dixon wondering what they had to say.

'She's on the phone,' was the slightly unusual response to his warrant card, the receptionist hardly looking away from her computer screen while she carried on typing.

'Who is?'

'Natalie.'

'What about Clare Pring?'

'Gone.'

'Where?'

'You'll need to speak to Natalie about that. May I?' she asked, picking up the phone when it rang on her desk. 'Bristol Recruitment Solutions. She's on a call at the moment, with someone else waiting. Yes, I'll tell her. Thank you.'

The red light on the switchboard went off, then the door opened. Must have been alerted by an email, thought Dixon.

'I'm Natalie Corfield.' Short dark hair, sharp two-piece suit, red shoes. 'Can I help you?'

'We wanted to have a word with you about Godfrey Collins,' replied Dixon.

'Oh, God, not that again.' She folded her arms tightly across her chest. 'I've been dealing with the tax office in Cardiff and it's all sorted.'

'Not about the loan charge, if that's what you're referring to.'

'What then?' A sharp edge of impatience was creeping into her voice. 'It's nine-thirty on a Monday morning, my busiest time.'

'Would you like to do it out here, or should we step into your office?' Dixon knew the answer to that one before he asked it, given that there were two people sitting on the far side of the waiting room.

Her office was small, an empty cereal bowl on the corner of her otherwise tidy desk; a laptop, a phone and a pad of forms, a piece of carbon paper sticking out of the side. Phone calls and filling in forms – recruitment was sounding a lot like police work already.

Cole must have been briefed by Louise, sitting down and taking his notebook out of his pocket.

'Do sit down,' said Natalie, her impatience slipping into sarcasm.

Cole was about to reply, but Dixon beat him to it. 'What's happened to your co-director? Your receptionist just said that Mrs Pring had gone.'

'The loans thing was my idea and when it all went bang Clare wanted none of it, so I bought her out and she's resigned her directorship.'

'It's not updated at Companies House,' said Dixon.

'She said she'd deal with that and it's her problem if she doesn't.'

'Do you have any other staff?'

'One part-timer who comes in on Monday and Friday, ten till four. They're the busiest days, really.'

'And your relationship with Godfrey Collins?'

'*Business* relationship, just to be clear. Look, I met him at some business networking event and he said he could save me thousands of pounds a year. It was as simple as that, really.'

'When was this?'

'At least ten years ago, so maybe 2008, thinking about it. I'd not long started up and was doing the rounds of those tedious networking events trying to meet employers, contacts, clients, anyone.'

'And he came here?'

'I was working from home back then, but we met and it all seemed perfectly legit. He'd got the offshore trust in place and everything. He said it was legal and he was an accountant. He took whopping fees, but we were all still better off.' She slumped down into the leather chair behind her desk. 'If only I knew then what I know now.'

'How many staff were paid using the scheme?'

'Ninety-three over the course of seven years. Some of them I got to know quite well over that time and it was devastating when that tosser Osborne changed the law in 2016.'

'I was over at the tax office yesterday and they have a slightly different take on it.' Dixon softened the blow with a smile. 'I'm paraphrasing, but it was something along the lines of: *Do they seriously expect us to believe it never occurred to them there was something wrong with using loans they didn't have to pay back?*'

'They do have a point, I suppose, with hindsight, but I was assured by Collins it was legal and I always told anyone going into the scheme to get their own advice as well. Look, what's this all about?'

Dixon was standing with his back to the window, the view of the block opposite not terribly inspiring. 'How many of the ninety-three would have had any direct contact with Mr Collins?'

'None.'

'Would they have known who he was?'

'I don't think so. The loans were paid by bank transfer and any queries came through me. You said *was*.' She sat up. 'What's happened?'

'Mr Collins is dead, Miss Corfield,' replied Dixon. 'This is a murder investigation.'

'You're joking.'

'And a Mr Keith Finch, who was the head of the enforcement team at the tax office in Cardiff.'

'Bloody hell. It was his name on all the letters, but I dealt with someone called Sanjay.'

'Do you recall any of your agency workers being particularly aggrieved by the loan charge?' Dixon was admiring the bewildering array of certificates hanging in frames on the wall.

'Not really. Some of them had put money aside for the tax because they thought someone would come after them sooner or later. I've even got a few still on the books.' Natalie leaned forward and closed the lid of her laptop. 'Most have settled, but a couple joined the action group and campaigned against the charge; letters to their MP, that sort of thing. I don't think any of them would have killed Collins, that's in the unlikely event any of them knew who he was. And the taxman's just doing his job, isn't he?'

'What's the biggest bill any of your workers was landed with?'

'Two hundred and ten grand. He sold a rental property and paid it off. Not everyone was so lucky.'

Chapter Fifteen

The notice of possession pinned to the door of the office on Queen Square had been ominous, and a quick check of Google had come up with a company winding up petition issued in the High Court by HM Revenue and Customs. Someone hadn't checked the agencies properly, but then it had been the weekend, so he decided to let it go. And Jones's assurance that no one had been bankrupted clearly didn't extend to companies, although it may have been unrelated to the loan charge.

'Get someone to speak to the directors on the phone,' had been Dixon's response, and Cole was organising that as they drove out of Bristol.

'There's a bloke in Weston on the crossbow list,' said Cole, when he rang off. 'We could pay him a visit after the next employment agency.'

'Which bow did he buy?'

'A Desert Hawk, two hundred and twenty-five pound recurve bow.' Cole was looking at his notebook. 'It fires twenty inch bolts and you'd need to add three for the broadhead so it sits off the end of the rail, and that fits with the twenty-three inch bolts found in Collins and Finch.'

Dixon reached behind his seat and felt for the body armour in the rear passenger footwell of his Land Rover.

'I got Type IV, Sir,' Cole said. 'Solid Kevlar plates. It'll stop a crossbow bolt, don't you worry.'

Dixon parked on the double yellow lines opposite the Worlebury Hill Residential Home and looked up. It was the last building before the road disappeared into the trees on the top of the hill, set over three floors in grey stone with bay windows and a new annex on the left.

The Worlebury Hill Care Agency occupied what looked like a converted double garage by the roadside.

'Hardly looks like a den of tax avoidance and criminality, does it?' muttered Cole.

The front of the garage had been replaced by a floor to ceiling window and a glazed door; three women visible inside, sitting at desks, two of them on the phone. Filing cabinets along the back wall were covered in lever arch files, just enough room left for a kettle.

'I suppose they nip up to the house if they need the loo.'

'I'll leave that question for you if you'd like to ask them.' Dixon was undoing his seatbelt.

'I was just thinking out loud.'

'Best avoided in my experience.'

'We're being watched, Sir,' said Cole, as they walked across the road, the phones ringing but going unanswered.

'Can I help you?' asked the woman striding towards them from the back of the office as Dixon opened the door, the dark blue nurse's uniform reminding him of his last visit to hospital. There was even that hospital smell.

Cole was first to produce his warrant card, the response an exaggerated sigh.

'Do we have to do this now? It's Monday morning, our busiest time.'

'Yes, we do.'

'And you are?'

'Detective Chief Inspector Dixon.'

'It's not Mrs Featherstone claiming someone's stolen her jewellery again, is it?' She shook her head. 'She hides it and forgets where she put it.'

'It's a murder investigation.' Matter of fact.

'Not one of our clients?'

'No.'

Dixon waited; curiosity would get the better of her sooner or later. Sooner, as it turned out.

'Who's been killed?'

Time to turn the tables. 'And you are?'

'Liz Goodall. I'm the manager here.'

'Is there somewhere we can talk in private?' asked Dixon.

'Take a comfort break, girls.'

'What about the phones?' asked Cole.

'They'll go through to voicemail and we'll call them back later.'

The two staff members filed out of the back door, Dixon watching them walk up the drive towards the house. Cole had been right, after all. 'How long have you worked here?'

'Seventeen years.'

'And who owns the business?'

'Hugh and Veronica Middlebrook. You can find them up at the house,' replied Liz. 'So, are you going to tell me who's been murdered or not?' She leaned back against her desk and folded her arms.

'Godfrey Collins and Keith Finch.' Slow, deliberate and watching for any reaction.

'Who's Keith Finch?'

'He was the head of enforcement at the Cardiff tax office.'

'I don't know him, I'm afraid.'

'It was his job to recover the back tax owed by workers paid using the loan charge schemes run by Godfrey Collins, who I assume you did know.'

'Yes, poor Godfrey.' Liz walked around her desk and sat down on her swivel chair. She pulled a tissue out of the box on the desk and dabbed her dry eyes. 'It's about the loan charge, is it?'

'We believe so.'

'He was as much a victim as everyone else.' Liz blew her nose. 'Poor bloke.'

'How many staff did you pay under the scheme?'

'All of them, for a time. It was *his* idea.' She glanced over her shoulder at the main house. 'Said it would save him thousands.'

'How many?'

'Oh, maybe a hundred or so over the years. Nurses, domestic help, carers, cleaners, shoppers, that sort of thing. This is a care agency, so no one was raking it in. We started using the scheme in 2011 and it all seemed perfectly legal at the time. My husband is an accountant; he looked at it and said it was technically legal, and I filed tax returns declaring it for five years and no one said anything until George bloody Osborne changed the law in 2016. Not a single worker had a tax return queried, to my knowledge, and then all of a sudden you're a bloody criminal!'

'You were paid using the scheme?'

'I had to use an inheritance from my mother to pay off the back tax,' she said, tucking her bleached hair back behind her ear.

'Did you know Godfrey Collins?'

'Yes, I knew Godfrey. I met him several times. He was a lovely man, running perfectly legitimate schemes that we all benefitted from, none of them ever queried by the taxman and then, wallop, they put the poor sod out of business and practically bankrupt him.'

'The tax officer we spoke to said that people should have known the remuneration was disguised and—'

'If that's right, then why didn't they say something before? I filed annual tax returns for five years and I know people through the action group who'd been filing returns declaring the scheme for longer than that. Some even received tax rebates. What the bloody hell was that all about if it was illegal?'

'Did any of your staff have big bills?'

'Not huge. Some of the private nurses, perhaps, but the carers and domestic helpers . . .' She grimaced. 'I think the biggest was about eighteen thousand. Mine was thirty. Look, there are some out there who no longer work for us who don't even know there's an issue. The taxman still hasn't caught up with them yet.'

Dixon was looking up at the house, watching the two women who had abandoned the phones standing outside holding mugs of coffee and cigarettes. 'What about the employer's bill?'

'Mr Moneybags Middlebrook took it in his stride.' Liz jabbed her thumb in the direction of the house. 'Sent them a cheque and forgot about it. His view was it had been worth a try and it didn't work; easy come, easy go.'

'How the other half live,' mumbled Cole.

'Quite,' replied Liz.

'Did any of your workers know Mr Collins?'

'I doubt it. And even if they did, I'd be surprised if anyone blamed him for it. Like I say, he was as much a victim as the rest of us.'

'Anybody get unusually angry about it, perhaps?'

'These are all low paid workers you're talking about, all bar two of them women. "If I haven't got it, they can't have it" was the view most of them took, and I shouldn't think for a minute any of them got excited enough about it to kill someone. Some of them were part-time and not making enough to have to file a tax return anyway.'

◆　◆　◆

'D'you ever get the feeling we're barking up the wrong tree?' asked Dixon, as they drove down into Weston.

Cole was sitting in the passenger seat of Dixon's Land Rover, trying to find Loxton Road on his phone. 'Maybe that last lot, but if you were facing a bill of two or three hundred thousand pounds you'd feel a bit pissed off, I reckon.'

'And you'd want to blame somebody.'

'You would.' Cole jabbed his finger at the screen. 'It's a maisonette above a shop. The entrance is round the back and up some steps.'

'Are Collins and Finch the right people to blame?'

'Who else is there?'

'The government.'

'You can't kill the government, but you can kill the man who ran the scheme and the taxman chasing you for the money.'

'It makes sense.' Dixon was looking at the dog walkers on the promenade as he drove along the seafront. 'And if we're right, who's next, I wonder?'

'Go left at the roundabout, then left again into Loxton Road.'

Dixon parked on the forecourt outside a parade of small shops, two of them closed, the shutters down; the others a fish and chip shop, a launderette and a charity shop. The two storeys above – of sandstone yellow brickwork – were the maisonettes, 'To Let' signs in the windows of at least three of them, or two perhaps; it was difficult to tell.

Round the back and up the steps. They were walking along the first floor balcony when Cole broke the silence. 'Why would you want a crossbow, living here? It's not as if there's a big back garden for target shooting, is it?'

'What's his story?'

'It's a council flat and he's not long finished a twelve month stretch for two offences under the Computer Misuse Act. That's it, really.' Cole stopped outside the last door. 'It's this one.'

Dixon tapped the Kevlar body armour under his shirt before knocking on the glazed front door, a large figure soon looming in the frosted glass.

'Let me, Sir.' Cole stepped forward. 'Gavin Curtis?' he demanded, his foot blocking the door from closing.

'Yes.'

'Police.'

Curtis stepped to one side, his eyes fixed on the floor in front of him; clearly compliant, an air of resignation about him, like a prisoner about to have his cell turned over. 'What d'you want?'

'Can we come in, Gavin?' asked Dixon.

'Yes.'

Cole closed the door behind them and they followed Curtis into the living room at the back of the flat. An old leather sofa against the wall on the left and a television on a corner cabinet, a table and chairs against the back wall.

'No computer?'

'Not allowed one. Can't get the internet on my phone either.' Curtis gestured to an old Nokia on the table.

'How long have you been out?' Dixon was looking at the small DVD collection on the corner unit.

'A couple of months.'

Saving Private Ryan possibly, but the rest he wouldn't give house room to. 'What were you in for?'

'Hacking. It was just a bit of fun, really.'

'Who were you hacking?'

'DVLA. I was selling the records on the dark web. And GCHQ.'

Cole looked up from his notebook. 'You tried to hack the spy headquarters?'

'No, I *did* hack the spy headquarters.'

'You got caught though,' said Dixon.

No reply.

No pictures up, no ornaments, nothing. 'You rent the flat?' he asked.

'Housing benefit.'

'And the furniture?'

'It came from a charity.'

'Where's all your personal stuff?'

'I haven't got any. My mum threw it all out when I was sent down.'

Dixon was watching Gavin. No more than early twenties, tall enough to have played in the second row; a little overweight perhaps, the wire arms of his glasses digging into his temples; clearly gifted, if hacking GCHQ was anything to go by. A touch of acne too, probably caused by living above a chippy.

'Where were you?'

'Bristol, then Ford.'

Dixon perched on the windowsill, his back to the view of the industrial estate beyond the railway line. 'What are you doing for money? Are you working?'

'Universal credit. The housing charity helped me with the forms.' Curtis's eyes were still fixed on the floor in front of him, but it was about more than avoiding eye contact. This was a comfort zone, thought Dixon. A place to retreat to, even.

'Do you mind if we search the flat?'

'No.'

Dixon looked at Cole and nodded, waiting until he got up and left the room before speaking. 'You didn't ask me why, Gavin. That would be most people's first question.'

Gavin shrugged. 'You get used to it inside. And I've got nothing to hide.'

'You don't know what we're looking for.'

'Doesn't matter. Whatever it is, I haven't got it. I haven't got anything.'

'There's nothing, Sir.' Cole reappeared in the doorway. 'Just a bed and a pile of clothes on the floor. Nothing in the kitchen or bathroom either.'

'Loft?'

'There isn't one.'

Gavin was still standing with his back to the television, rubbing his hands together and rocking ever so slightly backwards and forwards.

'What d'you do all day?' asked Dixon. 'D'you go out much?'

'I watch the TV.'

Locked in a room watching daytime TV; it was beginning to sound as though he had never left prison.

'Have you bought a crossbow online recently, Gavin?'

'No. I told you, I don't have the internet so I couldn't even if I wanted to.'

'Well, someone did. We're following up purchases of crossbows in Avon and Somerset and your name and address came up on a list from an online retailer.'

'Merlin Archery in Sunderland,' offered Cole.

'It wasn't me.'

'Have you had any parcels delivered here in the last six weeks or so?'

'No.'

'What about identity theft?' Dixon frowned. 'Have you had your identity stolen by someone?'

'Not that I know of.'

'Has someone else used this address to buy a crossbow recently?'

'No.'

Chapter Sixteen

'Where to now, Sir?' asked Cole, when Dixon started the engine.

'Back to Portishead. Then we've got six more on the crossbow list for this afternoon.'

'I can do them on my own, if you like?'

Dixon was stationary, staring at a green light. 'Did you believe Gavin?'

'It's gone green, Sir.' Cole turned in his seat to glare at the driver in the car behind when she hooted her horn. 'I don't think Gavin's capable of lying. He wouldn't know how.'

'Get on to the Prison Service and get his medical records. I wouldn't mind betting he's on the autistic spectrum somewhere.'

'Hard on him if he is, his mother kicking him out.'

'And find out if he pleaded not guilty when he went to court.'

Dixon was just about to pull away when the traffic light went red, prompting the car behind to hoot again. Then his phone rang on the dashboard. Cole picked it up, leaning forwards even though there was plenty of slack in the charging cable.

'DCI Dixon's phone. Yeah, hang on.' He turned to Dixon. 'Someone's come up on both lists, Sir.'

'How the hell did we miss that?'

'It's the partner of someone on the loan charge list who bought a crossbow online. They live at the same address, but they're not married. Pound Lane, Nailsea.'

'We'll go there now. And we'll have Armed Response on scene just in case.'

'Did you hear that, Lou?' asked Cole, turning back to the phone.

'Find out if there's a settlement agreement with HMRC in place too.'

Cole rang off. 'She says there isn't.'

Forty minutes later they picked up the Armed Response vehicle parked on a roundabout on the edge of Nailsea; a wave from Cole did the trick and the marked car pulled out behind them, following them along Pound Lane.

Number 37 was a semi-detached house with a red garage door, the next door neighbour's bright blue. Sandstone brick with dark brown tiles; upstairs were dormer windows so they may have started out as a pair of bungalows and both had loft conversions. No one could have designed them like that, surely?

Dixon parked across the drive, blocking in a white BMW parked in front of the garage.

'Tell the Armed Response team to show themselves. I want whoever's in there to know they're here,' said Dixon, watching Cole walk back a couple of paces towards the marked car parked behind them, waving at them to pull forward.

'Battering ram, Sir?' Cole was clearly unable to contain his excitement.

'Let's try the doorbell first, shall we?'

A dog started barking, closely followed by a shout of 'Shut up, Winnie, for God's sake. I'm on the phone!' Dixon rang the doorbell again, setting the dog off one more time; whoever was inside would arrive at the door nice and flustered.

The sight of two burly police officers with gun-toting Armed Response officers behind them on the drive clearly had the desired effect. 'I'll call you back,' mumbled the man in flip-flops, shorts and a T-shirt, disconnecting the call with one hand, a West Highland white terrier wriggling under his other arm.

'Police, Sir. May we come in?' Dixon didn't wait for a reply.

'Er, yes, of course.'

'Mr Tressider, isn't it?'

'Yes, that's right. Mark. Just give me a sec and I'll put Winnie in her cage; it's in the corner of the dining room.'

Dixon followed him, keeping him in sight, if only to make sure he didn't reach for a crossbow.

'Now, what's this about?' Tressider's eyes were bloodshot, the pupils a touch dilated for a bright day.

'We're lucky to find you at home, Sir.' Dixon was peering at the photographs on the wall.

'I'm a graphic designer. I work from home.'

'And Nicola Pate?'

'She's at work. She sells advertising space in the local newspapers.' Tressider took up position in the kitchen doorway, his arms folded. Behind him the patio doors were open, leading to a long garden, a carpet hanging from scaffolding poles at the far end.

'We're following up sales of high powered crossbows and we've been informed that you purchased one online from Hampton Archery about six weeks ago.'

Tressider arched his back. 'How did you get that information? I thought there were data protection laws.'

'It's a double murder investigation, Sir.' Dixon was craning his neck, making it obvious he was looking past Tressider. 'So, data protection goes out the window, as you might imagine. Is that a shooting range I see in your garden?'

'Target practice, that's all.'

'May I see the bow?'

'Which one? I've got three.'

'All of them, in that case. And your collection of bolts.'

Soon there was quite an armoury laid out on the dining table: a pistol crossbow, a compound bow with telescopic sights and an Anglo Arms Jaguar, the very model picked out by Bowman.

Tressider pointed to the Jaguar. 'This is the new one.'

'Why did you buy it?' asked Dixon.

'Nicky thinks I'm nuts, but I'm a bit of a prepper.' He gave an embarrassed shrug. 'There are quite a few of us around. Tins of food in the loft, that sort of thing.'

'And what exactly are you preparing for?'

'The end of the world.'

Cole tried to stifle a chuckle and failed dismally.

'You can laugh, but all it requires is a breakdown of law and order and we'll all be defending our properties from looters.'

'What else have you got?'

'Survival kits, rations, a couple of respirators. Look, I just bought some stuff and put it in the loft, but I do enjoy target shooting with the bows as well.'

Dixon gestured to the collection of bolts. 'Do you have any broadheads for these?' He glanced over at the DVDs lined up along the mantelpiece, the presence of the *Walking Dead* box set coming as no surprise.

'Don't like broadheads. If the shit hits the fan you'll need to be able to get the bolts back quick and easy,' Tressider said, miming the pulling of a bolt out of God knows what.

'PC Cole here will ask you where you were on a couple of specific dates, while I have a look at your targets, if I may?'

'Of course.' Tressider stepped to one side, although Dixon was already brushing past him.

Twenty paces: a collection of perforated plastic milk bottles, shoe boxes taped shut, sand leaking from round holes; a couple of archery targets scrunched up on the ground, the holes grouped tightly in the gold. Dixon checked for any sign of a curved broadhead and found none; there were none in the carpet used as a backstop either.

'He says he was here with Nicky both nights, Sir,' said Cole, when Dixon stepped in through the patio doors.

'And the nights of the sheep killings?'

'Give me a minute.'

Dixon busied himself trying to cock the compound bow while Cole checked the dates with Tressider – business trip, at home with Nicky, cinema with Nicky then at home.

Tressider kept a watchful eye on Dixon throughout. 'You need a string for that one,' he said, turning away from Cole.

Dixon replaced the bow on the dining table. 'Wouldn't be much good if you were surrounded by a horde of zombies.'

'It's a herd, not a horde.'

'If you say so.'

Cole finished scribbling in his notebook and looked up. 'We will be checking, Sir, as you might expect.'

'That's fine.'

'Tell me about Nicky's loan charge debt,' said Dixon. 'How much does she owe?'

'Oh, God, that.' Tressider puffed out his cheeks. 'It's just over twenty-seven grand, but the interest is racking up on top of that. It dates from her agency work; she was with Bristol Recruitment doing sales for about six years.'

'And she's not reached a settlement agreement with HMRC?'

'No, why should she?' Tressider lurched forward off the door frame he had been leaning on. 'They've only just changed it, so they can't go back beyond 2010, and that saved her eight grand. You never know what might happen if she waits a bit longer.'

'Is she in dispute with HMRC?'

'Not a dispute, as such. She's just ignoring them, taking it right to the wire. If they ever commence court proceedings against her, she'll pay up. Actually, she hasn't heard from them for a while, so we were beginning to wonder if it had gone away.'

'Could she pay it?'

'It would take the money we'd set aside to get wed, but she could, yeah.'

'Does the name Godfrey Collins mean anything to you?'

'Nope, never heard of him.'

'What about Keith Finch?'

'Sorry, no.'

Dixon was halfway along the corridor back to the front door. 'Can you ask her to ring PC Cole when she gets in, please? He'll have a couple of questions for her.'

'Of course.'

Dixon stepped out into the porch when Tressider opened the front door. 'Whose is the BMW?'

'That's Nicky's. She takes the bus to work.'

'And where's your car, Sir?'

'In the garage.' Tressider grinned. 'It's a BMW M3; shit off a shovel, it is.'

'Colour?'

'Red, why?'

Chapter Seventeen

Cole was looking around a deserted Area J as he dropped his sandwich and a bag of crisps on a vacant workstation. 'They must all be out and about.'

.'Dave and Kevin are in the CCTV suite.' Louise's head popped up from behind a computer screen. 'Mark's gone to get something to eat and the rest are out interviewing people on the loan charge list.'

'Any other connection between Collins and Finch?' Dixon chose to ignore the 'HR Dept' label on the kettle.

'There's nothing,' replied Louise. 'We can't find anything at all, apart from the loan charge business.'

'Tressider's got three crossbows and a red BMW.'

'I printed off the photos Mr Finch took and stuck them on the whiteboard.' Louise pointed over her shoulder with her thumb at a sequence of three grainy colour photographs sellotaped along the top of the board, taken sideways on as the car passed the gate. 'He'd got Live Photos switched off, so it's just three stills, sadly,' she continued. 'The more you zoom in, the blurrier they get too. I've pinged them over to High Tech to see what they can do with them.'

'The best you can say is it's a saloon.' Cole was squinting at the photographs. 'But you don't get the whole car in the one shot.'

'Cut and paste, the old fashioned way.' Louise held up two photographs taped together, the paper fluttering in the breeze from a fan on the windowsill. 'Mark sent them over to Traffic as well, just to see if they've got any ideas.'

The door pillar obscured the driver, not that the picture would have been good enough to have identified him or her anyway.

'It could be a Beamer,' said Cole, peering over Dixon's shoulder. 'Or one of the older Volvos, possibly.'

'What about a Passat?' asked Louise. 'The old shape.'

'That too.'

'There's an Audi that looks a bit—' Cole stopped mid-sentence, mercifully getting the message from Dixon's weary sigh.

'What about the computers?' Dixon asked, ripping the film off a pack of egg and cress sandwiches.

'I've printed off the HMRC file on Collins – all the correspondence and what have you.' Louise gestured to a pile of paper in a wire basket on the corner of her workstation. 'I've still got to sort through it. There's nothing on the old hard drives from his office computers, except a few emails from people complaining about the loan charge thing when it kicked off in 2016. I've printed those off as well and they're being spoken to this afternoon: top of the list. There's nothing on his laptop, either, really, except the HMRC correspondence.'

'Web browsing history?'

'You wouldn't want your grandmother to see it.'

'Emails?' mumbled Dixon, through a mouthful of sandwich.

'There are some Zephyr might be interested in. From a while ago, mind you. And he's got that encrypted chat thing installed; I don't know whether they can crack that. Otherwise the emails are about the boat.'

'And the micro SIM?'

'It's a Vodafone pay-as-you-go. I've been on to Voda and no calls have ever been made or received on the number, just data usage and not much at that – less than half a gig. Email, they reckon, or WhatsApp, something like that. Whatever it was, it was encrypted. There are no contacts on it either and it's never been topped up since it was bought.' Louise glanced down at her notebook. 'That would've been at the Tesco Express in Victoria Street.'

Footsteps running towards them along the aisle between the workstations; Dixon turned to see Mark, a bacon roll in each hand, tomato sauce dripping off the paper napkins. He started weaving through the vacant desks, taking a shortcut to the gap in the Area J partition nearest Dixon.

'Stand by to repel boarders,' he whispered, his eyes wide.

More footsteps now, several people walking purposefully; Dixon was about to ask who it was when Charlesworth, Potter and the press officer, Vicky Thomas, came striding along the aisle from the lift. Potter and Vicky Thomas diverted into a vacant meeting room while Charlesworth stopped by the open door, beckoning him. 'Have you got a minute, Nick?'

'No' was tempting, but the truth of the matter was he did have a minute. The investigation was going through the motions, ticking the right boxes; everything that should be done was being done, but still he couldn't shake it off – that feeling of working on a jigsaw puzzle when you know there's a piece missing.

'How's it going?' asked Potter, when Charlesworth closed the meeting room door behind them.

'Slowly.'

'I can't argue with your decision making, if your Policy Log is up to date.'

'It is.'

'Two o'clock this morning.' Charlesworth sounded impressed. 'Burning the midnight oil, I see.'

'Catching up on Zephyr's file; you know how it is.'

'We do.' Potter looked almost apologetic; it made for an uneasy feeling.

Almost as unnerving as Charlesworth smiling at him. 'Deborah's got some news.'

'We've got two more.' Potter blurted it out, making no attempt to soften the blow. 'The same distinctive pattern on the bolt.'

Dixon reached into his pocket, took out the broadhead and slid it to the middle of the table.

Charlesworth picked it up and rolled it around in the palm of his hand. 'How the bloody hell this stuff is on sale is beyond me.'

'A Mr James Bowen and his partner Ms Miranda Mather, both British citizens and both killed with a crossbow bolt to the head.'

Potter's reference to British citizens was telling. 'Where?' asked Dixon, trying to remember where he'd put his passport.

'Sitio de Calahonda.' Charlesworth sounded like a pisshead in a tapas bar on a Saturday night. 'It's between Marbella and Fuengirola on the Costa del Sol.'

'When?'

'They were found yesterday morning by their cleaner.' Potter was watching Charlesworth still fiddling with the broadhead. 'This is what we've got on them,' she said, sliding a thin document file across the table. 'You'll need to send someone over there to liaise with the Spanish police.'

'Were they on holiday or living there?' asked Dixon, reaching for the file.

'Hiding there is probably a more accurate description. They're both wanted in this country. I've asked someone from the Economic Crime Unit to brief you.'

Charlesworth passed the broadhead to the press officer. 'Vicky's going to put out a release saying we're liaising with our European partners etcetera etcetera, and I've asked Jesminder to rustle up some more people for you as a matter of urgency.'

Dixon turned back to Potter. 'Wanted for what?'

'Pension fraud.'

◆ ◆ ◆

'OK, let's start with the basics, shall we?'

'Like what's the Economic Crime Unit?' Dave's brow furrowed.

'Fraud squad to you.'

'Just shut up, Mark, and let her get on with it, will you?' Dixon had never met a criminal intelligence analyst before. Sharon Beech wore a sharp suit, hair tied back tight; only the red braces were missing.

'We all build up a pension fund while we're working, don't we?' She paused, but not long enough for anyone to draw breath. 'Well, we're supposed to. We do it through an employer's pension scheme and some people do it through a private pension, but the idea is that you have a pension pot built up during your working life to provide you an income in retirement, on top of the state pension – what's left of it.'

Dave and Kevin were sitting on the windowsill, grateful to get out of the CCTV suite for a minute or two, by the looks of things. Mark and Louise were sitting with their backs to Dixon, with Cole behind him slurping his coffee. All seemed to be paying attention, although Dixon suspected they were more interested in who was going to the Costa del Sol.

'That pension pot is transferrable. So, let's use you as an example, Sir.' Sharon turned to Dixon. 'You decide that your pension would give you a better return if you transferred it out of the police pension fund and invested it in, say, XYZ Pensions Plc. You're allowed to do that, and if XYZ Pensions are regulated and authorised there are no tax implications; the transfer is tax free. You'd take independent financial advice and—'

'The problem comes if your financial adviser's a crook,' muttered Kevin.

'Exactly.' Sharon took a deep breath. 'So, if your financial adviser transfers your pension to a fund that is *not* regulated and authorised, then that is treated as a withdrawal from your pension fund and *not* a transfer. And a withdrawal is subject to income tax on top of your earnings for the year.'

'So, they're landed with a big tax bill as well?' asked Louise, turning to Dixon.

'Yes, but that's not all. A lot of people who withdrew their money moved it to overseas pension funds, and some ripped them off with huge fees and made bad investments; others were scams and just blatantly stole the money. There are lots of people out there who've saved for their retirement all their lives and now find themselves with nothing to show for it. Not only that, but they've got the added headache of the taxman after them for a big income tax bill.'

'You can just imagine the bitterness, can't you?' Cole grimaced. 'I'd be bloody livid.'

'There are police officers who've been caught by it; armed forces, fire service, doctors, nurses, solicitors; tens of thousands of people,' continued Sharon. 'It adds up to billions of pounds scammed off unsuspecting people doing their best to plan for their retirement.'

'Motive enough.' Dixon sat up.

'Imagine being caught by both the loan charge and this?' said Louise, shaking her head.

'We can soon cross-check the lists,' replied Mark.

'Tell us about James Bowen and Miranda Mather then,' said Dixon.

'He ran Clearwater Wealthcare in the UK.'

'Wealthcare?' Mark threw his pen on to the desk in front of him. 'Snappy.'

'They had an office in Bristol,' continued Sharon. 'And Miranda Mather was down on the Costa del Sol, running Clearwater Pensions. Needless to say, *not* authorised and regulated.'

'How much did they take and from how many people?' asked Dixon, cutting to the chase.

'Thirty-one million from two hundred and two clients. The average pension fund size was one hundred and fifty thousand pounds, but some were much bigger.' Sharon paused, allowing that to sink in for a moment. 'They had some private pensions, but their clients were mainly police, fire, prison service, armed forces, NHS, people like that.'

'And the pension fund trustees allowed these transfers?'

'He's a solicitor,' whispered Louise, leaning forward.

Sharon raised her eyebrows, her surprise thinly veiled. 'Clearwater Pensions were registered with HMRC so they looked above board on the face of it. That was part of their marketing: "We're registered with HM Revenue and Customs", but it's just a few clicks to register online. It's *not* the same thing as being authorised and regulated by the pension regulator.'

'Which idiot was responsible for that?' asked Kevin.

'Tony Blair.' Sharon rolled her eyes. 'It was a bit of a free-for-all after that. The Wild West, someone said; pension scams became big business and pretty bloody easy too. There are still hundreds, possibly thousands, of people out there who have no idea their pension pots have been ripped off.'

'They're in for an unpleasant surprise when they get to retirement.' Cole cleared his throat. 'I transferred my pension; I suppose I'd better check it.'

'Who to?'

'I can't remember. It was a couple of years ago.'

'Did you get advice?' asked Sharon.

'Yeah, it was some bloke in Weston.' He looked ashen faced. 'I get a pension statement every year, but I just stick it in a box file. I don't remember it being overseas. I think I'd better ring my wife.'

'Do it now,' said Dixon.

Cole broke into a trot along the aisle, his mobile phone pressed to his ear.

'So, you work hard and save hard all your life, only to find your pension has gone.' Dixon stood up and started pacing up and down between the workstations. 'You blame HMRC because they registered the fraudulent pension company, thereby giving them some credibility, and HMRC's only response is to come after you for a big income tax bill.'

'How big?' asked Louise.

'The fund withdrawn is treated as extra income for the year,' replied Sharon. 'So, a fund of three hundred thousand on top of a salary of, say, thirty thousand, would push you into the forty-five per cent additional rate tax bracket. That's a bill of roughly a hundred and thirty grand.'

'And you've lost your pension fund, don't forget,' said Dixon. 'So, Bowen is the rogue financial adviser, Mather is the rogue pension fund trustee and Finch is the taxman pursuing the income tax bill.'

'At least the loan chargers had had the money in the first place.' Kevin leaned back against the glass. 'It makes a lot of sense.'

'More sense than the loan charge. We've got the agencies telling us their staff probably didn't know who Collins was anyway and—' Dixon hesitated. 'In fact, it makes perfect sense apart from Collins. How does he fit into it?'

'The accountant?' asked Sharon.

'He had nothing to do with the pension scam, did he?'

'There's no mention of it anywhere in his stuff, Sir,' replied Louise. 'Nothing.'

'You two.' Dixon turned to Kevin and Dave. 'Next plane to Malaga. An Inspector Alvaro will meet you at the other end.'

Mark folded his arms. 'Why Dave?'

'I'm not fussed, Sir,' said Dave. 'I never do well in hot places; I get prickly heat.'

'You're going precisely because you don't want to. And you're not going, Mark, precisely because you do.'

'Yes, Sir,' sighed Mark.

Cole came jogging along the aisle. 'It's all right, it's legit.' Beads of sweat were drying on his temples.

'What have you got on Clearwater, Sharon?' asked Dixon.

'Lots. We were working on a prosecution with the Serious Fraud Office when Bowen and Mather did a runner. We did get someone for it, though: their junior salesman was sent down for eighteen months.'

'Name?'

'Craig Pengelly.'

Chapter Eighteen

A sensational luxury property on a large plot above the beach with unrestricted views of the shimmering Mediterranean sea; it had sold for 3.7 million euros four years earlier, according to the old listing on the Spanish property website. The pool on the terrace looked nice, sun loungers and all. Palm trees and a perfectly manicured lawn too.

Dixon scrolled through the gallery: terracotta roof tiles, free-standing kitchen, double beds overlooking the sea; undoubtedly nice, but he was more interested in the next set of photographs, taken that morning and marked '*Policía, privado y confidencial*'.

Bowen had been enjoying a smoke on a sun lounger by the pool; the crossbow bolt embedded in his eye socket up to the fletch, his head tipped back, the broadhead resting on the back of the lounger, blood staining the white fabric. The remains of a dinner enjoyed al fresco were visible on the table in the background. A trickle of blood had followed the edge of the floor tiles and reached the pool, the few drops that had made it all the way having long since dissolved in the crystal clear water.

A single shot, probably from behind the balustrade on the terrace; ten paces at most.

Miranda Mather was lying face down on a king sized bed, the broadhead clean through the back of her skull and pointing at the mirror on the ceiling. The white duvet was stained red beneath her head.

Clean kills, both; in, out and back to the airport before the bodies had been found. Louise was checking flights to and from Malaga during the two days since Keith Finch had been pinned to the tree in his back garden. Another list to cross-check.

'Craig Pengelly's still at Leyhill, Sir,' said Cole, his hand over the speaker.

'We'll need to see him this afternoon,' replied Dixon. 'And ask them to notify us as soon as he gets a release date.' He was watching Louise pin a photograph on the whiteboard; three blue rings of different shades. It looked like someone had been colouring in the outline left by the broadhead with crayons – turquoise, sea and sky blue. 'What's that?' he asked, frowning.

'I thought you might be interested in that, Sir,' replied Louise. 'It's the Clearwater Pensions logo.'

◆ ◆ ◆

'Do I need a solicitor?'

'No, Craig,' replied Dixon. 'You can have one if you want, but you don't need one.' He'd had a bit of trouble getting the broadhead past security at HMP Leyhill, but had got there in the end; another advantage of his new rank. 'James Bowen and Miranda Mather were found dead at their villa on the Costa del Sol yesterday.'

'Best news I've had in a long time.' Craig glanced up at the prison officer standing with his back to the door of the interview room. 'Did they top themselves?'

'They were murdered.'

'Can't say I'm surprised.' Craig's eyes were glazed over, the pupils dilated. 'And I was in here, before you ask.'

In here and topped up with spice, no doubt, thought Dixon. 'Can you think of anyone who might have wanted to kill them?'

'Any one of two hundred clients. And me. Look what they've bloody well done to me. I was a trainee, sitting my exams, and they stitched me up.'

'Any clients in particular?'

'Mine were mainly the small fry.' Craig's speech was slow and deliberate. 'I was getting nurses and a couple of soldiers; a couple of your lot. The commission was hardly enough to get by on, really. Bowen dealt with the bigger clients.' He paused. 'There were a couple who were ex-SAS. Good funds too, they had. And some bloke came charging into the office with a pension statement in his hand; he was a planning officer at Sedgemoor District Council. He had a temper on him.'

'Did anyone have a go at you?'

'I had a few stroppy emails and calls, but it never came to anything. I just explained that I'd been conned too. And I'd left before the shit hit the fan anyway; got out when I realised what was going on.' Craig gave a half-hearted sneer. 'Still got sucked back in, didn't I?'

Dixon leaned back in his chair. 'My understanding is that the pension pots were transferred to a non-regulated fund run by Miranda Mather, so they were treated as withdrawals by the tax-man, triggering an income tax bill.'

'That's right. So what?'

'The head of enforcement at HM Revenue and Customs in Cardiff is also dead.'

'Karma, they call that.'

'Do they?' Dixon took a deep breath. 'He was just doing his job.'

'So was I.'

'Which of the clients had the biggest tax bills?'

'Fuck knows.'

'The Serious Fraud Office—'

'Don't talk to me about those tossers.' Craig folded his arms. 'I had a deal with them, then when James and Miranda ran for it the deal was suddenly off the table. My solicitor said it was because they had to be seen to be prosecuting someone and there was only me left.'

Dixon slid the broadhead across the table, the prison officer watching intently. 'They were killed with a crossbow and the bolts had one of those on the end.'

'Nice.' Craig resisted the temptation to pick it up.

'Recognise the pattern?'

'No.'

'Pick it up and have a look at it.' Dixon was watching for any reaction. 'Think about the shape of the entry wound.'

Craig held the tip of the broadhead between his thumb and index finger. 'The Clearwater logo.' He was looking at the curved blades from behind, a wry smile creeping across his lips. 'Someone's got a sense of humour.'

'We think you might be next, Craig,' said Dixon.

'Whatever. Hardly matters now, does it?'

'You're safe while you're in here and I've asked the governor to cancel your temporary licence, so no day passes for the time being.'

'Thanks a bunch.'

'Have you got a release date?'

'Not yet.'

'Well, let's hope we can catch whoever it is before you do.'

Dixon arrived back at Area J to find all of the workstations occupied and the phones buzzing. Cole was still working his way through the crossbow sales lists from the archery retailers; the rest of the major investigation team now following up the pension clients – victims – of Clearwater Wealthcare.

Wealthcare.

The word jarred every time, reminding Dixon of hours wasted at networking events when he'd been a trainee solicitor, listening to financial advisers drone on about wealth management and holistic approaches as if they had something different to offer.

'There's no one on both lists,' said Louise. 'Loan charge and pension.'

'No one's bought a bow either.' Cole spoke without looking up. 'We're checking their cars now, and passenger manifests in and out of Malaga for the last seventy-two hours.'

Dixon knew they were wasting their time, but it had to be done, or seen to be done. Unless and until he had something better to go on, it would be old fashioned police work: cross-referencing, checking, following up.

The killer could have flown via pretty much anywhere to cover his tracks. Or taken the train to Paris and flown from there. Or even driven all the way – he frowned – not that there would have been time for that. Plymouth to Santander on the ferry was definitely out; that would have taken far too long. Finch had been killed at nine in the morning in Bristol, and Bowen and Mather, say, twelve or fifteen hours later on the Costa del Sol; easily doable, but the killer must have flown. It would help if they had a name, though; checking two hundred would take far too long.

'Where are Dave and Kevin?'

'Somewhere over the Channel by now, I expect,' replied Louise. 'They took off about half an hour ago.'

Another waste of bloody time, but it was something else that had to be seen to be done. He had learned all he needed to know from the crime scene photographs and the Economic Crime Unit file, and the killer was too clever to leave any trace. Still, boxes to tick and all that.

'How did you get on with Craig?' asked Louise.

'He'd been at the spice again,' replied Dixon. 'He did say there'd been a couple of ex-SAS soldiers who'd kicked up, and a planning officer at Sedgemoor District Council.'

'I just spoke to one of them.' A voice he didn't recognise behind him. 'Seemed quite pleased they'd been killed, but then just about everyone's said that so far. "Got what they deserved" is a common response.'

Dixon turned round, but whoever it was had already ducked down behind her computer screen.

'What about the soldiers?' he asked, turning back to Louise.

'The list we've got doesn't specify an occupation, but we're filling it in as we speak to them, so we'll be able to search the database as soon as everyone's been spoken to.'

'Interviews being set up?'

'And Jez is sending over ten more bods too, so we should get through them quite quickly.'

Mark leaned back in his chair, his hands behind his head. 'We still can't find any connection between Collins and Finch, or Collins and the pensions thing. He seems like the odd man out.'

'Craig is the connection,' said Dixon. 'He's up to his neck in the pensions scam and his pregnant fiancée drowned on Collins's boat.'

Mark and Louise frowned at each other.

'Yeah, but how does that fit in with what we know?' she asked.

'It doesn't, which means it must fit in with something we don't know.'

Louise's text had arrived when Dixon was in the shower the following morning.

A couple of hours spent going through the Economic Crime Unit file; witness statements complaining of retirements lost and dreams shattered – it had been a familiar refrain – and he had finally got home just before midnight. A turn around the field at the back of the cottage with Monty while a curry was in the microwave, and he had been sound asleep by a quarter past.

The shower had woken him up, although he could probably have done without Jane getting in with him, not that he would tell her.

He tapped out a reply with one hand, a piece of toast in the other: *Briefing at 8. On way*

'I'm not sure I like it with you at Portishead after all.' Jane was holding her mug in both hands. 'We hardly get to see each other.'

'It's only while there's a flap on,' replied Dixon, watching through the windows behind Jane as her sister walked along the pavement outside the front of the cottage, the sound of a car speeding off in the distance. 'And it'd be the same at Express Park.'

'I've sort of got used to you hiding in my office, that's all.'

'Where's Lucy?'

'Still in bed. She had a study day yesterday and stayed over. I'm dropping her at the station on my way to work.'

'I'd better go.' He turned for the back door, stopping to scratch Monty behind the ears. 'You'll have to referee again, old son, sorry.'

Jane frowned. 'Referee what?'

The shouting still hadn't started by the time he was sitting in his Land Rover, so he wound down the window and listened, Jane's shriek carrying easily over the rumble of the diesel engine. 'What bloody party?'

Someone had moved the partitioning overnight, expanding Area J by two more blocks of four workstations. Maybe they would have enough people to check the various travel permutations to and from Malaga after all, although that remained very much a last resort.

Dixon stared at the list of twelve missing pension scam victims: four soldiers, a locum doctor, a midwife, a police officer, three fire-fighters and two prison officers.

'We need the service history for the soldiers. Prioritise any special forces first. All right?'

'Yes, Sir,' replied Louise.

'Tell me about the murder/suicide.'

'A retired police officer. Here's the file.' She handed him a thin plastic document wallet. 'It looks like it might have been a suicide pact, but then she couldn't go through with it, so he killed her, then himself.' She shrugged. 'Sad.'

'Who was he?'

'A superintendent from Wiltshire, retired to Weston. He wasn't drawing his pension yet because he was still working part-time as a security consultant. It would've been a big fund, though.'

'Better speak to the family.'

The briefing lasted twenty minutes: a recap for the newcomers to the team followed by a summary of the change of direction forced on them by the Costa del Sol murders. Dixon thought it was probably another waste of time, because most of them had seemed up to speed anyway and he felt almost as though he was interrupting them. But at least it was one more box that could be ticked; no one could complain the SIO hadn't kept them informed.

'Stay on Collins,' Dixon said to Louise and Mark when the briefing finished and most had drifted off in the direction of the kettle or the canteen. 'And find those soldiers.'

'Yes, Sir.' Louise's computer pinged. 'Hang on, there's an email.' She sat down and reached for the mouse. 'The locum doctor's in Belfast and we've got the midwife as well; she had her phone switched off.'

Dixon turned to Cole. 'How are you getting on with the bows, Nige?'

'Er, all right, I think. I've almost contacted everybody.'

'Pass the list on to someone else for the interviews and come with me.'

'Where are we going?'

'HMP Bristol.'

'Eh?'

'Both of these missing prison officers worked at Bristol.'

'The autistic lad, Gavin Curtis, started his sentence at Bristol.'

'He did, and so did Craig Pengelly.'

Chapter Nineteen

HMP Bristol: four storeys, red brick, behind the obligatory high wall, and no bloody visitors' car park; his warrant card hadn't worked with the jobsworth on the entrance to the staff car park either.

Dixon drove round and round the adjacent streets, all of them residents' parking permits only. Mercifully, the gate was open to the allotments behind the prison.

'We'll be buggered if someone locks us in,' Cole had said.

'It's a thin chain and this is a Land Rover.'

The admin block looked more like the temporary prefabricated office space he'd seen on the construction site at Hinkley Point, although the security checks to get in there had been more strict than for a prison visit.

'Wait here,' had been the instruction, and they were obliging; Cole reading the newspaper, Dixon pacing up and down.

'Come through to my office, I've got a computer in here.' Regulation black trousers, white shirt and clip-on tie; she was waving at them from halfway along the corridor.

'Shirley Adebayo?' Dixon had never understood the prison service insignia, nor the police insignia, come to think of it.

'You'll be Inspector Dixon, we spoke on the phone.'

'We did.'

Her office was at the back of the admin building, offering a view of the main prison block; the shouting just about discernible over the noise of the alarm bells and the traffic on the A38. It didn't help that her window was open. 'Always shouting about something,' she said, slamming it shut.

Dixon sat down on the chair in front of the desk, Cole leaning against a filing cabinet behind him. 'You were going to help with information on a couple of former inmates and two of your officers.'

'Who?'

'Let's start with Craig Pengelly. He's at Leyhill at the moment, not far off release.'

One finger typing. 'You'll have to excuse me.' Adebayo looked up, aware she was being watched. 'You learn a lot of things being a prison officer, but typing isn't one of them.' A few clicks of the mouse. 'Here we are, Craig Pengelly. Came here on twenty-fourth March and was D-catted June thirtieth – we're cat B here – then it was off to Leyhill the next day. Good report, no demerits. It says here he was a listener, which is always good for getting early D status.'

'Visitors?'

'Looks like his parents and girlfriend registered. No one else.'

'When I saw him yesterday he was high on spice.'

'We have a bit of a problem in here with spice.' Adebayo leaned back in her chair. 'You may have read in the papers, apparently one third of the inmates here are hooked on drugs. I was surprised by that to be honest.'

'Why?'

'I thought it was at least fifty per cent.' She smirked. 'Look, it's not as bad as that, but spice is virtually impossible to stop. It's a liquid, so they soak a letter in it, send it in and then the recipient smokes it. I've seen soaked Rizlas, even books. I didn't know Craig was taking it though.'

'He certainly is now.'

She shook her head. 'I remember he saved another inmate's life. He was a good listener. It was a young lad, mentally ill, been slashing himself with a razor, the cell was covered in blood, and I mean *covered*. The PO on the landing sent for a listener – they just go in and listen – but no one would, so Craig went in, even though he was off duty. Calmed him down so the doctor could get in there. D'you know, I think that was his last night here.'

'Is there anything else on his record?'

'No.'

'Tell me about Gavin Curtis then.'

More one finger typing. 'D-catted a month earlier – thirtieth May – and off to Ford Open Prison after that.' Her eyes were scanning the screen, following her mouse clicks. 'There's a diagnosis of level 1 autistic spectrum disorder. Not a single visitor, either; he's got next of kin listed but they never registered to come and see him.'

'Who did?'

'No one, according to this.'

'Who were his cellmates?'

'He had one of the single cells. There are a few on the top floor. You can't risk . . .' Her voice tailed off.

'Would they have known each other?'

'I wouldn't know, I'm afraid. I wouldn't be surprised, but the best I can say is they were here at the same time.'

'Prison officers then; there are two. Let's start with John Sims.'

'I took over from John as supervising officer.'

'We're not saying he's done anything wrong, just that we need to speak to him and we can't get hold of him.'

'He's probably gone fishing; mad on fishing, he is.'

'Do you have his latest contact details?'

Control P, an index finger on each. 'The printer's on the cabinet behind you,' she said, to Cole. 'Who else?'

'Francis Allan.'

'Frank's off long term sick. Got caught in a cell with a prisoner off his box on spice and was beaten to a pulp, sadly. It left him with neurological problems and a nasty back injury. Last I heard he was going to take early retirement, if he hasn't done so already.'

'Would either of them have come into contact with Craig Pengelly?'

'Probably, why d'you ask?'

'Because both were victims of the crime for which Craig was sent here.'

'Really?' Adebayo scowled. 'That shouldn't have happened.'

'What the hell is that?'

'Dave, Sir. You'll have to excuse his shirt,' replied Louise. 'He's video conferencing from Spain. They can hear you.'

Dixon glanced down at Louise's computer monitor, the screen subdivided into four. He recognised Dave and Kevin, but not the other two. 'Can't he just use the phone like everyone else?'

'Then we wouldn't have to look at that bloody shirt,' said Mark, under his breath.

'That's Detective Alvaro.' Louise pointed to the top left pane. 'And this is their pathologist, Dr Camilla Garcia.' She pulled up a chair. 'This is Detective Chief Inspector Dixon.'

'*Buenos días*, Chief Inspector,' said Alvaro.

'*Buenos días*,' replied Dixon, sitting down; conversational French, at a push, but Spanish was a mystery to him.

'They speak very good English,' said Louise.

Dixon leaned over the back of his chair and passed a piece of paper to Mark. 'These are the latest contact details for one of the missing prison officers. Check them out, will you?'

'Yes, Sir.'

'Sorry about that.' He turned back to the screen. 'What have you got for us?'

'You know the victims, I think,' replied Alvaro. 'Two British citizens. We've been fully informed of the situation by Detectives Harding and Turner.'

'There's not a lot, to be honest, Sir,' said Dave. 'We think the bolts were fired from the clifftop about twenty-five to thirty yards away. It's simply too steep to get up to the balustrade on the terrace, but there's a bit on the cliff that sticks out further along and you can get to the top of that from the road.'

'We've got some boot print which we send over for comparison,' said Alvaro.

'How far is it exactly?'

'Twenty yards to James Bowen on the sun lounger,' replied Dave. 'More to Miranda Mather.'

'The shot was fired through the open window. Closer to twenty-five metres.' Alvaro shrugged. 'Someone will be going up there today with a laser to measure.'

'It was fired from further away, of that there is no doubt,' said Camilla Garcia. 'Both have hit in the eye socket, but the bolt on the woman has not gone in as far. Death would have been instantly.'

'Anything on CCTV?' asked Dixon.

'No, Sir,' replied Kevin.

'It is coast road,' said Alvaro. 'Cameras in the town two kilometre away.'

'House to house?'

'They're all clifftop villas, Sir.' Kevin again.

'No one see anything,' said Alvaro. 'We stopping traffic on the road this afternoon and tomorrow morning to see if they remember see anything.'

'You'd better stay for that,' said Dixon, to Dave and Kevin.

'Yes, Sir,' they replied in unison, both trying to look hard done by at the prospect of another night on the Costa del Sol. Maybe he should have gone himself, thought Dixon.

'What about the broadhead?' he asked.

'It is the same,' replied Garcia. 'Your Dr Petersen emailed me some photos and it is a clear match.'

'The bolts are the same too, Sir,' offered Dave. 'They're both the Easton FMJ carbon fibre, twenty inch.'

'OK, let's assume the killer is British and returned home before the bodies were found—'

'We are checking the airports,' interrupted Alvaro.

'My guess is he or she wouldn't want to risk the return journey with the bow,' continued Dixon. 'So that will have been dumped somewhere.'

'There are miles of coastline, Sir,' said Dave. 'It was night time so he could have pulled up anywhere and chucked it over into the sea.'

'Can you check the sea directly opposite the villa?'

'We can do that, for sure,' replied Alvaro.

'Then we need to think about how he got the bow into Spain. It's mainly plastic and the limb is fibreglass; easily dismantled and hidden in a suitcase. Even the bolts come to bits.'

'He'd have struggled to get the broadheads through security,' said Kevin. 'Even if he got the rest through.'

'We check.' Alvaro was making notes.

'He could have posted it; even ordered the broadheads online and had them sent direct to a post office box perhaps.'

'We check that too. Of course, he could have bought the bow here. It is legal, as it is in your country.'

'Don't remind me, Inspector.'

Dixon left Louise to complete the meeting, having thanked Alvaro and Garcia profusely for their help and cooperation. Then he caught up with Mark, perching on the corner of his workstation.

'One of your prison officers had been fishing for a couple of days at Longleat,' said Mark, handing back the piece of paper. 'He's home now.'

'What about the other missing pension victims?'

'All accounted for bar one: the other prison officer.' Mark looked at his notebook. 'Two of the soldiers are in Thailand and the SAS lads are doing security work in Iraq; all verified. Everyone else checks out and is being spoken to as well.'

'John Sims and Francis Allan first then.' Dixon was sipping the coffee handed to him by Cole. 'Still no connection between Collins and the pensions thing, I suppose.'

'No, Sir. Just Craig and the boat.'

Chapter Twenty

'Were you listening to the video call from Spain?' asked Dixon, as he drove out of Portishead towards Bristol twenty minutes later.

'Yes, Sir.'

'What did you make of it?'

'Not a lot we didn't know already.' Cole was staring out of the passenger window and spoke without looking away. 'Except for the fact his aim's improving.'

'Thirty yards to Finch and he hits him in the cheekbone, so he has to close in to twenty for the eye shot. Now he's hitting Miranda Mather in the eye first time at twenty-five metres.'

'Practice makes perfect.'

'Or a lucky shot.'

'Where are we going?' asked Cole.

'A new development off Staunton Lane, Whitchurch.'

'Bet you never thought a few dead sheep would lead to all this, eh, Sir?'

Cole's question brought an abrupt end to the conversation. The answer was obvious – *maybe not four murders, but murder, certainly* – Dixon choosing to leave it unsaid as he waited at the traffic lights at the bottom of Whitchurch Lane.

EASTFIELD HOMES – BUY FOR AS LITTLE AS £490 PER MONTH – DEPOSIT PAID!

The sign and the muddy tyre tracks on the road told Dixon he was getting close to the housing development along Staunton Lane.

He turned left into Eastfield Park, a line of flags fluttering in the breeze along the road frontage, and left his Land Rover in the perfectly manicured bays outside the immaculate show home. Beyond that, the houses either side of the dirt track were in various stages of construction, apart from the first six, which appeared to be occupied, large 'SOLD!' signs still stuck in the recently laid turf outside. The windows were just going in on the next six, and further along the track a digger was excavating the foundations of six more.

'Four hundred and ninety a month is a sod of a lot to live on a building site,' muttered Cole.

Dixon was watching the sales assistant in the show home, taking a keen interest in their movements through the front window. She was already holding a handful of leaflets and looked ready to pounce.

'It must be that one.' He was looking at the first house on the right, an old Ford Mondeo parked in the drive with a fishing rod bag on the roof rack.

The house number, 2, had been printed off on a computer and taped to the inside of the sitting room window.

'You'd have thought they'd have screwed a bloody house number on to it for them, wouldn't you?'

Dixon decided Cole's question was rhetorical.

The lawn resembled a patchwork quilt, some of the rolls of turf doing better than others, the lines between them still visible and widening, if anything. A bloody good water might help. Dixon looked up at the house: a small bay window, open plan inside; he could see the rear garden through the patio doors at the back.

'This must be one of the two bedroom ones. Two hundred and twenty-five thousand.'

'You've been watching daytime TV again, haven't you, Nige?'

'Escape to the Country.'

The front door opened before Dixon had a chance to knock, which spared his knuckles, there being no doorbell or knocker either.

'Inspector Dixon?'

He answered with his warrant card.

'They told us you were coming.' A round face and short dyed hair; she had her coat on too. 'John's in the bath, I'm afraid; I'll let him know you're here.'

She disappeared up the stairs, pushing open the door at the top abruptly. 'They're here. And you've left all your crap in the car. How can I go shopping with that in there?'

'Just give me a minute.'

She took off her coat and threw it over the banister when she reached the bottom. 'Useless bugger would spend his whole life at that bloody lake if I'd let him. Tea?'

'Yes, please.' Dixon followed her into the kitchen.

Someone had made an effort with the back garden, the lawn lush green and tightly mowed, a stone path weaving its way to a shed at the far end; geraniums in pots, a small bed of roses along the fence to one side, threadbare conifers at the far end – eventually they'd be tall enough to offer some privacy from the houses behind.

Cole sat down at the glazed dining table. 'How long have you been here?' Dutifully making polite conversation.

'Three weeks. We were the first ones.'

'Noisy, is it?'

'It's going to be like this for a while, but at least we're in. The mud's the worst part; it gets everywhere. That's why I went for the hard floor.'

A figure appeared at the bottom of the stairs. 'Just let me get my fishing stuff out of the car,' he said, leaving the front door standing open.

Dixon watched him unload the Mondeo. A large trolley first – a bit like the ones you get at B&Q; a tackle box, several bags, a tent, a cool box, then lastly he lifted the rod bag off the roof.

'He takes more care of that stuff than he does of me.' Mrs Sims was watching her husband carefully loading it all on to the trolley before wheeling it into the garage.

'No room in there for the car, I suppose,' said Cole, smiling.

'It's too bloody small anyway. They always seem to build them like that these days; cars are getting bigger and the garages smaller. But, no, there'd be no room anyway.' She was putting her coat back on, any hint of a smile lost in the act.

'I've left the keys in it.' John Sims slipped his Crocs off on the doorstep. 'Don't forget my beer. I'm gagging for a pint.'

'I won't. I was making them tea.'

'Now then, what's this all about?' He turned to Dixon and Cole. 'They wouldn't say on the phone, but it must be serious if there's a detective chief inspector knocking on my door.'

What little hair he had was still wet and he was fiddling with his glasses, moving them up and down his nose.

'Are you all right, Sir?' asked Dixon.

'I've been wearing my contact lenses for a couple of days while I've been fishing, and my eyes always take a bit of time to adjust to my glasses.'

'Did you catch anything?'

'Only a couple of tiddlers this time, but I had a new PB last time out.' Sims was grinning from ear to ear. 'Personal best.' He slid his phone out of his back pocket and opened it at a photograph of him holding a large carp in the dark, the beam of his head torch and the camera flash lighting up the scene. 'Thirty-five pound twelve.'

Dixon glanced at the photo and the date and time at the top of the screen: a week ago, at 21:16.

'Where were you?'

'Longleat. I had a three-nighter last week and I'm just back from a four-nighter.' Sims was dropping a teabag into each of three mugs lined up by the kettle. 'Making the most of the weather before the winter sets in. The bailiff will vouch for me. Why?'

'Does the name Godfrey Collins mean anything to you?'

Sims left the carton of milk on the side and turned to face Dixon, standing in the patio window. 'No, I'm afraid not.'

'How about Keith Finch?'

'Nope.'

'James Bowen?'

'I know Bowen. The tosser ripped off my pension. Why?'

'He's dead, Sir,' replied Dixon.

'Something suitably gruesome, I hope?'

'He was killed with a crossbow at a villa on the Costa del Sol three days ago.'

'What about that bitch Miranda Mather?'

'Her too.'

'Can't say I'm surprised. Or sorry.' Sims was filling the mugs with boiling water. 'It couldn't happen to two nicer people. Fucking parasites.'

'And you say you were at Longleat the whole time?'

'I don't *say* I was at Longleat, I *was* at Longleat.' Indignant now. 'As I said, the bailiff there will vouch for me. I got there on Friday. Four days and four nights. Peg six, Woods Bank, Shearwater Lake.'

'What about your previous trip, when you had the PB?'

'I got there on the Sunday and fished for three nights: Sunday, Monday, Tuesday.'

Dixon waited for Cole to finish scribbling the details in his notebook. 'How long were you with the prison service?'

'Thirty years.' Sims placed the three mugs and a sugar bowl on the table, then the milk, before sitting down opposite Cole. 'I started at Belmarsh, then did a few years at Exeter and finished my career at Bristol as supervising officer. Eight years there until I retired in July.'

'Tell me about your pension.' Dixon was looking along the photographs on the bookshelves against the far wall of the open plan dining room; cookbooks obscured by pictures of family holidays, dogs and fish.

'I only really looked at it for the first time a couple of years ago, when I was coming up for retirement, I suppose.' Sims sipped his tea. 'I was planning to work part-time somewhere and wasn't going to start drawing it, but I thought I'd have a look at transferring it to see if it might do a bit better. That's when I met James Bowen.'

'When was this?'

'A couple of years ago.'

'Why Bowen?'

'He was recommended to me by a colleague. He seemed very knowledgeable – had a posh office, filter coffee – was absolutely convincing, and he came up with this plan to transfer the fund to Clearwater Pensions. It was an offshore fund, investing in property, he said. It was registered with HMRC so I thought it would be fine.' Sims wiped the bottom of his mug on his trouser leg. 'And he was telling me it'd get an eleven per cent return per annum instead of the one point something per cent it's been getting.'

'And what happened?'

'There was forty-seven grand left that my accountant was able to recover. That would've got me about fifty quid a month when I hit sixty-five, but I took some of it out to help buy this place.' He sighed. 'Not much to show for thirty years in the prison service.'

'How big was your pension fund originally?'

'Four hundred and twelve thousand.'

'Were you landed with a big income tax bill?'

'Bowen didn't bloody well tell me about that either, did he?' Sims was turning his mug on the table, watching it leave a ring on the glass. 'We had to sell our house to pay it off. Thank God there was just enough left to buy this place or we'd be at her bloody mother's now.'

'Mrs Sims's mother is still alive?'

'I know what you're thinking, but there won't be much of an inheritance; she's one of six children.'

'What did you do when you found out about the scam?'

'Went to your lot, obviously. There was a group of six of us and we instructed a pensions specialist at a law firm in the city and he did what he could, which was basically fuck all. He got the funds frozen, I suppose, so we eventually got back the pittance that was left.'

'Did you sue?'

'We were going to, but in the end there was no point. Yes, we would have won, but there was no money to be had. The companies had been wound up and all the money had just disappeared.'

'They were living in a villa on the Costa worth three point seven million euros,' said Cole, looking puzzled.

'Owned by an offshore trust, according to the solicitor.' Sims bared his teeth. 'You try proving where the money for that came from.'

'You mentioned a colleague who put you in touch with James Bowen,' said Dixon. 'Who was that?'

'Frank Allan. He introduced several of us to him, the silly sod. Lost the lot as well, mind you.'

'Where is he now?'

'No idea, I'm afraid.' Sims tipped his glasses on the bridge of his nose, peering at Dixon over the top of them. 'Last I heard he was living in a campervan; one of the little ones that looks like an ordinary van. He was in a terrible fix. His wife took him to the cleaners when they got divorced, took the house and even took half his pension – they split his fund – so he only had half after that. That's why he was trying to increase the return, I suppose. Pleased as punch he was, telling everyone how well James Bowen had done for him, and I was one of the stupid buggers who got roped in as well.'

'And he was at Bristol at the same time as you?'

'He was, until he got the shit kicked out of him and went on sick leave; forced into early retirement only to find his pension's gone. And I thought I had it bad. At least I can still afford to go fishing.'

'Does the name Craig Pengelly mean anything to you?'

'He was a listener on the third floor, from memory. Why?'

'He was an employee of Clearwater Wealthcare and was serving time for offences arising out of the pension scam.'

'Was he, the little shit? I certainly didn't know that. I always dealt with James Bowen anyway.' Sims frowned. 'Pengelly shouldn't have been at Bristol at all, in that case. There's a clear conflict.'

'Last question, then we'll leave you to it,' said Dixon.

'Catching up on sleep.' Sims yawned. 'It's the one problem with carp fishing.'

'You said your accountant was able to recover some of your fund.'

'He did his best, but the damage had been done by then. It was a bloke called Staveley over at Weston.'

Chapter Twenty-One

'Frank Allan's wife has just walked into the Patchway Police Centre.' Cole slid his phone back into his jacket pocket. 'She got Lou's messages, apparently, and is happy to help. She works part-time at Cribbs Causeway and is on her way home from work.'

'Tell them to keep her there, whatever they do.'

'It's all right, she's waiting for us. She only lives over the road anyway.'

Dixon parked in the visitors' car park twenty minutes later and walked into reception, his warrant card at the ready.

Patchway resembled a smaller version of Express Park, the same concrete and floor to ceiling windows dominating the front of the building. Hardly inspiring; Dixon had been surprised the architect had got away with it once, but twice?

'She's in there,' said the receptionist, pointing to an interview room without looking up. 'I gave her another cup of tea.'

Mrs Allan looked startled when Dixon opened the door. 'They told me I'm not under arrest,' she said, her voice tremulous, her hand shaking as she reached for the plastic cup on the table in front of her.

'You're not, Mrs Allan, we just wanted to talk to you about your ex-husband.' Dixon sat down opposite her, Cole next to him.

'What's he done?' she asked.

'We're not sure he's done anything. We just need to speak to him about his prison service pension.'

'I wouldn't get him started on that if I were you.'

'Not happy about it, is he?'

'Blames me for it; he said the divorce was my fault and if it hadn't been for that he wouldn't have been looking at his pension at all, let alone trying to transfer it out of the prison service scheme.'

'You split the pension when you divorced?'

'That's right. I got the house and half his pension. After that it was a clean break.'

'What did you do with your half?'

'Left it in the prison service scheme.'

'When was this?'

'About three years ago. I can't remember the figures, but it was something like one hundred and fifty thousand each. It doesn't kick in until I'm sixty-five.' She shrugged. 'Not as long to go as I'd like.'

'Was the divorce amicable?'

'Hardly.' She winked at Cole. 'He obviously hasn't met Frank yet.'

'My first one wasn't amicable,' replied Cole. 'I'm hoping the second one will be.'

'When did you last see him?' asked Dixon.

'My grandson's christening two years ago. We nearly had a fight at the meal afterwards. That's when he told me he'd lost his pension.'

'D'you know where he is?'

'No, sorry. Our son doesn't speak to him either, which is sad; hasn't seen him since the christening either.'

'Why did you divorce?'

'Like I say, you obviously haven't met him yet.' She stifled a sigh. 'Look, I met someone else if you must know. It just happened, but we'd have divorced sooner or later anyway, even if it hadn't. He changed after the assault. Became temperamental – took all his bitterness and anger out on me.'

'This is the assault at work you're talking about?'

'He was doing the late shift and got dragged into a cell by a prisoner high on drugs. Spice, or whatever it is they take these days. Three broken ribs, a punctured lung, fractured cheekbone, concussion. I suppose we should've been grateful the bloke didn't have a blade, but Frank was in a bad way after that. He tried to sue and got a medical report that said he had a brain injury and post-traumatic stress disorder, which probably explained the change in him.'

'He *tried* to sue?'

'They defended it and said he disobeyed the protocol and shouldn't have gone in the cell.'

'You said he was dragged in?'

'He said he was dragged in; they said he went in of his own accord.'

'And the claim failed?'

'He was forced to withdraw it. The No Win No Fee solicitor pulled out and that was that.'

'Has he worked since the assault?'

'Not in the prison service. He was on long term sick, then took early retirement. It was after that we divorced and he lost his pension.'

'Did he tell you what he was doing with his pension?'

'First I heard of it was at the christening and it was done, dusted and gone by then. And anyway, it's none of my business, really, is it?'

'Does the name Craig Pengelly mean anything to you?'

'No.'

'James Bowen and Miranda Mather?'

'No.' She folded her arms. 'Look, what's he supposed to have done?'

'We're keen to speak to him to rule him out of four murders that have taken place in the last seven days. Two in this country and two on the Costa del Sol. All of the victims were involved in some way in the pension scam that cost your husband his pension.'

Mrs Allan took a deep breath, exhaling slowly through her nose, her fingers twitching as if she was holding a cigarette. 'It's just one of those things you say, isn't it?'

Dixon waited.

'At the christening. He said he was going to see to it they got what was coming to them, the bastards who'd ripped him off. He'd had a few and I thought it was just piss and wind.'

'And you still say you have no idea where he is.'

'Frank, you bloody idiot,' she whispered. 'Last I heard he was living in a van and doing cash-in-hand work in the arcades down Burnham and Brean, places like that. A friend of mine said she saw him in the kiosk at one of them.'

'Which one?'

'She didn't say.'

'Can we speak to her?'

'I'd really rather not trouble her.'

'We need to find him, Mrs Allan.'

'This was a couple of months ago, but she said she saw him at Brean Leisure Centre, in the amusement arcade there.'

'Look after that for me, will you?'

Cole knew better than to ask, sliding Dixon's wallet into his jacket pocket. Dixon had noticed the frown, too, when he had emptied all his change into the driver's door pocket of the Land Rover.

Cole didn't know, didn't understand, but then how could he when nobody did?

Fruit machines.

He'd taken refuge in the flashing lights, the bells, the whistles; saved only by his friend Jake and their rock climbing partnership that long hot summer all those years ago. Getting the next nudge hardly matters when you're clinging on by your fingertips several hundred feet off the ground.

Dixon stopped in the doorway of the amusement arcade at Brean Leisure Centre, a cold sweat gathering in the small of his back. He felt the same sickening feeling in the pit of his stomach all over again. It was a mild form of self-harm; he'd been told that by at least two beer-swilling amateur psychiatrists in the pub, trying to analyse his apparently irresistible urge to push all his money into those bloody machines.

But the simple answer was that it was an escape: from the pain of loss. Or was he just replacing the pain of losing Fran with the pain of losing all his money? Either way, he'd stand there until he had.

Dixon had never thought of himself as stupid. He knew the seventy per cent rule, and he knew full well he'd lose in the end, no matter how many times the jackpot came cascading down the hopper into the metal tray; in tokens usually, so you had no choice but to push them straight back in again.

And that noise!

Even when the arcades were empty you could hear it from time to time, played on a loop by one or more of the machines. It reminded Dixon of a duck caller, attracting birds to the slaughter.

He walked along the line of machines, mesmerised already by the lights, some of the wheels spinning even though there was no one standing there feeding coins in; the sound of a jackpot behind him – there was no one there, either.

Cole appeared behind him. 'They've paged the manager, Sir. Are you all right?'

'I'm fine.' Dixon had his hands in his pockets, rummaging amongst his keys for any loose change.

'You left it in the car,' said Cole. 'I think I might have a go, though.' He was looking down at three one-pound coins in the palm of his hand.

'You might as well save yourself the trouble and just give it to the manager when he gets here.'

'I might find a machine someone's filled up and it's ready to drop the jackpot.'

'It doesn't work like that.' Dixon sighed. 'If only it did.'

'Someone told me—'

'He's right. Sorry.' Jeans and a blue Brean Leisure Centre polo shirt. 'It's all random. There's no such thing as a full machine bursting to pay out; not any more.'

'Mr Jackson?' asked Dixon, his warrant card in hand.

'Yes.'

'Tell him about the seventy per cent rule.'

'The machines are set to pay out seventy per cent of the money paid in to them. That's it, really.'

'Seventy per cent?' Cole made no effort to hide his disgust. 'Is that it?'

'Some used to pay out more, up to ninety per cent, but then the government capped the stake at two quid so that was the end of that.'

Cole stuffed his coins back in his pocket. 'Bloody fruit machines.'

'Fixed odds betting terminals, to give them their proper name, Nigel,' said Dixon.

'People enjoy them.' Jackson was bristling visibly now.

'People get hooked on them,' Dixon snapped back, hoping no one had noticed the beads of sweat on his temples. 'We're looking for this man,' he said, changing the subject with his phone held out in front of Jackson. 'We've been told he worked in your kiosk.'

'That's Frank Allan.' Jackson nodded at the photograph on the screen. 'He was here for about four weeks earlier in the season, then we had to let him go.'

'How much was he paid?'

'Ten pounds an hour. He did the late shift; four till eleven and then closed up.'

'Have you got an address for him?'

'He was staying on a local campsite and it was cash in hand. Sorry.'

Dixon waited for another vacant machine to finish its jackpot jingle. 'And why did you let him go?'

'The usual reason,' replied Jackson. 'We had money going missing. Nothing we could prove, though, so we just let him go. We didn't notice it for a few weeks, until the machines were cashed up.'

'Not the kiosk?'

'We'd have noticed the kiosk float down straight away; that gets balanced daily. No, it was a couple of the machines were well down on where they should have been for the height of the season. We had no way of proving anything, mind you, because the CCTV was switched off every night, late, for a couple of hours like.' Jackson was sucking on his e-cigarette, but hadn't switched it on. 'The bloke from the supplier said there was no way it could've been done, but that's bollocks. We're talking two machines, a couple of hundred quid down every day for three weeks. It's no bloody wonder Frank was happy to work seven days a week.'

'Where is he now?'

'God knows.'

'Which machines were they?' Dixon was watching an elderly lady pick coins out of her purse by a machine on the other side of the small arcade.

'We got rid of them. Look, I suppose I should make it clear we never proved anything, and the bloke from the supplier said it was impossible, so it could just have been a software glitch that caused the losses. We weren't taking any chances, though, so we got rid of Frank and the machines.'

'Why was the CCTV switched off?' asked Cole.

'Quite.' Jackson gave an emphatic nod.

'Can you let me have the supplier's contact details?'

'It's on the back of that machine,' replied Jackson. 'There's a sticker.'

Dixon slid his iPhone out of his pocket and took a photograph of the information he needed. 'And the machines, what were they called?'

'There were two, both the same. Called Crossbow Ninja.'

Chapter Twenty-Two

The ping of Louise's text arriving had been lost in the bells and whistles of the amusement arcade.

Ian Staveley 5pm with his solicitor at Weston, interview room booked

Cole leaned across from the passenger seat of the Land Rover, craning his neck to read the message on Dixon's phone. 'Wonder why he's bringing a solicitor? It always makes me think they've got something to hide.'

Dixon was watching the rollercoaster looping the loop in the park behind the amusements. It was bigger than the old wooden one that used to be there; his one brush with cash-in-hand work, a few weeks one Easter spent bolting the track on to the high rails with Jake, their head for heights and rock climbing equipment proving ideal for the job. It had been great fun, and had paid for a trip to the Alps. The rollercoaster had even passed its inspection too, much to his surprise.

A big dipper, spinning things that would have had his breakfast making another appearance, giant swings and waltzers, dodgems, go-karts; he could hear the screams inside his Land Rover on the far side of the car park.

'I went on a rollercoaster once.' Cole cringed. 'Never again.'

'You threw up?'

'Worse. The kid in front of me did.'

Dixon turned the key, the diesel engine drowning out the shrieks and screams. The sounds had gone but not the smells, the sickly sweet stench of fish and chips, coffee and candyfloss all rolled into one still lingering in his nostrils. Low tide and an onshore breeze didn't help, the mudflats adding a fetid tinge.

'Where to now?' asked Cole.

'We've got time to drop in on Arbern Gaming. Then it's over to Weston to see what Staveley's got to say for himself.'

Half an hour later he parked on the forecourt of a small industrial unit on the outskirts of Clevedon. The units either side announced their occupiers with huge signs, Avon Kitchens on the left and Brightview Windows on the right, but Arbern Gaming obviously wished to remain anonymous. Dixon knew he was in the right place all the same, the roller doors at the front open and revealing lines of fruit machines standing idle; no flashing lights or jackpot jingles. It felt a bit like a graveyard, or a mortuary perhaps.

The only flashing lights came from the charger on a forklift truck and the small red dot on a CCTV camera watching their approach. Lights were on upstairs, on the mezzanine floor, the office door open.

'I'll call you back.' Then a figure leaned over the metal balustrade. 'Can I help you?'

Warrant cards were followed by footsteps on the metal staircase.

Dixon noticed the tattoos first, then the earrings and grey stubble; ripped black jeans and a sleeveless Motörhead T-shirt. The only thing missing was the leather waistcoat.

'And you are?'

'Andy.'

Dixon waited.

'Andrew Digby.'

'Are you the owner?' Dixon was wandering along the lines of dead fruit machines, strangely comforted by the peace and quiet, at the same time not dropping his guard in case they woke up; a bit like a gazelle stumbling on a sleeping cheetah.

'That's Phil and Lynn. They own it and I do all the bloody work.'

'What work?'

'Servicing and repairs, all the installations. They deal with the contracts and the money, I s'pose, but I do everything else.'

Dixon stopped in front of Crossbow Ninja and looked down at the reels, shrouded in darkness; two crossbows on the winning line and one just above. 'Tell me about this machine.' He resisted the temptation to put his hands in his pockets.

'It's an upgraded version of Agent Crossbow that came out in 2017. It's quite popular. What more can I say?'

'Why have you got four of them here? Surely they should be in arcades and pubs?'

'We've had a couple of them returned, if you must know.' Andy picked up a cloth and started dusting the machines, slowly working his way along the line to where Dixon was standing. 'They were losing money.'

'Start from the beginning and treat me like an idiot.'

'They're category B3 machines; so that's a maximum stake of two quid and a top jackpot of five hundred. You'll only see them in betting shops, bingo halls and what they call "adult gaming centres"; they're the adults only sections of ordinary amusement arcades. They're always near the kiosk so they can be supervised, like.'

'Still subject to the seventy per cent rule?' Cole was leaning on a machine with his notebook in his hand.

'It's not just us, that's the industry standard.'

'How much money is in one of these machines at any one time?' asked Dixon.

'A lot.' Andy start polishing the first of the Crossbow Ninja machines. 'Stands to reason, dunnit, if it pays out five hundred quid. I dunno, three grand maybe?'

'And how does it work?'

'It's all computer generated these days, not like the good old days when you could watch out for some pillock to fill up the machine and then use a magnet.' Andy gave a sheepish grin. 'We've all got to learn somehow.'

'There's a computer in there?' Cole failed to hide his disbelief.

'A hard drive, yes. The machine works on a computer algorithm; it's basically just a random number generator. Impossible to crack.'

'Why were these machines losing money then?' asked Dixon.

'Fuck knows. A design flaw in the software maybe. We got on to the manufacturer and they said they'd have a look at it and issue an update.'

'Then what happens?'

'I'll have to go round and update all the machines.'

Dixon dragged the Crossbow Ninja machine out into the aisle. 'Show me,' he said, gesturing to the lock in the rear panel.

'This one's open.' Andy pulled open the panel in the back of the machine. 'I had a look at it when it came back; these two from Brean Leisure Centre, this one from the Pavilion at Burnham and that one was at Sedgemoor motorway services.' He squatted down and pointed at a black box inside. 'See, here's a USB port so I connects my laptop and can update the software.'

'What other maintenance do you have to do?'

'There really isn't any these days. Back in the old days we'd have to oil the reels and make sure it was all working like a clock, but nowadays it's just software updates and cleaning.'

'And everybody who's returned a Crossbow Ninja gave the same reason?'

'Yeah.'

'Have you got any others out there?'

'A few. There's one at Burnham in the arcade along from the Reeds Arms, a couple over at Minehead; one at Bridgwater services, there's one in the Ritz at Burnham as well. That's it, I think. I can let you have a complete list on the email.'

'Who holds keys to those panels?' Dixon was watching Andy close it and push the machine back into line.

'We do.'

'Not the arcade wherever they are?'

'No.'

'So, if you wanted to hack one of them, what would you do?'

'Way beyond me, I'm afraid.' Andy puffed out his cheeks. 'I just update the software, I don't write it. Wouldn't know where to begin.'

'But it could be done?'

'I suppose it could. You'd need to pick the lock, take the back off and connect a computer, write the software program to hack it, but I s'pose it could be done, yeah.'

'If you can get the back off, why not just take the money?' asked Cole.

'That box is separately locked,' replied Andy. 'And it's built like a mini safe.'

Dixon leaned back against a machine and folded his arms. 'So, while your laptop's connected at the back you play the machine and take it to the cleaners.'

'I couldn't see that anything had been uploaded to the hard drive, so that's the only way it could be done.' Andy frowned. 'Hang on a minute, are you telling me that's what someone's been doing?'

◆ ◆ ◆

Put a tail on Gavin Curtis. He'll lead us to Allan.

'Why don't we just pick Gavin up?' asked Cole, reading the text to Louise over Dixon's shoulder.

'We're trying to catch a multiple murderer, not a thief, Nigel,' replied Dixon, tapping out a second message. 'He's doing cash-in-hand work, almost certainly under a false name, so we'll let Gavin show us where he is.'

Check if Allan has worked at the Burnham Pavilion and Brent Knoll mway services

'Shouldn't we warn the other arcades that have got a Crossbow Ninja in them?' asked Cole, putting on his seatbelt.

'We need one of them to give him a job and if we warn them, they won't. And if I'm right, we'll catch him before they have the chance to hack the machines anyway.'

Dixon parked in front of the bike racks outside Weston police station twenty minutes later and watched Staveley having an animated conversation in the reception area with a woman in a grey two piece suit. Arguing with your solicitor – never a good sign.

'We've booked an interview room for five o'clock,' said Dixon to the receptionist when he walked in.

'Number one, Sir. Just through there.' Gesturing towards the door, the lock buzzing.

'This way, Mr Staveley, if you will.' Cole was holding the door open.

Dixon waited until everybody had sat down. 'You're not under arrest, Mr Staveley, and I'm not recording this interview. You're simply helping us with our enquiries and I'm most grateful to you for that.'

Staveley visibly relaxed, although the sigh of relief came from his solicitor.

'I brought Miss Smith along, thinking I'd—'

'My client has been dragged through investigation after investigation purely by reason of his business association with Godfrey Collins, so I'm sure you'll forgive us if he, and me on his behalf, are a little defensive.'

'It's quite understandable.' Dixon gave his best disarming smile. 'What I'm trying to do is understand why Mr Collins was murdered.'

'You've ruled my client out of that, surely?'

'That's part of why we're here.'

Staveley glared at his solicitor. 'It's fine.'

'Mr Collins,' continued Dixon, 'was one of four people killed with a crossbow within the last week. For reasons I needn't go into now, we believe the killings to have been committed by the same person and whilst we have established a motive for three of the murders, we have thus far been unable to find any connection with Mr Collins.'

'Thus far?' Staveley frowned. 'You've found a connection now?'

'We have, Sir.' Matter of fact. 'You.'

'Me?' Several octaves higher.

'We believe three of the murders relate to a pension transfer scam, but Mr Collins seems to have played no part in that whatsoever. His only connection to the pension scam is you, because you acted for at least one of the victims of the scam in trying to recover what was left of their funds.'

'That's exactly what I did do, for some of them. What's wrong with that?'

'Nothing, on the face of it,' replied Dixon. 'Who did you act for then?'

'There were two prison officers, a police officer and a couple of others. They were referred to me as a group by Bob, er Robert Harden, he's a pensions specialist in Bristol. He managed to get the remains of the funds frozen in a Spanish court – Clearwater

Pensions, that was it – and then referred them to me when the court action was over. I was mainly dealing with HMRC on their behalf because of the income tax liabilities, but when the funds were released they came to me; only a couple of them had anything left though.'

'Was Frank Allan one of your clients?'

'He was.' Staveley was leaning forward, his hands interlocked on the table in front of him. 'He had nothing left, sadly. Just the income tax bill. I told him to declare himself bankrupt.'

'And did he?'

'I really have no idea.'

'Look, maybe if you told us who else had been murdered, my client might be able to shed some light on it for you.' Smith glanced up at the clock on the wall; either clock watching or time recording, Dixon couldn't tell which, but suspected both.

'James Bowen and Miranda Mather were killed at their villa on the Costa del Sol three days ago. Mr Bowen ran Clearwater Wealthcare, who sold the pensions, and Miss Mather ran Clearwater Pensions. The third victim is Keith Finch, the enforcement officer at HM Revenue and Customs in Cardiff.'

'Not Keith!' Staveley let out an exaggerated sigh. 'I met him once on a tax enforcement course. The poor sod.'

'He was in charge of recovering the income tax due on the pension transfers that turned out to be withdrawals.'

'No, he wasn't. He was just the office manager,' replied Staveley. 'His name was on the correspondence, but that doesn't mean he wrote the letter.'

'You and I know that, Mr Staveley,' said Dixon. 'But someone didn't. And they shot him in the eye with a crossbow bolt.'

Staveley flinched.

'Do you own a crossbow?' asked Dixon. 'Forgive me, but I have to ask.'

'No, I don't.'

'And where were you on Saturday morning, between say eight and ten?'

'At home. My wife will vouch for—' He slapped his forehead with the palm of his hand. 'No, wait, I had a training course on the Friday in London. My wife came with me and went shopping and we stayed Friday night in the Premier Inn at Wembley. That means we were on the train home on Saturday morning. We didn't get home until lunchtime. My wife can confirm that and the hotel will be able to confirm when we checked out, won't they?'

Dixon glanced at Cole who was busy scribbling in his notebook. 'Had you ever come across Clearwater Wealthcare before?'

'I'm sure I'd met James Bowen a couple of years ago at a networking event somewhere; some lunch club, something like that. He had some young lad in tow, if I remember rightly. Financial advisers do the rounds of these sorts of things, don't they?'

Dixon remembered it well. It was the junior trainee solicitor's lot to represent the firm at networking events, usually when no one else could be bothered to go.

'It might even have been one of those speed networking breakfast things,' continued Staveley. 'A high price to pay for a bacon roll.'

'At the moment, the only victim of the pension scam unaccounted for is Frank Allan. Do you know where he is?'

'No. I only met him the once and haven't seen him for a couple of years at least. My file's closed and archived.'

'Was he angry enough to have resorted to this, d'you think?'

'To murder? What sort of question is that?'

Dixon waited.

'They were angry; they were all very angry and bitter about it. Wouldn't you be? They'd saved into their employer's pension schemes all their lives and then decide to transfer out to a new scheme that was registered with HM Revenue and Customs, so it should've been safe, shouldn't it? You tell me, would you have been angry enough to kill?'

'No, Sir.'

'Me neither.' Staveley was clearly backtracking, making an effort to calm himself, as if he'd suddenly remembered where he was and who he was talking to. His solicitor placing her hand on his forearm had helped snap him back to the present.

'The income tax bills.' Dixon was scrolling through an email on his phone. 'Who had the largest?'

'They were all much the same. I suppose John Sims had the biggest, but not by much; and he agreed a settlement over ten years. I thought the taxman was quite reasonable to be honest, bearing in mind these were people approaching retirement who'd just lost their pension pots. Most agreed settlements, but a couple weren't able to make any payments at all. Frank Allan was one, and the ex-police officer, Brian Willcocks. He was reluctant to cooperate with me, let alone HMRC.'

Time for a question or two that Dixon knew the answers to. Louise had been thorough in her research even though time had been short, and her email had arrived just as he was parking outside the station.

'How far is your villa in Marbella from Sitio de Calahonda?'

Staveley swallowed hard. 'About twenty miles.'

'It says nineteen kilometres on Google.'

'Twelve miles then, Sir,' said Cole, without looking up.

'We've only got it because we can't sell it; one of my wife's bright ideas when the kids left home. Now we're stuck with it unless we want to take a huge hit.'

'Do you rent it out?'

'We tried that a few years ago, but the place kept getting trashed so we don't any more. Not even to friends.'

'When did you last visit?'

186

'We had a couple of weeks there in August. It's easy enough, fly from Bristol and twenty minutes in a taxi.'

'D'you keep a car out there?'

'A Fiat Punto; just a little runaround. It gets us to and from the golf course and the shops.'

Dixon kept them waiting while he tapped out another text message to Louise: *Check Staveley at Premier Inn Wembley three nights ago, and flights out of Hrow and Gatwick to Costa del Sol. City too.*

'Look, I've been quite upfront with you,' said Staveley. 'I was when you came to my house.'

'Your house?' demanded his solicitor.

'He just turned up, caught me as I was going to work.'

Dixon was quite happy listening to their conversation.

'I told him I had a motive for wanting Godfrey dead, there's no point in hiding that. Godfrey nearly wrecked my business and my life, so yes, I'd have cheerfully killed him, but I didn't.'

'I think you've said enough, Ian.' Smith tried her hand on Staveley's forearm again.

'Think about it, though,' he continued. 'What possible motive could I have for wanting the others dead? I only gained out of the pension scam; I got several new clients out of it and lots of work that kept me busy for months, for heaven's sake! Why would I want them dead?'

Chapter Twenty-Three

'Fish and chips?' Cole frowned. 'Have we got time?'

'Plenty.' Dixon was leaning back against the window in the small chippy just around the corner from Burnham Library. 'If we make an arrest it'll be hours before we get a chance to eat.'

They were well hidden from the seafront and the amusement arcade next to the Reeds Arms, an unmarked Armed Response vehicle waiting further along the seafront.

Cole gave the thumbs up sign when the assistant waved the salt pot at him. 'How do we know Allan's in Castle Amusements anyway?'

'We don't, but if Gavin heads for Bridgwater or Minehead we can catch up with him while he's still out on the motorway. He's got to go past Burnham, hasn't he?'

He was wiping the last chip around the inside of the bag fifteen minutes later when a text arrived from Louise: *Gavin's on the move. A red Daewoo saloon 98 plate*

'A red saloon,' Cole said. 'Maybe he killed Collins?'

'You've met him, Nigel.' Dixon scrunched up the empty bag and dropped it into the passenger footwell.

'Yeah.'

Time to move from their picnic spot above the beach at the top of Allandale Road; Dixon crept along the seafront, parking on the double yellow lines beyond the Pavilion.

'Why don't we just go in?' Cole was clearly champing at the bit.

'Too many people.'

The sun had slipped below the horizon and the lights along the seafront were taking over, the scene flickering from the flashing bulbs on the Pavilion behind them and Castle Amusements a hundred or so yards ahead. People were milling about outside the arcade, more piling out of the Reeds Arms. Mercifully most disappeared around the corner, heading for the Pier Tavern or the Somerset and Dorset possibly.

Dixon's phone rang and he flicked on the loudspeaker.

'What is it, Lou?'

'He's just turning on to the seafront now, Sir, from the Seaview Road end.'

'All right, tell them to stop him now.'

'Don't we want to catch him in the act?'

'No, we don't.'

He watched the blue lights come on in his rear view mirror, Cole watching in the passenger wing mirror.

'What do they nick him for?' asked Louise.

'Theft. Get them to take him to Express Park; his car and laptop need to go to Scientific. And we'll need the interview team down from Bristol.'

'Yes, Sir.'

'Where's the Armed Response team?' he asked, his question soon answered by flashing headlights on a car parked opposite the hovercraft station. 'All right, let's get the local team in Pier Street and we'd better have a dog here too, in case he gets away and heads for the beach. It'll be pitch dark by the time we make the arrest.' He took off his jacket and tie, throwing them on to the back seat of the Land Rover. 'While you set that up, I'm going in for a look around.'

Dixon walked along the seafront until he was opposite Castle Amusements, looking straight in through the large doors that were standing open; the sounds of the arcade carried even over the roar of the waves breaking on the jetty behind him, the tide on its way out.

The arcade was large, people milling about inside; shooting at a screen with guns, dropping two pence pieces into cascades, more coins rattling as they dropped out the bottom. Someone was using the racing car simulator, the noise of screeching tyres followed by a loud crash and a cheer from the family gathered around the machine.

There was even a young girl shooting zombies with a crossbow.

The 'clack' of the air hockey table on the left, a father and young son playing with unusual venom and sending the puck towards a smaller boy playing whack-a-mole, with the mother, presumably. Beyond them a counter offering sweets and cuddly toys in exchange for their winning tickets, each machine pumping out rolls of paper tickets like streamers to the winner. There was a kiosk too, operated by a young man with dark hair – more student than retired prison officer.

Dixon's eyes were drawn to the opposite side of the arcade, where the fun turned to gambling and lines of fruit machines stood around the wall ready to empty the pockets of the unwary.

A small man with a beard was sitting in a kiosk at the entrance to a separate room with a large sign over the entrance: *Adults Only*. He appeared to be reading something and Dixon wondered whether that was 'adults only' too.

A quick glance at his phone and the HM Prison Service photograph of Allan, then Dixon took out his wallet. Two ten pound notes; a small price to pay, and he could always claim it back on expenses.

The machines either side of the front doors offered him the chance to grab a teddy bear with a crane, although he'd fallen for that one before – the arms always opening on the way to the chute, not much, just enough to drop the stuffed toy. Still, rather that than pushing his money into a fruit machine, although Crossbow Ninja was tempting.

He stood in front of the kiosk and slid a ten pound note under the Perspex screen, the sigh making it obvious that Allan would have preferred him to use one of the change machines, tearing himself away from his newspaper just long enough to press a button, Dixon's change sliding down into the hopper.

'They take notes, y'know.'

You'll have plenty of time for reading where you're going, matey.

He walked along the line of machines in the adults only area and stopped in front of Crossbow Ninja: five spins of the wheels for ten quid. Still, in for a pound . . .

Less than sixty seconds later he was back at the kiosk, sliding his last ten pound note under the Perspex screen.

'You should have taken the multiple,' said Allan – it was definitely him behind that beard. 'If you get it again, press the gold button.'

'Thank you.' Dixon made a conscious effort not to make eye contact; time enough for that in the interview room.

'Where's the nearest cashpoint?' he asked, back at the kiosk a minute later.

'There's one over there.' Allan waved his hand towards the back of the arcade.

Dixon resisted the temptation and drifted towards the door. A cashpoint in a fruit machine arcade? Someone must've thought it was a good idea.

He was soon sitting back in his Land Rover, putting on his tie. 'Remind me to claim twenty quid on expenses when we get back to Area J, will you?'

'Is he in there?' asked Cole.

'In the kiosk by the adults only bit.' Dixon was wriggling into his jacket. 'We can take him now, there's no one playing the fruit machines. Tell uniform to give us two minutes and then follow us in. We'll need to get him out of the kiosk; the door's on the far side as we go in. I'll get him out, you play the nearest machine to the kiosk and nick him as soon as he opens the door. Have you got handcuffs?'

'Yes, Sir.'

'One last thing. You'll have to lend me ten quid.'

'Back again so soon?' Allan's voice was impassive when Dixon slid the ten pound note under the Perspex screen.

'You know how it is,' replied Dixon, picking his change out of the hopper.

Five spins of the wheel and the money was gone; Crossbow Ninja again, Allan watching him from the kiosk.

'Bloody machine,' yelled Dixon, thumping the coin slot with the side of his fist. Then he reached up and rocked it backwards and forwards, the rear panel swinging open. A kick for good measure, then the alarm went off, the high pitched klaxon failing to drown out Allan and his frantic scramble for the keys to unlock the kiosk.

'Oi!'

The kiosk door opened outwards, just a fraction, and Cole was on it in a flash. He wrenched open the door and wrestled Allan to the ground, handcuffing his wrists behind his back before he had a chance to draw breath.

'What the fuck?'

Dixon left the Crossbow Ninja machine turned sideways in the aisle, the rear panel standing open.

A small crowd was gathering by the pool table, a large man elbowing his way through, more keys jangling from his belt on a chain. 'What's going on here?' he demanded.

Dixon watched Cole drag Allan to his feet with the help of the two uniformed officers who had now arrived, slightly out of breath.

'Francis Allan, I am arresting you on suspicion of the murders of Godfrey Collins, Keith Finch, James Bowen and Miranda Mather.' He waited for the gasps from the crowd to subside before continuing. 'You do not have to say anything but it may harm your defence if you do not mention when questioned something you later rely on in court.'

Allan looked up and smirked at him.

'Anything you do say may be given in evidence.'

'Where's Gavin?'

'Same place you're going.' Dixon turned to the two uniformed officers. 'Take him to Express Park and get him checked in. Search the kiosk too, before you go; and make sure you find his phone.'

'Yes, Sir.'

'What's happened to that machine?' asked the big man with the keys.

'And you are?'

'Luke Newman. I run this place.' He folded his arms. 'His name's not Frank Allan either. It's Harry.'

'You may want to check that machine, Sir; I think you'll find it a few quid light. Andy at Arbern Gaming can explain. In the meantime, my colleague here will need a statement from you.'

◆ ◆ ◆

Dixon was sitting in his Land Rover when Cole came trotting across the road from the arcade. 'Luke says our man's living in a converted minibus on the Grange campsite at Edithmead. It's a DIY Transit van conversion; Harry was very proud of it, apparently.'

'Let's cut the Harry bollocks,' snapped Dixon. 'We know who he is.' He turned the key. 'Get Scientific over to the Grange now and then get uniform to drop you down to Express Park when you've finished here.'

There was an uneasy feeling in the pit of Dixon's stomach as he drove out towards Edithmead. It all felt too easy by half – either that or it was losing thirty quid on a fruit machine – and it hardly felt like the moment of triumph when he parked outside the office at the Grange campsite and rang the bell. An Entryphone at a campsite – whatever next?

'I'm sorry, we're closed.'

'Police.'

'What d'you want?'

Dixon said nothing. It was a tactic he always used with telephone call centres that insist you key in your card number or crap like that before they put you through; stay silent, wait, and you soon get through to a real person.

A light came on in the back of the office, then the outside light, the door opening just as Dixon raised his warrant card.

'You've got someone staying here in a converted Transit minibus; goes by the name of Frank Allan, or he may be calling himself Harry.'

'He's been here a couple of weeks,' replied the woman. 'Harry, he said his name was. He's down there on the left, pitch twelve. He'll be at work now if you want to speak to him.'

'Is he alone?'

'Yes.'

'Are there people either side of him?'

'Just the far side; a couple in a campervan.'

'You'll need to move them, please.' He was already on his way back to his Land Rover. 'And if you can lift the barrier and leave it up, there's a Scientific Services team on the way.'

'Look, what's this all about?'

Proud of a long wheelbase minibus with black curtains up at the side windows? It had better be nice inside, thought Dixon as he parked facing it, his headlights on full beam.

The minibus had been reversed on to the plot, its rear doors facing the hedge. An orange cable ran from the electric hook-up and in one of the side windows that had been left open a crack. A canopy had been attached to the roof rack and offered some shelter to sit out at night, a pair of deck chairs lying on the ground under the bus.

Dixon flicked on the light on his phone and walked around, peering in the windows, listening to the animated conversation taking place on the far side of the campervan parked on the adjacent plot. Then an elderly man in pink boxer shorts and a vest appeared around the front.

'What's this about? Why have we got to move?' He was standing with his hands on his hips. 'It'd better be something bloody important, like a murder.'

'Four murders, actually, Sir,' replied Dixon, allowing the pain to shine through in his expression.

'Oh, I see. Well, that's all right then.'

'If you say so, Sir.'

All six wheels were rusting, P registration – although that was probably false – so at least twenty-five years old; older by the looks of things. It was miracle it had got through its MOT, assuming it had.

He slipped on a pair of latex gloves and tried the doors; locked. Then a uniformed officer appeared, rattling a set of keys.

The seats were new and rotated to face into the rear of the minibus, where there was a bed at the far end, a small kitchen area with a sink and hob, and even a shower cubicle. Dixon disconnected the gas bottles behind the passenger seat and began opening the cupboards one by one, using the light on his phone.

The uniformed officer was standing on the ground outside, leaning in the driver's door.

'Where would you hide a crossbow?' asked Dixon. 'Assuming it comes to pieces.'

'Under the bed, Sir?'

Dixon lifted the thin mattress clear and shone his light down between the slats; two suitcases, an overnight bag, and an air rifle with a telescopic sight. 'Looks like we're getting warm.'

'What about under the—?'

'Out!'

Dixon recognised Donald Watson's voice and knew arguments with the senior Scientific Services officer never ended well. It was Watson's crime scene now, and that was all there was to it.

'We're looking for a crossbow.'

'I know.' Watson was shining a torch in through the windscreen.

Dixon slid out of the driver's seat. 'You got here quick.'

'Bloody good job, with you stomping about in there in your size tens.'

'There are a couple of suitcases under the bed.'

'I'll be sure to look there, fear not.' Watson's frown was visible even in the half-light from Dixon's Land Rover. 'Haven't you got somewhere you need to be?'

'I have. And it would be useful if I had a crossbow tucked under my arm when I got there.'

'Give me a minute, will you?'

The campervan pulled off the adjacent pitch and Dixon watched the headlights in the dark as it made its way across the site to the far side, reversing on to a pitch near the shower block. By the time he turned around more Scientific Services officers were setting up arc lamps and the photographer was in the minibus, flashes going off one after the other.

'There's nothing in these suitcases,' shouted Donald Watson. 'D'you want the air rifle?'

'No!'

'There's a Sainsbury's carrier bag full of old correspondence in this cupboard above the bed.'

'Better have that.' Dixon was watching through the rear doors, which had been opened to allow an arc lamp to light up the interior.

Watson dropped the file into an evidence bag. 'No telly. Probably watches stuff on his phone.'

'We've got that.'

'It's not a bad job, y'know,' said Watson, looking around. 'Just a shame he's gone to this much trouble on such an old heap of a minibus.' He turned on the tap and watched the water running into the sink. 'It even drains.'

'There's a hole in the floor.' Dixon's attention had been drawn by the sound of running water under the minibus. 'It's pouring straight out on to the ground.'

'Well, at least the loo doesn't.' Watson grinned. 'It's a cassette so it collects underneath.'

'Any sign of the crossbow?'

'There's fresh silicone around the shower tray. Hang on. Pass me a Stanley knife, someone.' Watson appeared at the back of the minibus a few minutes later holding the shower tray. 'Cut the silicone and it just slides out. The pipe goes straight out through the floor just like the sink, the cheeky sod.'

'And the crossbows?'

'They're here.' Watson turned the shower tray upside down to reveal two crossbows taped to the underside: a smaller recurve pistol crossbow and a larger rifle bow. Both were in pieces, the stock of the rifle bow taped diagonally across the underside of the tray, the limbs either side. The smaller pistol bow sat under the rim of the tray.

'I was wondering why it was up on a little plinth.' Watson shrugged. 'It makes a nice little hidey-hole and a nice change from the old bath panel, I suppose.' He set the shower tray down on the end of the bed and turned back to the shower cubicle. 'These were in there too.' He leaned over and picked up two sets of bolts held together by elastic bands, one set short and the other much longer. 'It'll all need to go for DNA testing. With these.'

Dixon recognised the same size of padded envelope. 'What's the address on it?' he asked.

'Gavin Curtis, 13b Loxton Road, Weston.'

'How many are left?'

Watson reached in and pulled out a small plastic bag. He held it up to the arc lamp, the light glinting on the razor sharp curved blades of the broadheads. 'Two,' he said. 'Nasty bloody things, aren't they?'

Chapter Twenty-Four

Charlesworth and Potter were waiting for him when he arrived at Express Park just before midnight. Dixon spotted their cars in the visitors' car park as he turned in and so opted for the staff car park, the top floor deserted apart from Louise's old Ford Focus.

'You're flavour of the month, Sir.' She was holding open the back door for him. 'The bad news is they know you're here.'

'Where's Nigel?'

'He got a statement from the bloke at the arcade, then went back to Portishead with Scientific. He said he'd come down in the morning with the bow.'

'All right, Gavin first.' Dixon was watching over Louise's shoulder, Charlesworth and Potter striding towards him along the landing. 'We'll interview Allan in the morning.'

'Sam West's here and ready to start the interview. He's just waiting for Gavin's solicitor to finish with him; they're in a private conflab now.'

'Well done, Nick!' Charlesworth was beaming. Potter looked less impressed, although that may have been because she'd been dragged out of bed. 'I've asked Vicky Thomas to lay on a press conference tomorrow afternoon. You should have it all sewn up by then.'

'Why did you intercept Gavin Curtis?' Potter was standing with her hands on her hips. 'I thought the plan was to catch them hacking the fruit machine?'

Dixon had known that was coming, but had expected it from Charlesworth. After all, catch Gavin in the act and it's an easy addition to the statistics: another crime committed and solved in double-quick time. Always looks good for the force performance tables. 'The plan was for Gavin to lead us to Allan, which he did.'

'Nick's right.' Charlesworth smiled, which was always disconcerting. 'We've got him as accessory to four murders, so what's a bit of theft between friends?' It was probably a good job Charlesworth hadn't been pulled over on the way to Express Park; he'd have failed a breathalyser, judging by his breath. 'He was arrested for the murders, wasn't he?'

'Only the theft, Sir.' Dixon took a step back. 'Just watch his interview.'

'You've got the team down from Bristol, I gather?'

'Yes, Sir.'

'Well, Sam West is a trained psychologist. He'll get it out of him,' said Charlesworth. 'We'll see you downstairs.'

'Where can I find Sam?' whispered Dixon to Louise, when Charlesworth and Potter drifted off along the landing.

'Down in the custody suite, prepping for the interview.'

Training as a psychologist and then joining the police; it had virtually guaranteed Sam West the shit end of the stick, spending his entire life locked in a room with no windows interviewing other people's suspects. Dixon had thought training as a solicitor before joining the police was bad enough, but maybe not.

'Prepping for the interview' turned out to be listening to music on his earphones.

'Sorry, Sir,' said West, sitting up.

'What d'you know about Gavin?' asked Dixon, sliding a chair out from under the table.

'I've seen his prison record and the statement you got from him. I know he's on the autistic spectrum.'

'He was a vulnerable inmate at Bristol. Allan would have known that, and it's my belief that he's used him and his flat.'

'A form of cuckooing then?'

'Pretty much. I'm getting some house to house done in the morning. I want to know from the neighbours exactly how much time Allan spent there and what he got up to, but my guess is Gavin had no choice in any of it.'

'Acting under duress.'

'Exactly.' Dixon nodded. 'Ask the questions and rearrest him if you have to, but start on the basis he was an unwilling participant throughout.'

'A witness rather than a suspect. Yes, Sir.'

Dixon stood up. 'And I hope to God I'm right.'

Charlesworth and Potter had already nabbed front row seats in the anteroom, the screens on the side showing the view from above an empty interview room.

Four chairs were lined up side by side opposite the recording machine that was sitting on a small table bolted to the wall. The new layout always irritated Dixon – designed by someone who had never conducted a police interview; although, thinking about it, maybe this was one interview where building a rapport with the suspect might prove useful. That said, more often than not, a table between interviewer and suspect was invaluable.

Sam West and Louise filed in and sat down, soon followed by Gavin and his solicitor.

Gavin was shuffling along, the laces removed from his trainers, both hands thrust deep into the pockets of baggy trousers.

'If he takes his hands out his pockets, his trousers will fall down,' said Charlesworth, laughing at his own joke.

Dixon stopped himself just in time; a reminder that it was either that or risk Gavin hanging himself in his cell with his belt would hardly foster good relations with the ACC. Jane – his anger management counsellor – would have been proud of him.

'My name is DS Samuel West and to my left is DC Louise Willmott. Please confirm your names for the recording.'

Gavin's solicitor nudged him with his elbow.

'Gavin Curtis.'

'My name is Jasper Sullivan from Cartwrights.'

'This interview is being audio and visually recorded on to a secure digital hard drive,' said West. 'You've been arrested on suspicion of theft, Gavin, and cautioned. Do you understand?'

'Yes.'

'It's late and I'm sure we could all do with getting some sleep. But there are some questions we have to ask you, Gavin. All right?'

'Yes.'

'When did you first meet Frank Allan?'

'Two years ago.'

'Where?'

'Bristol prison.' Gavin was rocking backwards and forwards perched on the edge of his plastic chair, his eyes fixed on the recorder on the table in front of him.

'Then you went to Ford before you were released. Is that right?'

'Yes.'

'When did you see him after that?'

'He came to my flat.'

'Did you let him in?'

'No.'

'Did he force his way in?'

Gavin hesitated, his movements faster and more agitated.

Charlesworth turned to Potter. 'Whose side is West on, for heaven's sake?'

'Mine, Sir.' Dixon was standing behind them, his arms folded.

'It's all right, Gavin,' continued West. 'He can't hurt you now.'

'He took my money and my bank card. I had to sleep on the floor. He took my car too, used it all the time. I had to fill it up with petrol and he used it all.'

'Did he buy things on the internet and have them delivered to your flat?'

'Yes.'

'What things?'

'A crossbow.' Gavin stood up and dropped his trousers, pointing to a scar on the outside of his left thigh. 'He shot me with it.'

'We'll get the police surgeon to look at that as soon as we've finished, all right, Gavin?'

'Yes.'

'Tell me about the crossbow.'

'That was the first one. It was small and the bolts were this long.' Gavin held up his hands, the tips of his index fingers six inches apart. 'It was cheap and not very powerful. Not powerful enough, he said. The second one was bigger, and the bolts were this long.' Fingers two feet apart now.

'Not powerful enough for what?' asked West.

'He didn't say. He took my phone as well.'

'Did you see him use the crossbows?'

'He fired them in my flat, at empty milk cartons filled with water. Then I had to clean up the mess.'

'The larger bow, what was it like?'

'Bigger, like a rifle, with a telescopic sight on top that used a red dot. He told me if I said anything I'd never see the red dot until it was too late.'

'He threatened to kill you?'

'I think that's the implication from what my client just said, don't you?'

'Bloody solicitors,' muttered Charlesworth, turning away from the screen.

'Were you there when he killed Godfrey Collins?' West's voice was suddenly stern.

'No.' Arms clamped across his chest now, the palms of his hands tucked in his armpits. 'He told me he'd killed someone but he didn't say who.'

'Did he say why?'

'He said they'd taken his money.'

'Did he mention the name Keith Finch?'

'No.'

'Did you go with him to Spain?'

'No. I haven't got a passport.'

'Where did you get your laptop?' asked West.

'I'm not supposed to have one,' mumbled Gavin. 'I'm sorry.'

'Who bought it?'

'Frank did. He told me to write a program to override a random number algorithm that he'd downloaded. That was easy. He let me have a burger and chips when I did that.'

'Then you started taking money from the fruit machines?'

'He said if I didn't help him he'd use the red dot on me. And on my mother too.' Tears started to trickle slowly down his cheeks. 'He'd sit in the flat all day with the crossbow loaded, and shine the red dot at me. I'd try to curl up and hide, but he'd kick me and then shine the red dot at me again.'

'I've heard enough.' Charlesworth jabbed the mute button on the remote control. 'It seems the poor lad is a victim in all of this.'

'Unless Allan blames him for everything when he's interviewed tomorrow,' said Potter, turning to face Dixon.

'We'll see what Gavin's neighbours say in the morning,' he replied. 'And his story is corroborated by the injury to his leg. High Tech are checking their phones overnight too. Subject to what comes of that and what Allan says, I'll be releasing Gavin pending investigation.'

'On your head be it,' said Potter, solemnly.

Charlesworth had perfected the conciliatory smile. 'All part and parcel of being the senior investigating officer.'

Dixon arrived home just before 3 a.m. Time enough for a few hours' sleep, then back to Express Park to interview Allan at nine.

He parked in the pub car park and walked across to the cottage, hoping to get in without waking everybody up, although Monty started barking before he had turned his key in the back door. Then the landing light came on.

'Is that you?'

'Yes.' He was watching Monty cocking his leg against the corner of the shed in the back yard.

Jane was leaning against the door frame, her hair covering her face, Dixon's favourite T-shirt on inside out.

'Tea?'

'Thanks.' She yawned, covering her mouth with the back of her hand. 'How's it going?'

'We've arrested a retired prison officer,' replied Dixon, getting another mug out of the cupboard above the kettle. 'I've not interviewed him yet, but it looks like he was taking his revenge on the people who'd conned him out of his pension. He's been living in a van and cuckooing on a vulnerable former inmate, which made him a bit more difficult to find.'

'A good quick result.'

'A little too quick for my liking. They'd been ripping off fruit machines too; four hundred quid a day – nice work if you can get it.' He glanced into the back yard. 'Come on, in!' he said, shutting the back door behind Monty, who came trotting in; either the obedience training had paid off or it was the packet of biscuits in Dixon's hand. 'Where's her ladyship?'

'Gone back to Manchester. She'll be down for the weekend on Friday night. I said I'd pick her up from Highbridge station at nine.' Jane brushed her hair back off her face. 'I had another visit from Charlesworth today, or yesterday I suppose it was. He wanted to know if you'd had any further thoughts about the superintendent's job. There's a vacancy for a DS in CID, apparently; mine if I want it, he said, but not while there's a conflict, what with you being—'

'What did you say?'

'I said I hadn't seen you for a few days – which is true – and that he'd need to ask you what you wanted to do.'

Dixon handed her a mug of tea. 'How about Christmas Eve?'

'What for?'

'Getting married. There might be some decent snow and ice in the Lakes for our honeymoon.'

Chapter Twenty-Five

'Don't forget, Sir, this interview is being audio and visually recorded on to a secure digital hard drive.'

'The wonders of modern science.' Dixon sighed. 'You'll have to operate the machine. I must've missed the training.'

He had pulled rank to get the interview room with the table, and now Dixon and Louise were sitting opposite two empty chairs.

'Bet you he goes "no comment".'

'Did you get home last night?' asked Dixon.

'Yes, Sir. Gave Katie her breakfast too.'

A hushed voice outside: 'If you accept my advice, you'll answer no—' Stopped mid-sentence by the door opening.

Frank Allan walked in briskly and sat down on the plastic chair in the corner, sliding it back until he was able to lean against the wall behind him, arms folded as he watched his solicitor sit down next to him, notebook and pen at the ready.

Thinning closely cropped hair, shorter than his greying beard, and piercing eyes. Allan was wearing grey tracksuit bottoms and a blue sweatshirt – standard issue when your own clothes have gone to Scientific. He rested his head back in the corner of the interview room and closed his eyes.

Louise switched on the recorder.

'This interview is being audio and visually recorded on to a secure digital hard drive,' said Dixon. 'You have been arrested on suspicion of four murders and remain under caution, Frank. D'you understand?'

'It's Mr Allan to you.'

'Identify yourself for the recording, please. Frank.'

Allan's eyes opened and focused on the camera above his head. 'Francis James Allan.' Then he closed his eyes again.

'Katherine Bradbury, Harding and Rowe Advocates, Bridgwater.' She looked up from her notebook. 'For the record, I have advised my client not to answer any questions at this time.'

'You had a busy day on Saturday, didn't you, Frank?' Not a hint of sarcasm in Dixon's voice – he could have gone on the stage, he really could. 'Keith Finch in the morning, then you got all the way down to the Costa del Sol in time to kill James Bowen and Miranda Mather later that same day.'

Allan sat forward and took a deep breath through his nose.

'Miranda Mather in the left eye at twenty-five point two metres,' continued Dixon. 'So, what's that in yards?'

'Twenty-seven and a half.'

'Was there a crosswind?'

'It was downwind.'

'We've got the weather report here somewhere.' Dixon was flicking through the papers in the file on the table in front of him. 'Here it is. From the south-west, seven to ten, gusting to ten to fifteen; that's kilometres per hour, mind you.'

'I had to wait for the wind to drop,' Allan said, smugly. 'She was moving around the bed too. The bolt's a bit heavier with the broadhead on it – four hundred and twenty grains – so that's a drop of about seven inches at twenty-five yards from my bow. I was aiming above her head to make allowances. There was no time to adjust the sight after I killed Bowen, either. It was a hell of a shot, even if I say so myself.'

'Bowen was easy, by comparison; a sitting target.'

'He saw me. Sat up on the sun lounger and looked straight at me.' Allan closed his left eye and mimed the pulling of a trigger. 'I couldn't miss.'

'They measured that one at nineteen metres.'

'I was lying down on the top of the outcrop – a single shot fired up through the balustrade.'

'The bolt was on a rising trajectory, according to the post mortem.' Dixon closed the file in front of him. 'Let's deal with the mechanics of it then, so we can verify the details. You know what the CPS are like for details. How did you get down there?'

'No comment.'

'You must've flown, otherwise you wouldn't have got there in time. Where did you fly from?'

'No comment.'

'Bristol?'

Allan sighed, a faint smile creeping across his lips. 'I took Gavin's car, that's all I'm saying.'

'We'll talk about Gavin in a minute, if that's all right. How long's the flight?'

'You know you've got to pay extra for a meal these days. It's a bloody rip-off.'

'Where did you fly from?'

'No comment.'

'And you hired a car down there, I suppose?'

Silence.

'How did you get your crossbow on the plane?' asked Dixon.

'I bought one down there.'

'Where?'

'I don't remember.'

'Where is it now?'

'I dumped it in the sea opposite their villa.'

'So, that's six hours travelling and, say, twelve hours down there.'

'I was away for two days all told.'

'Were you working at Castle Amusements at the time?' asked Dixon.

'I started that job on Monday when I got back. I was in between jobs when I went to Spain.'

'Why did you kill them?'

'You know why! I wouldn't be here if you hadn't worked that out.'

'I need you to tell me, for the tape. You know how it is.'

'They ripped off my bloody pension, didn't they? And now they've got left exactly what I've got.' Allan sneered. 'Nothing.'

'When did you first meet James Bowen?'

'I dealt with that little shit Craig Pengelly, and he put me on to Bowen. That was two years ago, maybe. Craig contacted me on Facebook; saw that I was a prison officer, I suppose, and suggested I transfer my pension. I was getting divorced at the time and *she* wanted half of it, so it seemed like a good idea to try and increase the return on what was left.'

'You transferred your pension on the say-so of someone you met on Facebook?' Dixon tried to hide his small laugh of disbelief. Maybe a career on the stage wasn't an option.

'I'm not that bloody stupid.' Allan cleared his throat. 'I met him for a beer and then had a follow-up meeting at their offices in Weston. That's when I met Bowen.'

'How long did it all take?'

'About four months. The trustees of the prison service pension fund approved it because Clearwater was registered with the tax office and that was that. The next thing I know Clearwater's gone under and your lot are on their tails. That's when I checked my pension statements. Then the tax bill arrived.'

'How much did you have left of your fund?'

'Nothing. Absolutely bloody nothing.'

'What did you say to the other prison officers you'd recommended to Bowen and Clearwater?'

'What could I say?'

'How many were there?'

'Six that I referred to Bowen.'

'Did you get a referral fee?'

'A two hundred quid M&S voucher,' whispered Allan, clearly too embarrassed to say it out loud.

Dixon decided it was time to change tack. 'How many times did you meet Ian Staveley?'

'Who is Ian Staveley?' demanded Allan's solicitor.

'He's the accountant who tried to help us get our money back,' replied Allan. 'He was dealing with the income tax demands for us as well.' He turned to Dixon. 'We were referred to him by the solicitor; a fat lot of bloody good he was. Ramped up the fees with court proceedings in Spain and we still got sod all back. I met Staveley once. Why?'

Dixon picked up a large evidence bag on the floor next to his chair and dropped it on the table with a thud. 'Did you use this bow?'

No reply.

'We found it under the shower tray in your minibus.'

Allan gave an almost imperceptible nod.

'For the tape, Frank.'

'That's my crossbow and I used it to kill Godfrey Collins and Keith Finch.' He was tipping his head from side to side as he spoke. 'I used an identical one to kill James Bowen and Miranda Mather.'

'Why did you choose a crossbow?'

'Why not?' Allan clearly thought it an odd question, turning to his solicitor and frowning. 'They're cheap, legal to buy and own, silent, accurate. What more d'you want?'

'Let me ask you about Keith Finch,' said Dixon.

'The taxman?'

'Tell me about his murder.'

'I was in the field at the back of his house and shot him when he was pruning his roses.'

'Range?'

'Twenty yards, I suppose.'

'What sort of tree was it?'

'How the hell am I supposed to know that? I'm not Monty bloody Don.'

'How many shots?'

'One.'

'You're sure you fired one bolt?'

'Yes.'

'Where did you hit him?'

'In the eye.'

Dixon took a deep breath and exhaled slowly through his nose. 'You see, Finch was hit by two bolts. The first, as far as we can tell, was fired from thirty yards away and hit him in the left cheek, just below the cheekbone.' He was pointing at his left cheek with his right index finger. 'About here. The killer then closed in to twenty yards for the kill shot that hit him in the eye.' He squinted at Allan. 'And the wind was lighter, if anything, according to the weather report.'

'Yes, two, sorry. The first one pulled a bit. I snatched at it.'

'Why him, though?'

'He was pursuing me for an income tax bill, for fuck's sake.' Allan's fist slammed down on the table. 'They said I'd made a pension withdrawal and taxed me on it. I'd lost everything and then he lands me with this fucking great bill and tells me to pay up. Just like that!'

'That wasn't him,' said Dixon, calmly. 'He was just the office manager – the poor sod who had the misfortune to have his name on the letters.'

Allan's breathing quickened. He looked up at the ceiling, tearing at strips of dry skin on his lips with his teeth.

'What about Godfrey Collins then? Why did you kill him?'

'He was the accountant, wasn't he?'

Dixon sensed he was losing Allan, his answers getting shorter as he retreated into his shell, his bragging done; the reality of his situation was sinking in, perhaps. It wouldn't be long before the 'no comments' started coming thick and fast.

'Let's talk about Gavin.' Dixon tried a change of subject. 'When did you meet him?'

'At Bristol. I worked my entire life in the prison service until I got the shit kicked out of me, and I've got absolutely fucking nothing to show for it, and that little scrotum is released from prison straight into a flat they even furnished for him. And he gets bloody benefits to piss up the wall.' Allan's voice was getting louder and louder. 'While I'm living in a sodding van. So, yeah, I moved in.'

'Did he invite you in?'

'No.'

'Say you could stay?'

'Of course he didn't. "Leave me be," he kept saying, over and over.'

'Whose idea was it to hack the fruit machines?'

'Mine. It was easy money once you got the back panel open. A couple of jackpots and leave it at that.' Allan looked at Dixon and shook his head. 'Hope some other mug comes along and tops it back up again for you.'

'Was Gavin a willing participant?'

'Look, I tormented the poor lad. It's not his fault. Really. I suppose I threatened him with the crossbow and the red dot on the sight. I kept shining it at his forehead until he stopped crying and did as he was told.' He was plucking hairs from his beard and flicking them on the floor. 'I feel bad about it now.' Shaking his head at the memory.

'But not the murders?'

'No, not the murders.'

'Did Gavin lend you his car?'

'I took it.'

'Did he know about the murders?'

'No.'

'OK, let's clear up a few loose ends while we're here. Why the sheep?'

'Got to start somewhere. And you know what they say, practice makes perfect.'

'Why the broadheads with the curved blades?'

'I saw them online and thought it might be fun. They were just like the Clearwater logo and I enjoyed the joke. Let's leave it at that, shall we?'

'I think my client has cooperated fully, Chief Inspector.' The solicitor closed her notebook.

'One last question.' Dixon fixed Allan in a hard stare. 'How did you kill Godfrey Collins?'

Allan rolled his eyes. 'I shot him with my crossbow in Harptree Combe.'

'How many times?'

'Eh?'

'How many times did you shoot him?' Dixon was sliding his pen into his inside jacket pocket. 'It's a simple enough question. How many bolts?'

'I . . .' Allan hesitated. 'I don't remember.'

'I think I'd remember,' said Dixon, turning to Louise. 'Wouldn't you, Constable?'

'Yes, I would.'

'He was the first and I panicked,' mumbled Allan. 'I really can't remember how many shots I fired.'

'Was he sitting or standing?'

'I can't remember.'

'You said Collins was *the* accountant. He was *an* accountant, yes, but he had nothing to do with the pension transfer scam; he played no part in it whatsoever. So, I'm wondering why you killed him?'

Allan bared his gritted teeth. 'No. Fucking. Comment.'

Chapter Twenty-Six

Charlesworth and Potter were lurking in the corridor when Dixon and Louise emerged from the interview room.

'Well done, Nick.' Charlesworth was rubbing his hands together. 'I'm looking forward to this press conference.'

Dixon turned to Potter, hoping the inferences to be drawn from Allan's interview had not been lost on her, at least. Her response – a shrug – was not altogether encouraging.

'What?' demanded Charlesworth.

'Do I really have to—?' Dixon stopped himself just in time, the answer to his question blindingly obvious. 'Every single piece of information he gave us about the killings on the Costa fits,' he continued. 'I have no doubt whatsoever that he was the shooter, but why wouldn't he tell us how he got down there?'

'I don't know.' Charlesworth seemed taken aback. 'Why?'

'Because he knows we'll check.' Dixon was on a roll now, his voice gathering momentum. 'Either way, he didn't kill Finch, and I don't believe he killed Collins either. Every single piece of information he gave us about both of their murders is wrong. And look at the accuracy, or rather the lack of it. It must be a different shooter.'

'He admitted it,' protested Charlesworth.

'He lied. He couldn't even remember how many bolts he'd fired. And if you look at the accuracy with which he despatched Miranda Mather in particular, it's painfully obvious Collins and Finch were killed by someone else.'

Charlesworth rubbed his forehead with the palm of his hand, then allowed his hand to slip down over his eyes. 'We'll end up having to extradite Allan to Spain unless you find something on him.'

'A fruit machine scam hardly trumps two murders,' grumbled Potter.

'There's conspiracy to murder,' said Dixon. 'We can hold him on that and I've no doubt the CPS will authorise a charge. There's clear planning: they're using the same weapon, the same broadheads, and whoever reconnoitred Finch's bungalow also used Gavin's car to do it.'

'Well, Allan's not going anywhere, is he?' said Charlesworth. 'He'll have spent his whole bloody life in prison by the time he snuffs it.'

'What do we tell them at the press conference?' asked Potter.

'Nothing,' replied Dixon, turning for the door. 'Cancel it.'

Dixon, Cole and Louise were back in Area J by lunchtime. Allan's further detention had been authorised and he remained in custody, while Gavin was on his way home to Weston.

Mark was sitting in front of his computer and some of the other workstations were occupied, but most of the major investigation team were out and about. 'Jez was looking for you, Sir,' he said. 'Something about moving some of the team to other duties now you've made an arrest.'

'It's not over until I say it's over.'

'She said she'd come back later.'

'How have you got on?'

'Nothing from Bristol airport, so I'm trying Cardiff, Exeter and Birmingham now. That's just ticket bookings in his name; if he travelled on a false passport then we're looking at hours and hours of CCTV. It'll take months.'

'Anything on Gavin's bank account?'

'Nothing.'

'Let's assume I'm right and someone else really did kill Finch. Why kill him the same day Allan kills Bowen and Mather?'

'Finch would have been at work Monday to Friday,' offered Cole. 'So, Saturday morning would have been the first chance to catch him in his back garden.'

'We're supposed to think all four were killed by the same person, aren't we, so maybe they timed it deliberately to make us think the killer flew down to the Costa del Sol?' replied Louise. 'If he went another way, we'd be checking flights to and from Malaga from here, there and everywhere, chasing our tails for months on end and coming up with nothing.'

Dixon turned to Mark. 'Check the ferries and Channel Tunnel. Give them Gavin's car registration number and see if it pops up anywhere.'

'Yes, Sir.'

'What about fingerprints?'

'The bolts had been wiped clean and there was no DNA either,' replied Louise. 'Apart from the victim's, of course.'

'Finch was killed by someone else.' Dixon was sitting on the windowsill talking to himself. 'Someone who must have been driving a different car because Allan had Gavin's. Let's get the crime scene photographs from the sheep killings over to Scientific, Nigel.

Ask their photo boffin to see if they can identify three sets of foot-prints. Allan's, the farmer's and A. N. Other's.'

'Yes, Sir.'

'We need Dave to start checking cars again, really. When are they due back?'

'They get in at ten-thirty tonight and he said he'd come in,' replied Mark, his hand over the mouthpiece of his phone.

'Anything popping up on the mobile phones?'

'Allan's had a pay-as-you-go SIM in it, Sir,' replied Louise, from behind her computer screen. 'Only activated a couple of days ago. A trace shows he never left the Burnham area in that time, just moving between the seafront and the campsite.'

'No calls on it?'

'None. Just data usage.'

'How are we doing with the rest of the pension scam victims?'

'We're going through them now, Sir.' Louise sat back in her chair and pushed herself away from her workstation. 'None own a crossbow, or rather none will admit to owning a crossbow. We found a couple more who'd used Ian Staveley to help them with the income tax. He'd done a bit of advertising, apparently. "Have you transferred your pension and been landed with an income tax bill?" – that sort of thing. He picked up a few clients from that. Oh, and that prepper bloke Tressider, it turns out his stepfather is one of the pension scam victims.'

'He was on the crossbow list,' said Cole, looking up.

'His stepfather's lost his pension, his fiancée's up to her arm-pits in the loan charge thing and he owns three crossbows.' Dixon sighed. 'Let's pick him up and see what he's got to say for himself.'

'Shall I see if Nailsea police station have got an interview room?' asked Louise. 'Although it's only a back office in the fire station, these d—'

'You're sure?' Mark's voice had gone from background murmur to drowning out those around him, the phone still clamped to his ear. 'Thursday night; Plymouth to Santander. Who was driving the car?' He turned to Dixon and raised his eyebrows. 'You don't know. What about the ticket?'

Dixon waited.

'A prepaid credit card in the name of Gavin Curtis; departing Plymouth Thursday night, arriving Santander Saturday morning. What about CCTV at the ferry terminal and on the ferry? Yes, Portishead. Thank you.' Mark finished scribbling a note of the conversation before replacing the handset.

'Get on to Sergio Alvaro and see what they've got at the Spanish end,' said Dixon. 'And we'd better get someone down to Brittany Ferries to keep on top of that CCTV footage.'

'Yes, Sir.'

'I wonder how long it takes to drive from Santander down to Malaga?'

'Nine hours and thirty-seven minutes. I'm googling it now,' replied Cole. 'The crafty buggers.'

'That's it then.' Dixon curled his lip. 'Allan couldn't have killed Keith Finch – he'd have been on a Spanish motorway at the time – which means there really is another shooter with a crossbow out there.'

'We were supposed to believe his confession and not be looking for anyone else.'

'You're starting to sound like the assistant chief constable, Nigel,' said Dixon. 'We'll use Weston to see Tressider. Then we'll go and see Craig; see what he remembers about Frank Allan.'

'I'll ring Leyhill.' Louise picked up her phone.

'Then there's Collins,' said Cole, nodding. 'Did you see Allan's reaction when you asked him why you killed him?'

Dixon had become distracted listening to Louise's end of the conversation with someone at Leyhill open prison.

'What? When?' She looked at him, her mouth pinched in fury. 'You were supposed to let us know when he was being released! What address did he give?' She was scribbling on the notepad in front of her. 'Postcode? Yes, I know it's not your fault.' She mouthed 'his parents' as she handed the notepad up to Dixon, who was leaning over the partition. 'I'm sorry if I—' She stopped mid-sentence when she heard the dial tone.

Dixon had disconnected the call, his finger still pressed down on the hook. 'No, you're not,' he said. 'There's someone out there killing the people who ripped off his pension and some bright spark at Leyhill has just released his next target. "Sorry" doesn't come into it.'

'I came in here for a burglary once.' Cole was admiring the immaculate front lawns as Dixon turned in to Wavering Down Rise. 'They've all got alarms on them now; the crime prevention officer saw to that.'

'They're nice houses.'

'Prime targets, more like. You've got the A38 and the A371 for your getaway, then there's the motorway. And they stick out like a sore thumb on the side of the hill here.'

That much was true. Dixon had often noticed the small development of big houses as he sped by on the A38. Maybe on a detective superintendent's salary he might just be able to afford the smallest one, tucked away in the corner?

Cole was scrolling furiously on his phone in the passenger seat. 'Number one went for six hundred grand in 2006, according to the sold prices on Rightmove.'

Maybe not, then.

'Who needs a six bedroom house, I ask you?' Cole was warming up, his rant gathering pace and volume.

'A family with four kids?'

'Bollocks. Get 'em bloody bunk beds.'

Number fourteen was in the far corner. The view from the back might be worth seeing – looking south-east over Cheddar Reservoir, unless it was blocked by a hedge or trees.

'They bought it in 2007 for five-seven-five.' Cole swiped across, glancing at the old estate agent's photographs. 'And what's that small bay window above the front door all about? The flat roof's a recipe for disaster.'

'We're not here for a bloody viewing, Nige,' said Dixon, looking up at the house as he turned off the engine. Rendered and painted cream, three dormer windows on the second floor set into the terra-cotta roof tiles; and he had to admit Cole had a point about the bay window, perhaps. The leaded windows would be a pain to clean too.

Dixon knocked on the solid oak front door, peering through the narrow windows either side. They looked more like the arrow slits you'd find in the ruins of a medieval castle and were a trifle disconcerting, given the current situation.

'Mrs Pengelly?' he asked, when the door finally opened. 'Detective Chief Inspector Dixon, and this is Constable Cole.'

'What's he done now?' She sighed. 'Is he even out yet?'

'I take it Craig isn't here?'

Her eyes narrowed. 'He's not welcome here. He knows that, even if you don't.'

'Only he gave this address.'

'Well, he shouldn't have done.'

'May we come in?' Dixon was conscious that the neighbour pruning the hedge was craning her neck to listen.

Mrs Pengelly stepped back into the hall. 'I was just going out.' She gestured to a Land Rover Discovery parked on the drive, two black labradors watching them from the side window at the back. 'This way,' she said, making no effort to hide her reluctance. Blue jeans, a navy blue pullover, blue waxed jacket; at least the wellington boots sitting on the mat inside the back door were green. Someone was sitting on the verandah outside, his or her face buried in a broadsheet newspaper. 'That's my husband. He's a management consultant and works from home.' She leaned out through the open patio doors. 'Michael, the police are here. Again.'

Cole sat down at the kitchen island and placed his notebook on the black granite worktop, the rustle of the broadsheet newspaper outside carrying over the scraping of the wooden stool on the tiled floor. There was a good deal of huffing and puffing too, although Dixon couldn't hear what was being said; apart from the expletives.

Michael slammed his folded newspaper down on the worktop as he stepped into the kitchen. 'I take it this is about Craig?' Red corduroys and a check shirt open at the neck.

'Yes, Sir,' replied Dixon.

'Is he out yet?'

'He was released this morning and gave this address.'

'He's not here.' Michael was filling the kettle, an offer of a cup of tea not forthcoming even when his wife glared at him and nodded in Cole's direction.

'How many children d'you have?' asked Dixon, turning his back on the view of Cheddar Reservoir.

'Three.'

'Two,' snapped Michael. It was his turn to glare at his wife now. 'Jasper is up at Oxford and Charlotte works in the City. She's a solicitor at Clifford Chance.'

'And what about Craig?'

'He's no son of mine.' Calm and detached.

Dixon had guessed as much from the photo montage mounted on the wall in the hall. He had glanced at it on his way through to the kitchen; a boy and a girl at various stages of growing up. And not a single picture of Craig. 'Either he is your son, or he isn't. Now which is it?'

'We no longer have any contact with him,' said Mrs Pengelly. 'He's our eldest and let's just say he went off the rails.'

'You saw him at Laura's memorial service,' said Dixon.

'We went out of respect for her parents, really. Not for Craig.' She turned away. 'We didn't speak to him.'

Now was not the time to pull punches. 'Let me be absolutely clear about what's going on here.' Dixon was bristling and making no real effort to hide it. 'There's someone out there with a crossbow killing the people involved in the pension transfer scam. James Bowen is dead; Miranda Mather is dead; Keith Finch is dead; Godfrey Collins is dead. And that leaves Craig.'

'Well, that's his lookout, isn't it.' Michael Pengelly remained oddly impassive as he poured himself a coffee.

'Who's Keith Finch?' Mrs Pengelly spoke idly, pretending to look for something in her handbag. 'I don't remember that name.'

'He was the enforcement officer at HM Revenue and Customs.'

'Just doing his job.' Michael sneered. 'Did he have family?'

'A wife and daughter.'

'There's a grandchild too,' said Cole, looking up.

'Another of Craig's victims.' Michael tipped his coffee down the sink and reached for a tumbler. 'I don't remember a Godfrey Collins either.'

'Michael, it's too early for that,' whispered Mrs Pengelly, watching her husband take a bottle of Scotch from the cupboard.

A measure of whisky to match the measure of defiance as he raised his glass to her and took a swig.

'When I met him,' said Dixon, 'he told me that he was an innocent victim of the pension scam; that he'd been used by Bowen and Mather. Wasn't he a trainee financial adviser at the time?'

'He never studied a day in his life and certainly never sat any of the exams. And he knew full well what he was doing.' Michael drained his glass and reached for the bottle. 'The jury didn't believe that innocent victim story and neither did we.'

'You were at the trial?'

'We were.' Mrs Pengelly jabbed her car keys at Dixon. 'Each and every day. We've stood by that boy through thick and thin, but the guilty verdict was the end. No more.' Her jaw was clenched, no sign of a tear, let alone a hint of regret. 'Everyone has their breaking point.'

'Talk to me about the thick and thin.'

Michael let out an exaggerated sigh, long and loud. 'It started when he was expelled from school.'

'What for?'

'Drugs.'

'He was an occasional user.' Mrs Pengelly spoke softly, almost embarrassed to say it. 'That's all he'd ever admit to anyway.'

'Then there was the vandalism.' Michael raised his eyebrows at his wife. 'D'you remember that? Cost us a pretty packet to get him out of that.'

'And he burgled a neighbour's house. We paid for him to go travelling after that; Australia and the Far East. Then when he got back things started going missing. We didn't notice it at first, until he took that painting of your mother's.' Mrs Pengelly was watching her husband taking another swig of whisky. 'He was stealing from us, selling it at auction and buying drugs and alcohol. So, we did what we had to do.'

'Rehab?' asked Cole.

'God, we tried that. Three times at the Priory and each time he was back to his old ways within a month. No, we kicked him out.'

'He went to Bristol for a while and then came back; ended up living in some shithole in Burnham.' Michael was leaning against the worktop and starting to sway, a slight slur creeping in. 'That's when he met Laura.'

'A ray of sunshine, she was.' Mrs Pengelly managed a smile at the memory. 'He got a job, not that he kept it for long. They had this idea they were going to buy a derelict barn in France and do it up. They were going to live in a caravan and do the work themselves, then sell it on and do another and another.'

'He came to us for the money,' mumbled Michael. 'And we gave it to him.'

'No, we didn't. We said we'd buy the barn for them, but we wouldn't just hand over the cash. God knows where it would have ended up. So, we bought the barn.' She shrugged. 'We've still got it. The bloody thing's crumbling away in a field just outside Plouvien. It'd make a nice little *gîte*, or whatever they call it.'

'D'you know where he is now?'

'No.'

'Would Charlotte or Jasper have spoken to him?'

'No. I'm not sure he'd even know where they are,' replied Mrs Pengelly.

'Where d'you think he could be then?'

'Laura had a friend in Bristol and they were sleeping on the sofa when Craig was on bail. They had to give an address and we said no.'

'What about Laura's parents?'

'They knew nothing about it until he was sent down. They didn't even know she was pregnant.'

Dixon thought he saw the first sign of a tear in the corner of Mrs Pengelly's eye.

'He or she would've been our first grandchild,' she said, wiping her cheek with her finger.

'So, what you're saying is you have no idea where he might be.'

'He spent time living on the streets in Bristol. Maybe he went back there?'

'I can tell you exactly where he's gone.' Michael was waving his tumbler at Dixon. 'Back to the bloody gutter where he belongs.'

Chapter Twenty-Seven

'Looks all right when the tide's in, doesn't it, Sir?'

'It's going out.' That much was clear from the wet sand under the wheels of his Land Rover as Dixon drove along the beach at Uphill towards the Weston Bay Yacht Club. People were moving about on several boats moored on the River Axe; others further out and motoring in after an early morning's sailing in the Bristol Channel.

The clubhouse was up on stilts, a line of black seaweed marking high water at the bottom of the steps, the waves now lapping on the sand some twenty yards down the beach, the sun shimmering on the first sliver of grey mud as the water receded along the banks of the tidal river. Another couple of hours and the yachts would be sitting on the mud, their keels buried deep until the tide lifted them off again.

Beyond the clubhouse a line of cars and vans had been reversed as tight as possible to the dunes, the high water mark a few feet from their front bumpers.

'It was a ten point two metre tide.' Cole was looking at his phone. 'I suppose they get to know when it's safe to park on the beach and when it's not.'

'I suppose they do.' Ten point two metres wouldn't have left enough room at Berrow, but there was always the church car park.

'They had a spate of break-ins a couple of years back.' Cole slid his phone into his jacket pocket. 'Some of the boats and the old clubhouse.'

'Don't tell me, that was Craig as well.'

'No idea, Sir. We never nicked anyone for it.'

Dixon was backing up to the dunes. 'We'll ask in the clubhouse. Someone's bound to know where they are.'

Five minutes later they were walking along the beach towards the pontoon, a small yacht moored on the end facing towards them and out to sea. 'Summoning up the courage,' the bar steward had said. 'It's their first time out since . . . you know . . .'

Dixon knew.

'You're looking for a boat called *Laura's Dream*.'

And there it was. They'd managed the short trip from the marina at Uphill on the last high tide, but had sat this one out at the pontoon. It would be dark for the next and they'd only booked the pontoon for three days. The bar steward had been a mine of information.

Louise had rung ahead, so Geoffrey and Pamela Dicken were expecting them, Geoffrey most anxious that they shouldn't have to go over it all again. He'd been at pains to impress that on Louise and she had passed it on, as she promised she would.

Geoffrey was waiting for them on deck, making a half-hearted effort to polish something.

'You'll be the police.' He was watching Dixon and Cole walking along the pontoon.

'Yes, Sir.'

'Come aboard. We're sitting on the mud already here, so you'll be quite safe.'

Laura's Dream was a small yacht, twenty feet or so, the odd footprint here or there on the deck, but otherwise immaculate. Dixon climbed down into the cockpit while Cole stayed on the pontoon.

'The police are here, Pam.'

'What's this all about?' she asked, as her husband helped her up the steps.

She looked older than her years. Retired, yes, but Dixon suspected it had more to do with losing her only daughter at sea.

'We're looking for Craig Pengelly,' replied Dixon. 'He was released from Leyhill this morning and he's not at his parents' address.'

'You were at Laura's memorial service.'

'I was.'

'You didn't know her, did you?'

'No.'

'He wouldn't go to his parents.' Pam dropped a coil of rope on the deck and started coiling it up all over again. 'He'd never go there.'

'It's the address he gave to the prison service.'

'It may have been.'

'Have you seen him?' asked Dixon. 'It's very important we find him. For his own safety, I should add. Not for any other reason.'

'What's going on?' Geoffrey had finished polishing the wheel and was now working his way along the boom.

'We suspect that one of the victims of the pension scam is settling scores. Four of those involved are dead and Craig is the last person left alive. He was safe while he was in Leyhill, but he was released this morning.'

Geoffrey looked at his wife and raised his eyebrows.

'He came here this morning,' she said. 'A couple of hours ago; you've not long missed him.'

'What was he wearing?'

'Blue jeans and a black top, I think; a sweatshirt thing with a hood on it, so I suppose it's one of those hoodie things they wear these days.'

'Shoes?' asked Cole, from up on the pontoon.

'Don't remember, sorry,' replied Geoffrey. 'He was carrying a small blue rucksack though.'

'What did he want?'

Geoffrey took a deep breath, blowing the air out slowly through his nose. He glanced at his wife. 'Pam's applied to the High Court for a declaration of presumed death and he wasn't happy about it.'

'He was furious.' Pam was dabbing her eyes with a tissue.

'He seems to think it should've been his responsibility, but they weren't married and the law is quite clear. She was my stepdaughter, so it's for Pam to apply as her mother.'

'He said we should have told him first in that case, and I suppose we should have done,' said Pam. 'But we just didn't think.'

'Is there a hearing fixed?' asked Dixon.

'Monday at two,' replied Geoffrey.

'He's not a bad lad.' Pam leaned back against the railing. 'Not that his parents would agree, mind you.'

'How did he meet Laura?'

'Burnham Sailing Club,' said Geoffrey. 'She was there sailing and he was picking up litter as part of one of his Community Service Orders; possession of cannabis that time, I think it was. He had to do two hundred and fifty hours' unpaid work or something like that.'

'When was this?'

'Five years ago.'

'That sounds about right,' said Pam, coiling the rope for a third time. 'She was keen on her sailing. Good at it too; she raced the small yachts – lasers – and crewed on the bigger yachts as well. There's good money to be made at that. *Sunset Boulevard* was going to be her first transatlantic trip.'

'There's been a suggestion it was a drug run,' said Dixon, tentatively. 'That *Sunset Boulevard* was carrying drugs in her keel.'

'Rubbish.' Geoffrey threw his cloth into the cockpit and started retying the rigging. 'I don't believe it for a second. There's no way Laura would have gone knowing that.'

'Or coopering, perhaps. That's where they meet a larger boat and transfer the drugs.'

'No, I said.' Geoffrey turned his back on Dixon. 'You never met her.'

'No, I didn't, I'm afraid.'

'She sorted Craig out.' Pam sat down behind the wheel, licked the tip of her thumb and started rubbing at a smudge on the stainless steel. 'She got him off the drugs and alcohol; he even got himself a job. Then he decided to train as a financial adviser.'

'Did you go to his trial?' Dixon let Pam's change of subject pass.

'We went for the start, and then the verdict and sentencing. It was for Laura's sake as much as anything; to support her.'

'Did you believe his story that he was a victim, that Bowen and Mather had used him?'

'We did.'

'I know his parents didn't,' said Geoffrey. 'But they'd washed their hands of him long before that. The first time they kicked him out he was just eighteen and ended up on the streets in Bristol. "Tough love", they called it.'

'More like no bloody love at all,' sneered Pam.

'He was never going to live up to their expectations, not like his siblings who were top of the class at everything, first team colours and all that.' Geoffrey pulled on a rope, unfurling the sail a few feet. 'He just isn't made that way; poor lad never stood a chance. He tried, though, for Laura's sake, and was doing really well; he even went abroad for work a couple of times, to Spain, I think.'

'Were you disappointed when he and Laura got together?'

'Not really. He was her choice.'

'Every parent wants the best for their daughter, so I'd be lying if I said I was thrilled.' Pam was still rubbing at the mark on the wheel. 'But he tried to turn his life around, he really did, and Laura was happy, wasn't she, Geoff?'

'She was.'

'Did they mention a barn in Brittany?'

'It seemed like a mad scheme to us.' He curled his lip. 'But they were keen and it would've been fun, if nothing else.'

'His parents bought it, is that right?'

'We both put in the money.' Pam sounded indignant now.

'Look, let's not get carried away here,' said Geoffrey. 'It was only twenty thousand to buy it and we put in half each. It's not as if we bought them a chateau, for heaven's sake. It's registered in Laura's name, which is why we need the presumed death thing, so we can sell it and give his parents their money back.'

'Would he have gone there?' Dixon was glancing over the side rail, the yacht listing slowly as it settled on the mud, the ropes lashed to the pontoon creaking under the strain.

'He'll have gone back to Bristol. He had friends there.'

'There's nothing in Brittany,' said Pam. 'It's just a shell. There's not even a roof on it at the moment.'

'Did he give you a mobile phone number?'

Geoffrey handed Dixon a piece of paper, which he passed up to Cole.

'That's the same one he gave the prison service.' Cole shook his head. 'It's not in service.'

'Why would he give us a number that's no good?' asked Pam.

'Maybe he knew you'd give it to us.' Dixon stepped up on to the side deck. 'You will tell him to get in touch with us immediately if you see him or hear from him again? It's for his own safety.'

'We will,' replied Geoffrey.

'Are you going out on tomorrow's tide?' Dixon asked.

'We haven't got the stomach for it any more.' Pam blinked away a tear. 'We thought we did, but we don't.'

'We'll motor back round to the marina in the morning,' said Geoffrey. 'Then it's out of the water and on the market. You don't want to buy a yacht, do you?'

'The end of *Laura's Dream*,' said Pam, the tears flowing freely now.

'They've got Tressider at Weston,' said Louise. 'He's been there about an hour now.'

Dixon was holding his phone to his left ear with his right hand while he put on his seatbelt. 'We'll go there now. Is the tail in place to pick him up when he leaves?'

'Yes, Sir.'

'Good. In the meantime, get the CCTV ops room at Bristol city centre looking for Craig – Nigel's emailing you the description now – and we'll head up there when we've finished with Tressider. Anything else going on?'

'Not really. Dave's back and working on the Daewoo with Kevin. The rest are working their way through the pension victims, checking alibis and such. No alarm bells so far. Oh, and Jez was on the prowl again, looking for a chat with you about personnel.'

Dixon transferred his phone to his left hand and turned the key, the diesel engine rumbling to life. 'What did you tell her?'

'There wasn't anything I could tell her.'

'What about Gavin's neighbours?'

'They confirm Allan moved in. His van was parked at the back for a while and the bloke in the upstairs flat said he heard banging and shouting. He even saw Allan driving Gavin's car.'

'That's enough to put Gavin in the clear, but no doubt Charlesworth will want the CPS to have a look at it.'

'Better go, Sir,' whispered Louise. 'Incoming; Potter with Jez in tow.'

Dixon rang off. 'Right, let's get this Tressider bloke out of the way and then get up to Bristol, see if we can't find Craig before someone else does.'

'Someone with a crossbow,' muttered Cole.

'You're not under arrest, Mr Tressider,' said Dixon, sitting down opposite him in the interview room at Weston-super-Mare police station twenty minutes later.

'Do I need a solicitor?'

'I don't think so. Do you?'

'Well, I've not done anything wrong, apart from a bit of speeding maybe. So, no, I don't think so either.'

'That was your M3 in the car park?'

'Lovely, isn't it?'

'I'm not really a car buff, I'm afraid.'

'He drives an old Land Rover.' Cole arched his back. 'Bloody uncomfortable, it is.'

'We're investigating four murders, Mr Tressider. One of the victims was involved in the loan charge scheme that your fiancée, Nicky, was caught up in; two victims were involved in a pension transfer scam and the fourth was a taxman who seems to have played a part in both.'

'What's this got to do with me?' Tressider frowned. 'You checked the dates I gave you. I know you spoke to Nicky.'

'A fiancée is never the best alibi,' said Dixon. 'And we've got a couple more dates to check now, sadly.'

'Fire away.' Tressider sat up, his arms outstretched, the palms of his hands open. 'I've got nothing to hide.'

'Have you been to Spain recently?'

'No. We went to Faro for a week a couple of months ago, and had a weekend in Amsterdam, but that's it. And we're off to Rome for three nights next month. It's useful living near Bristol airport and the flights are dirt cheap.'

'Does the name James Bowen mean anything to you?'

'Yeah, I did the graphics for Clearwater; designed their logo and did them a website. I'm assuming it's the same James Bowen?'

'It is.'

'I'd not long started on my own and it was one of my first jobs. Nice bloke, easy to deal with. Prompt payer too. Is he all right?'

'He's dead, Sir.'

'What was it, an accident or something?'

'A crossbow.'

Blood drains from people's faces at varying speeds; some faster than others. Dixon had learned that a long time ago, but the change in Tressider was dramatic – from flushed to deathly pale in a jiffy.

'And you think I . . . ?' His voice tailed off.

'We have questions we have to ask, boxes we have to tick.' Dixon offered his best pained expression, almost apologetic even as he watched Tressider leaning on the table with his head in his hands.

'I . . . I didn't, of course I didn't. What possible reason would I have for doing that?'

'James Bowen and Miranda Mather were involved in a pension transfer scam that fleeced hundreds of people out of their pension funds; lifetimes of savings and dreams of retirement gone in a flash. And my understanding is that your stepfather is one of those victims.'

'He said he'd had the police around, but didn't say what for. So, what, do you think I lent him one of my crossbows?'

'There's an interesting idea, Constable.' Dixon leaned across and tapped Cole's notebook. 'Make a note of it.'

'You're taking the piss now.' Tressider glared at him.

'Did you know he'd lost his pension?'

'No.'

'Your mother never mentioned it?'

'She said he had a big tax bill, but not what it was for. Look, they only married a couple of years ago. I was an adult and had left home long before that, so it's not like he was a big part of my life or anything. We don't discuss that sort of stuff. Never have.'

'What about your pension?'

'I can't afford to pay into a private pension, so I'll just have to worry about it when I get there.'

'Have you ever come across someone by the name of Francis Allan, or Frank perhaps?'

'No.'

'Ever play the fruit machines in the arcades?'

'That's a mug's game.'

'You see, I'm struggling, Mark,' said Dixon, squinting at Tressider. 'I've got four murders, all of them clearly connected by the same weapon, and yet the motive for one seems to be different to the other three. And the only person I've come across who might have a motive for killing all four is you.'

'Me?' Tressider managed to force a sarcastic chuckle. 'You're barking up the wrong tree then, mate.' He stood up. 'You said I was free to go?'

'You are.'

'Right, that's it then. I'm out of here.'

Dixon watched him snatch open the door and stalk off along the corridor towards the front desk.

'What was that all about?' asked Cole.

'Now we've ruffled his feathers, we'll put a tail on him,' replied Dixon. 'See where he goes. Otherwise known as clutching at straws.'

Chapter Twenty-Eight

'And what's Craig wearing?'

'Blue jeans and a black hoodie,' replied Cole, sliding an empty chair across from the adjacent workstation.

'So's about half the adult male population of Bristol. Anything else?'

They were sitting in the CCTV Hub, Dixon and Cole either side of Maria Willis, who had been assigned to help them, somewhat reluctantly judging by the frequency and volume of her sighing. The office housed the emergency, traffic and community safety control rooms, covering a total of seven hundred CCTV cameras across Bristol.

White workstations with blue desktops and lighting in the footwell, presumably so you could see if your shoelaces were undone, thought Dixon; he couldn't see any other reason for it. Every workstation had two large computer screens on it, most of them running split screens as well. Then there were the twelve larger screens mounted on the wall, all of them showing scenes from the city centre in black and white, apart from the one top left that was running BBC News.

Cole was flicking through his notebook. 'I haven't got a note of his shoes.'

'He's carrying a small blue rucksack,' said Dixon.

'How up to date is this description?' asked Maria.

'This morning,' replied Cole. 'He paid his fiancée's parents a visit.'

'His fiancée? Where's she now?'

'At the bottom of the Atlantic Ocean,' said Dixon. 'She was on a yacht that sank a few months ago.'

'Not something you hear every day.' Maria's eyes were darting between the split screens in front of her. 'And you think he's come to Bristol?'

'*Back* to Bristol. He was living rough for a time a few years ago. So, he knows his way around.'

'Any idea where?'

'No, sorry.'

'Well, he might be sofa surfing if he's got any friends.'

'We've got one address we can try,' said Cole.

'If he's not there then perhaps try the Hobb's Lane Collective. It's a charity up behind the Hippodrome; they might have seen him. And then there's the St Govan's hostel in Old Park Hill. He might go there, I suppose. Is he on drugs?'

'Spice,' replied Dixon.

'The Trenchard Street car park might be worth a look then.' Maria clicked on a menu in the top right corner of one of the screens and selected 'Trenchard Main' from the dropdown list. 'This is outside the front.' She was pointing at the screen. 'We've got other cameras on each of the floors by the paystations.'

A few people were coming and going, walking past a person sitting cross-legged on a sleeping bag with a sheepdog. He or she had their head down, long hair covering their face, an empty coffee cup on the pavement in front of them. A passer-by stopped to drop a few coins in.

'It's a good car park for them,' continued Maria. 'It's on the go almost all day with shoppers and then later on they get the audience at the Hippodome. The Broadmead shopping centre's good too, obviously.' She leaned forward and looked at her notes. 'I'll circulate Craig's details and we'll keep an eye out for him. No doubt your lot are looking for him too?'

'They are.'

'What's he done?'

'Nothing,' replied Dixon. 'He was released from Leyhill this morning and we believe his life might be in danger.'

'How's he travelling?'

'Rail to Weston and he'll be hitch-hiking now, I imagine. We've got patrol cars looking out for him on the A38 and the A371.'

'Surely he'll have gone to a bail hostel?'

'He was supposed to go to one in Weston, but they've not seen hide nor hair of him,' replied Cole.

'If he knows someone's after him, he'll be trying to stay off the radar and that makes him harder to find.' Maria picked up the handset and immediately replaced it when the phone rang on her desk. 'He might be down the Bearpit too, come to think of it. Always worth a look; a bit of a community in the underpass and the collective run a food bank down there.'

'What's the Bearpit?' asked Dixon.

'You're not from Bristol, I take it?'

'Bridgwater.'

'It's the St James Barton roundabout. There's an underpass and an area in the middle. It used to be a popular spot for the homeless – there were shelters under there and then one day the council went in, cleared it all out and fenced it off.' She selected

239

'St James 1' from the dropdown menu and jabbed her finger at the screen. 'See here, there were shelters all along this back wall and now they're gone. Occasionally you'll see people sleeping rough, but it's nothing like it was. Sad, really. I mean it's not as if there's anywhere else for them to go.'

Dixon took out a business card and dropped it on to Maria's keyboard. 'Let us know if you see him,' he said. 'Any time of the day or night.'

'I'll circulate his details now.'

'And if you could email any footage you get of him to me, that would be great.'

'Where to now?' asked Cole, when they stepped out on to the pavement.

'We'll start with the address he gave when he was on bail, then we'll try the Hobb's Lane Collective. If they haven't seen him yet they can keep an eye out for him.'

'Let's hope we find him before the killer does.'

'Before would be good, but I'd take at the same time. It's finding him after the killer does that worries me.'

◆　◆　◆

'It looks like a squat.'

'That's because it *is* a squat, Sir,' replied Cole.

'You'd have thought they'd have bloody well checked when it was a bail condition that he stay here.' Dixon let out a long sigh as he stepped over the bags of waste blocking the gate. Some of them had been ripped open by seagulls, spilling the contents across the front garden: beer cans and pizza boxes, with the occasional foil tray thrown in for good measure. The gravelled garden, once someone's pride and joy, was littered with fly tipped rubbish – a rolled up carpet, a fridge with the door ripped off lying on its side, a television, two rusting bicycle frames.

The drive was blocked by a skip, so someone had been making an effort to tidy the place up. A layer of plasterboard and smashed kitchen units in the bottom; the rest of the stuff in it appeared to have been thrown in from the road and consisted almost entirely of fast food packaging of various shapes, sizes and brands. The seagulls had had a go at that too.

Two posters had been taped to a metal shutter covering the front door, although Dixon chose not to linger long enough to read more than the headings: *Bristol County Court: Notice of Possession* and beneath that *Environmental Health: Notice* . . .

He looked through the bay window, his hands shielding his eyes from the reflections in the glass. The front room had been stripped to the floorboards, only the fireplace remaining, a single beer can sitting on the mantelpiece.

'Looks like the owner's taken possession and boarded it up.' Cole was stepping over a shopping trolley. 'This side's the same. Cleared out.'

'Let's try round the back.'

The windows at the side and rear had been boarded up and a steel shutter covered the back door.

'What was the bloke's name, can you remember?' asked Dixon, looking up at the first and second floor windows.

'No, Sir. I've got the address but not the name of Craig's friend.'

'Get Louise to see if she can find him.'

'Yes, Sir.'

Cole turned away, talking into his mobile phone, although his stroll down the back garden was blocked by a gas oven and an old enamel bath.

A flat roof gave access to a first floor window, so Dixon stepped up on to an old washing machine and was able to reach the edge of the roof. Seconds later he was peering in, rattling the old sash frame.

'Any luck?'

'There's a lock on it.' Dixon was picking his way back along the edge of the flat roof. 'It's been cleared out anyway.'

'Lou's going to see if she can find him. She's already tried once and got nowhere, she said, but she'll have another go.'

'What's his name?'

'Jasper Fish.'

Dixon lowered himself down off the roof until he was standing on the washing machine, then dropped down on to the small area of patio that wasn't covered in litter. He turned to find Cole waving his warrant card at a neighbour peering over the fence.

'Is there anyone living here?' asked Cole.

'Not for a while,' came the reply. 'The owner's applied for permission to turn it into flats.'

'We're looking for Jasper Fish.'

'Not seen Fish for a while. He used to sell the *Big Issue* down the Broadmead shopping centre. Still does, I think; I saw him only a couple of weeks ago. Nice lad.'

'Fish's pitch is just inside the entrance to the Galleries, the bloke said. Along from Gap.' Cole rang off. 'He's probably gone by now, though. The afternoons are quieter and sometimes they sell out anyway.'

'What did he say when you asked for an address?'

'He laughed.'

'We'll park in here and try the collective,' said Dixon, turning into the Trenchard St multistorey car park. 'Then we'll try St Govan's.'

The stale smell of urine hit them before they had even parked the Land Rover.

Cole shuddered. 'I'd park on the ground floor if I were you, that way we won't have to use the stairs.'

Several people were begging by the paystations, leaning on the bollards placed by the council to stop rough sleeping in the alcoves by the machines; hands outstretched, one rattling a cup, the elderly couple feeding coins into the slot trying to avert their gaze. The same scene would be unfolding at the paystations on each of the six floors above them.

Straggly dark hair, her face pallid; the girl was standing next to a younger man, unshaven with short matted hair, wispy beard and a torn padded jacket, the stuffing hanging down. No laces in his boots either.

'Blue jeans and a black hoodie,' said Cole. 'He's not here.'

'Maria at the CCTV Hub would have told us if he was. And besides, he only got out this morning so he should be clean shaven.'

Hobb's Lane was narrow and spent its life in the shadows; high buildings on either side saw to that. Maybe an hour or two of warmth in the summer when the sun was directly overhead. Double yellow lines on both sides, needles and syringes in the doorway of the old warehouse, it was a rat run behind the Hippodrome, the music from a rehearsal for something or other following them around the corner as they turned into the lane.

Opposite the warehouse – Dixon peered through the window – *converted* warehouse, stood a terrace of two-storey buildings, rendered and painted cream with a black band along the base and newly painted sash windows. There was an Entryphone on the wall beside each of the four black front doors.

Dixon brushed past Cole on the narrow pavement. 'It's that end one.' He stopped outside number one and pressed the buzzer.

The sound of a phone being picked up, followed by 'We're closed now. You can get something to eat at the Bearpit or there's the St Govan's hostel in Old Park Hill.' Then the phone was slammed down.

Dixon rang the buzzer again. 'It's the police,' he snapped, before the voice on the other end had a chance to say anything.

'Oh. How can I help?'

'You can start by opening the door.'

'Er, right. I'm on my way down.'

She sounded young, but then the line had crackled as only Entryphones do. Dixon heard footsteps, the faint metallic click of the cover on the spyhole sliding to one side. Then the door opened slowly.

'Yes?'

The rainbow sweater must have been hand-knitted, the sleeves pulled up to her elbows revealing a new and painful tattoo of a red rose on her left forearm. Her hair was bleached blonde and cut short, very short; studs in her nose and tongue.

'And you are?'

'Maisie. I work here.'

'Is there anyone else here?'

'Molly's upstairs. She runs the place.'

Dixon waited patiently for the invitation; Maisie got there in the end.

'D'you want to come in?'

'Thank you.'

They followed her up the stairs into an open plan office on the first floor. The sash windows were open, allowing a cool breeze to drift in, carrying with it the noise from the Hippodrome.

'That's Elvis, isn't it?' Cole was craning his neck to listen.

'*This is Elvis* opens tomorrow night,' said the older woman at the far end; a red T-shirt with *Hobb's Lane Collective* on it, a fleece with the same logo on it hanging over the back of her chair. She was looking them up and down. 'You must be detectives. How exciting! How can we help?'

Dixon chose to ignore the hint of sarcasm. After all, he may have been wrong. 'We're looking for a man who was released from HM Prison Leyhill this morning. He has a history of rough sleeping in Bristol and we believe he may have come back here.'

'He hasn't wasted much time, has he, if you lot are after him already?'

Dixon was watching a group of people milling about in the lane outside. 'He hasn't committed an offence; we believe his life may be in danger. That's why we need to find him sooner rather than later.' He handed Molly his phone. 'His name's Craig Pengelly and this is a picture of him.'

'You'd better have a look, Maisie,' said Molly, handing her Dixon's phone. 'You were on duty downstairs.'

Maisie stared at the phone. 'We had a few in today, but not him.' Her hesitation was just long enough to be noticeable. 'I'd have remembered him.'

'He was in Weston earlier so he wouldn't have got here until after lunch.'

'Not seen him. Sorry.'

'What do you do here?'

Molly stood up. 'We're a port in a storm, so to speak. We find them a bed for the night, if we can – it's not always easy – treatment for the drug users, help them with benefits; we've got a small food bank downstairs, clothes, sleeping bags, that sort of stuff, and we run a food stand in the Bearpit, although for how much longer I don't know. Bloody council . . .'

'So, you're a registered charity?' asked Cole.

'We are. Staffed by volunteers in the main, but we have a couple on the payroll. Maisie is one; joined us a couple of months ago.'

Maisie leaned out of the sash window. 'Oi, you lot, clear off.'

'There's a group of kids hanging around, up to no good.' Molly curled her lip. 'A couple of our clients have been picked on, their belongings set fire to. Little shits, they are.'

'What did you mean when you said his life was in danger?' asked Maisie.

'He was involved in a pension scam and one of the victims is taking his or her revenge.'

'Killing people, you mean?'

'The body in Harptree Combe just over a week ago; the tax officer over at Bradley Stoke.'

'I saw that on the news,' said Molly.

'There were two more on the Costa del Sol at the weekend.'

Maisie was still watching the group of youths out in the lane. 'Does Craig know you're looking for him?'

'No.'

'Should we tell him if he comes in?'

'Please do, but stress it's for his own safety.' Dixon looked out to see the small group of teenagers drifting up the lane. 'I'd rather he was a witness than a victim.'

'Where would he be likely to go if he came to Bristol and knew his way around?' asked Cole.

'St Govan's, if he needed a bed for the night, although they're full at the moment. Unless he's got a tent, I suppose. Then he might be up on the Downs, most likely,' replied Molly. 'The Bearpit for food. Is he on drugs?'

'Spice, we think,' replied Dixon.

'Not as easy to come by on the streets as you might think, that. There's no shortage of crack and heroin, but I'm not sure where he'd get his hands on spice.'

'He has a friend known as Fish.' Dixon was listening to a commotion at the far end of the lane, the shouts drowning out

'Suspicious Minds'. 'Jasper Fish. He's a *Big Issue* seller down at the Broadmead.'

'I know Fish,' said Molly. 'He's been around for yonks. Used to live in a squat up in St Paul's. Then he had one of the shelters in the Bearpit until the council cleared them out. I think he said he'd got himself a bedsit last time I spoke to him. He was one of our first success stories; pitched up in a hell of a state, but we got him clean and then he started selling the *Big Issue*. Saved his life, that did.'

Dixon stopped on the way out to empty the contents of his wallet into a collection box on top of a filing cabinet. A nudge prompted Cole to do the same.

'Thank you very much.' Molly raised her voice as they disappeared down the stairs.

'You'll have to use a card when you pay for the parking,' said Dixon, when they stepped out on to the pavement.

'That Maisie's seen him,' whispered Cole, with a nod towards the open window just above his head. 'Did you see her reaction?'

'I did.'

They turned the corner into Denmark Street, Dixon dragging Cole back into a doorway. 'You can see the front door of the collective in the reflection in the window of that Italian restaurant over there,' he said. 'Any second now . . .'

Then the black door opened and a young woman in a rainbow pullover sprinted off in the opposite direction along Hobb's Lane.

Chapter Twenty-Nine

'They lost her behind the hospital, heading up into Montpelier. The CCTV thins out up there.' Cole slid his phone into his jacket pocket. 'She could've gone anywhere after that.'

'Let's try in here then,' said Dixon. They were standing on the pavement outside the St Govan's Community Project in Old Park Hill. 'We'll try the Bearpit next if he's not here, then take a turn around the Downs before the light goes completely.'

Dixon pushed open the heavy glass door, a shout going up before he had even stepped into the hall.

'Police!'

'We're not even in uniform, for heaven's sake.' He glared at Cole.

'They say it's the smell, Sir,' said Cole, rolling his eyes.

'It must be you.'

Three people sitting on the far side of the reception area turned their backs, pulled up hoods or buried their faces in copies of the *Big Issue* that were scattered on the plastic coffee table.

'You got a warrant?'

The question came from behind a Perspex screen to Dixon's right. Black everything: lipstick, hair dye, nail polish, T-shirt, tattoo ink; hostile with it.

'No.'

'Why not go and harass someone else then?'

'I wasn't aware I was harassing anyone.' Dixon was watching the split screen CCTV monitor on the side in the small office: four cameras, one showing outside the front door, the others flicking from the corridors on the three floors upstairs to the lifts, the stairwells, landings and back round again. 'We're looking for this man.' He pressed his phone to the Perspex screen.

'Not seen him.'

'It might help if you looked at the picture.' Dixon was quite calm; Jane would have been proud.

The woman looked up from her computer and stared at the photograph, her impatience softening. 'What's he done?'

'Nothing. He's in danger and we need to find him for his own safety.'

'Does he know?'

'No.'

The woman took a deep breath. 'What's his name? I can check the register if you like, but most of the names on it are false anyway.'

'Craig Pengelly.' He watched her scrolling through something on her screen, the reflection in the mirror on the mantelpiece behind her partially blocked by her hair. 'You didn't say whether or not you'd seen him?'

'He's not been in, no.'

'I didn't ask that.' Dixon was still holding his phone to the screen. 'I asked whether you'd seen him.'

'When?'

'It would've been today.'

'I told you, I've been here all day and he's not been in.'

'So, you haven't seen him?'

An exaggerated sigh. 'No.'

'What's your name?'

'People call me Riz.'

The hand rolling tobacco and packet of Rizlas on the desk next to her explained that, possibly, but it still wasn't getting any easier. 'I didn't ask you what people call you. I asked you what your name is.'

'Andrea Lukic.' She smirked, an eastern European accent suddenly more noticeable. 'I came here from Slovakia before Brexit so I get to stay.'

'And most welcome you are too.'

'I live here and volunteer.' She pushed her mouse away with a flourish. 'There's no Craig Pengelly on the list.'

'Can we have a look around? Show the photo to people, see if they've seen him on their travels?' Dixon tried his best disarming smile.

'You're not here to arrest anyone?'

'We're not interested in drugs either.' Dixon had stopped sniffing the air when he walked in, although Cole seemed determined to inhale as much of it as he could.

'We don't tolerate those in here.'

'I'm pleased to hear it.'

'I'll have to come with you,' Andrea said. 'Give me a minute.'

A noticeboard was mounted on the wall next to the fireplace, the original ground floor of the big old house having been knocked through, and a whiteboard was on the wall above the mantelpiece, felt pens scattered on the marble top. Various messages had been scrawled on the board: a couple of mobile phone numbers and several asking people to get in touch; probably the same people whose missing person posters crowded the noticeboard.

Dixon sat down opposite the group of three sitting in the corner of the reception area, rucksacks and rolled up sleeping bags on the floor next to them; they looked as if they had settled in for the night. 'You seen this lad?' He held his phone out with Craig's picture still on it. One of them took the phone, looked at the picture and passed it to the next with a shake of his head.

'May have seen him down the Bearpit a few days ago,' mumbled the third.

'Thanks. We'll try down there.' Dixon dropped his phone back in his pocket.

'Any luck?' asked Cole. He was standing in front of the noticeboard with his hands in his pockets.

'One of them saw him a couple of days ago down at the Bearpit.'

'He was only released from Leyhill this morning.'

'Quite.'

Andrea hung a sign in the Perspex window – *back in 5 minutes* – and then locked the door of the office behind her. 'You said he was in danger.' She hesitated by the keypad to the inner door, her finger hovering over the numbers. 'What sort of danger?'

'We have reason to believe someone will try to kill him if they find him before we do.'

'And he's done nothing wrong?'

'Nothing that he hasn't already been punished for. He was released from prison this morning.'

She turned to face him, her face paler, if that was possible, although it may just have been the light. 'He's not here.' Her eyes darted from Dixon to the three in the corner and back again, clearly nervous at being seen talking to the police. 'He came in this afternoon, but we're full, so I had to turn him away. He said he's got a tent so he could be anywhere. He had money for food too.'

'His fiancée's parents gave him fifty quid,' said Dixon.

'Fiancée?' Andrea frowned. 'There was nobody with him.'

'She drowned. She was on a yacht that capsized.'

'A sad story. Everyone here has one of them.'

◆ ◆ ◆

'Let's try the Downs,' said Dixon, when Cole climbed into the Land Rover in the Trenchard St car park. He'd watched Cole pay for the parking on a card and keep the receipt, even turning out his pockets to prove to the young couple still hanging around the paystation that he had no change.

The light was starting to fade as they drove along Circular Road, a few dog walkers on the Downs to their right, the cliffs of the Avon Gorge to their left, warning signs at regular intervals along the wall in front of the seating areas: *Danger, Cliff Edge, Keep Out.*

An easterly wind cooling the air was bringing with it the smells of the zoo. Dixon wound up the window of the Land Rover. 'Cows I can deal with, but that.'

'Beats the car park,' said Cole.

Dixon was inclined to agree. 'You'd be in or near the trees, wouldn't you, rather than out in the open.' He was thinking aloud as he drove. It was a familiar spot, although it had been a while, and he'd never lingered long at the top of the cliffs anyway; loop the ropes round a tree and abseil straight back down to start another climb had always been the order of the day. 'Plenty of time to rest when you're dead,' his old climbing partner, Jake, had said with a broad grin the last time they had climbed together. Dixon smiled at the memory.

Jake was getting lots of rest now.

'There are some down there.' Cole was pointing into the trees out of the passenger window when Dixon parked the Land Rover. 'There's a light on in one of them.'

They followed the path behind the bin at the end of the seating area, the undergrowth opening out into a small clearing, the light going off in the tent furthest from them as they approached.

'Hello?' Cole grabbed hold of the hooped tent pole and shook it. 'Police, we saw the light. You're not in trouble and we won't be moving you on. We just need to ask if you've seen someone.'

No reply.

'They're not in trouble either, so you won't be snitching.'

The zip started to open slowly, then a head poked out, blinking furiously in the light from Dixon's phone. 'I haven't got any drugs.'

'We're not buying, thanks,' he said.

The girl gave a nervous smile before crawling out of the tent on her hands and knees.

'Is there anyone else in there?' asked Dixon.

'Just me.' She stood up and began zipping up her padded coat.

'We're looking for this man.' Cole held his phone out. 'He's got a tent, so we wondered if you might have seen him up here?'

'No, sorry.'

'What about that tent over there?'

'They've gone down the Bearpit for some food; won't be back for ages.'

'You got money?' asked Dixon.

'Some.'

'Does anyone know you're here?'

'Nobody gives a shit.'

'Eighteen or nineteen, I'd say,' Cole said, when they climbed back into the Land Rover a few minutes later.

'Tell uniform and get them to keep an eye on her.' Dixon turned the key, the diesel engine taking longer than usual to stop rattling. 'Make sure they don't move her on.'

'Yes, Sir.'

'We'll try down the Bearpit, then call it a day, I think.'

The damp, stale smell of urine – the stench of despair; at least the wind had whistled through the car park, but the Bearpit was underground. Five pedestrian subways leading to an open space in the middle of the A38, oddly quiet despite the traffic racing around the roundabout above their heads.

Flickering streetlights casting an orange glow added to Dixon's feeling of unease as they walked down one of the tunnels, two people sleeping in the gutter beside them.

All the cafes and kiosks had closed some time ago, and metal shutters protected what was left of them. High metal fencing blocked the areas around the edge that were under cover of the road, where the homeless had built their shelters.

'You need to watch yourself down here, Sir. I don't care what that Molly says, there's lots of spice about and most of it'll be down here.'

Dixon was stepping over pavement art chalked on the ground. 'A good place to find Craig then.'

One kiosk remained open. Dixon watched the queue shuffling forward; food and a hot drink handed out, no money taken. The sign over the shutter explained why: *The Hobb's Lane Collective.*

'They'd be better off filling it in with concrete and putting footbridges over the roundabout,' said Cole.

Suddenly the people at the far end of the Bearpit started to disperse, some running down the subways.

'Hello, Nige! What are you doing here?'

Dixon turned at the sound of a hand landing on Cole's shoulder, to find two uniformed officers standing behind them.

'We're supposed to be making discreet enquiries as to the whereabouts of a witness, Constable,' said Dixon, impatiently.

'This is DCI Dixon.' Cole dived in before anyone could put their foot in it.

'No chance of that down here, Sir.' The officer was shining his torch at Dixon's warrant card. 'They're all off their boxes on spice. It's not safe down here, either, so I wouldn't hang about if I were you.'

'Thank you, Constable.'

'If it's that Pengelly lad you're after, we've had the alert and we're keeping an eye out for him, Sir, don't you worry.'

Chapter Thirty

It had been an unfortunate turn of phrase and Dixon was still stewing on it when he arrived home; the idea of anyone 'keeping an eye out' was enough to turn his stomach at the moment. Still, the uniformed officer couldn't have known – the murderer's preferred kill shot having been kept a closely guarded secret.

The familiar sound of his diesel engine had been enough and Monty was waiting for him behind the back door when Dixon pushed it open, the cottage dark except for the flicker of a black and white film on the television screen.

'What's she fallen asleep in front of this time, old son?' whispered Dixon, squatting down and scratching his dog behind the ears.

'*The 39 Steps.*' Jane sat up on the sofa, yawning and pausing the film with the remote control.

'Has he been out?'

'Just in the field at the back.' Another yawn as she walked into the kitchen. 'I ripped my jeans on that bloody barbed wire. I was going to cut it, but if he reported it, that'd be criminal damage, wouldn't it? Career over.'

'I'll cover it with some tape when I get a minute, or maybe some polystyrene. Then we haven't damaged anything, have we.'

Jane held up the kettle. 'Tea?'

'Ta.' Dixon was squatting down in front of the fridge, his fingers hooked in Monty's collar.

'There's one of your Slimming World veggie things in the freezer.'

'That'll do.' He dragged it out and started piercing the film lid with a sharp knife. 'Is Lucy still down at the weekend?'

'She's grounded.' Jane shook her head. 'You wouldn't believe me if I told you.'

'Try me.' Dixon was watching his curry on the turntable, waiting for the ping.

'Judy caught her exchanging messages with grown men in some online chat room. She was telling them she was fourteen and had even arranged to meet one of them at Birmingham New Street; paedophile hunting, apparently.' She banged two mugs down on the worktop. 'The idiot. She'd been in touch with one of those vigilante groups on Facebook, so it seems to be true.'

'Silly arse could've ended up in deep shit.'

'I spoke to her and she promised me faithfully she wasn't going to the meeting on her own. And she'd probably have chickened out anyway.' Jane handed Dixon a mug of tea. 'Judy threatened to tell her social worker, which put the fear of God into her, so hopefully that's the end of it. I told her it would be the end of any chance of a career in the police, so she's promised me she's not going to do it again.'

'How long have we got?' Dixon couldn't help a mischievous grin.

'She's grounded for two weeks.' Jane smiled as she blew the steam off her tea.

'I wonder if he turned up?'

'Judy told the local police, so if he did the nonce would've got more than he bargained for.' Jane watched Dixon sit down on the sofa, Monty jumping up next to him, sniffing his curry. 'Shall I switch the film on?'

'Don't bother.' He pushed Monty on to the floor. 'And you can hop it.'

'How's it going?'

'Two shooters, one still at large and the powers that be at Leyhill decide to release their next victim from his comfy cell.'

'Marvellous.'

'You couldn't make it up.' Dixon took a mouthful of curry. 'We've spent the day traipsing around Bristol looking for him; just missed him at St Govan's and he told them there he'd got a tent, so the local lot are keeping an eye out for him on the Downs. He'd been at the Hobb's Lane Collective too, I think.'

'Knows his way around then.'

'He certainly seems to. And he'll know we're looking for him by now as well.'

'How's Lou and everybody getting on at Portishead?'

'Fine, I think. Nigel's enjoying swanning about in plain clothes.'

'Is he any good?'

'He is, actually. And when the shit hits the fan, he's the one I'd want watching my back.'

'Let's hope it doesn't.' Jane stood up and kissed him on the forehead. 'Rural Crimes team, my backside.'

'Mine too.' Dixon was holding the empty plastic tray for Monty to lick the last of the curry sauce. 'I'm going to take him out, I think. Clear my head; too many unanswered questions going round and round. I'll never sleep.'

'Wake me up when you get back,' she said, turning for the stairs.

Cold nights and warm days; autumn had arrived with a vengeance, a week or two early compared to last year, thought Dixon, as he reached into the back of the Land Rover for his coat. It was no time to be bedding down for the night in a shop doorway somewhere, and even a tent would be pretty bloody miserable come winter. He'd done it, of course he had, ice climbing in Scotland and the Alps, but then he'd had the proper stuff: winter sleeping bag, down jacket, thermal boots. Craig and the other poor buggers on the street had none of that, and what little they did have some hooligan would merrily set fire to if he had half the chance. Now there was someone for Dixon to focus his energies on; maybe he'd pay the would-be arsonists a visit when this crossbow business was over.

One way or the other.

The spice sellers too. How hard could it be? He'd never worked the Drug Squad, so maybe there was more to it than following a drug dealer home and then raiding his crack house; following the county line back to London perhaps? No matter how many you arrest, more step forward to take their place and off you go on the merry-go-round again.

Maybe he'd stick to murder after all? At least murder cases have a beginning, a middle and an end.

A walk up Brent Knoll by moonlight always helped to clear his head, although tonight was more about identifying the questions than finding answers to them.

He started counting them out on his fingers, but didn't get past number one: what was the connection between Godfrey Collins and the other victims? Try as they might, Louise and Mark had still drawn a blank. There was that twerp Tressider, but was he really going to kill four people because his stepfather had lost his pension and his fiancée owed twenty-seven grand in tax? Was he even capable of it?

Was he bollocks.

Dixon had looked plenty of murderers in the eye, all of them different, with different methods and motives, and one thing he knew for sure was that Tressider was no killer – capable of theft, and speeding in that flash car, drugs possibly, but killing?

So, round we go again: what is the connection between Godfrey Collins and the other victims?

Dixon lifted Monty over the stile into the field at the top of the lane, the dog landing in a puddle on the other side. 'You'll have to go in the bloody bath when we get back now.'

There were other questions as he scanned the night sky for that comet that was doing the rounds, but whatever they were, they paled into insignificance next to the Godfrey Collins question. Even Frank Allan had resorted to 'no comment' when he'd asked him that one.

Don't bloody blame him.

He squatted down and shone the light on his phone at Monty's paws. 'You're covered in mud, old son,' he said. 'Just make sure you sleep on your mother's side of the bed. And for God's sake don't wake her up. I'm tired enough as it is.'

The knock on the door and Monty's growling were both gradually increasing in volume, Dixon finally being dragged back to his senses by loud banging and barking. Then Monty jumped off the bed and ran downstairs, the thud signalling that he had launched himself at the front door.

Jane's eyes were still closed. 'What time is it?'

Dixon reached for his phone on the bedside table. 'Ten to seven.' He ignored the three missed calls.

'You were supposed to wake me up when you got back.'

He shrugged. 'It was late and you looked so peaceful.'

Jane sat up and stared at the duvet. 'You didn't wash his legs off when you got back last night, did you?'

'I'll go and see who it is.'

Dixon hastily pulled on a pair of trousers and ran downstairs, catching Monty scrabbling at the front door. The figure visible through the frosted glass could only be one person, judging by the size. 'It's the Rural Crimes team,' he shouted to Jane, who was by now standing at the top of the stairs in Dixon's bathrobe.

'Invite him in for a coffee.'

'What is it, Nigel?' Dixon hid a yawn behind the back of his hand as he opened the door.

'It's not Craig, Sir, don't worry. I just thought you'd want to make an early start.'

'Have you been into Area J?'

'Yes, Sir. Lou's there, and Mark. Still no sign of Craig, but then I had a bit of a thought overnight.'

Dixon stepped back. 'You'd better come in.'

Jane appeared at the top of the stairs in jeans and a T-shirt. 'Hello, Nige, how's life in Rural Crimes?'

'My wife's loving it,' he replied, with a grin. 'She's not seen me for days.'

'Coffee?' asked Dixon.

'Thank you, Sir.'

'You eaten?'

'I don't tend to bother with breakfast.'

Dixon busied himself with the coffee, Monty sitting by the dog food cupboard wagging his tail. 'And you, don't panic.'

'To what do we owe the pleasure . . . ?'

'At this time in the morning,' muttered Dixon, finishing Jane's sentence for her. 'He's had a thought, apparently.'

'Yeah,' said Cole. 'I'm not sure how far it takes us, but . . .' His voice lost momentum and he frowned, clearly unsure that what he had to say was worth the trouble after all.

'Let's hear it then.' Dixon handed him a mug of coffee. 'There's no sugar in the house, but there's a—'

'Without's fine.'

'C'mon, Nige, the suspense is killing me,' said Jane.

'Right, well, let's say for the sake of argument, you've got an old photo on your phone and you want to make it look like you took it a couple of days ago. You open the photo, zoom in a bit maybe, and then take a screenshot of it. Then, when you look at the new photo it'll show the date and time the screenshot was taken at the top,' continued Cole. 'Not the original photograph.'

'There's a separate album for screenshots,' said Jane.

'Yeah, but you don't see that if someone just shows you the photo on their phone.'

Dixon leaned back against the worktop as the significance of what Cole was saying hit home. 'Someone checked his alibi?'

'They did, Sir,' replied Cole.

'Actually went to Longleat and checked?'

'Yes, I think so.'

'Let's hope they asked the right questions.'

'Whose alibi?' asked Jane.

'John Sims.' Dixon gritted his teeth. 'Mr squeaky-clean, happy-to-help, prison officer John Sims. He said he'd been on a three day carp fishing trip when Collins was killed and showed me a picture of the fish he'd caught.'

'Or a screenshot of a fish he'd caught years ago,' said Cole, raising his eyebrows.

'Let's get a team outside his house, discreetly, and we'll need Armed Response. I want everyone on scene wearing body armour too.' Dixon emptied his coffee into the sink. 'We'll catch them up later.'

'Where are we going?' asked Cole.

'Longleat.'

Chapter Thirty-One

'You been to Longleat before, Sir?'

Dixon was sitting in the passenger seat of Cole's pool car as they sped east on the A361, looking at the map on his phone.

'It's a grand day out.' Cole was adjusting the rear view mirror. 'I'd take Jane's car though, if I were you. The monkeys will have your windscreen wipers and your aerial. They'll love that snorkel you've got on your air intake too.'

'I'll try to remember that.'

'The house is a far cry from the Bearpit too,' continued Cole. 'How the other half live, eh, Sir.'

Dixon was busy dialling a number on his phone.

'Tim Robinson, Shearwater bailiff.'

'Detective Chief Inspector Dixon, Avon and Somerset police. You gave a statement a few days ago about John Sims.'

'I did.'

'I'm on my way now and I'd like to speak to you about it. Are you at the lake?'

'I'm a bit busy . . .' Robinson admitted defeat before his protest had really got going. 'I'm on the other side of the estate; I can be there in half an hour.'

'Thank you,' replied Dixon. 'We're in a dark blue Skoda.'

'I'll keep an eye out for you.'

Cole followed the track past the Shearwater Lake Tea Rooms and along the side of the lake, the concrete slabs making a dull rhythmic thud under the wheels of the car. 'You wouldn't want to fish too near this, the noise'd put the fish off.' He was craning his neck to see the nearside as he squeezed past cars parked on the grass verge.

'They get used to it,' said Dixon. 'On a quiet evening they'll patrol up and down here looking for the bread people have thrown in for the ducks.'

There were a few cars scattered around the gravel car park in the trees, rowing boats lying upside down on the grass. And a dark green Land Rover, sign written *Longleat Estate*.

'That must be the bailiff's.' Dixon was out of the car before Cole had taken off his seatbelt, striding out along the vacant pontoon, his reflection following him on the surface of the lake. Small fish were flitting in and out of the weed, which was starting to die back as the nights drew in.

A light drizzle smoothed out the faint ripple on the surface, blurring the mirror image of the trees on the near bank, a few anglers occupying pegs, the tips of their rods sticking out into the lake from between the bushes.

'You a fisherman, Inspector?'

He turned to find the bailiff walking along the pontoon towards him. The logo on his green coat was the giveaway: *Longleat Estate: Water Bailiff*.

'When I was a lad.' Dixon smiled – best to get him onside before asking the difficult questions. 'I keep threatening to dig out my rods. They're in the loft, I think.'

'You'd be most welcome here.' Robinson was rubbing his hands together. 'We've got some great fishing.'

'Pike?'

'Carp, mainly.'

Dixon nodded his 'oh, well' rather than saying it out loud, but Robinson understood it well enough. 'We need to ask you about John Sims.'

'I've printed off the bookings sheet so you can see when he was here.' Robinson took a piece of paper out of his coat pocket and handed it to Dixon. 'He's become quite a regular since he retired. Three nights most weeks, sometimes longer. What's he been up to?'

'Didn't our colleagues tell you when they took your statement?'

'No. It was just a phone call, to check he was here when he said he was. And he was.'

'We'll come on to that in a minute.' Dixon unfolded the piece of paper, shielding it from the rain as best he could. 'He told me he was here for four days last time. On peg six.'

'It's along that bank.' Robinson gestured along the near bank.

'You allow night fishing?'

'We do.'

'Let's go and have a look then.'

Dixon and Cole followed Robinson along the narrow path that weaved through the trees, tyre tracks from anglers' trolleys visible in the wet mud. Dixon could just imagine Donald Watson's reaction if he asked Scientific to take plaster casts of the tyres; and besides, there was no question that Sims's fishing tackle had been at the lake. Robinson had been quite clear in his statement that it had been on peg six for the days and nights booked.

Robinson tiptoed past a zipped up tent in the trees by the path, turning to Dixon with his index finger across his lips. Opposite the tent were three fishing rods on a stand, little red lights on bite alarms ready to wake up the slumbering angler inside if – or when, if you believed Robinson – a fish took the bait.

'They'll have been on the go all night, I expect,' whispered Robinson. 'It fishes well along this bank in the dark. Just before dusk and just before dawn are the best times.' The trees opened out again at peg four, an elderly man sitting on a deck chair, his one rod propped up on a small tackle box. 'Some just come for the day,' said Robinson. 'Night fishing's not everyone's cup of tea.'

Another gap in the bushes along the water's edge, vacant this time, an overhanging tree jutting out into the water, its lower branches submerged.

'I've got to do something about that.' Robinson was talking to himself now, surely? 'Get a good fish on and chances are it'll snag; another job for the winter.'

He stopped in the next swim; vacant, but there were footprints in the soft mud down at the water's edge, holes in the ground where bank sticks had been driven in for fishing rods to sit on, and an area of grass behind the path flattened, presumably by a tent or bivvy.

'This is peg six,' said Robinson. 'John was here.'

'Where was his tent?'

'It was here.' Robinson gestured to a narrow strip of grass on the lake side of the path. 'It's not flat but he'd have been nearer his rods. Most people camp the other side of the path.'

'Let's start with his most recent visit. How many times did you see him during the four days and nights he was here?' asked Dixon.

'Several times.' Robinson frowned, maybe sensing he was in for a rigorous cross-examination. 'I saw him the first morning to take his money in the lodge over there. Then I'd do my rounds every morning and late afternoon.'

'And what does doing your rounds consist of?'

'Just walking around the lake, chatting to people, seeing if anyone's had any good fish overnight, that they've got the proper kit and are complying with the rules.'

'The bloke asleep in the tent back there, have you seen him this morning?'

'I didn't want to wake him up. He's there, though. You can tell because he's cast out. He'd never have left his rods unattended in case a fish took the bait. And if I found anyone doing that they'd get a ban as well.'

'And John Sims the same. You didn't actually see him because you didn't want to wake him up. Is that right?'

'His rods were in the water, so he must've been there.' A slight tremble was creeping into Robinson's voice. 'And he's one of our regulars.'

'So, he'd have known you wouldn't wake him up in the morning?'

'I suppose.'

'Let me make sure I understand this correctly then,' said Dixon, ignoring the smile creeping across Cole's face. 'You didn't actually see him. You made an assumption he was here because his rods were in the water and his tent was zipped up.'

'Er, that's right.'

'Let me give you another scenario then,' said Dixon, scuffing the ground with his foot. 'He needs an alibi, so he comes here, pays for four days and nights, sets up his fishing tackle, casts out without any bait on the hook, zips up his tent and buggers off in the sure and certain knowledge that you'll tell us he was here all the time.'

'Oh, shit.' Robinson's face flushed. 'I've mucked up, haven't I?'

'He'd have been back by lunchtime, all smiles when you *did the rounds* in the evening.'

'Yeah, he was. I definitely saw him each evening.'

'Time?'

'About five or so.'

'So he could've gone anywhere after that too?'

Robinson was making eye contact with Cole, but avoiding Dixon. 'His car was here.' Defensive now. 'I've got it on the CCTV on the lodge.'

'Easy enough to park another car on the grass verge or down at the tea rooms.' Dixon sighed.

'Allan had taken Gavin's car down to Malaga,' offered Cole.

'He could've hired one. We'd better get that checked.'

'Yes, Sir.'

Dixon turned back to Robinson. 'Did he catch anything?'

'Not this time, not that he told me anyway. He's had some good fish in the past.'

'He showed me a picture on his phone of a large mirror carp he said he'd caught on his previous visit: thirty-five pounds twelve ounces.'

'Did it have a slightly deformed mouth?'

'It did.'

'That sounds like Little Orphan Annie. John caught her last year at thirty-five pound twelve. She was the only big mirror we had.'

'*Was?*'

'Yeah, she died in February. I found her one morning over by the far bank, upside down in the margins.'

'Did anyone know?'

'A couple of lads were here on the day and saw her, but we kept it quiet. It's not something you want to advertise too much, is it.' Robinson's face reddened. 'Hardly a great selling point for a fishery – your biggest fish is dead. We've got a common called Big Orphan Annie, but she was only thirty-three the last time she came out.'

Dixon looked at Cole and nodded. 'Tell them to go in now. Get Scientific on scene and get a trace on his phone. We're on our way.'

'Please tell me John hasn't killed anyone.' Robinson was watching Cole sprint off along the path towards his car.

'Anyone *else*.'

Dixon squeezed past the concrete mixer truck, its huge drum rotating slowly, and ducked under the blue tape, ignoring the small crowd gathered in the car park in front of the show home at Eastfield Park. Cole had left the pool car out on Staunton Lane, behind two more ready mix concrete trucks, and they had walked the rest of the way.

'Are you in charge of this lot?' A man wearing a white hard hat and fluorescent tabard was waving a clipboard at him.

'Yes, Sir.'

'How much longer are you going to be?'

'As long as it takes.'

'We're supposed to be laying foundations down the far end. I've got two mixers out on Staunton Lane and two more on the way.'

Cole stepped in front of the site manager. 'We'll let you know, Sir.'

It was self-sacrifice of the highest order, given that the residents of the other new houses on the small estate had seen them through the windows of the show home and were converging on them, red-faced, no doubt annoyed they had been told to evacuate their homes.

'They can all go home, Nigel,' said Dixon, ducking behind the first of the Scientific Services vans parked outside John Sims's house; an Armed Response car was still on scene, as well as two other marked police cars, their blue lights flashing.

'We've got an alert out for his car, Sir,' said a uniformed sergeant striding towards him down the garden path.

The Armed Response team had gone in as soon as Dixon left Longleat and he knew Sims was not at home, so it hardly came as an unpleasant surprise; unpleasant possibly, but no surprise. 'What about his wife?'

'She's in the sitting room. Not a happy camper.'

'Has she said anything?'

'Plenty of choice language. She did try ringing him for us, but it turned out his phone was on the bedside table.'

That ruled out a trace. 'Scientific?' Dixon asked.

'Mr Watson's in the garage going through his fishing tackle and there's someone else in the shed, I think.'

A battering ram was lying on the grass by the front step, but there were no corresponding marks on the door.

'She opened it in the nick of time, Sir,' said the sergeant.

Dixon stepped into the hall, all the doors on the ground floor open. He glanced into the sitting room, where two uniformed officers were trying to placate Mrs Sims, before walking through to the kitchen and into the garage.

Watson looked up. 'No sign of a crossbow.'

'He'll have it with him.'

'There's an old tin trunk under the workbench he probably hid it in.'

'Let me see.'

Watson dragged a black metal box out into the middle of the garage floor and lifted the lid, revealing several clear plastic boxes containing fishing tackle; enough to open a small shop. Plenty of room for a crossbow too. Dixon pointed to a piece of black cord with a plastic hoop on either end. 'Bag that up, will you?'

'What is it?'

'A crossbow stringer. You try putting the string on a powerful crossbow without one; it's impossible if you're on your own.'

'He *is* our man, then.'

'Let's see if his wife knows what he's been up to.'

He glanced into the back garden where a photographer in a hazmat suit was kneeling on the grass, pointing his camera at a post in the back fence with one hand, holding the conifer branches out of the way with the other.

'What is it?' shouted Dixon out of the back door.

'Whatever he was aiming at, he missed,' the photographer replied over his shoulder. 'There's a hole; the outline matches the broadhead.'

'Plastic milk bottles filled with water are quite popular, I'm told,' said Watson, still on his knees in the garage. 'But they'll have gone in the recycling, I expect. There's nothing in the bin. I did look.'

All was quiet in the sitting room, Mrs Sims having run out of steam. Both uniformed officers rolled their eyes at Dixon when he walked in and sat down on the armchair opposite her.

She looked up and glared at him. 'What's he done?'

'Where is he?' Dixon resisted the temptation to remind her that it was his job to ask the questions, hers to answer them.

'I don't know. I haven't seen him since yesterday.'

'He didn't come home last night?'

'No.'

'Does he own a crossbow?'

'A crossbow?' Her brow furrowed. 'Not that I know of, no. Why would he have a crossbow?'

Watson stopped in the doorway, holding up an evidence bag.

'That's a crossbow stringer,' said Dixon, pointing at the bag. 'We found it in the tin box in your garage.'

'That's his precious fishing tackle. I never go in there; more than my life's worth.'

'And there's a bolt hole in the fence post at the back of your garden. It seems he's not a very good shot.'

'News to me. I've never seen a crossbow and I've certainly never seen him shooting one, here or anywhere else. What's he been doing with it?'

'Killing people,' replied Dixon, matter of fact.

'You're joking! Killing people?' She forced a laugh. 'He's a terrible shot; I had to snatch the gun off him at the funfair.'

'You've got two armed officers standing on your front lawn, Scientific Services vans parked outside, people in hazmat suits searching your house, and you think I'm joking?'

'Who's he supposed to have killed?'

'The people who stole his pension.'

Mrs Sims took a deep breath as the possibility – probability – hit home, her eyes darting to a wedding photograph on the fake mantelpiece over the electric fire. 'Oh, John, John,' she whispered. She closed her eyes, releasing tears that trickled slowly down her cheeks. 'He never told me anything about it.'

'Forgive me, but you don't seem surprised,' said Dixon.

'I'm not, really. And I don't blame him.' She sighed. 'I'm not saying anything against him either. You can't make me.'

'We need to find him before he kills someone else.'

'You won't. And if you do, you won't take him alive. He always said an ex-prison officer wouldn't last five minutes as an inmate – worse than a copper – prisoners coming at him with razor blades and home-made knives. He'd seen it often enough and swore blind he'd never let it happen to him.'

Dixon stood up and walked through the arch into the open plan kitchen-diner, picking up a photograph of Sims holding a mirror carp from the bookshelves behind the dining table. Not the same picture he'd seen on Sims's phone – that one had been taken at night; the framed photograph had been taken in daylight, the fish kept alive in a carp sack until dawn broke.

He unclipped the frame and slid out the picture, turning it over and reading aloud the handwritten note on the back: *Little Orphan Annie, 35lb 12oz.*

'He had that printed online and I framed it for him.' Mrs Sims spoke quietly between the sobs.

'Trouble is, the fish died in February,' said Dixon. 'And he told me he'd caught it last week. Drives a coach and horses through his alibi, doesn't it?'

Chapter Thirty-Two

Dixon flicked on the kettle at the back of Area J half an hour later. 'Let's see if Sims's phone pops up at Harptree Combe and Bradley Stoke at the time of the murders. He probably left it at home, but it's worth checking.'

'Yes, Sir,' replied Cole. 'There's no sign of his Mondeo, but he may be on foot by now anyway. And I've been on to the CCTV Hub; they're keeping an eye out for him.'

Louise had spotted them and stood up behind her workstation, an empty mug in her hand. 'I've had Craig's parents on the phone,' she said. 'He turned up there late last night asking for money.'

'Did they give him any?'

'Three hundred quid.' She picked up the phone on her desk when it started ringing, pressing mute with her index finger. 'He said it was for the deposit on a bedsit.'

'What time was it?'

'Just before eleven. They asked him if it was for drugs and he said he was clean. They told him we were looking for him as well, and why, but he just left.' Louise ducked down behind her computer, talking into her phone. 'Sorry to keep you waiting . . . Oh, shit, really?' Hand over the mouthpiece. 'We've got Sims's car, Sir,' she said. 'The Mondeo. It's in the car park behind Gavin's flat. No sign of Sims.'

'What about Gavin?'

'They knocked but there was no answer. Shall I tell them to kick the door in?'

'Tell them to wait for Armed Response. They can go in as soon as they get there. We're on our way.' Dixon left the kettle boiling and ran towards the door, then stopped and turned back to Louise. 'Better have an ambulance standing by too.'

He'd got as far as the top of the stairs, Cole right behind him, when they were intercepted by Charlesworth and Potter.

'We were just on our way to see you, Nick.' Charlesworth's top button was undone, which was a first. 'Have you got a minute?'

'Not really, Sir.'

'Oh, well, it's another case safely put to bed anyway. Well done.'

'Hardly, Sir. We've got a killer on the loose with a high-powered crossbow and his next victim is on the streets somewhere.'

'Yes, but that's a job for uniform – a standard manhunt situation.'

Potter averted her gaze when Dixon glared at her; a slight raise of the eyebrows and the tiniest of shrugs was as close as he was going to get to an apology.

'It's just a matter of preparing for trial now, surely?' continued Charlesworth. 'We know who the culprits are and they'll both be in custody soon enough.'

'The reallocation of resources,' mumbled Potter.

Dixon had known it was coming, but had hoped they would at least wait until the arrest had been made, or Sims charged even; that would be traditional.

'There'll be witness statements and getting the file ready for the CPS.' Charlesworth was massaging the bridge of his nose between his index finger and thumb – probably snorting too much coke, thought Dixon. 'And we were wondering how many people you thought you might need, now the legwork's done, as it were?'

'As many as you can spare, Sir.' Dixon's voice was loaded with sarcasm as he and Cole set off down the stairs.

'I'll leave it to Deborah then,' replied Charlesworth, shouting over the echo of their footsteps in the stairwell.

'You have to deal with this sort of thing all the time, I imagine, Sir,' said Cole, when he judged that Dixon had finally calmed down enough for conversation. It had taken twenty-five minutes and they were turning off the M5 at Weston by then.

'Welcome to my world.'

'It's been tight in uniform for ages.' Cole shook his head, his unfortunate turn of phrase passing him by. 'Sending two to a disturbance when before they'd have sent four or six. It makes you wonder how they expect us to do the job at all, let alone properly.' He slid his phone out of his pocket. 'It's Louise.'

Dixon listened to Cole's end of the call, but somehow he knew what was coming.

'They've gone in, Sir,' said Cole. 'Gavin's dead.'

'Poor sod never stood a bloody chance, did he?'

'Dr Petersen's elsewhere, so Roger Poland's on his way from Taunton. She wants to know if she should get the local lot in Bath to tell his mother.'

'Better had, although I doubt very much she'll bat an eyelid.'

The car park behind the small parade of shops was full of vehicles by the time Dixon turned in ten minutes later, the sound of sirens still rising above the noise of the police helicopter hovering overhead.

Two Scientific Services vans, three ambulances, an Armed Response team in an unmarked car, and four other police patrol vehicles had crammed into the car park at the back. A Ford Mondeo was parked against the back wall, all four doors and the boot standing open, two Scientific officers in hazmat suits circling it with cameras.

A uniformed officer barring their way at the bottom of the steps soon shifted when he recognised Cole.

'All right, Nige?'

'Yeah.'

'It's a LOB, if you ask me. Got what he deserved.'

'A twenty year old autistic boy is dead and you think it's a load of bollocks, Constable.' Dixon glowered at the uniformed officer.

'Sorry, Sir.'

'Haven't you got somewhere else you need to be?'

'No, Sir.'

'Find somewhere. Now. And you'd better hope I don't remember your badge number.'

Cole raised his eyebrows and tipped his head sharply, the officer getting the message.

'He's not a bad bloke, Sir,' Cole said, catching Dixon up on the landing.

'I'll take your word for it.'

Scientific Services hadn't wasted much time, stepping plates leading through to a living room now brightly lit by arc lamps, the feet of a body lying on the sofa visible behind the door.

Camera flashes were going off at regular intervals, then a shout came from the bottom of the steps. 'Pathologist's here.'

Nice to see a familiar face, thought Dixon, watching Poland climb the steps and lumber along the landing, his metal case in one hand and three hazmat suits in the other.

'I thought you might need this,' said Poland, handing one to Dixon. 'What about you?'

'I'll wait outside.' Cole leaned back against the balustrade and folded his arms. 'Seen it all before; a crossbow bolt in the eye socket.'

'Has he been in there?'

'We've had four already, Roger.'

'Yes, of course.' Poland was steadying himself on a concrete pillar, sliding his feet into the legs of his suit. 'I suppose I'll be seeing less of you if you make the move to Portishead?'

'Maybe.'

'Right.' Poland paused while Dixon zipped up his own hazmat suit. 'Let's go and have a look at . . .' He raised his eyebrows.

'Gavin.'

'And what's Gavin's part in all this?'

'Victim. Used and abused by the prison officers charged with looking after him while he was in Bristol.' Dixon was following Poland along the stepping plates. 'Abandoned by his bloody mother and exploited by everyone else.'

Gavin was sitting up, a crossbow bolt buried in his right eye up to the fletch, the broadhead pinning him to the stud wall behind the sofa. A trickle of blood had run down his cheek, dripping on to his white polo shirt just above the Nike 'swoosh'.

'Do you know who did it?' asked Poland.

'I do.' Dixon was looking around the room; two mugs were sitting on the dining table, both full of cold tea. The television was on, the sound muted. The curtains were closed too, not that Sims could have been overlooked, unless a double decker bus had gone past, perhaps.

'Find out if this is on a bus route, Nigel,' shouted Dixon.

Cole was still out on the landing. 'Yes, Sir.'

'I take it you don't need a cause of death?' asked Poland.

'Just the time.'

Gavin's skin was pale but there was no discolouration yet.

'It's not overly warm in here.'

'The thermostat was on fifteen degrees when we came in, Sir,' replied a Scientific Services officer. 'And the front door's been open since then.'

'Four to six hours ago, then.' Poland looked at his watch. 'So, that's between eight and ten this morning. Rough estimate at this stage, with the usual caveats.'

Dixon leaned over and looked at the wall behind Gavin's head. The curved blades of the broadhead had left circular cuts in the magnolia paintwork, stained red with Gavin's blood; three red rings around the shaft of the bolt, strands of hair sticking out of the holes.

'The hair will be Gavin's.' Poland was looking over Dixon's shoulder. 'From the exit wound at the back of his skull.'

'I get it,' muttered Dixon, deliberately not looking too closely at the back of Gavin's head, the collar of his shirt stained red behind his neck.

'His social worker's here, Sir,' said Cole, from out on the landing.

'I'll be back in a minute, Roger.'

'Have you told his mother?' The question was abrupt and barked at Dixon before he had stepped off the last plate at the front door of Gavin's flat.

'Detective Chief Inspector Dixon,' said Dixon, making a conscious effort not to lose his cool. 'And you are?'

The man sighed, in his brown corduroys and cable sweater. 'Raymond Bryant. Gavin's social worker, as you well know.'

'I don't actually.' Dixon looked him up and down. 'For all I know you're here to read the electricity meter.'

Bryant placed his leather satchel on the balustrade and began rummaging inside, soon producing an ID card on a chain. He thrust it under Dixon's nose. 'There. Now will somebody please tell me what's happened to Gavin?'

'He's been murdered, Sir,' replied Dixon. 'And, yes, we've arranged for local police in Bath to visit his mother.'

'Murdered?' Bryant puffed out his cheeks. 'How?'

'It would have been quick, that's all I can say at this stage.'

'Failed by everybody at every turn; myself included.' Bryant gave a heavy sigh. 'He should never have been sent to prison. It was a feeble attempt to hack GCHQ and he never got close to getting in anyway. And all the pre-sentencing reports recommended a non-custodial sentence as well.'

'When did you last see him?' Dixon sensed that the wind had gone from Bryant's sails – another unfortunate turn of phrase.

'I'd see him once a week and he rang me yesterday. He told me about the fruit machine thing and his arrest.'

'Rang you?' Dixon frowned. 'We've got his phone.'

'He must've got a new one then. I'll have the number in my recents.'

'Not seen a phone,' said the Scientific Services officer who was waiting patiently in the doorway to get past Dixon. 'There's not even a landline.'

'It was a zero-seven number.' Bryant was scrolling through the recent calls on his phone. 'Definitely a mobile. I didn't recognise it to begin with. You know what it's like, taking a call from a number you don't know. Usually I put them through to voicemail, but I took it and it turned out to be Gavin. Here it is.'

'Let's get a trace on it, Nigel,' said Dixon. 'If Scientific can't find it in the flat, there's a chance Sims has taken it with him, thinking we don't know about it.'

'Either that or it's in one of the wheelie bins,' replied Cole.

'Good thinking.' Dixon turned back to the Scientific Services officer. 'No doubt you'll be checking them, if you haven't already.'

Chapter Thirty-Three

'What are you doing here?' asked Jane, when Dixon opened the back door of the cottage.

'Forgot my bloody insulin, didn't I. What about you?'

'I was so bloody bored I took a few hours flexi-time, thought I'd take Monty out. Have you eaten?'

'Not yet.'

'You might as well have something while you're here then. Where's Nigel?'

'I haven't really got time . . .' He gave up when he realised Jane wasn't listening and trudged to the front window, banging on the glass and waving at Cole. 'He's coming in.'

'You've got to eat. I was there when the doctor said you shouldn't skip meals, remember?'

Cole appeared at the back step, hesitating at the sight of a large Staffordshire bull terrier blocking the door.

'Let him in, you twit.' Dixon grabbed Monty by the collar and pulled him away. 'You know Nigel anyway.'

'Thanks.' Cole closed the back door behind him.

'I was just doing some cheese on toast,' said Jane, lying. 'And there's a tin of tomato soup in the cupboard, if you'd like that.'

'Lovely, thank you.'

She opened the cupboard, took out the tin of soup and lobbed it to Dixon. 'Here, make yourself useful.'

'It's called insubordination, Nigel,' Dixon said, making an effort to lighten the mood. He even managed a smile. 'I shall be raising it with her at her next performance review.'

'You could sell tickets for that.'

'How's it going?' Jane chose to ignore the banter.

'Gavin's dead.' Dixon's face hardened, the anger rising in him. Again.

'The autistic lad?'

Cole nodded when Dixon didn't reply.

'And was it an old photograph?'

'The fish died in February,' said Dixon.

'At least you know who it is.' Jane was watching the bread under the grill. 'Now all you've got to do is find him.'

'Before he finds Craig.'

'We've got uniform out in numbers all over the city, and the CCTV people looking out for him.' Cole pulled a chair out from under the small pine table and sat down. 'It's just a waiting game at the moment.'

'Craig knows we're looking for him, and why,' said Dixon, jabbing the button to set the timer on the microwave. 'I just don't get why he doesn't make himself known to us. Most people would want to be in safe custody when there's someone after them with a crossbow. Or am I missing something?'

'He's on spice, right?' asked Jane. 'Because that might be it. He's probably holed up in a crack house somewhere.'

'Out of it,' mumbled Cole.

'We tried all the obvious places yesterday, so word will have got round the police are out and about looking for someone.' Dixon was watching Jane slicing the cheese. 'What we need to do is put someone on the streets, someone who looks the part. We stick out like a sore thumb, apparently.'

'What about Louise?' asked Cole.

'She's got a three year old daughter, Nige. I'm not sending her and he knows what we look like. That leaves Mark or Dave.'

'What about me?' asked Jane, almost absentmindedly. She was placing the cheese on the toast, lining up the symmetrical slices in perfect straight lines. Then she bent over and slid the rack under the grill. 'I could be his sister looking for him, or an ex-girlfriend.'

'No.'

'Why not?' She dropped the knife on the worktop. 'I'm a police sergeant, let me do my bloody job instead of shuffling paper. I could have his photo on my phone and—' She ripped the elastic band from her ponytail and ruffled her hair. 'I've got an old dog walking coat in the shed; a green parka covered in mud where Monty keeps jumping up at me.'

Dixon was sucking his teeth. 'If he's holed up in a crack house we'll never find him.'

'Neither will Sims though, Sir,' said Cole.

'And if he's not, I might just be able to get near him.' Jane was squatting down, watching the cheese starting to melt under the grill.

Dixon took a deep breath and exhaled through his nose. 'Two cars. You and me in one, Nigel, Lou and Mark in the other. You're never more than a hundred yards from both; not one, both. Is that clear?'

'Yes,' huffed Jane.

'And you'll wear body armour and a wire.'

'Fine.'

'I'll charge up that old iPhone 5 in the drawer and you can have his photo on it; it won't matter if someone runs off with that old thing.'

'Fingers or a knife and fork, Nige?' asked Jane. 'The cheese has run a bit.'

'Fingers is fine, ta.'

'I've got an old sleeping bag you can stuff in your rucksack in case anyone checks it; if they pinch it, they're welcome to it.'

'Are you sure you want to do this?' asked Dixon, snatching a private moment with Jane when Cole was on the phone.

'Yes, I am. It's important and it's my job.' She kissed him on the cheek. 'It'll make a nice change to be doing something useful, instead of filing and looking busy.'

'You be bloody careful.'

'I will.' Jane rolled her eyes. 'I have done this sort of thing before, you know.'

'Better take your engagement ring off.'

'For the first and last time,' she said, sliding it off her finger and dropping it into Dixon's open palm.

'One last thing,' he said, when Jane slung her rucksack over her shoulder and turned for the door. 'You'll need this.'

She looked at the dog's lead in his outstretched hand, Monty sitting patiently at his feet, looking up at them. It would be a walk with a difference, but a walk all the same.

'Really?'

'How many homeless people d'you see with dogs? He'll help you look the part.'

'I'm not sure I want to be looking after him as well.'

'You won't be.' Dixon clipped the lead on to Monty's collar and handed the other end to Jane. 'He'll be looking after you.'

◆ ◆ ◆

They met Louise and Mark at Gordano services on the M5 half an hour later, parking in a quiet spot to fit the wire and body armour, then it was on into the city centre. Louise had got Jane's size just about right, but the Velcro was a bit tight around her waist. She winced, breathing in and tugging on the tab as hard as she could.

Must've put on a bit of weight, she thought, finally pulling Dixon's old polo shirt down over the solid Kevlar plates. Type IV, it would stop Harry Callaghan's .44 Magnum, he had assured her, let alone a crossbow bolt.

Not that she was the target, she reminded herself, sitting with her arm around Monty on the back seat of Cole's car.

As she walked down the subway twenty minutes later, she thought about Dixon's last words to her. Ever the romantic, he was: 'Got any dog poo bags?'

Jane made sure her hair covered her earpiece as she stepped out into the late afternoon drizzle of the Bearpit, the smell of stale urine hanging in the damp air. Louise and Mark had left their car in a loading bay just around the corner in the Horsefair and were idly strolling towards her, hand in hand. A nice touch, that.

'Got any change?' Jane asked, when they came within earshot. 'No.'

Mark wouldn't hear the last of that for a while.

In for a pound, in for a penny, she thought, walking up to the queue in front of the Hobb's Lane Collective food kiosk.

'You seen my brother?' she asked the person at the back of the queue, avoiding eye contact, the fingers of her right hand wrapped firmly around the old iPhone, Monty's lead wrapped around her left wrist. She knew Dixon was listening, and only a hundred yards away at most, but still her heart was pumping in her chest. She felt sure they must be able to hear it over the wire.

A shake of the head, then it was on to the next, working her way forwards; a girl, twenty or so, with straggly dark hair. 'You seen my brother?'

'No, sorry.'

On to the next; going through the motions this time, the lad swaying from side to side, his eyes glazed over. No response.

Jane held the phone up to the woman behind the counter. 'You seen my brother?' She was gaining in confidence now.

'He was here last evening,' came the reply. Jane could imagine Dixon sitting bolt upright in the passenger seat of Cole's car.

'D'you know where he is now?'

'No, sorry. He didn't say.'

'How was he?'

'Seemed fine. We gave him a burger and some soup. What's his name?'

'Craig.'

'He said it was Luke. I always ask for their name; sometimes that's all it takes to remind them they're human beings. Are you on the streets too, love?'

'I'm just looking for Craig.'

'And what's your name?'

'Georgie.' Dixon's voice in her earpiece, just in the nick of time.

'Georgie,' said Jane, turning away.

'D'you want anything to eat?'

'No, thanks. I'll be back later.'

'We shut at ten. Shall I tell him you're looking for him, if I see him?'

'No.' Dixon again.

'No, thank you,' Jane said.

Three figures were hunched over against the fencing on the far side of the Bearpit, sitting in the drizzle; they might have been dead were it not for the occasional twitch or random shout. Spice, probably.

'You seen my brother?' she asked, standing in front of them.

One looked up, his hood covering his face. 'Fuck off.'

Jane dragged Monty away when he started growling, heading towards a man standing in the entrance to another of the subways. He was leaning against the wall, smoking and inhaling deep, the sickly sweet smell of cannabis masking the stench of urine. Jane approached, tentatively.

'Twenty quid.'

'I'm not buying,' she said. 'I'm looking for my brother.'

He turned away as she held out the photo in front of her.

'He's into spice and I need to find him.'

'Maybe he doesn't want to be found? Maybe I should just take that phone?' The man leered at her, revealing a gold front tooth. 'And your dog. He'd be worth a few quid for fighting.'

'You can try.' Jane felt oddly calm, and not just because she knew backup was only seconds away. Monty's growl had turned to a snarl before the man had taken even one step towards her. 'Now, would you like to have another look at the photo?'

'Fuck off.'

She watched him turn and sprint off up the subway, disappearing around the corner towards the bus station.

On to the next. It must be a bit like working in telesales, she thought, looking around for someone else to ask.

'Have you tried St Govan's?' asked the girl from the queue. She had been watching Jane from the far side of the Bearpit and had finally summoned up the courage to make her approach. 'He might have gone there.'

'Not yet.' Jane shrugged. 'I thought he might be here, for the spice, y'know.'

'What's your name?'

'Georgie,' Jane lied. She was getting quite good at it.

'I'm Sam,' replied the girl. 'Are you on your own?'

'Apart from Monty here; he's my defence mechanism.'

'I'm on my own too. Can I see the photo again?'

She handed Sam the iPhone, the picture of Craig still on the screen.

'There were two coppers out looking for him last night,' said Sam. 'I've got a tent up on the Downs and they were out speaking to people. What's he done?'

'Nothing.'

'That's what they said, but I didn't believe that crap. Why would they be looking for him if he's done nothing wrong?'

'There's someone trying to kill him.' Jane was watching the queue for the collective kiosk on the far side the Bearpit, which had now grown to ten or twelve people. 'Give me a minute.'

'You're wasting your time,' Sam called after her. 'Nobody will tell you anything.'

It took two for her to work her way along the line and she'd got pretty used to being told to 'eff off' by the end of it. Some had been more polite, but the gist of it had been the same, and more importantly, no one had seen Craig.

Sam was still there when Jane had finished, but was now being jostled by two lads in the entrance to the bus station subway. One had managed to get his hand in her coat pocket, the other holding her arms behind her back.

Jane ran over. 'Can I help you boys?' Monty was up on his hind legs now, snarling and growling at the youths. 'Or I could let my dog off the lead.' She had her fingers hooked in his collar, the clip in the other hand. 'You choose.'

'Thank you.' Sam was watching them sprint off towards the bus station.

'Did they get anything?'

'Just some change I'd scrounged. Not much.' Sam smiled, her relief evident. 'You got somewhere to sleep?'

'I thought I might try St Govan's.'

'You'll be lucky.'

'Maybe see if Craig's there anyway. And the . . .' Jane hesitated. 'Trenchard Street car park, is it? I was told he might be there.'

'Tell you what, I'll come with you. We can try the car park and Broad Quay on the way, and if you don't get in at St Govan's you can sleep in my tent. How's that?'

'Go with her,' whispered Dixon in Jane's ear.

'Deal,' she said.

Sam was leaning over and stroking Monty. 'I like having your defence mechanism around.'

Chapter Thirty-Four

The streetlights had come on by the time Jane reached the far end of Broad Quay. She had spotted Dixon and Cole following them, Louise and Mark quickly taking their place when they sped off around the corner. If they weren't careful, uniform would be pulling them all over for kerb crawling.

A few people had been sitting around Broad Quay enjoying what was left of the evening sunshine, and Sam had taken the opportunity to ask a couple tucking into a takeaway for some spare change.

'Catch 'em when they're eating and they feel guilty,' she'd said, rattling the coins in her clenched fist.

The pavement outside the Hippodrome was busy, several people milling about dressed as Elvis Presley.

'We'll go this way,' said Sam. 'I want to show you something.'

It struck Jane as odd how the crowd on the pavement parted as they approached. She thought at first it might have been Monty making them nervous, but when the same people turned their backs, it hit home. Straggly hair, muddy parka, rucksack: homeless.

A puppy running loose and they'd have been falling over themselves trying to help.

Maybe they assumed she didn't want help, or was past help?

'Hold this.' She handed Monty's lead to Sam. Then she started pushing through the crowd, the picture of Craig on the phone in her outstretched hand. 'Anyone seen my brother?' Those who turned away were followed, the phone shoved under their noses. 'Please help me. I'm looking for my brother.'

'Do you want money?' asked one.

'No, thank you.'

'Oh, right. Let me see the photo.' A shake of the head. 'No, sorry.'

'Don't give her money, Simon, she'll only spend it on drugs,' a voice whispered behind her.

'There were several people by the ticket machines when we parked, he might be up there,' said another.

Then she felt someone pulling on her rucksack, dragging her back out of the crowd.

'You're not very good at this, are you?' said Sam, with a tired laugh.

'It just makes me so fucking angry. The assumptions they make and the way they turn their backs.'

'You'll get used to it. It's the nearest thing to being invisible. C'mon, round here.'

Jane followed Sam into the road beyond the Hippodrome and then stopped beside her on the corner, looking at Cole's car parked on the double yellow lines at the far end. Mercifully, Sam didn't appear to notice it.

'This is Hobb's Lane and that's the collective,' she said, pointing to the first black door. 'They run the kiosk down at the Bearpit. They might be able to help you, but the office doesn't open until ten in the morning now.'

'Thanks.'

'We'll try the car park, but it's not a place to hang about.'

Several people were sitting on the ramp up from the pavement, the bare feet of one poking out from the thin sleeping bag he had wrapped around himself.

Jane slowed and looked over her shoulder.

'Keep moving,' snapped Sam, grabbing hold of Jane's rucksack again.

'He's someone's son.'

'His parents are probably the reason he's here; mine are the reason I am. Is it Craig?'

'No.'

'We'll try the paystations. People have to get their money out and when there's a show on it's a popular spot.'

The sleeping bags in the alcove on the ground floor were empty.

'Probably gone off to get some food,' said Sam. 'You pay when you leave, so it'll get really busy from ten thirty onwards. We can always come back later as well.'

Jane's eyes were watering by the time they reached the top floor. There had been a few people – including Mark – loitering around the paystations, and one asleep in the stairwell, but no sign of Craig.

'We'll go down the way the cars come up.' Sam headed for the ramp. 'It avoids the stairs. And there's lots of fresh air up on the Downs.'

'What about St Govan's?' asked Jane, trotting after her.

'It's on the way.'

The heavy glass door was locked, so Sam pressed the buzzer and looked up at the camera above the door. 'I come in every day to see if they've got any room and the answer's always the same,' she said. 'I'd be in deep shit without my tent.'

The lock buzzed and she snatched open the door. 'You wait; no room at the inn.'

'No dogs, sorry,' said the voice behind the Perspex screen. 'Unless it's a guide dog.'

'I'm just looking for my brother.' Jane was holding the phone up to the window. She held it there for several seconds, waiting for the woman in the office to look up from her computer.

'Nothing for you yet, either, Sam, sorry. You're welcome to spend the night on the sofa.' Finally, she looked up, her eyes taking a moment to focus on the phone screen and Craig's photo. 'Your brother, you say?'

Jane nodded. Dixon had warned her about Andrea: black nail polish, eyeshadow, hair, clothes; it must be her.

'He is not here.' A hint of an eastern European accent.

'Have you seen him?'

'No. Sorry.'

'Leave a message on the board,' said Sam.

'Go ahead.' Andrea ducked back down behind her computer.

'Leave my number,' Dixon whispered.

Jane picked up a red pen: *Craig, ring Georgie pls x Am in a tent on the Downs love u*, followed by Dixon's mobile number.

'If he comes in, I tell him.'

'Thank you.'

'And you be careful, Sam,' Andrea said. 'Not everyone is who they say they are. We had police in here yesterday looking for this man.'

Sam waited until the door slammed behind them. 'She thinks you're a copper,' she said, grinning.

'What the hell gave her that idea?' Jane frowned, trying not to exaggerate too much.

'Oh, for fuck's sake!' Sam sighed. 'Who the bloody hell's done this?'

The light from Jane's phone reflected off Sam's sleeping bag, which had been dragged out of her tent and left in the mud. An open holdall was visible in the entrance, the contents strewn all over the groundsheet.

'Have you lost anything valuable?'

'I haven't got anything valuable. It's just clothes and a few bits. It's not the first time and I'm sure it won't be the last. It's just fucking annoying, that's all. At least they used the zip and didn't cut it open. Then we'd really be in trouble.'

Jane watched Sam on her knees, stuffing her clothes back into the holdall. 'They've had a bloody good rummage through my underwear. I'd only just been down the launderette too. Perverts.'

'What about your sleeping bag?'

'A bit muddy down by my feet, but it's not too bad.'

Jane was peering through the trees back towards the road. 'Can I come in?' She could just about make out Cole's car pulling in and watched him park behind Louise and Mark.

'We're here.' Dixon's voice in her earpiece. 'There's a patrol car doing the rounds and two PCSOs on foot.'

'Yeah,' replied Sam. 'Just do up the outer behind you.'

'Go on, in you go,' said Jane, pushing Monty into the tent. Then she squatted down and followed on her hands and knees, turning to zip up the flysheet.

'The shits have pinched my torch.'

'I've still got some battery on my phone. I charged it up on the train this morning.'

'Where have you come from?'

'London.' Jane sat down cross-legged and opened the top of her rucksack. 'Here.' She handed Sam a can of beer. 'This'll cheer you up.'

'So, what's Craig's story then?' asked Sam, her question punctuated by the snap of the ring pull. 'Why is someone trying to kill him?'

'Prison spice debt,' whispered Dixon. 'Gangs.'

'He got hooked on spice in prison,' said Jane. 'Now he owes people. When you get out the gangs expect payment.'

'I wouldn't touch drugs again if my life depended on it.' Sam took a swig from the can. 'Some people do it to help them get through the day, but I'd rather not get through the day to be honest.'

Jane had managed to balance the old iPhone on her rucksack so that it lit up the inside of the tent, and was sitting with Monty resting his head on her knee. 'How come you find yourself here? You said your parents . . .' Her voice ran out of steam, as if she had taken the question as far as she dared.

'My stepfather was a bit *hands-on*.' Sam's eyes glazed over. 'I told my mum, but she believed him when he denied it, so I left. And that was that.'

'He raped you?'

'It never got that far. He just kept trying it on. Even at their wedding, would you believe it?' Sam took another swig of beer. 'In the end I walked out, but had nowhere to go, so here I am.'

'What about your real father?'

'He's in a new relationship and doesn't give a shit.'

Voices outside the tent, hushed laughter; Monty started snarling. Jane felt a lump rising in her throat. A tent was a helpless place to be when people were lurking in the darkness outside.

'Oi, you lot, sling your hooks!' Footsteps, running, then a beam of light was bouncing around, illuminating the tent before swinging away again. 'Go on, I told you. And if I see you up here again, you'll be arrested.'

Sam looked at Jane and raised her eyebrows.

'They've gone now,' said a gruff voice Jane didn't recognise. 'Police. You all right in there?'

'Yes, thank you,' replied Sam.

'Just kids. They probably won't come back, but we'll check on you again later.'

'Thanks.'

Jane waited, listening to the footsteps fade into the night. 'What's your plan, then?' she asked.

'I haven't got one, really,' replied Sam. 'I'd like to get my own place and a job, but you need an address for the job and a job for the address . . .' Her voice tailed off.

'Would you let me help you?'

Sam sighed. 'I knew it. You're not really homeless, are you?'

'I never said I was, just that I was looking for my brother.'

'You've been wearing a ring recently too. I can see the mark on your finger.'

'I took it off and left it at home.' That bit was true, thought Jane.

'You're married?'

'Engaged.'

'Who to?'

Jane swept her hair back off her right ear and turned to Sam, revealing the earpiece. 'I need to watch what I say because he's listening to this conversation.'

'So you *are* police?'

Jane had expected a protest to come over the wire, but none came; Dixon clearly trusted her judgement. 'Yes, I am.'

'What about Monty, is he yours?'

'Sort of. He belongs to my fiancé.'

'Craig's not really your brother then, I suppose?'

'No, but his life is in danger; that bit's true. We have to find him before someone else does.'

'It's not just about spice, is it?'

'No.'

Sam drained the can and threw it into the corner of the tent. 'I'm sharing my tent with a copper. I thought you were too good to be true. And the bloke listening, where is he?'

'Parked over there.' Jane waved her hand in the direction of the road. 'You remember Hobb's Lane, the car parked on the double yellows? The couple walking across the Bearpit; the bloke at the paystation on the top floor of the car park.'

'Those two just then?'

'I didn't recognise them, but an increased presence was put in place up here yesterday when you were found camping on your own.'

'That was for me?'

'Just for you.'

'Got any more of those beers?' asked Sam.

Jane pulled another can from the plastic loop and handed it to her, watching her mulling something over; the vacant stare, her fingers fumbling for the ring pull. Sam was miles away. If only Jane knew where.

'He's really in danger?'

'Four people are dead already.'

'Five,' whispered Dixon.

'Make that five,' said Jane.

'The bloke listening.' Sam's brow furrowed. 'Was it him here last night?'

Jane nodded.

'He seemed nice.'

'He is.'

Sam took a deep breath. 'Further along, down by the Observatory, there's a seating area and a chicken wire fence with concrete posts along the top of the cliff. There's a gap in the fence this end and the path leads to the cliff top; only it doesn't. You can scramble down to a grassy terrace that's hidden from above. Plenty of room for a couple of tents. I went down there today, thought I might move and it seemed a quiet spot. Only there's a tent already down there and he told me to eff off.'

'Who did?'

'Craig.'

Chapter Thirty-Five

'All right, nice and calm, everyone.' Dixon glanced over his shoulder as Mark's headlights came on behind him, the sound of his engine spluttering into life at the same time as Cole's. 'We don't even know if he's down there yet.'

'What do we do then, Sir?' asked Cole, frowning at him.

'You and I will go down and see if he's there. Mark, you pick up Jane and we'll have those two PCSOs back up here to keep an eye on Sam.' Dixon's phone started buzzing on the dashboard. 'Hang on, Dave's on the phone.'

'Gavin's replacement pay-as-you-go phone's just gone live, Sir,' said Dave. 'If Sims has got it then he's the Bristol side of the suspension bridge, in the triangle between the zoo, the cricket ground and the Observatory.'

'Oh, shit.' Dixon sighed. 'That makes it an immediate threat to life. Let's get backup here now – Armed Response, dogs, and we'd better have the helicopter up as well. Give his position to the CCTV Hub too, Dave, get them looking for him in the right place.'

'Blue lights?'

'Nothing to lose now.' He was watching Jane running across the grass towards Mark's car behind them, Monty trotting along next to her. He rang off and tapped the dashboard. 'Right, go.'

Cole spun his wheels as he pulled out. 'I'll need to find somewhere to turn,' he said, reaching out of the window and sticking a magnetic blue light on the roof of the car.

'Bollocks, Nige. Go across the grass.'

The car slewed from side to side, Cole wrestling with the steering wheel to control the slide as he accelerated across the grass, churning the perfectly manicured turf to mud. Then it bounced off the kerb, the tyres spinning on the road surface.

Streetlights and the mass of bulbs on the suspension bridge lit up the trees in front of them as they accelerated off the roundabout and raced along Clifton Down. Dixon had forgotten Cole was traffic pursuit trained and made a conscious effort not to look across at the speedometer, not that there was much else to look at, apart from trees and startled pedestrians flashing by on the nearside.

Bulbs on the cables and the supports; the bridge at night was a spectacular sight, stretching across the Avon Gorge, the river far below in the darkness, the twinkling lights of the Bristol suburbs visible beyond. The moon was out too; not quite full, but near enough.

Right into Observatory Road.

'Is it your car?' asked Dixon.

'Pool car, why?'

'Go across the grass.'

The car bounced up the kerb, Cole following the footpath that offered the only gap in the trees. Then they were in the clear, the round tower of the Observatory directly in front of them, the bridge beyond.

'Over in that corner.' Dixon was pointing off to their right. 'And we can lose the blue light now.'

Cole slid to a halt on the grass behind a line of trees, empty benches silhouetted against the moonlit sky. Beyond the benches a line of concrete posts marked the wire fence and the top of the cliff.

Dixon had been there once before, finishing a climb on the buttress below the bridge with Jake, the fence posts offering sanctuary that time. He could picture the small terrace, too, and the two hundred foot drop below. Hardly a good place for a spice addict to camp.

'Let's go.' He jumped out of the passenger seat, leaving the door open, and set off across the grass to the gap in the fence hidden in the bushes beyond the benches, Cole right behind him.

Light certainly wouldn't be a problem, the display on the bridge casting an eerie orange glow across the cliff top.

He turned sideways and squeezed through the chicken wire fence, holding the metal links away from his jacket; snag that and the rattle would be enough to wake the dead. He looked at Cole and put his index finger across his lips. 'Shhhh.'

Tiptoeing down the path now, he stopped at the top where it took a sharp turn and dropped down into the void, two figures silhouetted out on the edge of the terrace ten feet below and maybe ten yards away at most. Sims was standing on the left, the unmistakeable outline of a crossbow in his hands, the red dot of the laser telescopic sight in the middle of Craig's chest, the curved blades of the broadhead on the bolt glinting in the orange glow from the lights on the bridge. Three more bolts were mounted in a quiver underneath the arms of the bow, each with a broadhead.

'John Sims!' shouted Dixon, just as the helicopter appeared over the Observatory, the powerful light mounted underneath sweeping the top of the cliffs as it moved towards them.

Blue lights raced across the bridge in the distance, more coming along the A4 far below, the sirens just carrying over the roar of the helicopter's engine, the downdraft sending fallen leaves high into the air all around them.

Then the helicopter was directly overhead, its beam lighting up the terrace.

The green flysheet of Craig's small pop-up tent was flapping violently in the rush of air from the rotor blades. It had been pitched at the back of the terrace, the guy ropes tied to large stone blocks and a sapling fighting for life in a crack in the rock.

Craig himself was bleeding from a head wound, his hair dishevelled and matted.

'How the hell?' Sims kept the red dot squarely in the middle of Craig's chest as he watched Dixon scrambling down the short section of cliff to the terrace.

'Get the helicopter higher,' Dixon said into his microphone. 'I can't hear myself think.' Hands behind him, he kept his eyes fixed on Sims as he picked his way down the top section of cliff, jumping the last few feet on to the terrace.

Cole followed, landing heavily beside him, the downdraft easing off as the helicopter climbed to a higher altitude.

'Hello, Craig,' shouted Dixon. 'You're not an easy fellow to find, are you?'

Craig was standing on the cliff edge with his back to the void, his eyes fixed on the red dot bouncing around in the middle of his chest.

'And as for you.' Dixon turned to Sims. 'Little Orphan Annie died in February, according to the Longleat bailiff.'

Sims shook his head. 'Is that it? Is that all it took?'

'That and a hole in your fence post.' Dixon took a step forward, Cole following without hesitation. 'You're not a very good shot, are you?'

'Good enough,' snarled Sims.

The wire fence started rattling along the top of the cliff as more officers squeezed through the gap and ran along the path.

'Stay back, all of you!'

The footsteps stopped at the top of the cliff. 'Armed Response are on scene,' said Jane, her voice in Dixon's earpiece.

He took another step forward, again matched by Cole to his left. 'So, this was all about your pension, John?'

'They took what was left of our lives, so we took what was left of theirs.'

'What about Gavin?' Another step forward.

'Collateral damage.'

'I'll tell his mother,' said Dixon, a sarcastic edge to his voice. 'That will be a great comfort to her, I'm sure.'

'It had to be done. And so does this.'

'How d'you expect to get away? Look around you.' Dixon craned his neck to look past Sims and over the cliff. 'We've even got the boat out on the river.'

'I've spent my entire working life inside and I'll be fucked if I'm dying inside as well.'

'Then you'll die here and now.'

'Not before I've taken this little shit with me.'

Another step forward. Cole followed.

'Frank kept his part of the bargain,' said Dixon. 'I'm guessing you planned it all between you?'

'Two each, that was the deal.'

'And if either of you got caught you'd confess to all the murders?' Keep him talking, at least until Armed Response could get into position.

'Neither of us are going to prison,' said Sims, his eyes darting from Craig to Dixon, to Cole, the top of the cliff and back round again. 'He knows what it'll be like for a prison officer on the inside; he'll never serve a single day. And neither will I.'

Dixon moved slowly, bringing his right hand up to the microphone pinned to his jacket and lifting it towards the corner of his mouth. 'Put Frank Allan on suicide watch now.'

Sims laughed. 'He's a prison officer, for fuck's sake. That won't stop him.'

'That's for our benefit, John, not his.' Dixon shrugged. 'We've got to have a tick in all the right boxes for the inquest. You know how it is.'

'I know how this is too. You keep me talking, edging ever closer until you can make a grab for the weapon. I've done it often enough inside to know the drill.' Sims took a step towards Craig, still holding the crossbow in both hands. 'Only that's not how it works this time.'

Two paces at most between Sims and Craig now; at that range the bolt would go clean through him. Dixon was losing control; things coming to a head before Armed Response had got their arses in gear.

Too bloody soon, by half. Fuck it.

He took two steps forward; Cole followed again – *good lad.*

Sims swung the crossbow towards Dixon, holding it in his outstretched right hand, his index finger clenched around the trigger, the red beam of the laser sight now pointing squarely at him.

'Oh, shit no, don't!' Jane's voice in his ear and up on the cliff top behind him, safely out of the way.

'That's far enough,' growled Sims. 'It ends now.'

Dixon looked down and watched the red dot hovering in the middle of his chest. He glanced at Cole. 'Five seconds, Nige,' he whispered, taking a deep breath.

Then he stepped forward.

Chapter Thirty-Six

A searing pain exploded across his chest. Then he was falling, a blood-curdling scream echoing in his earpiece. Dixon landed flat on his back, fighting for breath, gasping and sucking in gulps of air.

'You fucking . . .' A shout from near the cliff edge, the voice fading into the distance; the terrace plunged into darkness as the helicopter moved away, its light searching the void below.

Cole was shouting into his phone. 'We need an ambulance now. Officer down!'

Watching too many American cop shows on the TV, thought Dixon.

Odd, the things you think of at a time like this.

Then the coughing started, each rasp sending a stabbing pain tearing across his ribcage. He looked down at the crossbow bolt buried in the middle of his chest and grimaced. It had seemed like a good idea at the time.

Fighting for breath.

Cole knelt beside him. 'Breathe through your nose, Sir. Nice and easy.'

'Shit, shit, shit.' Jane's voice.

He felt hands clawing at his shirt, ripping at the buttons.

'You've got your body armour on, you beauty!' she screamed.

He watched the tears streaming down her cheeks as she tore at the Velcro side strips, releasing the front plate. She thrust her hand up behind the Kevlar, smiling down at him. 'It's not gone through.' Laughing and crying at the same time now, she leaned forward and planted a kiss on his forehead, holding his face in her hands. 'Just breathe,' she said, her voice soft and calm.

His gasps slowed, breathing through his nose now, filling his lungs with air. 'Where's Sims?' he spluttered.

'Gone over the edge,' replied Jane. 'Don't worry about him now. Craig's safe, we're all safe. That's all that matters.'

'But—'

'Don't. Worry.'

'Paramedics coming through!' The scene was lit by torches and phones held aloft. 'Let's get this off him.'

That was a decent shirt, Dixon thought, watching a pair of scissors working their way up the sleeves. Then the Velcro shoulder straps on the body armour were ripped apart and it was slid from underneath him, the bolt still sticking out of the front plate; an oxygen mask clamped across his face, the elastic snapping back behind his head.

'What's his name?'

'Nick,' replied Jane.

'You're going to be all right, Nick,' said the paramedic kneeling next to him. 'The body armour did its job and stopped the bolt, but you've been winded and you've got a blunt force injury to the chest. Just breathe normally. Can you taste blood?'

'No.'

'That's a good sign. Are you in pain?'

'Worse when I cough.'

'We're going to get you to the hospital as quick as we can. We need to get you checked over.'

'Where's Monty?' Dixon asked, holding the oxygen mask away from his mouth, his eyes wide looking up at Jane.

'Who's Monty?'

'His dog.' Jane smiled down at him. 'Lou's got him in her car.'

'Take him home.'

'I will, Sir.' Louise's face appeared from behind one of the phones being held aloft. 'Jane's given me her keys. I'll see to it.'

'His food's in the cupboard.'

'She knows,' said Jane, still smiling.

'Oh, no, you don't.'

Dixon slumped back into the pillows and closed his eyes.

'You're staying right where you are,' said Jane.

The worst part of it all had been getting to the top of the cliff strapped to a stretcher; bloody terrifying, that. He'd offered to climb up and had felt perfectly capable of it, but the paramedics had been adamant. And so had Jane. There really had been no escape.

Then had come the ride in the ambulance, various people poking and prodding his chest on arrival at the hospital, followed by an X-ray. Now he was lying in a private room, wired up to at least two machines. He turned his head on the pillow and watched the heart monitor, the line jumping at regular intervals, just as it should.

'They're wasting their time with that,' he said, from behind his oxygen mask.

'Why?'

'My heart always skips a beat when you're in the room.'

'You soppy sod.'

The cannula in the back of his left hand was a pain in the arse, if such a thing was possible. And there was something clamped to the tip of his right index finger; he'd found that out when he'd tried to scratch his nose. What's more, it had hurt like the devil when the nurse had stuck the heart monitor patches on his chest – and getting them off would be even worse.

The stabbing pain had gone at least, although he hadn't felt the urge to cough for a while; a side effect of the morphine, probably.

He was trying to focus on Jane sitting on the end of his bed. 'Have you got my insulin?'

'I gave it to the doctor and they've got you on an insulin pump to keep your blood sugar levels stable. That's the thing in the back of your hand.'

He noticed the clipboard first, then the woman holding it; peering at him over a pair of reading glasses, she was. Most unnerving.

'We've got the results of your X-ray,' she said, with a reassuring smile. 'You've fractured your sternum; or your breastbone, I should say.' She was rubbing the tips of her fingers up and down in the middle of her chest. 'Right here. It's a nasty one, I'm afraid, and there's not a lot we can do except give you pain relief. It's not something we can put in plaster.'

'Will he be all right?'

'It'll take a few weeks, but he should be fine.' She held the X-ray up to the light and pointed at it. 'You can see a nice clean crack here. And he's also got an eggshell fracture on the outer surface. Imagine hitting the top of a boiled egg with a spoon. It must have been one hell of an impact.'

'It was,' mumbled Dixon. 'Take it from me.'

'We'll be keeping you in overnight to monitor your heart and lungs.'

'Overnight?' He frowned. 'It must be two in the morning already.'

'Till later on today then. In rare cases we see soft tissue damage to the heart or lungs and sometimes both, so we need to check that before we let you go. Your heart is looking good.' She was watching the screen behind his bed. 'And your blood oxygen levels look fine too, so you may have got away with it.'

'Thanks.'

'More often than not these types of injuries are caused by seatbelts, so you're quite a novelty around here.'

'He's one of those everywhere he goes,' muttered Jane.

'It's going to be pretty uncomfortable for a while, so we'll let you go with some Tramadol. Have you had that before?'

'When I got stabbed.'

'Stabbed and shot? You have been a busy bunny.'

'And burnt,' offered Jane.

'Don't remind me.'

'The hardest part is going to be coughing, but you must keep doing it. Don't stifle them, whatever you do; you have to clear the gunk off your lungs or it might set up a chest infection and that can lead to pneumonia if you're not careful. Is that clear?'

'Painfully.'

'No driving for six weeks either, and if you get in a car, for God's sake put a cushion between you and the seatbelt. All right, that's it from me,' said the doctor. 'I'm back on duty at two o'clock tomorrow afternoon and we'll see if we can't let you go home then.'

'Thank you,' said Jane.

'And there's someone outside to see you.'

'At this time in the morning?'

The doctor hooked the clipboard over the end of the bed. 'He said he was the assistant chief constable, so I didn't really feel we could say no.'

'Brace yourself,' whispered Dixon.

Charlesworth walked in and dropped his cap on the end of the bed. 'How are you feeling, Nick?'

Full dress uniform? You needn't have bothered on my account.

'Fine, Sir.'

'Somehow I doubt that.' Charlesworth seemed mesmerised by the heart monitor, watching the flat line blip at regular intervals. 'I was at a dinner when I got called in to Portishead and I've seen the footage from the helicopter. I'll be putting you forward for a medal first thing in the morning.'

'I'd rather you didn't, Sir.' Dixon was trying to sit up. 'Give one to Nigel Cole, he was with me every step of the way.'

'I saw that.' He turned to Jane. 'And you've been undercover, I gather?'

'Yes, Sir.'

'And you authorised it, I suppose?'

'I did, Sir,' replied Dixon. 'It's one of the advantages of my new rank.'

'Yes, well.' Charlesworth cleared his throat. 'Well done anyway, Jane. You're wasted in Safeguarding and it'll be good to have you back in CID in due course.'

Jane looked at Dixon and offered a guilty smile.

'How long will you be in here?' asked Charlesworth.

'Tomorrow lunchtime, apparently. They just want to be sure there's no damage to my heart or lungs.'

'So do I.'

'I feel fine. Really. It's just cracked my breastbone.'

'Thank God for Kevlar. It's just a shame Peter Lewis wasn't wearing his.' Charlesworth was gesturing to the chair next to Dixon's bed. 'D'you mind if I . . . ?'

'Not at all, Sir.'

'Sims is dead, as you may have guessed. His body is on a ledge about twenty feet off the ground. The cliff rescue team are recovering him now. We've got the crossbow as well; that got caught in a tree on the way down.'

'What about Craig Pengelly?'

'We've put him up in a hotel and someone will be getting a statement from him in the morning. Deborah Potter will sort it out, you needn't trouble yourself with that.'

'Is there any other footage, Sir?'

'Uniform was on scene so there should be bodycam footage available as well.'

'What happened?'

'From what I could see, after you were hit, Sims made a lunge for Pengelly. The lad managed to wrestle himself free and that's when Sims went over the edge. Saves the taxpayer a few quid. And we've still got Allan.'

'We've got him for conspiracy to murder, maybe, but the chances are we'll end up extraditing him to Spain for the Costa murders.'

Charlesworth's eyes narrowed as the realisation dawned on him. 'Shame, it would have been a public relations triumph for us.'

'We'll live, Sir.'

'Well, listen, you take your time.' Charlesworth stood up. 'Put your feet up for a while, go walk your dog, and I'll ask Deborah Potter to wrap up the major investigation team. I do still need your application for the super's vacancy, don't forget.'

'Thank you, Sir.'

Jane waited until Charlesworth had disappeared along the corridor before softly closing the door behind him.

'So, that's it then?' she asked, placing the back of her hand on Dixon's forehead. 'Case closed.'

'Really?' He settled his head back into the pillows. 'Whatever gave you that idea?'

Chapter Thirty-Seven

'I've got you a clean shirt and a cushion off the sofa.'

'You could've left the cushion in the car.' Dixon sighed. 'People will think I've got piles.'

'I'll carry it if it makes you feel any better.' Jane dropped the holdall on the end of the bed. 'What did the doctor say?'

Dixon was sitting on the edge of the bed stamping his feet into his shoes. 'Heart and lung function are all perfectly normal, so I can go. I've got to take it easy and keep taking the painkillers. She said I'd "dodged a bullet", which was a rather unfortunate turn of phrase.'

'Louise took Monty home with her in the end. He's had a whale of a time playing with Katie and eating them out of house and home.'

'Where is he now?'

'At the cottage.' Jane looked at her watch. 'Lucy will be there by now. She jumped on a train when I told her what had happened.'

'I thought she was grounded?'

'There was no stopping her, apparently, so Judy gave her the money for the ticket rather than let her hitch-hike again. I said I'd give it her back.'

Dixon was trying to put on the clean shirt, but struggling to lift his arm high enough.

'Here, let me.' Jane pulled the sleeve down and hooked it over his hand. 'There.' She stepped back and watched him button the shirt. 'Good thing I didn't bring a polo shirt, you'd never have got that on.'

'What did you do about Sam?'

'I got her into a refuge in Bridgwater; pulled a few strings, called in a few favours.'

'Did you remember fresh insulin?'

'In the bag, but we're going straight home anyway so . . .' Jane's voice lost momentum when Dixon smiled at her. She sighed. 'Where?'

'Portishead first, then home.'

'Why?'

'I need to see the footage of what happened on the terrace.'

'Charlesworth told you what happened,' protested Jane, half-heartedly.

'I need to see it for myself.'

'You were shot in the chest!'

Dixon stood up and put his hands gingerly around Jane's waist. 'When were you going to tell me?'

It was mid-afternoon by the time they arrived in Area J. Louise was there, with Mark and Nigel Cole.

'What are you lot doing here?' Dixon asked.

'We're doing our witness statements, sir,' replied Louise. 'It was quite a night. Are you all right?'

'Fine, thanks.'

'He's broken his breastbone,' said Jane. 'Powerful painkillers and no driving for six weeks.'

'We thought you'd be putting your feet up, Sir,' said Cole, waiting by the kettle.

Dixon stopped in front of him, his hand outstretched, and managed to hide the wince when Cole clasped it firmly and shook it. He didn't feel the need to say anything. A handshake was enough.

'Mr Charlesworth rang me this morning.' Cole turned back to the kettle. 'He's putting me forward for a commendation. I suppose I have you to thank for that as well, Sir?'

'Don't thank me. I nearly got you killed, remember?'

'Bollocks.' Cole gave a dismissive chuckle. 'Coffee?'

'Thanks.'

'Deborah Potter's called a full team briefing for tomorrow morning at ten,' said Louise. 'I don't think she was expecting you in.'

'Where's the footage from the terrace last night?' Dixon asked, sitting down in front of a computer at a vacant workstation.

'We've got the helicopter camera and bodycam footage from two officers on scene so far. Why?'

'I need to see what happened after I was hit.'

Jane sat down on the empty chair at the workstation next to him and slid it across as he logged in and opened the footage from the helicopter first.

Filmed from above, the scene lit by the searchlight, Dixon could see the angle changing, the lens zooming in on the terrace until the helicopter was directly overhead, Cole following him down the cliff and then jumping the last few feet. Craig's tent, pitched at the back of the terrace against the cliff, reflected the powerful beam and appeared to glow.

Sims and Craig were standing on the edge of the terrace, the drop directly behind them, the trees at the bottom just visible in the gloom below. Sims was holding the crossbow in both hands, the stock tucked under his right elbow, his right index finger on the trigger. He was looking from Dixon to Craig and back again. Dixon remembered the conversation – 'Two each, that was the deal.' The phrase had been going round and round in his head all night; a night of broken, chemically induced sleep.

'Is there a transcript available?'

'They're working on it now, Sir,' replied Louise.

'Good thing we were wearing that wire,' said Jane.

The first step forward, figures on the terrace smaller now that the helicopter had increased altitude.

'You can zoom in.' Jane reached across and took over the mouse. A few clicks, a scroll and the terrace filled the screen, although slightly blurred now.

More back and forth, then another step forward.

Sims was clearly getting more and more agitated as Dixon and Cole approached. Craig standing still and appearing calm, despite the crossbow pointed straight at him; occasionally he glanced down at the red dot, but otherwise he was keeping his eyes fixed on Sims.

Two steps forward.

Jane took Dixon's hand and squeezed it. 'You don't have to watch the next bit.'

'Yeah, I do.'

Sims swung the crossbow towards him, another step, then Dixon was falling back.

'It knocked me a good few feet.' He was rubbing the back of his head with his hand. 'It looks like I hit my head, but I didn't.'

'Shame, it might have knocked some sense into you.'

Cole lurched forward to grab Sims, but he was already on the move, the bow in his left hand now, reaching out, trying to grab

Craig's coat. Arms flailing at Sims, Craig side-stepped the lunge and appeared to lash out as he threw himself away from the edge.

Then Sims was gone, falling away into the gloom, the helicopter camera swinging away, trying to follow his body down the cliff face.

'Rewind it.'

'Must I?'

'Yes.'

Ten minutes and twenty rewinds later Dixon looked away from the screen. 'Let's try the bodycam footage; see if that's any better.'

'Better for what?'

Jane opened the first piece of body camera footage. It showed the terrace from the top of the cliff – thirty feet at most – and started as Dixon and Cole were climbing down, Sims and Craig in view on the edge.

'I think the camera's on the bloke standing next to me,' Jane said. Then her voice on the footage: *Armed Response are on scene.* 'Yeah, he was right next to me; one of the Bristol lot.' She turned to Dixon. 'What exactly is it you're looking for?'

'I'll know it when I see it.'

Heads popped up from behind computer screens when Jane screamed on the film. 'God, that was me, wasn't it?' she said, her face reddening. 'Turn the volume down before you rewind it.'

The same scene unfolded in front of them time and again, albeit from a different angle: Dixon fell back; Cole lurched forward; Sims made a grab for Craig; Craig lashed out; Sims went over the cliff.

By the time Dixon had watched it ten times Louise was standing behind them with her arms folded. 'Sims tried to grab Craig and take him over the cliff with him, if that's what you're looking at, Sir. Craig may have pushed him away, but even if he did, it was self defence.'

'Looked that way to me,' said Mark.

'Who's taking a statement from him?' asked Dixon.

'Dave's gone over to the hotel, with Kevin,' replied Louise. 'Kevin'll be going back to Zephyr tomorrow, I expect. Deborah Potter was talking about wrapping the whole thing up once the statements had been done. All that's left after that is Allan's prosecution for conspiracy and whatever the Spanish want to do; the CPS will be liaising with them over that, so . . .' Her voice tailed off, her frown etching deeper into her forehead. She had worked with Dixon long enough to know the signs. 'What are you thinking?'

Mark's head popped up again from behind his computer.

'There are far, far too many unanswered questions left,' Dixon said, shaking his head.

'Like what?' asked Mark.

'Like why did Sims kill Godfrey Collins?' Dixon folded his arms. 'We still haven't found a connection between them. Both admitted pretty much everything; Allan in interview and Sims on the terrace. It was about their pensions, but Collins had nothing whatsoever to do with the pension scam. He was up to his neck in the loan charge thing, but not the pensions. So, you tell me, why did Sims kill him?'

'No idea, Sir,' said Cole, daring to speak out loud what everyone else was thinking; that much was clear from their blank expressions.

'Watch the footage again and read the transcript when it's available.' Dixon stood up. 'The key to this is what Sims says and does, not Craig.'

'What d'you mean?' asked Louise.

'Sims and Allan teamed up to get revenge for the loss of their pension funds. They've both admitted that. "Two each, that was the deal," he said. So why was Sims trying to kill Craig when they'd already killed their two each?'

Dixon waited.

'Two each is four and Craig would make five. Whatever Craig did on the terrace was self defence, we'll never prove otherwise,' he continued. 'But why was he having to act in self defence?'

'Craig was involved in the pension transfer scam, Sir,' said Louise. 'He was convicted of it and sent to prison.'

'Maybe Collins was killed by mistake?' offered Cole. 'Have we thought of that?'

'Collateral damage,' said Mark. 'Like that poor lad, Gavin.'

'Did Craig have a phone on him yesterday?'

'Yes, Sir,' replied Louise. 'He got himself a new pay-as-you-go when he got out of Leyhill.'

'Run a check on the calls, will you? And expedite it.'

'What do we say if Deborah Potter wants to wrap up the major investigation team tomorrow morning?' she asked. 'You're officially off sick, and she's taken over as SIO; that's what her email said.'

'Then you say, "Yes, Ma'am, three bags full, Ma'am."'

'Yeah, right.'

Dixon picked up his mug and took a sip. 'Stone cold,' he said. 'But it'll do.' He snapped a couple of Tramadol out of the foil sleeve and took them with a swig of cold coffee, swallowing hard. 'Lou, d'you remember that micro SIM card we found at Collins's bedsit? It was buried in a lump of Blu Tack on the back of a postcard.'

'We had it checked and there was nothing on it,' said Mark.

'I'm interested in the postcard, not the SIM.'

'There's a scan of it on the system,' said Louise. 'I'll print it off for you.'

'Thanks.'

'You really should be at home with your feet up, Sir,' said Cole.

'Too many questions going round and round in my head for that.'

'Here it is, Sir.' Louise handed Dixon a piece of paper off the printer. 'I've printed it double-sided, but there's nothing on the back to tell you where it is. It just says "Postcard of unknown beach" on the evidence log. Looks a bit like Scotland to me, though.'

He looked down at the picture: dark blue water, waves lapping at golden sand. 'A nice place for a dog walk.'

'Or a holiday.'

'Fat chance.'

'Thank you for looking after Monty, by the way,' said Dixon, with a sideways glance at Jane.

'We may have to get a dog,' replied Louise. 'Katie loved having him around.'

'Where will you be if anything comes up?' asked Cole.

'He'll be on the beach with Monty,' replied Louise, smiling. 'It's where he always goes to clear his head.'

Chapter Thirty-Eight

Dixon was deep in thought as they drove south on the M5, heading home. Questions, questions everywhere and not a . . .

Jane opening the driver's door and a dog barking dragged him back to the present; the Land Rover parked behind his cottage. Then the thud of paws up at the passenger door. She wound down the window and shouted across to Lucy who was standing in the back door of the cottage. 'Put him on his lead, will you? I don't want him jumping up at Nick.'

'I've got him.' Lucy hooked her fingers in Monty's collar and dragged him away from the passenger side of the Land Rover.

Dixon opened the door and slid out gingerly, Lucy laughing at the cushion in his hand. 'You got piles?' she asked.

'Nice to see you too.'

'I'm just kidding.' She waited while Jane took hold of Monty's collar, then threw her arms around Dixon, recoiling when he grimaced. 'Sorry!'

'It's fine.'

'There are some videos on YouTube of people firing crossbows at body armour.' She grinned. 'Hits it with a hell of a thwack.'

'Tell me about it.'

'You can watch them later, Nick,' said Jane, rolling her eyes. 'I'm sure you'll enjoy that.'

'And what's this I hear about you paedophile hunting?' He frowned at Lucy. 'Idiot.'

'I know,' she replied. 'I'm sorry.'

'If you want to do something about it, pass your exams and join the police.'

'I'm joining the Police Cadets. And I'm free on Christmas Eve.'

'You told her?'

'I had to,' said Jane. 'She's my bridesmaid.'

'There's no getting out of it now, then,' he muttered, with a rueful smile.

'I put the kettle on,' said Lucy. 'And I got a chocolate cake.'

'He's diabetic.'

'It's sugar free.'

'Is it?'

'Not really, but he can have a small piece. It's not every day you get shot by a crossbow bolt, is it?'

'A small piece then.'

Dixon was starting to like his future sister-in-law more and more each day. 'I can walk it off on the beach.'

'Are you sure you should be going?' asked Jane.

'We'll drive round and park on Berrow Flats.' He sat down on the sofa, patted the seat and Monty jumped up, sitting quietly next to him, nuzzling his ear.

'It's almost like he knows there's something wrong with you,' said Lucy.

'Of course he knows.' Jane was in the kitchen, raising her voice over the boiling kettle. 'And it's six quid to park on the beach. They don't stop charging till October.'

'I'll be able to afford it on a super's salary. And besides, the bloke in the kiosk will have gone by the time we get there.'

Lucy dropped down on to the sofa next to Dixon. 'Here.' She handed him her phone. 'This one's the soft Kevlar and the bolt goes straight through – it's the sharp point, it cuts straight through the fibres, only a couple of inches so you'd probably survive it.' She didn't take the hint and held her phone in front of him when he tried to ignore it. 'Was your body armour hard or soft?'

'Hard.'

'Let me see if I can find a video of that.'

'Really, don't bother.'

'For God's sake, Lucy, he doesn't want to sit there watching bloody videos of people firing crossbows at body armour.' Jane was standing over them with a mug of tea in each hand. 'Go and cut the cake.'

'Sorry.'

'How's your chest?'

'The bruise is coming out, and it's going all sorts of different colours.'

'C'mon, get this down you.' Lucy handed Dixon a wedge of cake, just out of Jane's reach. 'Monty's had a stressful time as well, y'know, and he needs a run.'

Twenty minutes later they parked on the beach at Berrow. The tide was out, revealing a vast expanse of glistening wet sand, mud shimmering in the distance down by the water line. Dixon opened the back of the Land Rover and Monty jumped out, heading for

Burnham. 'Looks like we're going that way. You'll have to throw this for him,' he said, handing the tennis ball launcher to Lucy.

'There's nothing in for supper,' said Jane, as they strolled along the sand.

'Red Cow it is then.' Dixon was watching Lucy playing with Monty, pretending to throw the ball then running off with it when Monty went in the opposite direction. He soon caught her up, until she did it again; the silly arse fell for it every time.

'I think I'm putting on a bit of weight.'

'You're probably pregnant.' Matter of fact.

Jane stopped in her tracks. 'What on earth makes you say that?'

'You're not eating any more than you were before, and we decided to let nature take its course, so what else could it be? It's obvious when you think about it.'

'It was supposed to be a surprise . . .' Jane jogged the few steps to catch him up.

'The obvious answer is always the best one. And the most likely.'

'How would you feel if I am?'

'Over the moon.'

'I haven't done a test yet.'

'Well, you'd better do one, sharpish. Until we know one way or the other, there's no gin for you.'

'Yeah, but I might not be!'

'If there's no sugar for me, there's no gin for you. Unless and until we know for sure you're not.'

'Fascist.'

'Now you know how it feels.' Dixon wrapped his arms around her waist and kissed her.

'Get a room!' shouted Lucy, throwing the ball at them, Monty tearing after it, spraying them with sand as he belted past.

'I suppose it is obvious, when you think about it,' said Jane. 'What other explanation could there be?'

'I wish you'd bloody well told me before you went undercover on the streets.'

'I didn't know for sure. I still don't.'

'What's that old wreck over there?' asked Lucy, running over with Monty jumping up at her.

'It's what's left of the SS *Nornen*,' replied Dixon. 'It ran aground in a storm in 1897. The local lifeboat got everybody off, even the dog. It's on the honours board in the lifeboat station.'

'The lifeboat was a rowing boat back then,' said Jane. 'Which makes the rescue even more impressive. Sort of makes you wonder where that yacht is now.'

'The *Sunset Boulevard*?' Dixon was staring at the wreck, deep in thought.

'And the people on board. How many was it?'

'Four.'

What other explanation could there be?

'Right then.' Dixon snatched the tennis ball launcher from Lucy. 'We need to go.'

'Where?' she demanded.

'There's a twenty-four-hour chemist in Bridgwater.'

'Are you all right?'

'We need a pregnancy testing kit,' he replied, smiling.

'Three Diet Cokes, please, Rob,' said Dixon, standing at the bar in the Red Cow an hour and a half later. 'Two fish and chips and a chicken curry.'

'Diet Coke? Are you all right?' asked the barman.

'I'm on painkillers and Jane's pregnant.'

'Congratulations!'

'Thanks.'

'We should crack open a bottle of . . .' He thought better of it. 'There's not a lot of point, is there?'

'Not really. Keep it under your hat, though. It's early days.'

'Yes, of course. Look, you go and sit down, I'll bring it over.'

Dixon slid into the corner of the bench seat, stepping over Monty who was stretched out in front of the fire, and downed a couple of Tramadol with a swig of Coke when Rob placed the drinks on the table.

'I should tell my mum and dad.' Jane leaned across and put her arm around Lucy – Dixon spotted the flash of guilt. Jane had been the lucky one, adopted at birth by parents who had doted on her ever since; Lucy, on the other hand, had stayed with their biological mother, although she had spent much of her time in and out of foster care.

'They'll be chuffed to bits,' said Lucy, still grinning from ear to ear.

'I think we should wait.' Dixon took another swig of Coke. 'You're not supposed to tell people until three months, or something like that.'

'It's thirteen weeks, I think,' said Jane. 'But, you're right. We'll wait. I must be about seven or eight now, so it's not long anyway.'

'Tell me about the case you're working on,' said Lucy.

'Everybody's either dead or in custody, but he still has questions, apparently.' Jane raised her eyebrows.

'Questions which you answered,' said Dixon.

'Me? What did I say?'

'You said, "It's obvious when you think about it, what other explanation could there be?" And it is obvious. Answer every single question with the most obvious answer there could be and the whole thing drops into place.' Dixon slid a piece of paper out of his pocket and handed it to Lucy. 'Here, clever clogs, tell me where this is.' He unfolded the printed copy of the postcard found in Godfrey Collins's bedsit. 'It doesn't say on the back,' he said, when she turned it over.

'It looks cold, so it's not tropical. Could be Scotland or some-where like that.'

'You're not far off. Actually it's Old Grimsby Beach on Tresco,' said Dixon. 'I put it on the force's Facebook page and someone identified it for me.'

'There you are, I told you.' Lucy looked at Jane and gave an emphatic nod. 'Where's Tresco?'

'The Scilly Isles.'

'Is it significant?' asked Jane.

'It's the missing piece of the jigsaw puzzle.'

The ripple of applause that started when Dixon opened the glass doors on the second floor of the operations building had become a standing ovation by the time he reached Area J.

Deborah Potter was standing in front of the whiteboard, the whole major investigation team assembled for debriefing and real-location; Jez was hovering at the back armed with her clipboard. Dixon knew the drill: a skeleton team would be left to prepare the file for the CPS and the rest would move on. It was a tried and tested strategy and it worked well, provided the current case had been resolved. And, contrary to popular belief, this one had not.

Much to his embarrassment, Potter ushered him to the front of Area J, stepped back and joined in the applause. Charlesworth too, striding along the aisle.

'I heard you were in,' he shouted in Dixon's ear. 'You're sup-posed to be off sick.'

'It isn't over,' said Dixon.

Potter frowned, shaking her head while she waited for the applause to subside. 'Take fifteen minutes, everybody,' she said, with a final clap of her hands.

Charlesworth gestured to a meeting room on the far side of the open plan office. 'Let's have a private chat.'

Dave intercepted Dixon on the way, handing him two documents. 'That's a copy of Craig's witness statement and the phone records you asked for, Sir,' he said. 'Craig obviously wasn't expecting us to find out about his new phone. There's a call to Sims's landline the day before yesterday and then two from Gavin's mobile yesterday, the last an hour before Sims died.'

'Which makes Craig's statement a pack of lies?'

'Pretty much.' Dave was watching Potter standing in the open doorway of the meeting room, her hands on her hips. 'They think it's all over, don't they?'

'They do.'

'Rather you than me.'

'Thanks.'

'Sit down, Nick,' said Charlesworth, when Dixon walked into the meeting room. 'How's the ribcage this morning?'

'Fine, Sir.'

'You said the case isn't over and yet we've got Allan in custody and Sims is dead. What else is there?'

'I was just going to wind down the major investigation team.' Potter failed to hide her exasperation. 'People are needed elsewhere.'

'You can let them go,' replied Dixon. 'I just need Louise, Dave, Mark and Nigel Cole. Nigel was in at the start so it's only right he should be in at the finish.'

'What finish?' snapped Potter.

Dixon took a deep breath. 'It was a hell of a coincidence, Sims being on the terrace with Craig Pengelly when we got there, don't you think?'

'Are you saying it wasn't a coincidence?'

'I am.' He slid the phone records across the table to Potter. 'That's Craig's phone records for the last forty-eight hours. He got himself a new pay-as-you-go phone when he was released from Leyhill – he had it on him last night and had no choice but to give us the number. There are three calls on it: one to Sims's landline and two from Gavin's mobile after Gavin's murder, so we know the calls were made by Sims. The last was an hour before we found them on the terrace.'

'Does he mention that in his witness statement?' asked Potter.

'No.'

'So, he's lying,' muttered Charlesworth.

'He is.'

'Do you know what's gone on?' asked Potter, holding eye contact with Dixon. 'And if so, will you please tell us?'

'I will,' he replied. 'Ask the right questions and apply the simplest, most obvious answer to each and the whole thing drops into place like a row of dominoes going over.'

Charlesworth folded his arms. 'Let's hear it then.'

'What's the connection between Godfrey Collins and the other killings? Allan and Sims were taking their revenge for the loss of their pension funds and yet Collins had nothing whatsoever to do with the pension scam. He was the odd man out.'

'You never found one,' said Potter.

'That's right, we never found a connection, for the simple reason that there isn't one.'

'Why did they kill him then?' Potter and Charlesworth in unison.

'Because Craig told them to. He was in Bristol prison at the same time Sims was a prison officer and he fed them the names and addresses they needed. Who else knew about the villa on the Costa del Sol? Because we sure as hell didn't. The Economic Crime Unit had been looking for Bowen and Mather for ages and yet Allan pitches up there and kills them both with a single shot.'

'And Craig knew about the villa?' asked Potter.

'He went there once or twice, according to Laura's parents.'

Charlesworth's brow furrowed. 'Who's Laura?'

'Craig's fiancée, Sir,' replied Dixon. 'You may remember I went to her memorial service with Detective Sergeant Winter? Laura died when the *Sunset Boulevard* sank mid-Atlantic; Zephyr thought it was a drug run.'

'I do remember something about it, yes.'

'So, Craig gives them Bowen and Mather?' asked Potter, getting the conversation back to where she wanted it.

'They'll have known about Finch anyway – after all, he was the taxman pursuing them as far as they were concerned. And I'm guessing Craig will say he did it under duress and that Sims was making his life hell in prison, threatening to kill him if he didn't, that sort of thing. And that might convince a jury, had he not given them Collins too. He'll have convinced them Collins was the driving force behind the pension scam, the scheme accountant, something like that, but it was entirely for his own ends.'

'What ends?'

'Well, for that you need to look more closely at the sinking of the *Sunset Boulevard* and the Marine Accident Investigation Branch report.' Dixon leaned back in his chair. 'The keel fell off in heavy seas; the yacht capsized, four sailors went into the water and yet only three personal locator beacons were activated. Why is that?'

Potter looked at Charlesworth and shook her head. 'Maybe the battery on one was flat?'

'Unlikely. These things are serviced annually and have a battery life of seven years. They emit a GPS signal that connects with low earth orbit satellites. But it's far simpler than that.'

'Occam's razor,' said Charlesworth. 'The simplest answer is usually the right one.'

'If only three beacons were activated,' continued Dixon, 'then only three people went into the water.'

Chapter Thirty-Nine

Dixon was standing on the pavement just outside the entrance to the St Govan's Welfare Centre, hidden from the CCTV camera mounted in the porch above the heavy glass door. Cole was standing behind him, with Louise and Mark on the pavement on the other side.

Louise stepped forward into the porch and pressed the buzzer, then the door was opened from the inside by a young girl in a hand-knitted rainbow sweater.

'Thanks,' said Louise.

Mark followed her in, then Dixon and Cole.

'It's Maisie, isn't it?' asked Dixon. 'From the Hobb's Lane Collective.'

'Er, yes.'

Andrea was sitting in the office; the same black hair and clothes. She looked startled, or maybe it was just the black eyeliner?

'Hello, Andrea.' Dixon offered his best disarming smile. 'We're back again looking for Craig Pengelly.' He held a photograph to the Perspex screen. 'We caught up with him yesterday and he gave us a statement, but he's disappeared and we need to find him. He gave us this address.'

'He's not here,' she said, her eyes fixed on the computer monitor in front of her. 'And he's not been in.'

'Do you mind if we have a look around?'

Andrea stood up behind the Perspex screen and trudged to the office door with a heavy sigh, then opened the inner security door.

'Has anyone written a message for him on the whiteboard?' Dixon asked, distracting her enough to allow Louise and Mark to slip through the inner door behind her as she walked into the reception area.

'I don't think so.' Andrea was pretending to look at the board.

'What about you, Maisie, have you seen him down at the collective?'

'No, sorry.'

'You're sure you've not seen him, Andrea?'

'No.'

He glanced into the office where Mark was holding up a bag in one hand and a phone in the other. Then Louise stood up, holding a baby in her arms. Dixon slid a small booklet out of his jacket pocket and held it in his outstretched hand in front of Andrea. 'How about this person?'

Her knees buckled and she slumped back on to the leather sofa. 'How did you know?' Fighting back the tears now.

'I went to your memorial service, Laura,' he replied. 'It's a nice photo of you on the order of service, don't you think?' Long ginger hair, a red sailing coat, holding the wheel of a yacht in the Bristol Channel, Steep Holm visible in the background.

A blink, and a tear was released from the corner of her eye. 'That was the first trip out on Mum and Dad's new boat.'

'I'm not sure how you're going to explain it to your mother. She'll be declaring you dead at the High Court at two o'clock on

Monday.' Dixon turned to Cole. 'That reminds me, we'll need to ring the court; find out which solicitors are on the record, then ring them and put a stop to it. Monday morning will do.'

'Yes, Sir.'

He turned back to Laura. 'Your mother is going to find out from her solicitor she can't declare you dead because you're still alive. And that she's a grandmother after all. Do you think she'll laugh or cry?'

'I get a phone call, don't I?'

'You do.'

'I'm sorry. It was supposed to be a fresh start.' She started to sob. 'When I was declared dead, the life insurance would pay out and . . .' Her voice tailed off.

Dixon picked up a pen and started scribbling on the white-board: *ANDREA LUKIC*, then beneath that *LAURA DICKEN*. He started crossing off each of the corresponding letters in turn. 'Whose idea was the anagram?'

'It was just a bit of fun. Please tell me it wasn't that.'

'No, it wasn't.' Dixon dropped the pen on the mantelpiece. 'Laura Dicken, I am arresting you on suspicion of the murder of Godfrey Collins.'

'Murder? I haven't murdered anyone!'

'You do not have to say anything, but it may harm your defence if you do not mention when questioned something that you later rely on in court. Anything you do say may be given in evidence.'

She was sobbing uncontrollably now. 'What about my baby?'

'What's her name?' asked Dixon, the sound of a baby crying carrying from the office.

'Abby.'

'She can go with you.'

Fighting for composure now. 'Look, there's been a mistake,' she said. 'I never killed anyone. Yes, we were trying to claim on the life insurance, but . . . it was all a fucking mess.'

Dixon waited. She'd been cautioned and if she wanted to talk, let her.

'I never knew it was a drug run. As far as I was concerned I was just crewing a yacht for a few weeks; hardly ideal being four months pregnant but we needed the money. Then I find out we're picking up some cocaine from a cruiser off the Azores and bringing it in via Burnham. I should have guessed, I suppose, but that was it for me, I was having none of that, so I got them to drop me off on the Scilly Isles on the way down. I said I wouldn't say anything and I haven't. Till now.'

Louise gently placed Abby in Laura's arms.

'Then the boat sank while I was still on Tresco and Craig said we should claim on the life insurance. Mine was the first policy he sold when he started doing financial services and he said it was time to cash in. Then we could go to France and do up the barn.'

'Not a spice debt then?'

'There is a spice debt, all of it from prison. He was clean when he went in that bloody place.' Laura was watching the baby sucking the tip of her little finger. 'There was a prison officer giving him the bloody stuff; he'd beat him up one minute, then give him spice the next.'

'D'you know his name?'

'Sims.'

They turned as one when there was a thump at the Perspex, Mark pinning a Brittany Ferries ticket to the inside of the screen. 'Today at five o'clock, Sir.'

'I guess we know where Craig will be,' said Dixon.

'It would've worked, too, if Godfrey Collins hadn't found out I wasn't on board his yacht when it sank. He'd had a satellite call with the skipper when *Sunset* started taking on water and he'd found out then. He was blackmailing us – half the payout, he wanted, or he'd tell the police. Craig said he'd deal with it and that I should leave it to him. So I did.' Laura frowned. 'Please tell me he didn't kill him.'

'He got someone else to.'

'Oh God.' The tears were flowing freely now, falling off the end of her nose on to Abby's pink onesie. 'We agreed that we'd pay him off. He wasn't supposed to have him killed. Oh, Craig, what the hell have you done?'

Chapter Forty

Dixon had spent much of the run down to Plymouth on the telephone to Brittany Ferries. Time was tight, and the last of the cars were queuing to get on when they finally arrived fifteen minutes before the scheduled departure.

Two cars: Dixon and Cole in an unmarked police pursuit vehicle; Louise and Mark behind in Mark's black BMW.

Security were expecting them and waved them straight on to the ramp, past the holidaymakers waiting in line.

'They think we're queue jumping,' said Cole. 'You don't have to be a lip reader to work that out.'

'They're not going anywhere for a while.' Dixon threw his cushion on to the back seat. 'Only they don't know it yet.'

Craig was travelling as a foot passenger, according to Laura, and would be waiting for her on the rear deck at the stern rail. Dixon resisted the temptation to look up as Cole drove up the ramp and on to the vehicle deck, in case Craig saw him; although he would probably be watching the foot passengers boarding, looking out for Laura in the crowd and no doubt getting more and more agitated as the scheduled departure time approached.

'Are you the two cars who'll be getting back off in a minute?' asked a security guard holding a clipboard.

'That's us,' replied Cole.

'Park behind that minibus. Up them steps takes you to the passenger area and the deck.'

'Thanks.'

'We've stopped loading until you're done, so the ramp will be clear when you're ready to go.'

Dixon leaned across from the passenger seat. 'Keep people off the vehicle deck.'

'We do that anyway.'

Laughter echoed down the metal stairwell, children shouting and crying; families starting their holidays.

People were milling about on the passenger deck too, some already sitting in the restaurant and the bar, others carrying hold-alls and looking lost; a few playing the fruit machines in the small arcade.

'The cabins are that way, Madam,' said someone in a white shirt and black tie, insignia Dixon didn't recognise on her shoulders.

Loose children raced past them with adults in pursuit.

'Are you the police?' asked the woman in uniform.

'Yes.'

'I've lined up a couple of people to clear the rear deck of passengers when you make your arrest. The last thing you want is an audience, I expect.'

'Thank you,' replied Dixon. 'All right, let's get it over with. Nige, you and me one side, Lou and Mark the other. I'll make the approach. He won't get past us, but what I don't want is him going over the rail. There's a corrugated roof that might break his fall, but if he misses that it's all the way down to the access ramp.'

They weaved through the few passengers taking in the evening air on the deck, Craig visible at the far end – exactly where Laura said he would be – leaning on the rail and staring across to the foot passenger ramp. He checked his watch, then his phone, then looked back down at the ramp, shaking his head.

Dixon stepped forward and leaned on the rail next to him. 'She's not coming, Craig.'

Craig turned his head slowly and swallowed hard. 'Who isn't?' His agitation was ebbing away, replaced by a sadness in his eyes. 'I don't know what you're talking about.'

'How do you think we knew where to find you?'

Craig looked over his shoulder at Cole to his left, Louise and Mark waiting by the rail to his right. Further along the deck two staff members were holding back the passengers trying to walk around the stern.

Quick as a flash, Craig was up and over the rail, standing with his hands behind him and his heels on the ledge. 'I'll jump,' he said. 'Don't think I won't.'

Dixon turned to Cole. 'Give us a minute, will you, Nige?'

Cole, Louise and Mark backed away, out of earshot.

'Laura said you might do something like this, but I said you wouldn't do that to your daughter.'

'Have you seen her?' Fighting back the tears now.

'She's lovely.'

'Have you got children?' asked Craig.

'My fiancée's pregnant,' replied Dixon. 'We found out yesterday and it hasn't really sunk in yet.'

'I can't go back to prison.'

'Yes, you can. And you'll get to see all her birthdays. This way you'll see none of them and leave Laura to carry the can for the whole thing. That's the murder of Godfrey Collins and the insurance fraud. She might be out for Abby's eighteenth, I suppose, but . . .' He let that thought hang in the air.

'She knew nothing about Collins.' Craig was gripping the rail tighter now as he rocked backwards and forwards.

'D'you think a jury's going to believe that? She's admitted she knew Collins was blackmailing the two of you. And if she was part of your plan to get Sims to kill him, then the law of joint enterprise makes her just as guilty.'

'She wanted to pay him off.'

'So she says, but without you there to corroborate that, the CPS will charge her with his murder and let a jury decide.' Dixon was watching an ambulance driving slowly down the outside of the queue of traffic waiting to board the ferry. 'On the other hand, if you're there telling us she knew nothing about it, then she probably won't even be charged with it; just the attempted insurance fraud and with a newborn baby she might not even go to prison for that.'

Craig was breathing hard now, staring at the vehicle access ramp far below.

Time to go in for the kill, thought Dixon – figuratively speaking, of course. 'You've got to ask yourself, Craig, what will happen to Abby if you're dead and Laura's serving life for Collins's murder. Her parents are a bit old and they don't have the money to fight for her through the courts, so my guess is your parents will end up looking after her.'

The blood drained from Craig's face as the realisation washed over him. 'My fucking parents, looking after my daughter.'

'I'm guessing Sims forced you to tell him where Bowen and Mather were?'

'He used to come to my cell and beat the shit out of me. Every bloody night, no bruises above the collar. When that didn't work he gave me spice and tried to get me to tell him where they were when I was out of it. I was hooked again then, wasn't I?'

'Where was he getting the spice from, d'you know?'

'An ex-prison officer called Frank. He used to supply it until he got the shit kicked out of him by one of his customers; nice little business they had going.'

'Did you report Sims?'

'I tried that, but no one did anything!' Craig's voice increased in volume to a scream that carried to the foot passengers at the bottom of the ramp, all of them looking up now. 'Then he was hanging around when Laura came to visit, and when she'd gone he told me he was going to have her killed. He knew people, he said. This went on for weeks, fucking weeks.'

Craig was holding on with one hand now, wiping the tears and snot from his face on the sleeve of his hoodie.

Dixon waited for him to regain his composure. 'Is there a record of your complaint?'

'Probably. In my medical records maybe.'

'There you are then. Look, I can't make any promises, but if there's independent evidence that supports your claim that Sims forced you to reveal Bowen and Mather's whereabouts, the chances are you may not even be charged with their murders. That just leaves Collins and he was blackmailing you, right?'

'I told Sims that Collins was the brains behind the pension thing. I had to do something.'

'That's a murder charge, Craig, but we'll let the lawyers argue the toss. Get yourself a good solicitor and you may get away with a single count of manslaughter. Conspiracy even. Who knows, that might see you out for Abby's twelfth birthday, maybe her tenth?'

'What about the insurance fraud?'

'I've stopped the hearing at the High Court to declare her dead, so that makes it attempted fraud. Any sentence for that would run concurrently so it shouldn't cost you an extra day.'

'And Sims's death?'

'What was he doing on the ledge?' countered Dixon.

'He said to contact him when I got out, that he'd have some money for me, so I told him where I was. Then he turns up with the crossbow and says I have to pay for tricking him into killing Collins. He was going to kill me. Loads of people saw it; he tried to grab me and take me over the cliff with him.'

'He did, and it'll go down as self defence, Craig. But you and I both know you made damned sure he went over the edge.' Dixon was watching for any reaction. 'I'd never be able to prove it, though, and he said himself there was no way he was dying inside, so maybe you did him a favour?'

'You know just what to say, don't you?'

'I know Abby will never forgive you if you jump. She'll lose her father and her mother. Still, she's got lovely grandparents, eh?'

'I was expecting you to try and grab me.'

'I couldn't hold on to you even if I did. Broken bones,' replied Dixon, with a wince.

'That was quite something, what you did the other night.'

'Thanks.'

'This conversation's inadmissible, isn't it, because you haven't cautioned me?'

'You haven't said anything I didn't know already, but it'll give the lawyers something else to argue about.'

'You'll say you were trying to save my life, I suppose?'

'For Abby's sake.' Dixon watched Craig mulling it over. 'C'mon, we need to let these good people get on with their holidays. The ferry's already twenty minutes late.'

Craig gave a sad smile, then started climbing back over the rail. Mark and Cole lunged forward and took hold of him by the wrists as Dixon sat down on a bench.

'Do the honours, Nigel,' he said, closing his eyes as Cole arrested Craig for the murder of Godfrey Collins.

'You talked him down. Well done, Sir.' Louise sat down next to him. 'What did you tell him?'

Dixon took a deep breath. 'A pack of lies, Lou. A pack of bloody lies.'

Author's Note

I very much hope you enjoyed reading *Dying Inside*. It was written during the coronavirus pandemic and provided me with something of an escape from the daily diet of bad news. I can only hope that life is starting to get back to normal by the time you are reading this, or better still that the nightmare is behind us.

I am grateful to Burnham-on-Sea Gig Rowing Club for holding their open evening at the sailing club in early February, just before the pandemic hit, and I am disappointed that I haven't been able to take them up on their kind offer of a rowing trip yet. I hope the offer still stands!

Otherwise, the various lockdowns and restrictions curtailed the research that I was able to do, the end result being that I stuck to locations familiar to me, such as the Avon Gorge and the fruit machine arcades of Somerset; signs of a misspent youth perhaps. The Bristol Hippodrome and surrounding area too.

Shillingford Wood, which is within walking distance of my house and became my lockdown dog walk, doubles for Harptree Combe. I hope the residents of East and West Harptree will forgive me!

There are several people to thank, as always. Not least my wife, Shelley, who reads the manuscript on a daily basis. I would also like to thank my unpaid editor-in-chief, Rod Glanville. And David Hall and Clare Paul who, once again, have been extraordinarily generous with their time – over Zoom rather than a long lunch, sadly!

And lastly, I would like to thank my editorial team at Thomas & Mercer – in particular, Jack Butler, Victoria Haslam and Ian Pindar.

Damien Boyd
Devon, UK
January 2021

About the Author

Photo © 2013 Damien Boyd

Damien Boyd is a solicitor by training and draws on his extensive experience of criminal law, along with a spell in the Crown Prosecution Service, to write fast-paced crime thrillers featuring Detective Inspector Nick Dixon.

Did you enjoy this book and would like to get informed when Damien Boyd publishes his next work? Just follow the author on Amazon!

1) Search for the book you were just reading on Amazon or in the Amazon App.

2) Go to the Author Page by clicking on the author's name.

3) Click the 'Follow' button.

If you enjoyed this book on a Kindle eReader or in the Kindle App, you will be automatically offered to follow the author when arriving at the last page.